The Fell Walker's Legacy

Michael Wood

Pen Press

This book is a work of fiction. References to real people, events,
establishments, organisations, or locales are intended only to
provide a sense of authenticity, and are used fictitiously. All other
characters, and all incidents and dialogue, are drawn from the
author's imagination and are not to be construed as real.

First published in Great Britain by Pen Press

All paper used in the printing of this book has been made from
wood grown in managed, sustainable forests.

ISBN13: 978-1-78003-694-6

Printed and bound in the UK
Pen Press is an imprint of
Indepenpress Publishing Limited
25 Eastern Place
Brighton
BN2 1GJ

A catalogue record of this book is available from the British
Library

Cover design by Jacqueline Abromeit

"I loved this book and would highly recommend it."

"Much better than some so-called best seller writers of late."

"Loads better than some well promoted thrillers."

Climate Change

"The story is well penned and has a great twist at the end. If you like a murder mystery you'll love this."

"This is a compelling read which is impossible to put down before you reach the very last page."

"A chilling tale of greed, passion and a meticulously planned murder."

"A definite page turner."

Acknowledgements

My thanks go to members of the Cumbria police force (they know who they are) for information on police procedures.

Thanks also to editor, Claire Spinks, and proof reader, Maureen Dorey, for their diligence and expertise.

And a special thank you to Dorothy, my partner in crime, for her support.

Surely, there is no other place in this
wonderful world quite like Lakeland..
no other so exquisitely lovely…

Alfred Wainwright

Even within the most beautiful landscape,
in the trees, under the leaves
the insects are eating each other; violence is a
part of life

Francis Bacon

Prologue

The slash was long and straight, the scar old but deep. It was as if a giant branding iron had been placed there years ago and little healing had since taken place. The man didn't like it. He didn't like its straightness, its uniformity, its regimentation. But it had its consolations; it allowed him to walk from the top of the steep fell right down to the lakeside, the wonderful, ever-changing view in front of him unimpeded by the tall, wounded forest that flanked him on both sides.

He appeared to belong to the old school – cloth cap, faded grey anorak, check shirt, brown trousers tucked into thick wool socks, exposing well-worn boots; canvas rucksack on his back. White hair protruded from the perimeter of his cap and travelled down his cheeks in trimmed sideburns. Gold-rimmed spectacles and a steel-stemmed pipe hanging from the corner of his mouth added a slight touch of modernity, but micro-fibres, Goretex, walking poles and multi-layers had clearly not insinuated their expensive benefits into his consciousness. Yet his stride was long and strong, as if a younger man hid within.

As his descent progressed so the fells on the opposite side of the lake became clearer. Ullock Pike, steep and rugged, its base ablaze with golden trees, rusting bracken below its peak, various shades of green sandwiched in between, the colours randomly daubed as if by Monet, yet creating a perfect picture to his distant eye. Behind it, the great grey hulk of Skiddaw, lying quietly, like a shy giant trying to hide its size and comparative drabness, unwittingly dominating the whole masterpiece.

Lower down the slope he sat on a tree stump and gazed up at the sky. He loved to watch nature in action, ceaselessly painting watercolours on the cerulean blue background. A dab of Payne's gray and rain was on its way, ivory black and storm clouds appeared. Alizarin crimson meant thunder and lightning, yellow ochre heralded the sun's return. On this mid-autumn day there was little painting going on. Only a few wisps of Chinese white broke the monopoly of blue, allowing the sun's glow to highlight the beauty before him.

Nearing the bottom of the slope he came to a T-junction, another arrow-straight, unsealed scar in the forest, this one as wide as a road, big enough for lorries to carry lumber away. He sat on a shelf of rock jutting out from the cut-away hill and took out a sketchbook from his rucksack. He drew with a charcoal pencil, quickly trying to capture the scene. The short, shadowed avenue of trees immediately in front of him led his eyes into the picture, where they were suddenly exposed to glistening water, backed by the dramatic fells beyond. He was about to add suggestions of colour with watercolour pencils when the distant, deep-throated roar of a car engine brought him to a halt.

He stood up and took out a small notebook and pencil from his anorak pocket. He was just in time to write down the number of the car as it hurtled past, leaving behind a fleeting image of two grinning faces topped by shaven heads, a mocking blast of the horn and a showering swirl of dirt and debris. He stepped forward into the road, turned left and watched as they sped into the distance. Suddenly, the car seemed to be bouncing. Then it was swerving. Then it jerked to the right, off the road, down the slope, turned somersaults and crashed into the trees.

The man put his notebook and pencil back into his anorak pocket, and his sketchbook and pencils back into his rucksack and hefted it onto his back. He walked along the road until he came to the scene of the crash and clambered down the slope until he reached the wrecked car.

Shattered glass, severed steel, splintered wood had all performed merciless deeds to soft flesh. Their bodies had been sliced, penetrated, crushed and butchered in an orgy of destruction. The eyes of one of them had survived undamaged and were still open, and his mouth still grinned even though the rest of his body was no longer connected. The man smiled back at him and kept smiling as he turned and made his way up the slope. Then he walked back along the road.

Chapter 1

Private Jamie Wilson and Private Hamish Craik were preparing vegetables when the first explosion shook the building. Tables shivered, plates clapped, cutlery danced on stainless steel. "What the fu—," Jamie shouted as his eardrums did a jig then took up singing shortly afterwards. Ninety per cent of all Jamie's sentences contained an unwarranted expletive, but he reckoned this one was fully deserved as he shot a glance at Hamish, saw the quivering in his eyes, grabbed his arm and led him outside.

It wasn't the harsh, ear-shattering sound of the blast that terrified them. It was the initial, emphatic THUD as the missile hit the ground, sending shock waves through their feet. There was no mistaking that dreadful sound. It was unequivocal. It was the sound of death. No drum had yet been made or music composed that could replicate it. Even Beethoven would be defeated.

It had been three months since the last Taliban attack on the base, and they had started to relax again. But it seemed that the insurgents had an endless supply of young men willing to die for Allah. Those who were firing at them now would certainly die. There would only be two or three of them who had sneaked through the outer perimeter patrols, carrying Russian grenade launchers and maybe a couple of anti-tank launchers. The latter were deadly weapons capable of penetrating walls before exploding, but they emitted a glaring flash when fired and gave away the position of the firer. The young men using them knew they would eventually be found and killed by the patrols. Such fanatical bravery was incomprehensible to Jamie and Hamish who did everything they could to avoid confrontation of any sort. That is why they had joined the catering arm of the Royal Logistics Corps. A steady job with decent pay was all they had been looking for, not trying to kill strangers in a foreign land.

Hamish was shaking as Jamie led him out. With Hamish it wasn't just the blast that made him shake. His street-tough exterior was a veneer hiding a timorous beastie within. He was a nervous wreck – always had been, apparently. Jamie had been his minder ever since they had teamed up, trying to avoid the police, the pushers and the gangs on the Dyke Estate in Edinburgh.

The routine for non-combatants was to grab your helmet and get to the shelter zone, about 100 metres away. They had walked a few metres, instinctively crouching, being overtaken by those running, dust from the explosion drifting in the hot air, Jamie still holding Hamish by his arm, supporting him mentally as well as physically, when Jamie cursed, "I've forgotten the fuckin' helmets….ooer late….we'll keep goin'."

Another explosion, to their left, smaller than the first one, probably a grenade. They saw a man keel over in slow motion, about 40 metres away. "You get to the shelter," Jamie shouted at Hamish. "I'll get that guy." He set off running towards the man on the ground. Hamish stumbled on towards the shelter zone.

Approaching the shelter, Hamish turned to check on Jamie's progress. He was just in time to see a volcanic eruption of dry brown earth and a nearby figure produce a clumsy display of aerial acrobatics, the blast noise reaching him a split second later. Jamie's body landed like a bag of sand thrown from a lorry. "Christ no…." Hamish shouted as he ran towards him, his own fear temporarily forgotten.

As he approached Jamie's body he expected the worst, the grenade having landed so close to him. But as he grew closer Jamie seemed to be whole. He lay on his back, legs and arms spread-eagled – all present and correct. Hamish hoped against hope. He would have prayed to God if he knew how.

Arriving breathlessly at Jamie's side he saw that Jamie was still breathing, his chest heaving. He seemed to be in one piece. Then, "ugh!" Hamish couldn't control his reaction as he recoiled from the sight. Jamie was staring up at him, his right eye focussed, but his left eye was outside its socket, lying on his cheek like a grotesque growth. It looked three times bigger than his right eye.

Hamish's stomach started to heave, but he gritted his teeth, knelt down and started to brush the dust and earth from Jamie's face. As he did so, a slow trickle of blood – disgusting, dark red blood – started to leak from Jamie's nose. And then from his ears.

Hamish took Jamie's hand in his. Jamie seemed to react, seemed to be able to focus on him with his right eye. "What the fuck are we doin' here?" he rasped.

He had said precisely those words two years ago as they both sat on the ground in an alley doorway, drinking from stolen cans of lager, watching Edinburgh rain running down a rusty pipe.

Jamie had been the leader, 18, numerically a year older than Hamish, but many years more mature. Hamish was happy to let him lead. He had never had a friend, never known a father. When Jamie had decided to join up, Hamish had gone with him in spite of it being the last thing on earth he would have done alone. Fortunately for Hamish they had managed to stay together in the army.

Now, here he was, his best mate, his only mate ever, needing him to take over, to rescue him, to sort it.

"Hang on, Jamie," Hamish gasped, his wild eyes looking around for help.

Jamie tried to reply, his mouth opening and closing like a landed fish, but all that eventually came out was an extra-long breath, and then his chest collapsed and it didn't come back up again, and his right eye lost its focus, but continued to stare. "Jamie!" Hamish shouted, releasing his grip on Jamie's hand and sliding it down to his wrist. There was no pulse.

For some reason Hamish's mind flashed back to Edinburgh, to a time when he had seen a Labrador pup knocked down by a car. It too had stared up at him and breathed weakly before dying. Both had looked strangely pathetic, vulnerable, soft; ill-equipped to face the hardness of the world.

Slowly, he stood up and looked around and lifted his head. "B-A-S-T-A-R-D-S!" he shouted as loud as he could.

It wasn't just the Taliban he was shouting at. He was shouting at all the politicians, megalomaniacs and religious fanatics who had created the war, all wars.

Now other soldiers, medics, had gathered around Jamie and the man he had attempted to rescue. They told Hamish to run for the shelter zone. But he didn't. He took a final look at his mate then set off walking slowly. He didn't care if he got hit.

In the shelter he sat on a bench and put his head in his hands and cried like a baby.

A day later, the death of Jamie was suddenly removed from the core of Hamish's mind when, just after he had finished breakfast duty, he was informed that his mother had died at their home in Edinburgh, and that he had been awarded 28 days' compassionate leave.

Two days later he was sitting in a Hercules aircraft taking off from Kandahar Airport along with 127 others, all having various reasons to return to the UK, including nine on stretchers and three in coffins, Jamie among them. Hamish dreaded what awaited him. Bad news came in threes they said.

Chapter 2

Hamish was still locked in his world of worry when he stepped off the plane. A drop of cold rain on his warm neck brought him back to the outer world. He glanced around at his surroundings, noticed a number of vehicles heading across the tarmac towards the plane, other planes toy-like in the distance, people ant-like.

He had arrived back in winter. He'd forgotten about the bleakness, the lack of light, of life; the stark, leafless trees swaying in the wind, clawing at the low, grey sky like manic skeletons. The coldness shocked him. It wasn't the dry cold of Afghanistan nights – but damp, penetrating British cold, threatening snow. He shivered and shrank inside his lightweight clothes, wishing they were thicker, warmer.

The procession of vehicles arrived alongside the plane headed by an army staff car. Behind came two ambulances and three buses. As he joined the crowd heading for the buses he saw a soldier jump out of the staff car and approach them carrying a placard with PRIVATE CRAIK written on it. He held up his hand and walked towards the soldier.

Inside the staff car – the warm, spit-and-polish staff car, the polish unable to mask the smell of the driver's cigarette – he was told he was being taken straight to Heathrow airport where he was booked on a flight to Edinburgh in three hours' time. The army was efficient with all aspects of death, apparently.

Soon they were passing through a town, crowds lining the pavements ready for the latest parade of coffins. A lump came into Hamish's throat. He had seen the parades on television, found them emotional, disagreed with Jamie who used to take the piss out of them. "Fuckin' English," Jamie would scoff. "Saft in the heed. We're in the army for Chrissake, we're in a war. What do they fuckin' expect - us and the Taliban to be dancin' round the fuckin' maypole? Standin' gawpin's not goin' to change nowt."

Now Jamie was going to be gawped at. He would be squirming in his coffin. Hamish felt dejected at the thought, yet found a smile creeping across his face as he imagined Jamie's reaction had he been able to see himself. He could imagine Jamie sitting astride his coffin, left eye dangling on his cheek, waving to the crowd, picking out an ugly man and shouting, "Hey Pal! Wanna change places, you look worse than me." And then Jamie would have got angry; the red mist would have descended. "Away back to your fuckin' work you bampots," he would have shouted. "We're not fuckin' heroes. I was a tattie peeler for Chrissake. And we ken we're all just cannon fodder anyway. We're the daft sods that couldnae get a proper job so we joined the army. We're the yobs, the anti-socials, the asbo boys what stole your cars. You were tryin' to lock us up not long ago, noo you want us to be your fuckin' heroes. Away hame to your semis and stop gawpin' at us. Go back to your tellies and your wee manicured lawns and your fuckin' en-suites and leave us to *requiem in* fuckin' *pacem* among our own."

Hamish had never got to the bottom of Jamie's contempt for the English, a contempt shared by most of the boys on the Dyke Estate. It seemed to simply exist in the air, in the water, in their genes. Somehow, although he had spent his entire life on the estate, that part of Hamish's education had passed him by. The only person he had contempt for was himself.

He was jealous of Jamie's anger, of the certainty of it, of the courage to express it. He found himself incapable of expressing much that he felt. His emotions stayed deep within the bottle, the cork immovable. He longed for the day when the cork would pop, when he would become a man like Jamie, when he wouldn't be afraid. He often wondered if that day would ever come.

Heathrow was chaotic as usual and without the help of the driver, who had his ticket and terminal details, Hamish would have been lost. By now he was thoroughly travel weary and feeling disorientated – the events, time and location changes of the past few days starting to take their toll.

He was not an experienced traveller. Before joining the army he had never left Edinburgh, never had a holiday. His mother said they couldn't afford one. She was right – welfare benefits couldn't pay for holidays, particularly when a big slice of them went on drink and fags. His holiday periods had been spent mostly at the local swimming pool where, being small, he had perfected a way of sliding underneath the entrance barriers. His entrance money had bought chips on the way home.

There was nobody to meet him at Edinburgh airport. The army would assume he had family or friends to meet him and take him home. Hamish knew there wouldn't be; his mother had been his only family, and Jamie his only friend.

Nothing much registered as he found his way out of the airport and onto a bus into town. Seated among the pale, pinched faces he became vaguely aware of coldness, dampness, tyres hissing on wet roads, traffic jams, his language being spoken, stone buildings, crowds, traffic lights, heavily clothed people walking quickly, familiarity. But none of it blotted out the overriding feeling of dread that persisted in his tired mind.

A second bus journey from the city centre, followed by a long walk, and he arrived on the Dyke Estate. Soon he stood outside the concrete, flat-roofed, small windowed building that others would have thought was a garage block or an industrial building, but which he recognised as home. It had two entrances for four families. The council called them maisonettes, the auld yins called them flats, he called them cells – all they needed were bars at the windows.

It was late afternoon, the winter light was fading and it was getting colder as he pushed the heavy communal door open with his back. He eased his two heavy holdalls into the dark concrete passageway that separated the two flats and knocked on his neighbour's door. It was Mrs Finnie who had found his mother at the foot of the stairs, the army had told him. The police, doctors and council social workers had done the rest, and now she lay in the local hospital mortuary awaiting cremation in two days' time. The post mortem had shown alcoholic poisoning causing failure of the respiratory system and aspiration of fluid into the lungs causing asphyxiation. In other words she had choked on her own vomit while unconscious. It was not clear whether the alcohol or the fall down the stairs or a combination of both had rendered her unconscious.

Hamish found it hard to care very much. She had drunk heavily as long as he could remember, and he had borne the brunt of her violent mood swings. She had shown more affection to her occasional "boyfriends" than to him. She had become just another Dyke Estate statistic, dying from the drink earlier than expected – 39 going on 55.

Mrs Finnie seemed to get smaller every time Hamish met her, his time away being long enough to render changes in people noticeable. Her hair didn't seem to have gone any greyer or her wrinkles any deeper, but it was difficult to judge with only the light from her hallway shining behind her. Something that never seemed to change, however, was her aura of genteel warmth and friendliness. Word was that she had once lived in a big house in a posh part of Edinburgh, but things had gone downhill after the death of her husband and the twists and turns of life had brought her corkscrewing down to the depths of the Dyke Estate. She had become a friend to the boys on the street, talking to them quietly, asking how they were getting on, bringing them her freshly baked oatcakes and biscuits. She always seemed to be cooking, often wearing her pinny when she came out to see them. They affectionately called her Finnie the pinny.

Peering up at him over her glasses, it took a second or two before she recognised him. When at last she did, she didn't speak. She took his right hand and wrapped both her small, bony hands around it and stood in silence. Initially, Hamish was slightly startled, not being used to physical contact, but he soon realised that she was just expressing her care and sympathy.

"Thanks for all yer help, Mrs Finnie," he finally managed to whisper.

"So sorry, Hamish… so sorry…" she replied, releasing his hand. "God will look after her now…"

"He'll hev a job on," Hamish quipped nervously, not sure what to say. "I couldnae manage her."

"Aye… you'll get some peace now, Hamish."

"Aye…"

"I've put a pie and some beans and bread and butter in your kitchen, Hamish. And I've put the heating on… oh, and there's plenty of tea and milk and some oatcakes… and the electric is still on."

"Thanks very much Mrs—"

"I'll go and get the key for you."

She returned with the key and handed it over. "If you need anything else, Hamish, just knock on the door."

"Thanks Mrs Finnie," Jamie said for the third time, unable to drag any conversation through the fog of his exhaustion.

A turn, one pace and he opened the door to his cell. He dumped his holdalls in the hall, switched on the light and stumbled upstairs, vaguely registering an unpleasant smell. In his single room his mattress lay in its usual position - on the floor in a corner. There were no bedclothes on it. He opened his single wardrobe and found a quilt squashed on the top shelf. He carried it through to his mother's room where he lay it on top of her double quilt. Sitting on the bed, he took off his boots, let out a deep sigh, slid under the quilts and was asleep within two minutes.

The smell and a noise from the street were the first things that proved his nose and ears were still functioning. A cobweb on the ceiling, highlighted by a weak winter sun coming through the window, confirmed his eyes were working. And an involuntary scratch of his stubbled chin checked out his touch. He was alive. He was going to have to face another day. The thought appalled Hamish. He wanted to roll over, hide under the bedclothes and never have to surface again. Let the world get on with its madness, leave him alone. He did roll over and try to get back to sleep, but it wouldn't happen. Flashes of the last few days kept pestering his mind, like flies round a wound. Jamie... his ma... both dead? Is it a dream...? The eye... Jamie's hanging eye... his mammy... only 39...

Eventually, it was the pressure of his bladder that forced him to get up and face the day. He looked at his watch, which he had altered to UK time on the plane from Heathrow. It was eleven o'clock in the morning and it was Wednesday; must remember that – Wednesday. Ma is cremated on Thursday.

Ablutions over and some unpacking done, he sat, with two pullovers on, at the table in the living room. A plate of reheated pie and a mound of beans filled his plate. He tucked in hungrily while watching the large television which dominated a corner of the small room. An earnest couple of English presenters were oohing and aahing about the wildlife of Africa as they bounced about in their Land Rover. Then they were on their knees, wetting themselves with excitement as they watched a beetle pushing an elephant turd along the ground. '*Need a life*,' thought Hamish as he shovelled the beans.

The programme finished as Hamish got up to make a cup of tea to go with his oatcakes. He heard the next programme start as he was taking the teabag out of the cup. "Over to Westminster for Prime Minister's Questions." He would switch it over, couldn't stand politicians, do anything to get your vote, send you abroad to get killed... bastards.

He carried his tea and oatcakes over to the table, set them down and stepped towards the television to change channels. Just then the Prime Minister said, "I'm sure the whole house will want to join me in paying tribute to the three brave soldiers who died in Afghanistan recently. Private Andrew McMahon, Private Jamie Wilson and Corporal Samuel Tyson were all serving with the Royal Logistics Corps. They were all brave men who gave their lives fighting for their country and we will never forget them. Our thoughts go out to their families and friends at this time of terrible loss." A chorus of hear-hears followed. Hamish threw an oatcake at the telly. "Shite," he shouted. "You're talkin' shite." He continued his rare outburst internally. *'Brave soldiers...? Jamie wasnae a fighting man... how brave do you have to be to chop cabbage? And he didnae give his life fightin' for his country. His life was taken from him. And he couldnae give a rat's arse about any country, 'specially England where he reckoned "men in suits blethered all day and couldnae fix a fuckin' puncture." As for "we will never forget them". I'll ring the Prime Minister tomorrow... ask him where Jamie Wilson's goin' to be buried. He'll say "who?" Then I'll thank him for thinkin' about me at my time o' terrible loss and he willnae ken what to say. Bags o' wind that's all they are... should be fixed to the pipes.'*

He switched over to another channel and watched a soap he hadn't seen for a long time while he supped his tea and ate some oatcakes. *'Mrs Finnie... now there's a proper hero... a brave woman... a good woman.'*

That afternoon he went to see his mother in the hospital mortuary. It felt good to walk along the streets again in civilian clothes, parka hood over his head to keep out the cold, trainers on his feet, feeling so light compared to his army boots he felt he might levitate. He seemed to bounce off the wet pavement as he swerved past the stampeding herd of people who incessantly came towards him, seemingly late for something important.

He'd been to the mortuary twice before to farewell two boys from his street who'd overdosed, so he knew the way. He hadn't known them well, and he wasn't keen to go, but Jamie had dragged him along to "show respect". But he had forgotten about the smell and it took him by surprise as he entered.

The next surprise was to see his mother looking so young and peaceful. Death seemed to suit her more than life. Life had made her look old, tired, haggard. She and life had not got on together. She had seemed determined to get rid of it as soon as possible. She had a death wish, Hamish had concluded in his mid-teens after years of trying to get her to stop drinking. Now her wish had been granted and she looked well on it. The lines on her face had gone, the skin was unblemished, her hair clean and shining. Now she looked her age.

Hamish had been looking at her dispassionately. There were few fond memories here, and thousands of bad ones. She had been uncaring, self-absorbed and self-pitying. He had had to fend for himself for most of his life. And yet... something about her age... only 39... tripped his mind. Then he noticed again how peaceful she looked...

Hamish felt a change entering him, like a tide in an estuary. Something inside his chest began to swell. His eyes started to moisten. His throat constricted, making him swallow. The umbilical cord that had once joined them seemed to be rewinding itself around his neck. An unexpected, overwhelming sadness swept through him. A visceral pain gripped his body, crumpling his features, turning him into a whimpering spaniel. She had been his giver of life and that simple, complicated fact inexplicably wiped the slate clean, and he looked at her with love in his heart, which was now breaking.

The following day, at the crematorium, Hamish found himself in the company of two middle-aged women he didn't recognise: the Pakistani owner of the local off-licence and a social worker from the council who had come along in case Hamish hadn't made it back from Afghanistan in time. The minister's well-meaning platitudes about his mother were as truthful as the Prime Minister's about Jamie.

He scattered her ashes in the crematorium grounds and watched numbly as a fine drizzle gradually merged her with the soil below, the elements seemingly in a hurry to claim her back.

Turning, he found the social worker patiently waiting. He handed Hamish a document explaining the things that needed to be done after the death of a relative, along with the original death certificate and a few photocopies. The social worker emphasised that he should look out for a will among his mother's possessions and to take it to a solicitor if he found one. Out of politeness, Hamish didn't laugh at him. People on the Dyke Estate left debts, not wills.

That night, after downing a fish supper he'd bought on the way home, he got steadily drunk on the vodka he'd found in a kitchen cupboard – she had left him something after all. There was a mid-week football match on the telly which helped to distract him while it was on, but afterwards the alcohol and the stress of the last few days caused him to sink into a dark, depressive mood. He had nobody left. His crutches had been removed. He was alone.

He had never felt sorry for himself in the past. He'd got used to somehow toughing things out even though he found the practicalities and responsibilities of everyday life difficult at best, terrifying at worst. But then he had been able to lean on Jamie, and his mother when sober. Now, alone, he was in danger of becoming a cripple without his crutches. A mental cripple. This was the thought that filled him with dread.

The next morning, he became aware of a throbbing in his head before he opened his eyes. Then he heard knocking. Somebody was knocking on the door downstairs. Wincing at the pain in his temples, he eased himself out of bed, discovered that he was still fully dressed, and shakily made his way down the stairs.

Mrs Finnie stood holding two dishes. "I've made you some porridge and a shepherd's pie," she smiled, offering them to him.

Hamish took them from her, trying hard not to shake. "Thanks Mrs F—"

"You might get two days out of the shepherd's pie... if you're not very... how did it go, Hamish? Is she at peace now?"

"Aye... she's at peace... she's away... it was okay... thanks Mrs—"

"And are you alright, Hamish?"

"Aye... I'm okay... just a wee bit tired ye ken..." His hands began to shake.

Mrs Finnie noticed and started to back away. "Aye... well... I'll let you get on, Hamish... you'll catch your death standing in the cold doorway." She turned and shuffled back across the passageway.

"Thanks again, Mrs Finnie," Hamish shouted after her, then wished he hadn't as the vibration of his voice drilled at the pain in his skull.

In the next fifteen minutes, in no particular order, he consumed three cups of coffee, two pain-killing tablets (there was always a large supply of pain-killers in the house) and a bowl of porridge. Then he went back to bed for half an hour.

Approaching midday, the call of nature forced him from his bed to the toilet. From there he drifted into the small bathroom. Absent-mindedly, he glanced in the mirror above the hand-basin. He had a slight shock when he saw a brown-faced person staring back; he'd forgotten about Afghanistan, the sun. But he soon ignored the brown surface and, as usual, gazed disdainfully at the features beneath it. If his mother had had a litter of children he would have been described as the runt. He was short, thin, sandy-haired. His head was narrow, as if it had been compressed between two vertical steel plates. Two small protruding ears had apparently been glued on afterwards. Over this bony head his skin seemed tightly stretched, like a burns victim, giving him a skeletal, sunken eyed look. Below his large, sepia eyes sat a narrow nose which flared alarmingly at the nostrils and took attention away from the wide, horizontal gash below it – his lipless mouth. Even his teeth were strange. As small as a child's, they made him look as if he had too many. They were embarrassing, rarely on show.

How he had come to look like this remained a mystery to him. His tall, heavily built, dark-haired, blue-eyed mother had always refused to tell him who his father was in spite of his endless questioning. For years he had tormented himself by trying to guess the reasons for her secrecy. Was he in gaol? Was he a dealer? Was he a banker? Was he a bailie? Was he a priest? Was he a Rangers supporter? Was she just too embarrassed to let on she had slept with the ugliest man in Scotland? Was he English?

That afternoon, using the list given to him by the council social worker, he set about searching his mother's room, looking for all the documents that connect the citizen to the state – council housing, benefits – and the suppliers of services such as gas, electricity, telephone, television, post, medical etc. He found most of them in the middle drawer of her small dressing table, scattered randomly among paper clips, rubber bands, biros, pencils, a few coins, cigarette butts and other detritus. Needless to say, there was no will. (But she had left him £7.35 in her purse in the cutlery drawer.)

He had to write to all these organisations, in some cases using their pre-printed forms, enclose a copy of the death certificate and tell them what was going to happen in the future – who remained in the house, who was going to pay for what, what was the name of their bank, account numbers and so on. He looked in horror at the volume of paperwork he confronted. His mind started to blank. He was no good at this sort of thing. He didn't know what to put on the forms, mainly because he didn't know what was supposed to happen to an empty council house while he was away in the army. He didn't know what his rights to the house were. Other questions to which he didn't know the answer started to overwhelm him as he went through the paperwork. It was all too much. He would deal with it another day, he was too tired today. He glanced at the window. The rain which had peppered the glass all afternoon was no longer visible because of the darkness outside. His watch told him it was only five thirty. He climbed into bed, pulled the quilts right over his head, and hoped he would sleep forever.

When he opened his eyes again there was a pale light in the room, but no traffic sounds from outside. Slowly, he eased himself out of bed and stepped to the window. There was the usual parade of early morning traffic, but a light covering of snow was cushioning its sound. He glanced at his watch. Seven thirty. He had been in bed 14 hours. That was probably why he was feeling better, clear headed; that and a lack of alcohol the night before, and the jet lag diminishing.

After breakfast of toast and tea, he went back upstairs to where the ominous pile of paperwork lay waiting on the dressing table. Even with his clearer head the thought of tackling it appalled him. He decided to put it off until the afternoon. He would spend the morning sifting through all his mother's belongings and place them into piles on his bedroom mattress. A pile of stuff to give to Mrs Finnie, a pile of stuff, mostly clothes, to go to the charity shop, and a pile of stuff to chuck out.

He opened her wardrobe and started to lift out her clothes, a waft of stale perfume accompanying them. He carried them to his bedroom and laid them on the appropriate piles. He returned for the shoes that lay on the bottom of the wardrobe, alongside three half-used rolls of wallpaper, an emulsion brush stiff with paint, five shiny-looking handbags, a hair brush, an electric plug, a roll of toilet paper, old-looking hair tongs and a pile of women's magazines. He transferred them all to his bedroom except the magazines which he decided to take downstairs to give to Mrs Finnie straight away.

As he bent to lift the magazines he noticed there was a small gap underneath the pile. They were sitting on something else. He lifted the pile and revealed a small, brown case, not much bigger than a briefcase. It was very old and cheap-looking, with a handle and a rusting metal keyhole mounted where the two halves of the case came together.

Hamish put the magazines down on his mother's bed, turned and picked up the case. It was fairly light and he felt something move around inside as he laid it on the bed to examine it. He tried to prise the two halves apart with his fingers, but they wouldn't budge. He tried banging the sides with his fist to loosen the locking mechanism, but nothing happened. Clearly, a key was needed to open it. But he had no intention of spending hours looking for it. He went downstairs and brought back up a handful of cutlery – knives, forks, spoons.

Instead of tackling the locking mechanism, he attacked the hinges on the bottom of the case, knowing these would be much weaker. By inserting and levering first a knife and then a fork, he managed to force the hinges apart and finally to break them away completely. He tipped the contents of the case onto the bed.

A pile of newspaper cuttings spread out before him and one or two handwritten letters peaked out between them.

He moved to the doorway and switched on the bedroom light, the weak winter daylight failing to send enough light for reading through the small window. He returned to the bed, sat on the edge and picked up a newspaper cutting. It had been cut from the body of a paper, so there was no paper title or date on it. The headline read: *"Filipino 'slave' case – search for best friend's husband"*. Beside the headline was a long-shot photograph of a small highland house standing alone, surrounded by hills and heather. Underneath it a caption said: *"Last known location of Vilma Tapales"*.

Hamish frowned in puzzlement, but read on. *"Investigations into the Filipino 'slave' case have moved to the tiny community of Strathy Point in Sutherland where Vilma Tapales was last seen, four years ago, at the funerals of her best friend, Mrs Leni Snodd, and Mrs Snodd's five-year-old daughter, Grace.*

After the funerals, she is known to have stayed for a few days with Mrs Snodd's husband, Hector, in his isolated croft house. When questioned by police, four years ago, about her non-arrival back in the Philippines, Mr Snodd is reported to have said that she left his house to catch her return flight, and that was the last he saw of her."

Hamish's frown deepened, but he carried on reading:

"In response to continued pressure from Ms Tapales's parents since that time, police had carried out further investigations throughout the country without success and she had remained on their 'missing persons' list, until the recent discovery of her chained body on the A591 in Cumbria."

'What the hell is this…? Why's she kept this…?'

"Police are now anxious to trace the whereabouts of Mr Snodd, who subsequently left the area a few months after his wife and child's death. Snodd, 33, who worked as a concrete laboratory technician at the nearby Dounreay nuclear plant, is reported to be 5' 5" tall, of slim build, with thinning, sandy coloured hair…"

Hamish stopped. He reread the last sentence. The man – Snodd – was small and slim and had sandy hair. A description of himself. Was it just a coincidence? There were millions of small, thin men about. But not that many with sandy hair. His mind started to race. Was this why she'd kept it secret? Could this be his father? He read on, hurriedly this time:

"Local police said he was known to have suffered depressive episodes after being made redundant, and he was charged with causing the death of his wife and child due to dangerous driving while under the influence of alcohol. For that offence he was given a two-year suspended jail sentence and banned from driving for five years, the judge in the case stating that the sentence was lenient because Snodd had 'already suffered irreparable loss'."

Hamish put the cutting to one side. He was still puzzled. Snodd had been a married man and a drinker. Was that it? Was that all? Okay, he'd been depressed and unlucky with his driving. Who hadn't? What was the big deal? Why keep him secret? He found himself feeling vaguely disappointed, because he'd fantasised about his father being somebody special. At the same time, he was puzzled as to how his mother and this man could have come together when they lived at opposite ends of the country. Must read on, find out more.

He picked up a large cutting. A quick scan of sundry stories and adverts told him he was looking at the wrong side. He turned it over – and almost fainted. He was looking at a photograph of a man's face. It took up half the front page of a national daily tabloid which was dated about six years ago, when he was 14. The caption beneath the photograph said: *"The face of a serial killer".* Under the bottom right corner of the photograph, in small print, the words: (photo: courtesy of Dounreay Security). The features were unmistakable – the sunken eyes, the narrow, skeletal head, the stretched skin, the flared nostrils, the lipless mouth. The man's hair was receding at the temples and lay flat and limp, unlike Hamish's bristling army short cut, but the colour was the same. He had no doubt that he was looking at his father.

Hamish swallowed and shuffled himself into a more comfortable position on the bed as he prepared to read on. The bold black headline alongside the photograph screamed: ***"SLAVE CASE UNCOVERS SERIAL KILLER HORROR".***

Hamish's heart thumped and a strange singing started in his ears as he read on: *"Police investigating the 'slave' case involving Filipino woman, Vilma Tapales, whose chained body was found beside the A591 near Keswick in Cumbria, claim to have identified a serial killer who has been operating undetected for a number of years. Cumbria's Chief Constable, Simon Crane, sitting alongside senior detectives from Cumbria and Metropolitan police told a packed gathering of shocked reporters that the killer's name was Hector Snodd, a man they had wanted to question in connection with the Tapales case".*

So much space had been taken up with the headline and photograph that readers were now asked to turn to page 5 to continue. Hamish put the cutting aside and hurriedly picked up the next one on the pile. It was page 5. He read on:

"We recently found Mr Snodd's body at the foot of a Lake District fell called Barf," the Chief Constable reported. *"Subsequent searches of his home and place of work, Scarness Manor near Bassenthwaite, revealed items and records that lead us to believe that he has carried out a number of murders over the past few years."* His voice went quiet and his head lowered when he said that the number was probably as high as 15 and could be more, but nobody would ever know".

Hamish closed his eyes tightly. Bad news number three had arrived. How much more was he supposed to take? He wanted to crawl under the quilts again. But he had to continue, he was a rabbit caught in the light of his father's staring eyes.

Hamish read on, finding himself holding his breath as details of Snodd's murderous exploits were slowly revealed to him. His father had, after all, been *very* special.

Hamish found himself horrified but also thrilled. Horrified at the brutality of the man, the killing of innocent people; thrilled at his strength of purpose, his certainty of mind, his bravery, his masculinity. In spite of his size and appearance, he had been all-man. He was everything that Hamish wanted to be.

By the time he had finished reading the long article, Hamish had recovered from the initial shock, and he even found himself looking forward to reading the other cuttings, which he assumed covered the same subject. He was not mistaken. They were from different national daily papers, all telling the same story in their own way, some telling the bare bones of the story, others digging deep into the case, revealing even more startling detail of Snodd's life and history.

There was also one cutting from the *Thurso Gazette* describing local reaction to the story about their, now famous, local man. Hamish wondered how his mother had got hold of it.

While reading through cutting after cutting, article after article, Hamish was desperately hoping and searching for a reference to his mother and himself, possibly as Snodd's first wife and child before divorce or separation. There was nothing.

Finally raising his head from the papers, Hamish tried to cast his mind back six years. This was a big story. It must have been on the telly as well as on the front pages of the papers. But he didn't remember it. If he had seen it, it hadn't registered with him. At 14, he'd probably been out on the street, or up in his room playing with his games or listening to the latest hits. He'd spent a lot of time alone in his room; he hadn't watched much telly in those days.

He turned his attention to the three letters he'd found among the cuttings. He picked out the one with the oldest date, about 21 years previously. It was from a Mrs Janette

Muir of 16 Bank Street, Thurso, and was handwritten. It was addressed to his mother:

"Dear Margaret,

I was so relieved to hear from you the state you were in when you left I wasn't sure what was going to happen to you. Im glad to hear youve found a place in Edinburgh I hope you find a job soon there should be plenty of work there at least. Your dads been asking me if I know where youve gone and I havent told him like you asked. Im already missing you but your best out of it, let him get on and manage on his own thats all he deserves."

A page of local gossip followed, then the letter ended:

"Keep in touch and let me know how you are getting on with jobs etc.

Missing you.

Love

Janette"

The second letter, also handwritten by Mrs Muir, dated nine months later said:

"Dear Margaret,

I cant believe it. A baby why didn't you tell me I would have come down and helped. Are you sure you are all right and going to cope. I dont know whether to say congratulations or sorry what with Hector being the father you say. Just that one night youve been so unlucky. Its best you didnt tell him he wouldnt be able to cope would he. Hes moved out of that flat over the butchers and hes in his uncles house on the croft at Strathy now. His uncle died and left it to him. They say you can here his loud music all over the place. I wont say a thing to your dad. Hes as miserable as ever the new barmaid wont last long she says she cant stand him."

More gossip followed, then the letter ended:

"Take care of yourself and the bairn. Let me know how your coping.

Love

Janette"

The third letter, also from Mrs Muir at the same Thurso address, was typed on a word processor and was dated about 6 years ago:

"Dear Margaret,

We havent been in touch for so long and Im not sure if you are still at the same address, but I hope you don't mind me enclosing this report from the Thurso Gazette. *Its all about Hector whose all over all the papers and on the television. I dont know what else to say but if you want to talk about it you can see my phone number at the top or you can send an email.*

Love

Janette"

Hamish shuddered as he put the letter down. A deep sigh left him as he stood up and stepped across to the window. The steel grey sky and the dark grey buildings did nothing to lighten his mood. His eyes aimlessly scanned the regimented rooftops, some starting to hold onto the light snow. Lights shone dully through smeared windows even though it was midday. A single jackdaw trying to keep its balance on a television aerial caught his attention. It seemed about to fall off at any moment, its wings fluttering every time it threatened to do so. Was it mocking him or imitating him? He was just hanging on to reality, felt about to fall off.

It was all there. The cuttings and letters explained it all. His mother had lived up in Thurso when young. She'd had a one-night stand with a guy called Hector Snodd and he was the result. It wasn't clear why she had run away to Edinburgh, but it seemed to be something to do with trouble with her dad, who probably ran a pub in Thurso. Mrs Muir was obviously a close friend, maybe a neighbour. She hadn't known his mother was pregnant when she left Thurso, but she did know about Hector Snodd. Maybe his mother didn't know she was pregnant when she left Thurso?

Hamish could see why his mother had kept Hector a secret from him after reading the papers. But he had been fourteen when all that happened. Why hadn't she told him about his father before that? He had asked often enough. There was no mention of crimes before that. Mrs Muir had said he wouldn't have been able to cope. Why? He had a job at Dounreay. He was coping with work. He was earning a living. Was it just because he had been a married man? Had he even been married at that time? Maybe not. Then why? Hamish wanted to know. No... he *needed* to know. He had yearned for so many years to know everything about his father that it had become an obsession. The fact that his father had turned out to be a murderer had not quenched that need. It may even have added to it. The most important thing to Hamish was that his father had not abandoned him and his mother, as he had always imagined. His father had not known he existed. He had not been told. He had not been given the chance to be his father.

Suddenly, a whirlpool of thoughts and questions filled his mind. If his mother hadn't run away from Thurso he might have been called Hamish Snodd or Alec Snodd or something Snodd. He would have been a different person living in a different place, and maybe having different thoughts. He wouldn't have met Jamie... he wouldn't have gone into the army... if Margaret had left him with Hector he would have been brought up by a Filipino woman... he would have had a sister... but maybe Hector wouldn't have married the Filipino woman if his mother had stayed in Thurso... maybe they would have been a happy family like those he saw on the telly... his father and him fishing in the highland lochs... playing football together... although if they both drank it didn't seem likely... but maybe they wouldn't have drunk if they had been happy together...

He was driving himself mad with questions, most unanswerable. But some were answerable, and he needed to know the answers. He wanted to go up north to find the answers. He *would* go up north. He would go to Thurso. He would find out.

He collected the cuttings and letters together, went downstairs and put them in one of the zipped pockets of his holdall. The rest of the day went by in a blur as Hamish tried to come to terms with his momentous discoveries. Some more tidying of his mother's belongings went on, some food was cooked and eaten, some telly watched, but all in a fog of distraction, his thoughts elsewhere. Only when climbing into bed did he remember that he'd forgotten to do the paperwork.

After a good night's sleep, Hamish woke up at seven thirty. He felt different. He wanted to get up and get on with things – a feeling he wasn't used to. Normally, he wanted to stay under the covers for as long as possible. Not today. He flung back the quilts and almost jumped out of bed. Today he had a reason to live. He was going to find out everything possible about his father. He was going to visit the places he had lived – from the far north of Scotland down to the Lake District. He was going to retrace his steps, talk to people who knew him, get to know what he was really like, not just what the headlines said. Nobody could be all bad.

Before he reached the bedroom curtains, another decision came to him. He was going to go AWOL. Tens of thousands had done it since the politicians had decided to go to war again in 2003, and there was usually a thousand out there at any given time. They were mostly men like him and Jamie who had not joined the army to kill or be killed, but just to find a job. Their punishment if caught could be severe, though execution by firing squad had been abolished some years ago. He would take his chances. He hated the army, the discipline, the rules, the routines. It had not made a man of him as Jamie had promised. It had made his nerves worse. He had been cowed by the absolute authority of those above him. He had felt small, frightened and weak. Without Jamie it would be unbearable. He had dreaded the thought of going back. Now he had a reason not to. His decision was made. Already he felt stronger, more assured… like Jamie… like his father… a proper man.

Chapter 3

Hamish lay in a single bed in a small room, staring at the plain white ceiling above him, trying to make sense of the incredible changes in his life. Staring, thinking, worrying had become his morning wake-up routine.

Two years had passed since he left Edinburgh and the military police had not yet traced him. He had changed his surname to Stott, to give himself the same initials as his father. He had let his military haircut grow and given it a dose of dark brown colour every few weeks. He had been to Thurso and talked to people about his father. Then he had made his way to Ullapool and jumped on a ferry to the Outer Hebrides. Here, as he had hoped, he found work in a remote island hotel where staff were hard to come by, and he laid low there for six months. Hoping that by now the army had given up their hunt for him and he had become just another of their AWOL statistics, he moved on to the Lake District to continue the journey into his father's life. Here he had visited Scarness Manor where his father had worked as a caretaker, and the nearby Scarness Cottage – home of Ben Foxley, the man responsible for his father's death. He had also walked up the fell called Barf where his father had died.

He had decided that the Lake District, with its many hotels, was a good place to get a catering job with accommodation and continue hiding from the military police, and he now had a job in a big hotel on the shores of Lake Windermere. Most amazing of all…

There was a gentle tap on the door and it swung open quickly. A small doll-like face beamed at him as he raised himself onto his elbows. She had short, jet-black hair, large brown eyes, a flat, oriental face, olive skin and pure white teeth. As she moved towards him, the smiling doll quickly discarded her clothes, revealing a boy-like figure. She hesitated momentarily, hands clasped together in front of her, waiting for his invitation. Hamish lifted the quilt to one side and smiled his welcome as she squeezed in beside him. …he had a girlfriend.

"Hi Hami," she giggled as she wrapped her arms and legs around him, seeking warmth rather than sex.

"Hi Sami," Hamish said through clenched teeth as he tried to absorb the shock of her cold limbs without flinching. The hotel's staff accommodation block was notoriously cold, the heating only put on when the owner gave the go-ahead.

"You still on two to ten?" Sami asked in her gentle, clipped Filipino accent.

"Aye," Hamish replied, wrapping his arms around her back. She was so small and child-like she made him feel relatively big and strong. She had changed his life. And he believed he was changing hers.

She was one of three Filipino girls among the staff of the 36-bedroom Greenstone Hotel, the rest of the staff coming from Australia, New Zealand, South Africa, Portugal, Poland, Ireland, Scotland and England. She worked as a general assistant in the kitchen, which is where Hamish also worked doing what he had done in the army. Her prettier friends had been given front-of-house jobs.

Hamish and a few others were working for below minimum wages, with no questions asked, no references required, no passport checks, no background checks. Word in the pubs was that the Greenstone had hit hard times after a boat speed limit had been introduced on the lake. Being on the lakeside the Greenstone had specialised in catering to waterskiers and powerboat enthusiasts, a young crowd who played all day and spent lots of money in the hotel's marina, boat supply and repair facility, restaurant and bars. Since they had left, times had been hard, money had been lost on the sell-off of boats and equipment and money had been borrowed to upgrade the hotel to appeal to an older, more sedate clientele. Keeping costs to a minimum was the hotel owner's top priority, hence the need to hire itinerants like Hamish who would work for low wages in exchange for anonymity.

The kitchen was run by a burly, shaven-headed bully with the inappropriate name of Tulip. He had spent 15 years in the army and insisted that the kitchen staff called him Sarge rather than Chef or Mr Tulip. Shortly after his arrival at the hotel, Hamish had been cornered by Tulip.

"You're AWOL aren't you," Tulip had accused in his broad Yorkshire accent.

"No…" Hamish had started.

"Don't lie…I can spot an AWOL before breakfast," Tulip had sneered. "Don't worry, I'll keep me mouth shut as long as you do exactly what I tell you. Understood?"

Hamish had nodded his agreement. Since then Tulip had given Hamish all the dirty, boring jobs in the kitchen, made him work extra hours without pay and generally taken pleasure in belittling him and making things hard for him.

Though seething inside, Hamish had put up with it as always. He was used to it; it seemed to be his lot in life to be dominated by people shouting orders at him. He didn't have the ammunition, physically or mentally, to retaliate.

But when he found that Tulip was pulling the same stunt with the shy little Filipino girl, had her literally running to meet his commands, found her crying in corners, he had been stirred to action. He had befriended and sympathised with the girl who eventually told him that time on her work permit had run out and Tulip had threatened to shop her if she didn't do as she was told. She had entered the country before the new points system had been introduced, and with low-skilled workers now being refused entry she thought she would not be allowed to stay if she applied for an extension.

Brought together by the similarities of their situation and their hatred of Tulip, they had become reliant on each other, found solace with each other, and eventually became lovers. Two small, insignificant people, they had created their own small world within the hustle and bustle of the hotel; a protective bubble in which they supported each other through the work with a look, a smile, a touch, and after work with a passionate love neither dreamt they would ever experience.

Each had struggled with the other's name and accent. Samuela Babalato had agreed to become Sami, and because she struggled to say the sh of Hamish, he had agreed to become Hami. And when Sami had jokingly suggested that her accented English was better than Hamish's Scottish version of English, Hamish had agreed with her.

The arrival of a Filipino girl into his life made Hamish wonder if in some strange, coincidental way he was destined to relive the life of his father, thereby getting to know the man he had always wondered about. His trip to Thurso had revealed a number of similarities between them. There he had met a man called Callum McDonald who had been his father's boss at Dounreay Nuclear Plant. McDonald told him that his father's mother had died giving birth to him, that his father's alcoholic father had died five years later and he had been raised by his Uncle Maurice on an isolated croft at Strathy Point a few miles from Thurso. McDonald told him that as a young man his father, Hector Snodd, had been a small, shy, loner who became obsessed about things he liked. He had been in a few scrapes with the police, mostly to do with petty thieving and his Uncle had thrown him out of the croft. He had moved to a flat in Thurso and became known as a heavy drinker. But he had been a very good worker and had been rewarded with a trip to the Philippines for special achievement at work. He had also been a good husband and father, and had obviously "gone mad with grief" when his beautiful wife, who he had met on his trip to the Philippines, had died along with their child in the car he was driving.

McDonald had been a helpful but formal kind of man who knew nothing of Mrs Janette Muir or Margaret Craik or her father. When Hamish suggested they might be connected to a pub or hotel, McDonald announced proudly that he never went near such dens of vice. And he became agitated and disbelieving when Hamish told him he was Hector Snodd's son by Margaret Craik. Soon after this revelation, Hamish had been shown the door.

Hamish had found Mrs Janette Muir still in residence at 16 Bank Street, the address on her letters to his mother. It turned out to be next door to the Central Hotel. After recovering from the shock of meeting him and learning of his mother's death and his discovery of her letters, she told him that Margaret had helped her father run the Central Hotel. Margaret's mother had left them because of the beatings she took from her husband. After she had left he had turned his aggression to Margaret who had turned to drink and her friendly neighbour for support.

One of the hotel's regulars had been young Hector Snodd who lived in a flat above the butcher's shop next door to the hotel, on the other side. He used to get drunk almost every night and then go back to his flat and listen to classical music. Margaret had told Mrs Muir that she felt sorry for him because he seemed so sad and lonely and one night when she had found him collapsed in the hotel hallway after a heavy drinking session, she had helped him back to his flat, and helped him into bed and he had clung onto her hand and begged her to stay. She had been drinking as well and she stayed with him and woke up beside him in the morning. He was still lying, flat out, when she went back to the hotel.

Her father had beaten her for staying out all night, calling her a whore like her mother. She had packed a few things, called to let Mrs Muir she was leaving, and caught the next train out of Thurso.

Hamish had been pleased with his trip to Thurso. He now knew much more about his father, knew that he had been a good father and a good worker, that he had not known he had a son by Margaret Craik, that he was not inherently evil, that a terrible grief had turned his mind to murder. His initial sympathy for him had developed into a feeling of affinity, sameness. He felt as though he was walking in his footsteps, taking on his identity.

Now, as *his* Filipino girl snuggled into *him*, in their routine get-together in between shifts, Hamish's thoughts drifted away from the happy bubble they had created and came to rest on the man who daily threatened to burst it. Tulip had continued to make their life difficult individually and when eventually he spotted the looks passing between them he had started to ridicule and abuse them as a couple, careful not to let the rest of the staff hear, as he knew they would have come to their defence. Hamish could take the snide jokes, such as "here comes the stallion with his little fili", but when Tulip began calling Sami a "husband-seeking foreign tart" and worse, he knew he had to do something about it. But what exactly? As he absent-mindedly stroked

Sami's shining black hair, he thought, as he always did these days *what would faither have done?*

Chapter 4

Ben Foxley let his left hand slide off the gear stick and come to rest on his wife's right knee. He gave it a gentle squeeze.

"Can you concentrate on the road please," his wife snapped with mock severity. She knew he was just larking about, but there were bends ahead and she would be glad if both his hands were on the steering wheel.

"Man who concentrates on curves of road instead of curves of wife goes round bend," Ben quipped in his best oriental accent.

Helen sighed. "How did I get landed with a 58-year-old schoolboy?" she chided.

"Beats me Miss, but if you would like to cane me…"

"Just concentrate please… you're going to miss the magic corner…" Helen was referring to the sweeping bend on the A66 which takes the traveller from the mundane to the magical; the bend that sneaks through a gap in the hills and delivers you into another world. The change is dramatic, otherworldly; the scene as you emerge – shockingly beautiful. To your left, the small town of Keswick, nestling in the foreground of an impossibly picturesque vale containing a lake surrounded by mountains. Ahead, more mountains – some bare, some coated with forest. To the right, more mountains, another shimmering lake. It is like entering the mythical valley of Shangri-La.

And so it is with all entries into the Lake District. Nothing prepares you for the sudden, stunning change of scenery that makes this small area of north-west England renowned throughout the world. Whether you enter from north, south, east or west, it is only when you crest a rise or turn a corner or breach a gap that the exquisite beauty suddenly presents itself to your wondering eyes.

Of course, you see the Lakeland Fells ahead of you as you approach, but they are just hills, just lumps on the horizon. It is only when you pass over them, through them, or around them that the magic they hide comes into view. Which is why Ben Foxley, on his second visit to the Lake District, 30 years ago, named the bend that led into the north-eastern corner of the Lake District, into the Vale of Keswick – the magic corner.

He had lost count of how many times he had driven round that bend and through that gap, but he never tired of it, never failed to slow and look, never failed to thank his lucky stars that this magical valley was now his home. He had no need of a reminder from Helen. He would never forget to slow down and take it all in as they rounded the magic corner.

Now here it was again, for the umpteenth time, bringing them back home after their spring holiday on a canal boat in the south of France, an experience that did not live up to expectations. How many people, he wondered, were as pleased to return home from holiday as to go on holiday?

Arriving in the centre of the vale, he turned right and joined the A591 heading north towards Bassenthwaite village. It was late afternoon, and the sun still held above the western fells, casting its welcome glow across the lake, lighting up the mighty slopes of Skiddaw and Ullock Pike. As he passed Dodd Wood, the sun's rays started a kaleidoscopic dance among the trees to his right. They were reflecting from the bodies and windows of numerous cars regimentally parked behind the trees, discordant amongst such verdancy. Clearly, the ospreys had arrived from Africa.

A mile later, he turned the car down the narrow, mile-long, tree-lined lane that led directly towards the lake, where only four properties had been allowed to be built so close to the lake. Their cottage was one of them. As they approached it, they had to pass the entrance to Scarness Manor, the scene of Helen's traumatic encounter with Hector Snodd a few years ago. After that event they had contemplated moving from the area because of the empty, sinister reminder they had to pass every day. But they loved where they lived, and when a few months later the Manor was bought by a developer and split into three apartments, it seemed to lose its empty menace, and life gradually returned to normal. The apartments were subsequently bought by three lake-loving families who were now friendly neighbours.

As expected, the pheasants and the mallards appeared as soon as they pulled up outside the cottage. From under shrubs and hedges around the lawn they waddled and quacked and flapped their wings, guessing that it would not be long before food was served. And out of the corner of his eye Ben spotted a red squirrel, no doubt with the same idea, scrambling down one of the giant trees that surrounded the cottage.

After emptying the car and downing a cup of tea Ben went out to oblige the waiting throng. He was delighted to see them again, their funny walks, their chattering, their fights. Above the shuffling mallards, who always stole the pheasant's food, the pheasants held their haughty heads high and strutted about like Mrs Thatcher at a cabinet meeting, occasionally stopping to deliver a vicious peck to the back of the neck of a minister pinching her biscuits.

Over the hedge and down a slope, Ben could see the lake and the little wooden jetty to which his rowing boat was tied. The sloping ground had been their saviour when the floods of 2009 struck. The unimaginable water rise, which seemed to double the surface area of the lake, had stopped at the hedge. It had been a close call, hopefully not to be repeated. The Lake District's rain was the price you paid to live amongst such beauty.

Back in the cottage, with Helen busily finishing off the unpacking and loading the washing machine, Ben went upstairs to the bedroom office and checked the answering machine. There was a message from his friend, retired police sergeant Bill Unwin, asking him to turn up an hour later than usual for their weekly golf round because the third member of their party, police sergeant Peter Murphy, was going to be delayed. They had become an inseparable trio ever since their involvement in the Hector Snodd case. The next message was from Sue Burrows, editor of the *Keswick Tribune*, for whom Ben worked as a part-time freelance journalist. She gave details of a couple of upcoming events which she wanted him to cover for the paper. Next came a call from a Grasmere hotel asking for a visit from Helen to advise on their proposed new swimming pool. Helen's recent move from being the manager of a Windermere leisure centre to being a self-employed consultant on all things aquatic was beginning to pay off financially, though Ben hoped it did not lead to the same level of time commitment Helen had given to her previous job. The last call came from an art gallery in Keswick advising Ben that one of his oil paintings had sold and would he like to pop in to pick up his cheque.

Ben went back downstairs happy in the knowledge that all was well, good things were happening, their pleasant, fulfilling life was about to get back into its routine. They hadn't really *needed* a holiday, life here was better than a holiday; they had just gone for a dose of sunshine and a change of scenery.

Downstairs, he picked up the pile of mail still lying on the floor beside the front door. Experience told him that ninety per cent of it would be junk-mail, most of their important correspondence now being done online. He was not mistaken. He took them into the kitchen and, after a cursory glance at each one, proceeded to drop them one by one into the cardboard box set aside for paper recycling.

After discarding a few, he came across a single sheet of white A4 paper roughly folded in half. He opened it up, and stopped breathing. In large capital letters, scrawled with a black marker pen, were the words *H S LIVES ON.*

Recovering from the initial shock, Ben decided it must be somebody's idea of a prank; somebody who was aware of the terrible events of that time, but unaware of the potential consequences of their action. If Helen saw the note she might be badly affected, even though she and the world knew that Hector Snodd was definitely dead. But now he began to recall the two deaths he had reported in *The Tribune* in the last three months. Two falls from mountains, both victims with severe head injuries, eyes missing. There was nothing in the Mountain Rescue Team reports or the police reports to suggest that they were anything but accidental falls; the missing eyes being ascribed to the usual attacks on bodies by crows and ravens. *A copycat killer* flashed into his mind. No… surely not… he was letting his imagination run wild, he was being ridiculous. No, it was probably a local kid carrying out some stupid dare, he rationalised.

He would not show the note to Helen. He would take it to his police friends and ask their opinion. What was starting to bother him more than the actual note was the fact that a stranger had been snooping around their cottage while they were away. The thought brought a sense of vulnerability with it and it stayed with him long into the night when he went to sleep listening to a sound that did nothing to reduce his creeping feeling of unease – the haunting hoot of an owl.

Chapter 5

Humans cannot resist a challenge, even if the challenge is ridiculous. Hence the compulsion to play golf. Ben Foxley had always loved it for reasons beyond the mere sporting challenge. The long, healthy walk, the company of friends, the beautiful environment, the physical satisfaction of a good shot, the mental satisfaction of making the right choice, the locker-room banter, the clubhouse drink.

Today, he had made his usual farrago of good and bad shots, good and bad decisions and had managed to finish second, and thus not had to buy the drinks. That duty fell to police sergeant Peter Murphy, the youngest of the three of them, the longest hitter, but, as with his road driving, occasionally too quick and inconsistent. Sergeant Murphy had matured, physically and mentally, since Ben had first encountered him as a young PC, driving the car in pursuit of Hector Snodd. He had added a stone of muscle to his tall, angular frame, giving him a powerful physical presence. And he was now sharp, confident and assertive. He was modern man personified – a technophile, bristling with the latest electronic gadgets, always in touch, always in fashion, coldly ambitious. It was expected that he would become an Inspector ahead of schedule. Yet he still had the charm of the country boy who showed respect to his elders and visited his mum on Sundays.

By contrast, his retired ex-boss had lost weight since his retirement. Bill Unwin had always been described as burly by his friends, fat by his enemies. Now, away from the patrol car and the desk, he spent most of his spare time on the golf course, in the garden and walking the fells, and had a part-time job doing manual work in a DIY warehouse. Un-ambitious, Bill was fitter and happier than he had been for years.

Ben was the outsider, the observer: aware, sensitive, intellectual but indolent. They were an unlikely trio, not having much in common except a love of golf and their shared experience when pursuing Hector Snodd, yet they enjoyed each other's company. Sitting at a corner table in the golf club lounge, in the shadows, away from the sun's rare intrusion, Ben was halfway through his pint of Cumberland Ale before he produced the note.

"What do you think of that?" he said plainly, as he handed it to Bill. This was in deference to Bill's seniority, though he knew Bill had switched off from police work, and Peter was the man to talk to. Bill glanced at the paper, looked up and raised his eyebrows questioningly.

"It was pushed through my letterbox while we were away on holiday," Ben explained.

"…and you think H S means Hector Snodd," Bill offered.

"Who else?" Ben said, slightly too sharply, his impatience with Bill's slowness not having improved over the years.

"Well it can't be, can it?" Bill said with certainty. "We all know he's dead and buried…" Before Bill could add to his statement of the obvious, Ben was relieved to hear Peter say "Can I have a look?", and watched him lean over and take the note from Bill.

Peter stared at the note for a long time. The swift dismissal Ben had been expecting was not forthcoming.

"Taking longer than his putting," Ben smiled at Bill, trying to lighten the mood suddenly darkened by Peter's serious demeanour.

Peter finally lifted his head from the note to find two anxious faces waiting for him. He smiled. "Relax… it's nothing. I was just running some recent cases through my head. There's been one or two odd ones in the past eighteen months…"

"You mean those two recent mountain deaths," Ben intervened.

"No…I wasn't thinking about them. I was thinking about a pedestrian accident and a drowning, and a couple of others. Anyway, it's obvious our mutual friend couldn't have been involved, so clearly this note is from some crackpot with a sick sense of humour. I'll pass it on to forensics, see if they can find anything on it, but don't hold your breath." With that, he wrapped the note in a paper serviette, placed it on the table, and picked up his glass of fruit juice. "Might be wise to check your security – doors, windows etc – just in case," he added.

Chapter 6

It was time for action, Hamish decided. Sami had come into his room red-eyed. She had arrived like that every night of that week. Hamish didn't need to ask. And he didn't want to be told what Tulip had said. Tulip's insults had reached new depths, become more frequent. Meeting no resistance from Hamish and Sami he had targeted them mercilessly, enjoying the feeling of power it gave him, turning it into his daily entertainment. Hamish feared that it wouldn't be long before Tulip's bullying became physical as well as mental. He feared every time Sami was left alone with him; he seemed to have a particular hatred for non-Europeans. Sami was becoming increasingly withdrawn and nervous.

They talked about leaving their jobs but decided against it. It might take a long time to find another place where they could work and live together, with no questions asked, well hidden from the authorities. Just looking for another job would expose them to the risk of discovery. And they didn't want to let the hotel owner down. Mr Robinson had been good to them. He had treated them well, even apologising for paying low wages and keeping the heating off. He was also risking a fine by employing foreigners whose work permits had run out. A local man, who had started in kitchen work just like them, he had worked his way up to owning a bed and breakfast, then a small guest house and then the hotel, which had been a big success until the speed restriction came in. Now, in unguarded drinking sessions after customers had left, he could often be heard cursing the authorities that had brought the restriction in. "Mostly bloody outsiders... know-alls... Nimbys... He seemed to have a particular dislike for the man who headed an organisation called *Lake District Fellowship*. He had been the main driving force behind the introduction of the speed restriction on the lake. "Bloody London barrister... gift of the gab...what chance did us locals have?"

Hamish and Sami felt sorry for Mr Robinson and they always worked hard in the hope that their small contribution would eventually bring better times to the hotel. Hamish had thought of approaching Mr Robinson to complain about Tulip but decided that it would be too risky. It would be his word against Tulip's and because Tulip had been there for many years he felt Mr Robinson would probably back him, and they could finish up losing their jobs.

Each night all Hamish could do was comfort Sami, stroking her hair while trying to think of a way to get rid of Tulip, if only for a few weeks. A small accident or an illness would give them a welcome break from his foul mouth. If he could find a way of dropping him in with Mr Robinson he might get him sacked. That would be great.

But no amount of thinking brought a worthwhile suggestion to his tired mind. So he had decided it was time for action rather than thinking. The action he had finally decided on was to follow Tulip on his days off to see if any opportunity to "take him out" showed itself. Hamish was thrilled to find himself thinking in such tough language. He was about to become a man of action. His faither would have been proud of him.

Chapter 7

When Giles Innes took early retirement at the age of 57 he promised himself he would spend much of his time in physical pursuits, trying to get rid of the weight he had, almost inevitably, accumulated during his career as a criminal barrister. Long hours at work, long working lunches, long dinner parties, a love of food and wine and a natural distaste for the sports of the common man, had left him wealthy but unhealthy.

That promise had been made nine years ago and had been partly kept. From his expensive home on the eastern bank of Lake Windermere he had taken daily walks, but they were not sufficient to burn off the calories he needed to in order to balance his still considerable intake of food. His weight had settled at a slightly firmer but stubborn 17 stone.

Six months ago, after his annual check-up, his doctor told him he *had* to lose weight or look forward to an early demise. The doctor had recommended that he continued with his walking but also added some swimming and gentle rowing, activities that would not jar his ageing joints but would burn off more calories. Never having swum and not keen on displaying his naked bulk to public gaze, Giles had decided to forego the swimming, instead investing in a rowing boat which he could launch from the small, muddy beach where his front garden met the lake.

Now, on a perfect, windless, late spring evening he and his wife stroll down the garden path towards the boat. He is wearing a peaked cap to keep the sun from his eyes and a thick wool pullover as there is a tendency for an evening chill to settle on the lake. They both wear Wellingtons to launch the boat, though his wife, as usual, will not be joining him. She, being as thin as an ex-model is expected to be, has no need to lose weight, is apprehensive when on water and prefers to read rather than row. As they near the bottom of the garden, a flock of geese appear in the sky, taking their eyes up and out and over the lake towards the distant Langdale Pikes. The sun is just starting to kiss their peaks as it descends in the west, highlighting a view so beautiful it causes them to stop and stare and hold their breath even though they have seen it every day for the past nine years. Only the rich can afford this view permanently, their elegant homes and four-star hotels claiming prime positions on the waterfront. The rest of mankind gets to see it when on holiday – cruising on the lake, or sitting on a bank or walking, or driving past on the road behind the waterfront.

Getting in and out of the boat is the hardest part of rowing, Giles has found, which is why he seeks help from his wife. Today's "launch", as he clambers into the boat while his wife holds it steady, is a bit better than usual.

Gripping the oars, he pulls slowly away from the shore, then releases one hand to wave to his wife who has turned to wave as she returns to the house. He is confident in the boat now, feels at one with it and the silken water beneath it, takes pride in his rowing technique, gently parting the water without splashing. It wasn't so to start with. Everything had felt so hard and heavy and clumsy. Worst of all was the life-jacket, which restricted his arm movement, dug into his protruding belly and was generally uncomfortable. Which was why, as his confidence and rowing technique improved, he got rid of it.

He pulls steadily towards the centre of the lake, then decides to swing the boat around and stop rowing. He wants to enjoy that view again – to see the sun setting behind the Langdale Pikes. And there it is in all its glory. He glances up and down the lake. Save for a swimmer, probably practising for the Great North Swim, he seems to have it all to himself. Such peace, such tranquillity. Such a contrast to the bad old days when they used to allow speedboats and waterskiers to roar up and down. He had taken great personal satisfaction in helping to persuade the National Park Authority to introduce a speed limit. That had certainly been his greatest achievement since taking over the leadership of *The Lake District Fellowship* shortly after arriving in Windermere. His eloquent way with words and confident delivery – the result of years of courtroom debate – had seen him quickly elected to replace the retiring leader of a small organisation whose stated aim was to keep the Lake District natural; unspoiled by inappropriate development and activities.

Now the lake played host to only sailing boats and cruisers, gently gliding along within the 10 miles an hour limit. And even they were missing tonight. Taking his time, he looked all around at the glorious scene – the shadowed fells, looking like giant resting creatures, the verdant forests, the glass-like lake. He felt like a monarch surveying his kingdom. The boat rocked slightly and he looked down and saw a pair of gloved hands come out of the water and grip the left side of the boat.

There was a sudden, violent jolt to the left as the pair of hands pulled down on that side, and Giles lurched over and tumbled head first into the water, adrenalin hitting his system like a hammer.

The coldness of the water shocked him, but he held his breath as he turned to right himself and soon he found his head above the surface. Gasping, he thrashed his arms and kicked his legs in an attempt to stay above water. He looked for the boat which he knew contained built-in flotation chambers which would keep it afloat even if capsized. He spotted it. It had not capsized, but he was shocked to see it so far away - about 15 metres. And it seemed to be moving. Now he realised it was being towed away from him – his assailant holding the boat's launch rope as he swam away on his back.

Giles knew he was doomed. His Wellingtons had filled up, forcing his legs down; his clothes seemed to weigh a ton and already he was exhausted. Even a good swimmer would struggle to survive this situation, he knew. He gasped and thrashed for a few more seconds, and then gave up. He took one last look at the paradise he was leaving before letting it slip from his view. As he sank down into the cold darkness, he found the words *I rest my case* repeating themselves in his mind, and he wondered if there was a judge to hear them.

Chapter 8

"I'm off", Helen shouted, from the bottom of the stairs.

Ben swivelled away from the desk, walked to the landing, and rushed down the stairs. She was only carrying her swimming gear, but he took the backpack from her and they walked outside together. It was one of those silly rituals that sometimes become habitual in a marriage. He couldn't let her go without seeing her off, without carrying her stuff to the car, without warning her about the dangers that lay ahead on that big bad road out there, without kissing her goodbye. The fact that Hector Snodd had almost snatched her from him now added poignancy to the ritual.

Helen had long ago stopped protesting her independence, that she was capable of carrying her own things, that she could look after herself. She knew exactly what was coming next, and she didn't mind. It was nice to be silly, nice to be cared for.

"Watch out for the cows..." he said

"And the uninsured..." she said

"And the addicts..." he said

"And the sheep..." she said

He had a list of about ten, but only three or four usually got mentioned before she started the car and he kissed her goodbye through the open window. Walking back into the cottage, thinking about the note that had been left, Ben hoped there wasn't going to be a sinister addition to his list.

The phone was ringing as he stepped into the hallway. He picked up in the hall.

"Can you get down to Kendal police headquarters tomorrow Ben?" Sue Burrows asked. Ben hesitated – the *Keswick Tribune* didn't usually cover stories that far south. "I suppose so," he replied thoughtfully.

"I know it's not usually our patch," Sue went on, "but this news is of interest to the whole Lake District. Giles Innes is missing, presumed dead. He went for a row on Windermere and didn't come back. His boat was found empty a couple of hundred metres offshore. The Underwater Search Team are out there as we speak. The police have called a brief press conference at two o'clock just to give out the basic facts. By then, of course, they might have more news."

"Okay, Sue, I'll get myself down there," Ben said, then added, "I hope the cynic in me is right this time. My first thought when you told me was that he's probably ran off with his mistress and faked his disappearance. He is a barrister after all, knows all the tricks of the trade."

"Whatever's happened, his poor wife must be worried sick. I'll leave it with you," Sue said, sharply. Then she hung up. Clearly, she had not been amused by his frivolous comment. And on reflection Ben decided she was right. He had allowed his dislike for Innes to cloud his judgement. That dislike was only based on the couple of times he had seen Innes on television interviews during the speed restriction debates, which had been big local news at the time. Ben could see both sides of the argument and didn't have a firm opinion as to who was right or wrong, but he had taken a dislike to the arrogant way Innes had put his case. Innes and his supporters had won the day but made lots of enemies, Ben remembered. Now his imagination took over and he envisaged a dastardly murder perpetrated by a bankrupt business owner.

Ben was chatting to a reporter from the *Westmorland Gazette* when Detective Chief Inspector John Menzies called them to attention. There was quite a gathering. Ben recognised one or two reporters from other local papers, but he guessed there were some there from the nationals as well. Innes had been a big name on the London legal scene before retiring to the Lakes and it looked like his name could still sell papers.

Occasionally glancing at his notes, DCI Menzies gave them all the relative information regarding time of disappearance, location etc, then added solemnly "divers found Mr Innes's body this morning. He was at a depth of approximately 45 metres and within approximately 50 metres of where his boat was found. His body was unmarked."

He then invited questions, to which his answers were: "There was no sign of foul play. His wife said he was happy and had no concerns, but as you know, we can never rule out suicide. No, there have been no witnesses come forward as yet. Yes, the boat did have flotation chambers. Mr Innes, unfortunately, was not wearing a life-jacket and was wearing Wellingtons." Other questions covering the minutiae of the event were asked and answered, and then DCI Menzies held up his hand and said, "Until further investigations take place we will be treating this as a tragic accident and I'm sure you will all join me in expressing our condolences to Mrs Innes and her family."

There was a general murmur of agreement, and people were about to leave when DCI Menzies raised his voice and reclaimed their attention, "Since you are all here I will give you the bare details of another fatality that has just come to our notice this morning. The usual press releases will follow later on." *Obviously not a big name like Innes,* Ben thought. "Early this morning a passer-by noticed a dog whimpering at the edge of a jetty in Bowness Marina. Its extendable lead was at full length, which is what attracted the man's attention. On looking over the edge into the water the man saw a body lying on the bottom in a few feet of water. On recovery it was found that the man had an injury to his head. The man's name is Daniel Tulip. He was employed as head chef at the Greenstone Hotel. That is all the information I can give you at the moment, so no questions on this one please." With that, the Chief Inspector gathered his notes and quickly left the room.

Chapter 9

"So what's the verdict?" Ben asked. His question was addressed in the general direction of his two companions, giving either of them the chance to reply. They had agreed not to talk about it while they were playing golf, but back in the clubhouse Ben expected it to be their sole topic of conversation. Such had been his eagerness to finish the round to get their opinions that his concentration had lapsed and he had ended up having to buy the drinks.

Picking his pint off the table, Bill said smartly, "My verdict is you were lifting your head just before the strike…"

"And mine is you weren't completing your backswing," Peter added, winking at Bill.

Ben smiled and took a drink of his Cumberland Ale. "Very funny, gentlemen. I hope your powers of deduction are as sharp as your wit."

Ten days had passed since Ben had attended the press conference in Kendal and he was keen to find out if there was anything he could now add to the factual piece he had written for *The Tribune*. Reluctantly, he had stifled the fact that the hotel Daniel Tulip worked for was one of the three which had suffered the most when the speed restriction was brought in. Had he not done so, he could be accused of implying a connection between the two deaths, a thought that had immediately crossed his mind when the Chief Inspector had announced Tulip's place of work.

"I'll put you out of your misery," Peter offered, "you've had a bad enough day already." Again he winked across at Bill, momentarily sharing that flash of power that comes with the policeman's job. "I've heard that the Coroner has released his preliminary findings to the families in both cases, and inquests will be heard in the next few weeks when final verdicts will be made." He leaned over and took a long drink of his fruit juice, deliberately stretching it out to playfully annoy Ben.

"And…" Ben came in urgently, as expected.

Peter took his time replacing his glass on the table, smiled knowingly at Ben, then went on, "In both cases the post mortems showed no evidence of unlawful killing. It is therefore likely that the final inquest verdicts will be death by accident or misadventure. If, during the inquests, the Coroner has any doubts about the deaths, he might declare an open verdict on one or both of them."

"What about the wound on Tulip's head?" Ben frowned.

"Apparently it was found to be consistent with striking it on the side of a boat or jetty structure just before he entered the water. The post mortem suggests that he was very drunk at the time, and Windermere Station took statements from neighbours who said he was usually drunk on his days off work, and he usually took his dog for a walk late at night. The fact that his dog's lead was found extended at the time of discovery has raised the possibility that he tripped over it while drunk, and staggered over the edge, hitting something on the way down."

Ben delved further. "He worked at the Greenstone – a hotel badly affected by the speed restriction, which was mostly down to Giles Innes. Bit of a coincidence don't you think?"

"So Tulip kills Innes then tops himself, is that what you're thinking?" Bill scoffed. "Come off it. There was more than the Greenstone affected, more big hotels and lots of smaller businesses. Dozens of people had reason to dislike Innes, and why would an employee do the dirty work for an owner, where's his motive?"

"Paid to do it?" Ben offered, hesitantly. "And he didn't top himself, his death was an accident after drinking to celebrate his earnings."

Peter joined in. "Bill's right, Ben, the link is too tenuous. Anyway, there is no evidence that Innes was murdered. Apparently, three witnesses have come forward to say they saw a swimmer in the lake at the same time as the boat, but none of them saw anything else. None of them witnessed Innes entering the water. The boat was quite a way out. Any swimmer that far out would have to be a good strong one. Tulip was flabby and overweight, apparently."

"Lots of good swimmers are flabby and overweight – that's why they swim rather than walk," Ben countered. "Has the swimmer seen in the lake been identified? Has he or she come forward yet?"

"Er… not that I know of," Peter said, slightly defensively.

"Then until he/she does, or evidence of Tulip's inadequate swimming ability appears, my theory still holds as much water as the lake," Ben said, defiantly.

Bill had been distracted by movement outside the window, on the eighteen green. He spoke while continuing to watch two shapely ladies go about their putting. "You see everything as a drama, don't you Ben? It's the writer in you, the journalist. It's a bit like that when you're a young copper, isn't it Peter? Then a few years later you get resigned to the fact that most of the work is very mundane. I think you'll eventually find that we are looking at a couple of routine accidental deaths here."

Ben wanted to remind him of the drama of Hector Snodd, wanted to tell him that his attitude probably explained why he never made Inspector in such a long career, but instead he said, "I hope you're right, Bill, but in my book when two unexplained deaths occur close together and there is a link between the parties, however tenuous, then I would expect the police to examine that situation until they can rule it out of their investigations."

"I'm sure they will," Peter intervened, sensing a slight friction between the two. "But what bothers me is, even if Ben's theory is eventually proved to be wrong, we will be left with yet more unexplained deaths."

Bill was still staring out the window. Peter and Ben followed his gaze. "Are you listening, Bill?" Peter raised his voice. "Or have you got more important things on your mind?"

"They need some putting lessons," Bill said, turning back to face them. "And I'm just the man to…"

"Your putter's too old and rusty for them, Bill. Best keep it in your bag," Ben quipped. And the laughter they shared seemed to blow the subject of death out the window and they turned to other matters.

Later, as they walked across the club car park to their cars, Peter suddenly turned to Ben and said, "Oh! I forgot to tell you, the forensic report on that note came through. There was nothing special about the paper or the ink and there was nothing on the surface. Whoever dropped it through your letterbox was probably wearing gloves."

Chapter 10

Ben was excited. He could well be the only adult in Cumbria, perhaps in the country, who was excited by watching grass being cut. The root of his excitement lay in his childhood when, as a toddler, he sat on the edge of a meadow burgeoning with buttercups, daisies and clover, and watched enthralled as rabbits and birds scurried and flew as the grass-cutter came along. Gangs of men turned up with pitchforks and turned the hay and made rows of stooks, then came again to collect them up and make giant haystacks. Wives and mothers brought food so the work could go on well into the long summer nights, which, strangely, seemed to last much longer in those days, the sunshine apparently more reliable. The completed stacks were works of art, built to stand up to all weathers, the temporary home of field-mice, and the secret refuge of trembling sweethearts.

Then it all changed when men were replaced by baling machines, clattering and chattering as they compressed the cut grass into giant bales. After school, in his teens, Ben had rushed to a local farm run by two cheerful, matronly sisters and helped out in the fields in the evenings. He helped to load the bales onto trailers pulled by tractors that took the bales back to the farm, where they were stacked in the barns. It was hard, hand-blistering work, the coarse string around the bales sawing into the joints of his young fingers. He couldn't keep up with the men, but he had never felt so alive or so worthwhile. At the end of the week the smiling, grateful, apron-clad sisters invited him into their stone-flagged kitchen, cluttered with milk churns, alive with dogs and pungent smells, and gave him half a crown and a bag of eggs to take home to his Mam.

Now, in a field close to his cottage, Ben watched as one man with two machines took only two days to turn a field of verdant, swaying grass into something utterly alien. Here, Ben was not excited by the machines that did this, amazing though they were, but by the visual impact they produced. To suddenly see large, round, black plastic bags where natural grass once stood always tripped his imagination, his artistic impulse. He saw them as the droppings of giant sheep, or as pods dropped from spaceships, soon to open up and unleash alien creatures bent upon world domination. Or, more seriously, as a symbol of the relentless march of science over nature, of man's careless pursuit of what he saw as progress. Visually, they excited his painterly senses – space, colour and texture. The simplicity of the scene they produced was, to Ben, captivating. A large expanse of blue sky above a large expanse of shorn green field, dotted with large, round, black, shining objects. It was both a natural landscape and an abstract one – a rare occurrence.

Ever since the black plastic bales came into the fields Ben had produced a painting of them each year, from different viewpoints but always kept it simple. Each year he had put them in a local gallery and each year nobody had bought them. Clearly, they did not see what he saw, and preferred his regular output of recognisable Lake District scenes.

This year was no exception and full of hope that eventually somebody would "get the message" he had delivered his latest "black bag" oil painting to a Keswick gallery while on his way to his weekly art lesson run by the council's Adult Education Department. Although he was proficient enough to produce paintings that sold to tourists, Ben was well aware of his limitations, particularly with watercolours.

Roger Coulson, his tutor this term, a retired art teacher who looked and acted like an absent-minded professor, arriving by bicycle, forgetting to remove his clips and backpack, "smoking" his unlit pipe, was particularly good with watercolours, and Ben had so far learned from him some of the techniques necessary to achieve better results. But he couldn't, as yet, produce them consistently. He shared the classroom with a diverse group of eight others, depending on the weather and other commitments. John and Mary Donaldson, in their eighties, were always there first. Ben suspected this was the highlight of their week. They took their lessons very seriously and tried hard to improve. Mary was quite good, but John was painfully slow and seemed unable to produce anything of the slightest merit. Sitting beside them was Tom Carter, in his thirties, out of work, full of artistic confidence but who did what he thought was right and not what the tutor told him. Three or four ladies in their sixties always sat in a row in the middle of the classroom, so that they could converse while working. The standard of their work indicated that it was more of a social occasion than an art class for them, although Jean and Claire occasionally sprang surprises, particularly with paintings of flowers. Always last in and seated on his own at the back was Alan Williams, a forty-year-old forestry worker. He was as dark and swarthy as his Welsh name suggested yet the few words he did utter were in a broad Cumbrian accent. Every class has an Alan – shy, quiet, doesn't join in the banter. His drawing was good, but he struggled with the mixing and application of paint.

Ben knew that he was more accomplished than his classmates, but he also knew that the people who were not there – the professionals – were streets ahead of him and were out there producing while he sat learning. But he wasn't concerned, he wasn't ambitious. He enjoyed learning and a level of socialising that was pleasant and undemanding.

At the end of the lesson Ben looked down at his painting with disgust. He would never master watercolours. He had failed to get the correct tone in his first washes and there were hard edges everywhere. He should stick to oils he told himself, but he didn't like to give up on a challenge. No doubt he would be back for more.

Before heading for home he called at the library to change some books, then at the supermarket to pick up a few things on Helen's shopping list. As he loaded his car he glanced upwards and around, as always. And, as always, he was struck by the beauty the surrounding fells bestowed on the town. A few high, white clouds drifting with the prevailing westerly breeze had gathered on top of Skiddaw, as if taking a breather before continuing their journey into infinity. Today, Skiddaw was as warm and friendly as a favourite aunt. Sometimes it was distant and aloof; sometimes a fearsome snow-capped alp; sometimes a close neighbour keeping a protective watch. How many supermarket car parks could boast such a view? How lucky he was to live in such a place.

His feeling of luck stayed with him as he weaved his way out of town. Then it grew as he wended his way through the sublime valley landscape, accompanied on the car radio by Beethoven's Pastoral symphony. And it continued when he remembered that Helen said she was having a baking afternoon.

Approaching the cottage he was momentarily surprised by the absence of Helen's car, then remembered that it had gone to the garage for a service. He offloaded and carried the shopping bags to the back of the cottage, to the kitchen entrance. The door was locked. He walked to the front of the house and found the front door also locked. Locked doors were routine for a couple of years after Helen's experience with Hector Snodd, but things had returned to normal since then. He returned to the back of the cottage. If Helen was baking she should be in the kitchen. He knocked on the kitchen door. There was no reply. He moved to the kitchen window and put his face to the glass to see inside. With a sigh of relief, he saw Helen appear from a shadowed corner and approach the kitchen door. The door opened and Helen emerged. She looked gaunt. She was holding one of his golf clubs in her right hand.

Hesitant, and scarcely audible she said, "I think... I'm going mad."

Chapter 11

A light shower flicked at the windows of the cottage; the ducks, having been fed, had waddled back down to the lake; the pheasants remained, goose-stepping around the lawn cleaning up the scraps. A police car sat cooling on the gravel.

Inside the cottage, around the kitchen table, Helen and Ben and an off-duty Sergeant Peter Murphy sat drinking a morning coffee. Ben had phoned him the night before, asked him to come and listen to Helen. Peter had his notebook and pen on the table in front of him. "So, Helen..." he invited.

A tired-looking Helen took a deep breath and spoke on the outward sigh, "I was working in the kitchen yesterday afternoon when I saw a man through the window. He was standing on the lawn beside the beech tree and was staring at the cottage. I wasn't concerned at first because we occasionally get tourists in the garden. They get mixed up with the paths down to the lake and finish up here. But when this man saw me at the window he suddenly hid behind the beech tree and stayed there. It was as if he thought he had been looking at an empty house and was surprised to find somebody in. That could be because there were no cars outside. Ben was out in Keswick with his and my car was at the garage for servicing. But I still wasn't concerned. He was only a small man and he had acted like a guilty schoolboy caught red-handed. So I went outside to reassure him that he wasn't trespassing, and to help him find the right path to the lake."

Helen paused, closed her eyes, took another breath, then continued, "When he saw me approaching, he stepped out from behind the tree and came towards me, and smiled." She stopped abruptly. There was a long pause, then, "Those teeth…those tiny teeth… I'll never forget them." She stared ahead in recollection. Ben reached over and took hold of her hand.

"Go on," Peter urged. "What happened next?"

"I screamed… yes… I screamed… and I ran back into the house and locked the door. I rushed to the window but he was gone… at least I thought he'd gone, but I couldn't be sure. Then I ran to the front door and locked that. I tried to keep calm, tried to work out what to do. I thought of ringing the police, but what could I tell them… a man had smiled at me… he looked like somebody who was dead…"

"You didn't phone Ben?" Peter queried.

"No… no… I should have… I didn't want to spoil his afternoon at the art class… I know I was stupid… but that's how I am… I… I…"

Ben came to her rescue. "Anyway, Peter," he said forcefully. "I would pity that man if he had come near her. She had my eight iron in her hand when I came home and I've no doubt she would have used it to good effect. A lost ball comes to mind."

Peter glanced at Ben, grimaced, and stayed on track, "Had you told Helen about that note before yesterday afternoon?" he asked.

Ben looked uncomfortable. "No, I hadn't. I didn't want to upset her if it was genuine, and you thought it was a prank anyway. I told her about it last night. I had to, of course, after what happened yesterday." He looked at Helen and squeezed her hand. "Weren't too pleased with me were you dear?"

Helen attempted a tired smile of forgiveness. "We're as bad as each other, trying to protect each other and doing the wrong thing in the process."

"So," Peter continued. "This man was the double of Hector Snodd... is that what you're saying?"

Helen hesitated. "Well... I only saw him for a few seconds. He wasn't his double, but I would say he must be closely related to be so similar. He had the same narrow face, the same features... the same teeth, the same mouth... and the same wide nose. But he was younger and his hair was a different colour... it was darker..."

"Ben told me what you said when he came home yesterday," Peter said, sympathetically. "No wonder you thought you were going mad. If it wasn't for that note I would have thought so too. But unlike biblical stories, dead men don't rise from the grave in real life, so until proven otherwise, we must assume that you are being targeted by a member of the Snodd family, somebody we didn't know existed until now. Perhaps a younger brother or even a son, although there is nothing in his records that show he had either. Hopefully – and I think you should both draw some slight comfort from this – he is just trying to frighten you. He has been here on two occasions we know of and had the opportunity to do harm to you or your property and has not done so. Unfortunately, until he does there is nothing much that we can do. Personally, I'd love to provide you with a 24-hour vigilance service, but I know my boss won't have it, not on the information I have here." He indicated his notebook. "What I think I can do is persuade him to order the night patrols in this area to call down your lane each night and check you out. The other thing I will do is take this info back to base and hand it over to detectives to investigate Snodd's family history and background. As well as the usual registrars, they will get in contact with the police up in Thurso and ask them to question the locals about Snodd's family history. Let's hope they come up with something quickly and we can get this joker found and dealt with. Meanwhile, I will alert everybody at the station to the situation, and tell them how to react if they get a call from you to say that he's returned. Just ring me personally, or the station, and we will come running, or driving even, and try to catch him in the act."

Peter took a drink of his coffee. A long silence followed. Helen flinched when the letter box slammed shut. She hadn't heard the postman's van arrive. "Any questions?" Peter asked.

Ben cleared his throat, "What would have happened if this man had come into the house and attacked Helen and she had clobbered him unconscious with the golf club?"

"Times have changed, thank goodness," Peter replied. "The law is now on the side of the householder. You can take all reasonable measures to protect yourself and your property without fear of prosecution."

"Looks like I'm going to have to buy a new eight iron," Ben quipped.

"Don't forget, Ben," Peter emphasised. "If we are dealing with a member of the Snodd family it will be you he's interested in, not Helen. Don't *you* forget to protect yourself at all times."

"What do you think the new eight iron is for," Ben joked. "I never could use the thing on the course."

Chapter 12

"Here is a charming and secluded natural sanctuary in an idyllic setting, a place of calm, where a peaceful farming community husband the good earth now as for centuries past. Every rod, pole and perch of it is delightful and unspoilt." Josephine Turner paused, looked up from the small book in her hand and smiled at the camera a few feet away. She continued, "This is how Wainwright described Wythop Valley, and I couldn't agree more." As she finished this sentence she turned with her right arm outstretched and invited the television audience to see what she could see. The cameraman followed her movements then proceeded to pan around the valley. These shots would later be mixed with shots looking down from the tops of the surrounding fells and from a helicopter which would circle the valley later that afternoon as they were finishing the day's shoot.

Dave, the cameraman, completed his circuit shots, cut the power and started to walk forward, up the narrow lane. The sound man, Steve, had already lowered his boom pole, reduced it to about a metre long with a twist of the telescopic mechanism, and set off to follow him. After a few paces, Dave turned and saw Josephine still stationary, checking her appearance in a mirror. "Howay, Jo," he shouted, "Move that lovely orse of yours, we haven't got all day."

Jo winced, even though she was used to his irreverent patter by now. It was that Geordie accent. He had reduced her best feature to an "orse". He and Steve had been hired from a small Newcastle independent because of their proximity to the Lakes and, no doubt, because they were twenty per cent cheaper than their competitors in Manchester. Dave was, however, good at his job and she had to admit she found his straight talking a refreshing change from the gushing insincerities of the London crowd. She also had to admit that she found *his* arse and the rest of his athletic physique very attractive. While she plodded breathlessly up the fells he could run up them effortlessly while carrying his heavy equipment.

This was the last day of shooting on another series of 'Walking with Wainwright' and Jo was sad. When she had been asked to take over from the usual presenter she had jumped at the chance. The series had been incredibly popular, pulling in far greater audiences than had been expected. She had seen it as a major step up in her career path, a chance to make a name for herself and thus increase her future income. But she had never been particularly interested in the outdoors and had never visited the Lake District. Her fit and healthy look had been bought in a London gymnasium alongside hundreds of other ambitious clones who knew that looks went a long way in the scramble to the top. Now, however, after a few weeks of filming among the fells and valleys, she was hooked. She had never realised that such wild beauty existed in England. The unique landscape had worked its magic on her and she had grown to love it. She saw now why people came back year after year: here they found an oasis of peace and spectacular natural beauty in an overcrowded, urbanised desert. It was very precious, and she was going to miss it.

"Coming," she shouted, as she slipped her mirror back into her backpack, and set off after them. It was a warm, clear-skied morning and the forecast was good. Good, that is, for the holidaymakers who liked to sunbathe by a lake and pop in now and again to cool off; perhaps not so good for a film crew with a fell to climb. Soon she caught up with them, and gave Dave a playful slap on the back of his curly hair as she passed him. "One orse coming through," she said, in her interpretation of a Geordie accent.

She was well aware that Dave had a genuine regard for her posterior. When watching playbacks of the previous days' shoots it had become noticeable that shots of her rear end were playing an increasing role as the days passed. She said nothing. She knew many of them would be edited out, and she actually felt flattered by Dave's attention.

It had been a long time since her husband paid her any compliments. Ten years her senior, and an established television performer, his flattery had stopped soon after their wedding. Gradually, he had "disappeared" in pursuit of his own ambitions, leaving her, the young journalist, to plough a lonely furrow. She had been too young, too naïve, too star-struck to see it coming. Now they virtually lived separate lives under the same roof, but it was her deepest wish to change that situation, and this new job was the stepping stone. She dreamt of the day when she would earn more than him, when she could show him her bank account, then show him the door.

A few hundred yards further along the valley she stopped to consult the shooting schedule with Dave. "What do you think… about here… this should do it?"

Dave looked ahead, into the far distance, then at her through the camera. "Aye… should be good… if you stand right there I'll have you well framed, and after you've finished speakin' I can zoom up behind you and finish on Skiddaw."

While Steve extended the boom pole again, linked it to the camera, and took up his position beside Dave, Jo studied her notes.

"Right, let's do it", she said suddenly, and took up her position. The camera light came on, her face came alive, and she said, "We are now about halfway along Wythop Valley travelling west to east, and it is from this point that you can best see what Wainwright described as 'The Great Illusion'. He also called it a 'geographical freak' and he got quite excited, and wrote about 'hearts quickening because you think you have discovered an unknown 3000-foot peak'. This is because, as you can see behind me, the valley leads to a large mountain at the end and you don't expect to see one there; it is not on your Ordnance Survey map. But study the map more closely, or walk with me to the end of the valley and you will see the reason for this illusion. It's because, although we are in a valley, it is 600 feet high and the land ahead suddenly drops down to Bassenthwaite Lake, which we can't see from here. We are therefore looking at 'dear old Skiddaw of course', as Wainwright put it." Jo looked down at her little book, and continued, "He said: 'It's not immediately recognisable from this angle... but how odd!... What an illusion!'" She looked up to camera. "And I think you will agree it is very strange indeed." She turned to look up the valley towards Skiddaw, and Dave followed with the camera and finished the take with a zoomed close-up of Skiddaw.

Moving on, they spent some time on the edge of Wythop Wood where she told a future audience that the woods and the surrounding area had once been home to a major pheasantry and was still the home of roe deer. Shortly afterwards they paid a fleeting visit to the ruins of a cottage that the pheasantry gamekeeper used to occupy. Then they made their way up the eastern slope of Sale Fell, where they spent much time filming the magnificent views overlooking Bassenthwaite Lake, pointing out the tenth-century church of St Bega on the lake's eastern bank and the two mansion houses – Mirehouse, famous for its literary connections, and Scarness, now known because of its infamous caretaker.

On reaching the summit of Sale Fell they pointed the camera north and west to show that it was possible to see the Solway Firth and the hills of Scotland, and, regrettably, a number of wind turbines that now desecrated the intervening landscape and infuriated the locals who had had them imposed on them against their wishes.

Not wishing to finish the day on a low note and tired of waiting for the helicopter which was scheduled to fly over the summit for the final aerial shot, they clambered down the southern slope of Sale Fell and finished with a brief visit to another rarity: the remains of a remote church called – so an inscribed tablet of stone told them – *Wythop Old Church*. It was one of two reserves on the shooting list, to be visited if time permitted. Speaking to camera, Jo said, "I'm told that once every year there is still a service held here among these ruins. What a romantic thought, and what a romantic valley Wythop is. I, for one, will also be returning here again." And she held her farewell smile as Dave finished the close-up, and the camera light went out.

"Phew! Long hot day, but a good one," Dave said, as he wiped his sweating face with his handkerchief and started to pack up his camera. He glanced at Jo and said, "You were really good today…you sounded so genuine…"

"I don't know whether to take that as a compliment or an insult," Jo frowned.

Dave hesitated, "Sorry… I didn't mean… it's just that you seemed to get better… more involved as the days went by."

"Yes, you're right," Jo acknowledged. "I just got to like this place more and more… it got under my skin."

"Nice place to be," Dave said, instinctively, then hurried on before Jo could comment. "Did you mean that just now about returning to this valley again?"

"I did actually. I'm going to come back to a lot of places…"

"It would be nice to see you again," Dave said, with a seriousness not heard before. Then in a hurried attempt at camouflage, he quipped, "Let's hope they make another series next year, eh!"

But it was too late. Steve as well as Jo had heard the smitten tone in his voice. They exchanged uncertain glances. Jo turned her back to Dave and pretended to look at the sky. Steve, who had already packed away his sound equipment, suddenly announced, "Look, I'm going to shoot off now. I've got me own car today, remember, and I'm in a hurry to get home. I'll probably see you next week, Dave. And I'll be seeing you on me telly later this year, Jo. It was good working with you... cheers." And he strode off without waiting for a reply from either of them.

They were left standing in a little amphitheatre – a small, sunken area of long grass surrounded by trees. Its geography had trapped the afternoon sun and the hot, humid air was almost edible. The only sound was the occasional call of a buzzard gliding in the thermals above. Jo turned and faced Dave, who seemed to be waiting for her. He smiled, "All alone, eh?"

Jo dropped her eyes from his and mumbled, "I think we'd better get going..." She started to move off.

Dave put his hand out involuntarily and touched her shoulder. "Hang on, Jo."

She stopped and looked at him. His eyes told her everything.

"I'm married, Dave... you're a great guy... but I'm married". Even as she said the words she was supposed to say, a part of her hoped he would ignore them.

Dave put his camera down on the grass. "Words, bonny lass...they're just words. Now with your permission I'm going to take hold of your hand, and I'm going to kiss it, and if you don't want that to happen just step away and we'll carry on as though nothin's happened."

Jo swallowed. Her brain told her legs to move, but they seemed to have a mind of their own. While she hesitated, Dave reached out and took hold of her right hand and raised it to his lips. And before the buzzard cried out again he had her in his arms and was lowering her to the ground as he kissed her.

Ten minutes later, engrossed in their passion, they ignored the sound of a helicopter circling the valley, and were unaware that a pair of joyless eyes was watching them from the nearby trees.

Chapter 13

"So here's the news," Peter said, enthusiastically, as he put his drink back on the table. Ben and Bill lowered their recently acquired pints of Cumberland Ale and leaned forward. They had shortened the round to nine holes due to light rain, and their eagerness to learn Peter's news as soon as possible.

"I've had some info from Windermere Station on their two recent deaths," Peter started. "It looks like you might have been right after all, Ben. That is, right to suspect murder, but not right about who murdered who. There is still nothing to connect anybody with the death of Giles Innes. No more witnesses have come forward and that swimmer has not been located yet. And Tulip was definitely not the swimmer. Everybody questioned – his friends, neighbours, staff at the Greenstone Hotel – laughed when it was suggested. They all said that his one and only leisure pursuit was drinking. Nobody had ever seen him swim or heard him talk about going for a swim. And the local swimming pools had never seen him. The owner of the Greenstone Hotel admitted his dislike for Innes but ridiculed the idea that Tulip had been doing his dirty work for him. He, himself, had a rock-solid alibi at the time of Innes's death, and anyway, he was too old to swim like that.

So, at the moment, the death of Innes is still looking very much like an accident."

"The swimmer is yet to be accounted for," Ben reminded him.

"That's true," Peter responded, "and since nobody local has come forward or been identified, they are working on the assumption that the swimmer was probably a tourist. As enquiries progress, they may eventually put out a national media campaign to ask him or her to come forward."

Ben nodded.

Peter continued, "Now, Tulip's death is another matter. While they interviewed everybody I've mentioned about the possibility of Tulip being a swimmer, they also asked if anybody knew of any problems he had in his personal life. Nobody knew of any, and bank checks showed he didn't have any money worries. So they concluded that suicide was unlikely. It was certainly looking like an accident caused by drink. Then two days after the official interviews, one of the Greenstone Hotel staff turned up at Windermere Station and informed them that two members of staff had left the hotel on the night of Tulip's death. He also said that Tulip had bullied both of them, hinting that they might have taken revenge. When questioned as to why he was, in effect, putting two ex-colleagues in potentially deep trouble, he eventually confessed that he was sick of foreigners taking all the local jobs. He explained that he was a local and he had a sister who had been unable to get work in the hotels because of foreigners working for low wages. Apparently, one of the two who had done a runner was a Filipino woman called Babalato. Her partner was a Scotsman called Stott."

"Surely the owner should have told the police about these two leaving when they did?" Ben queried.

Peter sighed, patronisingly. "Of course he should, Ben. And, of course, the police went back and asked him why he hadn't. He told them that they were decent young kids who wouldn't hurt a fly, and he hadn't wanted to waste police time by sending them after them on a wild goose chase. And he had no idea where they had gone. They had left without telling him. Needless to say the DI on the case took a very dim view of this and, apparently, gave him a severe dressing down. If it had been me I would have charged him with obstructing the police in the performance of their duties. The trouble is, in small towns like Windermere everybody knows everybody else, and you can bet that the DI knew the owner of the Greenstone, and knew him to be a decent bloke. The local DI wouldn't want to take a local man down, particularly one whose business had been hit hard by the speed restriction. And I wouldn't be surprised if the DI already knew that the hotel was operating with some illegal labour and had turned a blind eye to it. Anyway, Ben, here comes the interesting part. The description of the Scotsman given by the owner, and by the staff member who dropped him in it, tallies with the description Helen gave us of the man in your garden."

"What!" Ben gasped. "I don't believe it. We have had two hours on the course and then you've sat there calmly going through the investigations, then you spring this on me. How long have you had this information?"

"Late yesterday afternoon," Peter replied calmly. "That's why I left it until today, I knew we would be meeting up."

Ben tried to control himself. "I take it this means the police have found this man Stott and he is in custody?" he asked, pointedly.

"Er… no," Peter said, quietly.

"I don't believe it!" Ben seethed. "A man you obviously suspect of murder is seen in our garden a few days ago… you saw the state of Helen… and you sit here talking about it as if it is an academic subject on a training course. We need action now…we need some protection…"

"Take it easy, Ben," Peter interrupted. "It's almost certain that he's not in the area anymore. We will, of course, be checking every hotel and guest house in the Lakes to make sure they haven't found other work here. Where could they hide out without money? They can't pay rent without money. They can't sign on for benefits. No, they must have gone to find work somewhere as far away from here as possible. London would be my guess, hide in the biggest crowd. If Stott killed Tulip he'll have run a mile by now. If he's innocent you have nothing to worry about."

"Run a mile?" Ben gasped. "So how come he was seen in our garden two weeks after Tulip died. Popped back to admire our flowers, did he?"

Peter hesitated, clearly caught out. "…We don't know for sure that Stott was the man in your garden, do we? All we have are descriptions. Hopefully, we will be able to clear things up when Thurso police finish their investigations."

Ben snarled, "In the meantime, Helen and I can rest peacefully in our bed knowing with absolute certainty that a man who has called at our house twice, who is either a suspected murderer or a relative of a madman whose death I was responsible for, or both, will not come again?"

"Look, Ben," Peter insisted. "The police cannot provide twenty-four hour protection for everybody who *might* be in danger. We do risk assessments and at the moment your case has been classified as a non-specific threat. If things change, if Thurso establish that Snodd had a young brother or a son or a nephew, then we will reassess the situation. We would probably supply you and Helen with personal panic alarms that connect you directly to Police Headquarters where they can hear immediately what is going on at your end. All local officers would be briefed on the circumstances and provision made for an immediate response should it be necessary. You should also always carry a mobile phone so that HQ could phone you after you have pressed your panic button."

Ben stood up, took out his mobile phone, and walked to the corridor outside the lounge bar. Peter and Bill glanced at each other, pursed their lips, raised their eyebrows, but said nothing.

A few minutes later, Ben returned, sat down, and stared out the window.

Bill broke the silence, "Everything all right?"

"I was checking on Helen," Ben said, plainly. "She's working at home today. She's okay. I told her about Stott, and I reminded her about locking the doors."

Apparently unembarrassed by Ben's protestations, Peter addressed Bill, "This bloke, Stott, has opened up a whole new set of possibilities."

"How come?" Bill managed to say while downing a mouthful of ale.

"Well, think about it. *He* could be the killer of both Innes and Tulip. He kills Innes first, then pushes Tulip in the lake to make his death look like suicide, so that we will think Tulip killed Innes, then committed suicide."

"So what is his motive for killing Innes?" Bill queried.

"Don't know yet," Peter mused. "Maybe he thought he was doing the hotel owner a favour, without the owner knowing about it. Maybe the owner did know about it. If Stott is a relative of Snodd's, maybe he doesn't need a motive, maybe he is a serial killer like Snodd."

"Snodd did have a motive," Ben interjected. "At least *he* thought he had one which is the same thing."

"Fair enough," Peter agreed. "So maybe Stott thinks the same crazy way. Maybe he has some crazy motive for killing people. If it is found that he is related to Snodd, and he is a good swimmer, then I think a lot of old files will be getting opened for reinvestigation."

"Old files?" Ben queried.

Peter sighed, as if tired of having to repeat himself to an ancient relative, "Remember I told you there had been quite a few unexplained deaths throughout the Lakes in recent times. Well, Stott had been at the Greenstone for eighteen months, which is approximately the time period in which these deaths have occurred."

"It's a hell of leap from circumstantial suspicion of one death to serial killer, isn't it," Ben said, cuttingly.

"Not when you take those descriptions into account," Peter insisted. "Stott could well be the relative of Snodd we are looking for. Maybe killing is in the family genes."

"You were dismissing the veracity of those descriptions a minute ago," Ben argued, "and if Stott was a relative of Snodd he could not be a son or brother otherwise his name would be Snodd. That leaves only a nephew or a cousin."

"I know," Peter blustered. "I'm just theorising all possibilities now."

"What about the fact that Stott has a Filipino girlfriend. Snodd's wife was Filipino." Bill had decided to enter the debate in support of Peter. "You would normally say that that is a coincidence not to be ignored, wouldn't you, Ben?"

"...Yes," Ben nodded, grudgingly.

Peter went on, "Then there's that note left at your house – H S LIVES ON – that implies a continuation of Snodd's life or deeds. Maybe Stott is trying to emulate his famous relative... sort of relive his life... become famous... leave a mark. It's usually small, downtrodden, bullied men who have the urge to do that."

"You've been reading those profiler books again, haven't you?" Ben sniped,

"And I'm not ashamed to admit it," Peter countered. "That is how you become a good policeman. And besides, they are a damned good read... very interesting."

Bill cleared his throat, a sound that told Ben this time he was on his side. Old coppers like Bill didn't put much store by profilers. Bill looked at Peter, "So what kind of relative do you think Stott's going to be – a nephew or a cousin?"

Ben couldn't decide whether Bill's question was serious or rhetorical, and he doubted whether Bill either knew or cared. He was probably just trying to keep the conversation going until he finished his beer.

"Neither," Peter offered. "I'm betting that Stott is Snodd's brother, having changed his name to avoid the family slur. Remember, Snodd had a daughter and by all accounts was a decent father until he went mad. So surely a son would have been with the family as well as the daughter. And brothers, particularly brothers with a big age gap between them, often lose touch with each other. I suppose a cousin or nephew couldn't be completely ruled out, but it's not often they look so alike."

"A profiler and a genealogist," Ben scoffed, and then regretted it. "Sorry, Peter... I've been on edge ever since Helen came face to face with... whoever it was..."

"Forget it, Ben," Peter said. "It's not surprising."

There was a long silence, then in a conciliatory tone, Ben asked, "Can I use any of this in the paper? I'd like to get it in for obvious reasons... maybe somebody local will recognise Stott's description."

"No!" Peter said, firmly. "No... it's still unofficial... not to be released to the public yet."

Another silence followed. This time it was broken by Bill. "Did you hear that one about the eighty-year-old man with an eighteen-year-old wife?"

Chapter 14

In the Lake District a man in a suit is almost as conspicuous as a man in a tutu. Which is why Dominic Lund had disguised himself in the trappings of the outdoors – boots, walking stick, backpack and waterproofs. It was his first time in the District and he had been staggered by the number of shops selling such paraphernalia. How was it, he wondered, in an age when more time than ever is spent indoors – an explosion of shops selling outdoor gear takes place? The same could be said for sport – much less played, many more shops.

Something strange, even perverse, seemed to be happening as the technological age took over. Dozens of cookery programmes on television when fewer people cooked at home; programmes being watched avidly by people eating takeaways. The trivia of celebrity dominating the media when the world was in political and economic turmoil. Perhaps the growing displacement of the real world by the virtual world was causing these distortions.

These thoughts came and went in a few seconds of introspection as he hitched his backpack, changed his grip on his walking stick and continued walking along the grassy banks of the lake.

Dominic was a child of the virtual world, born shortly after an American company called Motorola gave birth to the first mobile phone. Since then, technology had dominated his life, his fascination with it bringing him great rewards but also great sorrow, with the death of his famous mother and six interminable years in prison.

It was on the point of destroying him, his brilliant brain slowly succumbing to the fog of routine, banal activities and conversation when, his colleagues, who had been sentenced to five years each, managed to smuggle in a smartphone with spare SIM cards and life became much more bearable. He was able to convert his electric shaver into a charger, and to keep in touch with them most of the time. Thus, he didn't fall behind in the fast-changing world of computer technology. An Elite Hacker couldn't afford to drop behind.

Dominic had met his colleagues at the SummerCon hacker convention in Barcelona. Alberto from Brazil and Vyan from India, both 18, had impressed him with their abilities and enthusiasm and they had agreed to team up in London to see if they could shake the world. They had started off as 'White Hat' hackers – the ethical arm of hacking – winning some contracts to test the vulnerability of company systems. But eventually they found this didn't stretch them enough or pay them enough, so they turned to 'Black Hat' hacking, just to make money. It was at this time they decided to call their group "Robin Hood" as they decided only to take money from the rich. Over a surprisingly short period of time they were able to relieve companies and wealthy individuals of considerable sums of money. Alberto did the targeting, Vyan the research and information gathering, and Dominic analysed their results and decided who to go for. This, too, eventually became relatively easy and unsatisfying, and so they decided to test themselves against the biggest, most powerful computer systems in the world. Their objective was not financial gain or anything of a criminal nature, though they realised that just the act of hacking into national systems would be classed as criminal. It was simply to test their capabilities, their expertise, their brain-power. They had no intention of disrupting or harming any of the systems they invaded – they would not use viruses, worms, rootkits, Trojan horses and the like – they just wanted to see if they could get in.

They started with the big international car companies, and they were soon successful. Having found their way into the head office central financial system they would typically leave a message on the personal computer of the finance director saying something like "good to see you made $19,591,341 profit last month. Robin Hood won't touch it, we have our own horsepower".

Gradually, as their exploits made international news, Robin Hood became one of the biggest names in the hacking fraternity, culminating in their recognition as Elite Hackers.

It was during this phase that Dominic's mother, ex-newspaper editor and TV personality, Sophie Lund, returned to London from France, having walked out on her French lover and his vineyard.

A few weeks after her return she contacted Dominic and asked him if he would hack into the Ministry of Defence systems to find what he could on "Operation Pluto". She told him that she had been tipped off by an old contact in the Ministry who had heard rumours about a proposed secret operation called Pluto. Apparently the contact owed her a favour from years ago when, as editor of a daily national, she had quashed a story she was going to run about the contact's extramarital affair.

Dominic, Alberto and Vyan had relished the task and risen to the challenge. After weeks of fruitless work and blind alleys they had finally found a file marked "Operation Pluto". The system's designers had not put it in the TOP SECRET zone, but left it amongst thousands of routine files with no special category annotated. They had, however, restricted its availability to a few named people.

The file contained records of meetings between political and military leaders from Britain and the USA regarding the possibility of transferring "material" from Sellafield to a US base in the Nevada desert. They had apparently agreed to look into the possibility of doing the transfer under cover of the decommissioning project taking place on the old Windscale Power Station site.

It didn't take Dominic's team long to learn that the "material" was weapons-grade plutonium and that the US base in the Nevada desert was probably still capable of making nuclear weapons. Further investigation showed that this went against all internationally agreed protocols, the latest being an agreement between Russia and the USA to each "dispose of" 34 tonnes of weapons-grade plutonium as part of their non-proliferation agreement. The USA was, in fact, currently in the process of building a new MOX plant to convert the plutonium into a fuel suitable for use in nuclear reactors producing electricity. So, it seemed that the USA, with Britain's help, was bent on getting rid of weapons-grade plutonium with one hand while replacing it with the other, thus deceiving the Russians and the rest of the world.

When Sophie Lund had received this startling information from Dominic, including all the names on the file, she immediately saw it as a way to get back into the headlines and secure another top job in the newspaper world. She couldn't, however, let the world know that her information had been obtained by her son hacking into government computer systems, so she set about making enquiries amongst her old contacts in a typical journalistic fashion to create the impression that her information, when revealed, had been obtained through routine investigative journalism.

One of her first ports of call amongst her old political contacts had been Jack Fraser, Secretary of State for Trade and Industry. She had known him for years when he held positions in the government's Press Relations and Culture departments, and she trusted him implicitly. She had been surprised to see his name among those who had access to the Operation Pluto file since he was not in the Defence Ministry. But she then realised that his current job would bring industrial complexes like Sellafield under his department's umbrella and would inevitably entail frequent contact with and visits to Sellafield. He was obviously in the "need to know" category rather than an active participant in an operation which, Sophie believed, Jack would have been horrified to learn about. She knew him as a man of principle and honesty.

When Sophie finally achieved a meeting with Jack Fraser she asked him immediately what he knew about Operation Pluto. He had tried to hide the instinctive, shocked expression on his face but knew that he had failed. After a long pause he said, "Let us say that I find most things in politics very worthwhile and elevating, and a few that are deeply disturbing and unforgivable. For the record, I know nothing about an Operation Pluto."

Two weeks after that interview Jack Fraser and his wife had been found dead while on holiday in the Lake District. Sophie had immediately suspected that Jack had been silenced by those in government who were afraid that a man of his integrity would not keep quiet about Operation Pluto. It was at this point that Sophie, during a visit to the Lake District immediately following Jack's death, had recruited a Lake District journalist called Ben Foxley to try to find out the truth behind the death of Jack Fraser. When Ben Foxley eventually told her that he needed access to police and mountain rescue team records and photographs in order to confirm his theory about Jack's death, she had turned to Dominic and his team. Dominic had questioned the wisdom of involving an outsider and it was with reluctance that he eventually obtained and handed over all the information that Ben Foxley had asked for.

A few weeks later his mother was shot dead in her London apartment, the victim of a burglary the police announced, pointing out that the apartment had been ransacked. Shortly afterwards, Dominic and his colleagues were arrested and charged with hacking into police and other records. During one of many interrogations by two men in plain clothes who did not introduce themselves, it was made clear to them, in a cold, matter-of-fact way, that they should forget about the existence of Operation Pluto otherwise they would meet the same fate as Dominic's mother. "You will not be safe from us in prison," they said. "And the Operation will be over by the time you come out, and all traces of it extinguished. If you tell your story at this point, nobody will believe you, but we will kill you just in case."

It was clear to Dominic that Ben Foxley had betrayed his mother to the police and that the subsequent search of her apartment had led them to Robin Hood.

The terrible tragedy of the whole thing was that, while awaiting trial, Dominic learned that the death of Jack Fraser had nothing to do with the government or Operation Pluto. He and his wife had been the innocent victims of a serial killer called Hector Snodd. This unbearable fact had plagued Dominic's mind every day of his six years in prison.

As the years slowly passed, his hatred of the person who had shot his mother lessened – he/she had been doing a job, following orders. But his hatred of the man who had betrayed her, thereby causing her death and his incarceration in prison, did not lessen. It grew year on year, and by the time of his release it had become a malignant black growth in his mind; something, he decided, that could only be removed by removing the man who caused it. Only revenge – good old fashioned revenge – could purge his mind, return it to its former brilliant clarity.

While in prison he had consulted with his fellow inmates on the best way to kill somebody. Surprisingly long discussions had ensued covering purpose, methods, motivation, possibility of detection, weapon reliability, strengths and weaknesses of perpetrator and victim etc. He was clearly among experts in their field. Some had offered to introduce him to people who could supply him with a gun; others, in the drug business, to people who could supply a syringe for the purpose of air injection into the arteries – voted the best method to avoid detection. They agreed that, if personal hatred and revenge was involved, by far the most satisfying method was personal contact, i.e. beating to death with fists or a heavy object. Though the most satisfying, this method was also the most risky if the victim fought back, and it was high on the possibility of detection list.

Dominic came away from these discussions with the disturbing realisation that man is more animal than he had realised. Another world existed out there, one far removed from civilised society. He had stepped outside the norms of this society when hacking, but he had been using his civilised brain. This other world was all about brawn – physical power, animal fear, survival of the strongest, bravest, cruellest. It was both terrifying and admirable, and it was his fervent intention to acquaint Mr Ben Foxley with it.

Now, as Dominic strolled along the eastern bank of Bassenthwaite Lake, he recalled those discussions, those terrible years in prison, his mother's death, and he felt again the malignant growth in his mind and he looked forward to getting rid of it.

He had been watching Ben Foxley for about three weeks, studying his physique, his fitness, learning how he spent his time, his routines, when he left the cottage, where he went, the geography in the vicinity of the cottage and the surrounding area, routes of entrance and exit. Only when he was sure of success would he make his move.

He carried with him at all times the weapon he was going to use. His walking stick came not from one of the local shops but from a dealer in London specialising in rare and traditional sticks. He had rejected those sticks whose handles could be withdrawn to reveal a sword or knife, and chosen instead a traditional old Shillelagh made from blackthorn, the large knob at the top having been hollowed out and filled with molten lead to increase its weight – the cudgel that had split a thousand heads down the centuries. He was taking the advice of his prison companions and going for the satisfaction of personal contact. However, it was because of this that he had regretfully come to the conclusion that now was not the right time. The long, light days of summer filled with hordes of people were not conducive to dark deeds, particularly when the deed would involve close personal contact in an outdoor setting.

This would be the last day of his reconnaissance. He planned to return when the days were short and cold, when the tourists had gone home and there would be nobody to witness a man dressed in black step out of the darkness and crush the skull of his enemy with one mighty, satisfying blow.

Chapter 15

A warm, late summer afternoon saw Ben practising his golf swing on the lawn outside the cottage. Helen had his eight iron in the boot of her car, which was probably parked outside a hotel in Grasmere where she was working on the new swimming pool project. He had insisted that she kept it with her at all times. After lunch he had started on a new painting, but during his afternoon tea break he had been tempted outside by the sunshine, where he grabbed his old seven iron which always leaned against the cottage wall ready for action.

The practising of his swing came secondary to the pleasure of seeing dandelion and daisy heads flying in the air as he made his way around the lawn; the pleasure being diminished when large divots of turf went with them.

Having taken a divot big enough to fill the Grand Canyon, he decided it was time to quit. He walked across the lawn and placed the seven iron back in its usual place. Ritually, before returning indoors, he glanced around his surroundings. Close by – giant trees, home to crows and squirrels; hedges, home to tits and finches, shelter to ducks and pheasants; mid distance – the shimmering lake, the towering fells; far distance – more fells, fading to blue, the ever-changing sky, often filled with flocks of geese visiting the lake. Whatever the time of year there was always something to make him stop and stare and wonder at its beauty.

His reverie was interrupted by that destroyer of contemplation – the telephone. He reached the hall phone just in time.

"Can you come down to the station?" Peter asked, breathlessly. "There's been some important developments about you know who. I'm on duty here, I can't leave and I wanted to let you know as soon as poss… so you don't jump on me again."

"On my way," Ben said, quietly satisfied that his tantrum at the golf club a few days ago had not been wasted.

Peter was sitting behind a desk, a loose-leaf file in front of him, other papers neatly stacked in three groups. He was immaculately dressed in police uniform. How remarkable is the effect a change of clothes and environment can have. Used to lounging in a clubhouse armchair, arguing with his pullover-clad friend, Ben now felt he should be sitting to attention, prepared to believe every word this officer of the state told him.

"Help yourself to paper and pen," Peter said, indicating some blank A4. "You might want to make notes."

Ben reached into his deep inside jacket pocket and pulled out his notebook with pen attached. "I'll use this, thanks." He was about to say something about not wanting to waste taxpayers' money but thought better of it. He and Peter still had a bit of bridge building to do.

Peter flicked open the file in front of him. "Cumbria, Thurso and Edinburgh police have been busy boys…"

"Edinburgh?"

Peter held up his hand. "You'll see in a minute. Thurso police had no record of Snodd having either a brother or a son or a cousin or a nephew, so they went around all their old contacts on the case and eventually came up with a woman called Mrs Janette Muir who lived next door to the Central Hotel which Snodd used to frequent. She gave them the fascinating news that a young man from Edinburgh called Hamish Craik came to see her about two years ago asking for information about Hector Snodd. Apparently, Craik's mother had died and he had found newspaper cuttings about Snodd in her wardrobe. To cut a long story short, she had no doubt that Craik was the son of Snodd. Snodd had had a one-night stand with the daughter of the hotel landlord, Margaret Craik, who had immediately moved to Edinburgh, leaving Snodd unaware that he would become a father. Mrs Muir confirmed that Hamish Craik looked very much like his father, and she also divulged that Craik was on compassionate leave from the army—"

"This all seems a long way from Stott," Ben interrupted.

Peter frowned. "Patience Ben… patience. Thurso police contacted Edinburgh police who went to the last known address of Margaret Craik. Here they interviewed a neighbour called Mrs Finnie. She confirmed the whole story and said she had not seen Hamish Craik since he left Edinburgh after his mother's funeral two years ago. She said the military police had come looking for him, so she assumed he had gone AWOL. Edinburgh police checked their records and found Craik was indeed still listed as AWOL. By now, Edinburgh had also been asked to check if Hamish Craik was known to be a good swimmer. Mrs Finnie said he had spent a lot of time at the local pool, and somebody at the pool remembered him as being a good swimmer. All this information was fed back to Cumbria. They checked the national records of people who have changed their names and lo-and-behold Hamish Craik became Hamish Stott 22 months ago. We have our man." Peter leaned back in his chair with a satisfied look on his face.

"Looks like you know who he is," Ben agreed, as he lifted his head from his notebook. "But I'd feel a lot happier if you did actually *have* him."

"Won't take us long now, Ben, now we know who we are looking for."

"He's been AWOL for two years," Ben pointed out. "Are you telling me nobody has been looking for him all that time?"

Peter shrugged. "More or less. If the military police don't find them early on, they don't spend much time on it. There are about 2000 AWOL's every year and not enough resources to chase after them."

"What about the civilian police… you?"

"Same here, not enough resources. Few are actively pursued. If they stay out of trouble they are unlikely to be caught."

Ben thought for a moment. "What if he ran away from the Greenstone only because he knew the police would turn up there to ask questions about Tulip and, in the process, they would find out about him being AWOL?"

"But police wouldn't have questioned him about him being AWOL, unless they had been tipped off that he was."

"He might not have known that, and didn't want to risk it."

"But he left on the same day that Tulip was found, not later on. Who told him about the death? It was only announced the next morning…you were there, weren't you? And at that stage he couldn't be sure that the police would be going to the Greenstone. No… it looks like the actions of a man who has left the scene of his crime as soon as possible."

"Mmmm," Ben mumbled. "Maybe you're right. And now you know he could swim I suppose you have him down for the murder of Innes as well?"

"Why not? Hell of a coincidence if it wasn't him."

"But you haven't got a definite motive yet."

"True, but once we find him I'm sure we will be able to persuade him to reveal what went on in that mind of his. Remember whose son he is. Maybe he is as crazy as his father."

"And maybe you should have given us more protection when I asked for it," Ben said, coldly. "Surely we are going to get some now. You have no evidence that he has left the area."

Peter leaned forward and scribbled a note on a paper in the file. "Yes, absolutely, Ben. We will issue you with two personal panic alarms which you wear at all times as I described to you before, and make sure you both have your mobiles on you at all times."

"Is that the best you can do? Ben questioned. "Have you had another *risk-assessment* meeting?" The emphasis in his voice carried his disapproval of modern management techniques and the naive faith put in them. In Ben's opinion they had ushered in the abandonment of common sense.

Peter reacted calmly. He was well aware of Ben's contempt for most things introduced after 1970. "Yes we have, Ben. And as you can see your status has been changed, hence the panic alarms. And until there is strong evidence that you and Helen are in imminent danger it will stay like that. We may have no evidence that Stott has left the area, but we still believe he has. He must have had enough money to stick around for a few weeks, maybe in a B&B, which is when Helen saw him, but after that he would have to move on to find work."

Ben wanted to protest further; to point out that evidence of imminent danger more or less implied that he or Helen had to be found dead before real protection could be offered; that it was unprofessional to make decisions based on belief rather than facts. But he was experienced enough to know that an individual has little chance of changing the procedures of a state organisation. "Are we calling him Stott or Craik from now on?" he asked.

"Stott. He's been Stott for the last two years, so if he has left a recent trail it will be using that name. You know, it seems to me that he chose Stott because it starts with the letter S, so that he has the same initials as his father. And the fact that he used those initials on the note he left you could indicate that he intends to relive his father's life. He didn't write Hector Snodd lives on, he wrote H.S. lives on."

Ben scratched his nose with his pen. "How come you're in uniform? How come you didn't go in for detective work, you seem to enjoy analysing things?"

Peter looked uncertain. "Are you being sarcastic, Ben?"

"No... no, not at all," Ben said. "It was a genuine question."

Peter relaxed and said quietly, "Keep it to yourself, but I have applied for a transfer to CID I'm hoping to make it within a year."

"Seems the right place for you," Ben said. "Good luck."

"Thanks."

Ben put his notebook away and rose from his chair. "Thanks for the info, Peter. You'll let me know what and when I can put anything in the paper, won't you?"

Peter nodded as he rose from his chair.

"Just out of interest," Ben said, as he made his way to the door, "are you going to reopen those files you were talking about?"

"In confidence, Ben, yes we are. There are a few cases all over the Lakes and each station has been asked to review them in the light of Stott's presence here over the past eighteen months."

"Good luck with that as well then," Ben said, as he turned and left the room.

Chapter 16

Colin and Judy Grant had been holidaying in the Lakes for 34 years. If you asked Colin he could tell you precisely the date of their first visit, and probably the time of their arrival such was the thoroughness of his diary keeping. One of his favourite pastimes was to browse through his old diaries and recall past holidays, recounting their adventures to a patient, half-listening Judy, intent on counting the stitches of her latest knitting project.

Knitting and reading was as exciting as things got in their Suffolk village; at least that's what the younger generation claimed as they slouched against the trunks of the trees surrounding the village green, eyes transfixed by the small screens in their hands. They were not to know that many of the silver-haired inhabitants of their village had led lives beyond their wildest imaginations; assuming, that is, that they had imaginations, that they had not been deadened by the incessant distraction of their electronic toys.

Colin and Judy, however, although silver-haired, did not belong to that group. They had not won medals in wars, or led expeditions across the Antarctic, or discovered an unknown tribe in the Amazon jungle, or built a business empire, or become film stars. They had passed all of their years in and around the village, as had their parents and grandparents, and now their children and grandchildren. Most of that time had been spent running the village post office.

They had wanted to lead adventurous lives, travel the world, explore the wild places, try their hand at business, but like the majority had been held back by responsibility and lack of resources. Essentially, they lacked the drive and selfishness that allows people to walk away from family and follow their singular ambitions. In recent years, looking after their ageing parents had been replaced by supporting children and grandchildren through the trials of modern life.

It was this life-long self-denial and the placidity of their Suffolk village life that made their holidays in the wilds of the Lake District so special to them. Getting away from the flatness of Suffolk to the mountains of Cumbria was, to them, escaping from monotony to adventure.

Over the years their accommodation in the Lakes had progressed from tent to caravan to guest house, and now to village pubs. Each year they based themselves in a different area and as a result had become broadly familiar with all that the Lake District had to offer. This year they were staying at the Britannia Inn in Elterwater village, undoubtedly one of their favourites, providing as it did a cosy atmosphere in the stunning surroundings of the Langdale Valley.

Each day, after a hearty breakfast, they couldn't wait to get into their boots, load their backpacks with a packed lunch, map, compass, whistle, torch and waterproofs, and set off to explore the fells. Being in their sixties, and having already visited the tops of all the major peaks, they now contented themselves with the lower altitude but no less captivating fells, and their beautiful valleys.

After six summer-long days of wonderful walking Judy's knees told her it was time to take a break. At least that is what she told Colin. The veracity of her claim was in some doubt because she proposed spending the next day visiting the shops in Ambleside. Since Colin couldn't abide shopping, and was feeling fitter and stronger than he had at the start of the holiday, they agreed to go their separate ways on day seven. The plan, which they formed while enjoying a drink in the tiny, crowded bar of the pub, was to jointly take the car into Ambleside, from where Colin would walk back to Elterwater via Loughrigg Fell, while Judy would spend the day in Ambleside then drive the car back to Elterwater later that afternoon.

Day seven looked like being a better day for shopping than for fell walking as a light rain settled over the area. Undeterred, Colin donned his waterproofs and, hoisting his backpack, took his leave of Judy in an Ambleside car park. He didn't need to consult a map to start with because he had done the walk before, but he knew he might be consulting it once on the top because of the many grassy paths that criss-crossed among the rocky knolls and undulations on its surface.

Leaving the town behind, he took the usual stone-wall-lined route via Browhead Farm and was soon on open ground heading up towards Ivy Crag. His spirits soared as he thought of the familiar journey ahead, one of his favourites, full of interest and beauty. With a schoolboy's enthusiasm he set off up the early slopes. Gradually, as he got into his rhythm, the special magic inherent in fell walking started to possess him. He found it difficult to explain to the uninitiated how the simple act of placing one foot in front of another takes on a transcendental quality when it is done with awareness and purpose in such challenging and beautiful outdoor surroundings. It took him back to basics, to his animal self, to an awareness of place and time and his capacity to enjoy the complex movement of his own body. It chased away his troubles, cleared his mind, put things in perspective and brought him to a blissful awareness and enjoyment of *now*.

On reaching Ivy Crag, Colin paused for a bird's-eye view of Windermere, a silver sheet under the light grey sky, the familiarity doing little to dull the wonder that such a view inflicts on the mind. He hoped Judy was enjoying herself, hoped she didn't spend too much money, knew that was unlikely as she would be buying presents to take back to the grandchildren.

Leaving Ivy Crag, he proceeded along the main path for a while then detoured off to the left to get his first view of Loughrigg Tarn and its pastoral surroundings, a beautiful setting more in keeping with the gentle south of England than the wilds of Cumbria.

Back on the path he strode along among the fairy-tale landscape – knolls like miniature castles, undulating mounds of lush green grass, fans of swaying, pungent bracken, shaded rocks thick with emerald green, coral-like moss, unshaded rocks clad in bright yellow lichen declaring the clarity of the air, everywhere the clean, fresh smell of Lakeland rain.

After a while he fancied a last look down on Loughrigg Tarn so he ventured left again, off the path, and took up a position right on the edge of one of the many rocky crags that flanked the whole fell. The sheer drop-away gave him an excellent view of the tarn, and he stood there for some time admiring the scene. He saw colourful dwarfs walking around the tarn, the shining tops of dinky cars moving between the hedges, sheep that looked like mice. He felt like an eagle surveying its kingdom. He heard the dull sound of a booted foot on the rock behind him just before he felt a powerful push in the small of his back. He was unable to stop himself from staggering forward and falling over the crag edge. He didn't cry out but thought of Judy as he flailed in the air. He bounced off a stony slope and somersaulted onwards and pranced and danced on all of his limbs and heard them break before he was stopped abruptly by an ice-age boulder which thankfully cleaved his skull and sent him into oblivion before he had time to feel the pain.

Chapter 17

Late August had Ben, yet again, wondering why agricultural societies chose it for their country shows. Everybody knew that it was one of the wettest months of the year, particularly in the Lake District. Occasionally, the August deluge was too much, fields got flooded and shows had to be called off. Even those that went ahead were often visited by rain, causing disruption and discomfort to exhibitors and spectators alike. But next year it would be August again.

Each year Ben vowed to find out why this was so, and each year he forgot to do so. Since the shows went back over a hundred years he guessed it must be simply the carrying on of tradition; maybe the Augusts weren't so wet in the old days. Whatever the reason, it was his job to cover the Keswick Show for *The Tribune*, and as he entered the show-field and showed his pass to the Wellington-shod gateman, he looked forward to doing it.

He liked agricultural shows, liked their atmosphere, the farmyard smell of grass and animals, the hustle and bustle of sideshows, the drifting smells of hot dogs and beer, of warm bodies inside big tents, craft displays, bygone games and sports, young men wrestling, iron-muscled fell-runners caked in mud, ancient tractors racing. Mostly he liked the idea that farming families – weather-beaten people with muscles on their fingers and earth under their nails, multi-skilled, hard-working, self-sufficient, unpretentious, stoical and probably the most valuable people in the country but rarely recognised as such – got their day in the spotlight.

Ben circulated around the large show-field for a few hours, took photographs of events as they took place, held brief interviews with the worthies he spotted, left his card with event organisers while reminding them to send their results into *The Tribune* office by the deadline date, and stopped to chat to one or two familiar faces in the arts and crafts tent. He kept himself going with a delicious local beefburger and plenty of tea. Later, at home, he would write a couple of hundred words giving general information about the number of visitors, the weather, mention any worthies who attended, and write captions to the selected photographs. The next day, at *The Tribune* office, he would link it all in with the long lists of event results which would be supplied by the organisers.

The following day, having worked alongside editor, Sue Burrows, while putting the agricultural show to bed, Ben decided to call at the headquarters of Keswick Mountain Rescue Team to pick up their news. He was certain they would have news as the summer holiday season always brought its share of unprepared, inexperienced and downright foolish walkers who inevitably got into trouble on the fells and needed rescuing. In the last few years the team had become busier than ever as new tourists arrived to gaze at the places they had seen on their television sets – two channels now running programmes about the Lakes. And the team's burden had been further increased by a new breed of walkers, particularly the young, who used their mobile phones to navigate – "often worse than useless" according to one MRT – and then to call for help when the situation they were in did not warrant it. Call outs by this method had trebled in recent years. As a result, the Lake District Search And Rescue Association (LDSARA) – the umbrella organisation of all 12 Lake District Teams – had issued written guidelines on when and how to use the mobile phone, and Ben and *The Tribune* tried to do their bit by constantly reissuing the guidelines in the paper before busy holiday periods.

The accident statistics put out by the LDSARA seemed, to Ben, to be more than a simple statement of figures; they were a reflection on the state of modern society. The most call-out requests were now made by young people, indicating a lack of self-reliance, and almost fifty per cent of deaths were caused by medical conditions such as heart attacks among the middle aged, indicating the weight-gain and lack of basic fitness in that age group.

As Ben expected, he found a small gathering of cars in the Keswick MRT headquarters car park, indicating a rescue was probably in progress. He climbed the stairs to the control room and found Ian Smith, the controller, busily writing. Ian had gone slightly grey at the temples since they first met eight years ago, but otherwise he was completely unchanged in manner or efficiency. Ben still didn't know him as a person, but nonetheless admired his dedication and efficiency.

"Afternoon, Ian," Ben said, brightly.

Ian swivelled his head slowly, like a turtle, and glanced at Ben. "Afternoon, Ben." His head slowly returned to his forms.

'Trying to get blood out of a stone' was how Ben described his meetings with Ian to Helen. The meetings could occasionally be the source of great amusement to them as Ben described Ian's slow actions and mimicked his accent. But they both laughed with affection rather than scorn as they never forgot that day on Barf when he saved Helen's life.

"Any news?" Ben always had to ask. Ian never offered. It was a ritual.

Ian picked up a *Summary of Incidents* page and handed it to Ben. Ben glanced at it, and noted that there had been three incidents since his last call. He would transfer them into newspaper-speak when he got home, along with the phoned reports he also received from Cockermouth and Patterdale teams. He had recently persuaded Sue to include all the northern teams' reports in *The Tribune* because their areas of operation overlapped and they were sometimes called upon to assist each other when a major situation arose. Mostly, he wanted to give their prodigious achievements as much publicity as possible in order to encourage a steady flow of donations to them.

"Got something on at the moment?" Ben enquired, hesitantly. The reply he received would depend on Ian's mood of the day. It could range from a grunted "na" to an effusive explanation of the whole situation.

"Just a wee one," Ian replied, quickly, indicating that he was in a cooperative mood today. "Woman on Glaramara…

near the bottom… sprained ankle… three lads gone to get her…"

Ben wanted to joke that he had never met a woman with an ankle near her bottom, but thought better of it – Ian's sense of humour had yet to make itself known to Ben or anyone in the team.

Keen to test Sergeant Peter Murphy's certainty that Hamish Stott had left the area, Ben asked with fake nonchalance, "Have any team members reported anything unusual lately… you know… people on the fells who look out of place… maybe an odd couple… maybe oriental…?" As soon as he had finished the question he realised how stupid it was, and he prepared himself for Ian's ridicule. It came in the form of a slow turn of Ian's head and a stare which was clearly checking whether Ben had suddenly gone mad or whether he was joking.

Ben held up his hands, "Okay… okay… I'll save you the trouble. Half the people you see on the fells look out of place, and how do you define an odd couple. But that leaves *maybe oriental?*"

"No, and I'm not going to ask why, I'm too busy." Ian's head had already turned back to his forms, and his tone told Ben that his brief spell of cooperation was at an end.

Before leaving the MRT headquarters Ben checked the LDSARA annual death statistics and found that this year's figure already matched last year's figure, and there were still four months to go. And last year's figure was slightly higher than average.

Chapter 18

Don Ivison didn't need to speak to give away his nationality. It was written all over his face, and the way he held his big, old body. Although obviously of Caucasian ancestry, his skin was every shade of brown – from light fawn to mahogany – depending on which bit was busy renewing itself. Untrimmed hedges of white wire sheltered his eyes which were barely visible slits of blue hidden by leather skin so deeply creased at the corners he could wedge his matches in them. His mouth was constantly at war with his cheeks which had turned into jowls as age and lifestyle took their toll. When he was relaxed the jowls had it all their own way and he looked like a benign St Bernard dog, but when he laughed his mouth had to lift the jowly flesh out of the way, leaving him with a somewhat forced, crocodilian grin. A full head of white, pan-scrubber hair, huge ears, long, strong nose, creased, tree-trunk neck, and hands made from grilled sausages completed the picture. In spite of his seventy years his back was ramrod-straight, giving him a posture which tended to emphasise his considerable beer-belly.

It wasn't so much the creased, leathery skin that told you where he came from, but the assured, masculine way in which he held himself, and the calm, confident yet unassuming manner in which he conducted himself. Only men who have spent most of their lives battling against nature's extremes end up with these attributes. And few places are as extreme as the Australian outback.

Don was a fifth generation Australian, a Queenslander. His great-great-grandfather, Henry, had been one of the last "convicts" to be transported from England in 1868, his crime being the stealing of one lamb from the farm where he worked, near the village of Eaglesfield in Cumbria where he lived. After surviving his ten years' hard labour working on the road gangs in New South Wales he was given his freedom and the chance to buy a plot of land to start his own farm. Since most of the prime land of New South Wales and Victoria in the temperate south of Australia had already been allocated during the previous one hundred years he ventured north into Queensland and, against much advice, bought a relatively small plot of land just west of the Great Dividing Range. Most of the land was lush and green when he arrived just after the wet season but rapidly turned to scrub as the sun took over. It was the climate they had all warned him about – unbearable heat, droughts, floods, humidity, snakes, mosquitoes. Anything north of Sydney in New South Wales was not considered fit for a white man to live in, a perception that still persists today, the southern half of the country believing that most Queenslanders are "as mad as cut snakes".

Don's great-great-grandfather had wanted to stock sheep, having worked with them in England, but they warned him against them because of constant attacks from dingos which were prolific in that part of Australia. This time he took their advice, bought a few cattle and started his new life.

130 years later, after the incredible hardship and hard work of his great-great grandfather and subsequent generations, Don now controlled an empire of eight cattle stations running over 140,000 cattle, covering an area approximately the size of England. All of the remote stations had their own runway, mechanics workshop, schoolroom, general store and entertainment area/bar for the staff.

Like his forebears, Don was no stranger to hardship, having seen his fortunes go up and down as disease, drought, floods and the 1970 beef depression struck. But somehow, with the grit and determination passed down in his genes, he had always lived to fight another day, and bring his stock back up to previous numbers. It was no wonder that the collective term for outback farmers became "battlers". In recent years technology had improved things considerably with the introduction of computers to do the administration, helicopters to do the big mustering jobs, and the cross breeding of Pakistan Zebu cattle with USA Brahman cattle resulting in an animal much more tolerant to the outback heat and the ticks.

Now, at 70, as he slowed down and let his two sons and two daughters take more of the strain, he looked forward to his first trip overseas. He had always intended to visit the old country to see where his family came from; his father and grandfather had told him a thousand stories about their family history and he wanted to go see for himself before it was too late. A recent diagnosis of lung cancer had brought some alacrity to his plans. He faced his illness stoically as always; he understood disease – the natural predator of man and beast. But he would be leaving Australia with a regret which had settled within him some twenty years ago when his wife, Kathy, left their remote homestead and went to live on the Queensland coast, intent on seeing the blue pacific from her window rather than the bush. She had always been a reluctant grazier's wife, sacrificing her love of the sea for her love of Don. She had done her duty and raised the four children into adulthood, and then decided it was her turn. They had parted amicably and stayed in touch by phone and email. But her absence had left a lead weight in his heart which had never lightened.

Don flew the 600 miles from his homestead to Brisbane airport in his own Piper Seneca V six-seater, accompanied by his two daughters who would fly it back and then return to pick him up in two weeks' time. The twin engines of the Seneca gave him some peace of mind when flying over such inhospitable terrain. The only other planes he had flown in were 30-seater inter-town commercials. He looked forward to seeing the inside of the mighty 300-seater jet that would take him to England.

Walking up the stairs that led into the Boeing 777 Don paused to look at the huge Rolls Royce engines. He had seen the planes before, of course, but never close-up. How on earth could something so large and so heavy take to the sky, he wondered?

He squeezed his large frame into his allocated seat and watched with some perplexity as hundreds of people came on board and sat so close together as to remind him of mustering the cattle into a branding pen. His daughters, who had travelled abroad, had tried to persuade him to buy a Business or First Class seat, but he had staunchly refused. Frugality had been hard-wired into his character many years ago when times were hard, and the idea of paying thousands of extra dollars just for a bigger seat was ridiculous to him. He didn't even agree with the principle of having different classes of seat. Class was not a thing of relevance in the outback. To get along in the outback you had to have the respect and trust of those you shared it with. You were all in the wilderness together and you needed to be able to rely on each other. The boss of any cattle station had to be able to ride, fix, drive, fly, muster, brand and even drink equally as well as his station hands if he was to earn their respect. Don had spent years doing just that, and though the boss, he had never felt like one; more like one of the boys. Now, as the giant plane taxied along the Brisbane runway, Don Ivison felt more like Crocodile Dundee on his first trip to New York than the millionaire owner of a livestock conglomerate.

Twenty-three hours and much discomfort later, Don looked down on the green chequered landscape surrounding Manchester airport. He had wanted to fly into London, spend a month doing the full tourist thing, visit the historic sites before heading for Cumbria, but his medics wanted him back as soon as possible. So it was to be Manchester, Yorkshire and Cumbria and back in two weeks.

The first three days he spent in Yorkshire, shivering in the cold September temperatures while visiting the woollen mills that still processed Australian wool, mostly Merino. In

Bradford's Industrial Museum he read with sadness how, in the days of his great-great-grandfather, children went to school for half a day, then worked in the woollen mill the other half. A supervisor was employed to stand at the mill entrance and whip the legs of the latecomers as they ran in from school. Once inside, the noise of the machines was deafening and many young ears were damaged for life.

Coming from a country with very strict immigration policies, and always being too busy to keep up with international affairs, Don was caught unawares by the number of brown Asian faces he saw in and around Bradford. His ignorance as to their exact nationality was soon corrected when a white shopkeeper said with a sardonic smile, "welcome to Bradistan". He wondered if he would find the rest of England like this.

He found it very difficult to drive his hired car around the narrow country roads and choked narrow streets of the towns, and unbelievable that houses were so close to the roads and the passing traffic. The houses shocked him; row after identical row, so small he couldn't imagine a family living in them, crowded together like animal pens, no garages, cars lined up outside, half on the road, half on the pavement. He wondered how people could live like that; how they could cope with such conditions; where were the open spaces, the grassland? Where did they go to stretch their legs, play some sport? It didn't look to him as if living conditions had changed much since his great-great-grandfather's day. Maybe the penal authorities of old had unwittingly done people like Henry a favour by transporting them to Australia.

Driving across the A66 into Cumbria his spirits lifted slightly when he saw more space, open moors instead of postage-stamp fields, fewer towns and villages. But the weather had changed for the worse, the grey sky oppressively low. He started to feel claustrophobic, as if he was about to be smothered by a malevolent grey blanket. He knew it was a reaction to his years of living under a high, bright blue sky, but the knowledge did nothing to alleviate his discomfort.

The amount of traffic on the roads and the small size of the cars continued to amaze him. Here, in what he took to be one of England's quietest country areas, an endless stream went both ways, all seemingly in a desperate hurry to get somewhere, overtaking on the twisting, narrow roads. Back in Queensland he was used to driving his four-litre Landcruiser on dead-straight roads where he would see more Emus than vehicles, where just for the heck of it he would spend an hour or two on the wrong side of the road, always knowing he would see any oncoming traffic in plenty of time.

Due to the grey, murky weather and his deep concentration on avoiding the other traffic, Don's entry into the Vale of Keswick, into the magic of the Lake District, was not particularly memorable. He was puzzled when he saw a sign before a roundabout pointing the way to "Ospreys". He was a keen bird man and could recognise all the 16 species of birds of prey that soared above the Queensland sky, from Kite to Goshawk, Osprey to Eagle, but he couldn't understand the purpose of the sign. He filed it away for future investigation.

He found his way to the village of Braithwaite and a small hotel called Middle Ruddings. He had picked it out of the brochures because he didn't feel comfortable in large, expensive hotels, but mostly because of its name – it sounded so intrinsically English.

The next morning, drawing back the curtains, Don saw blue sky and colourful fields and hills all around, and a particularly big hill across the valley which he would come to learn was called Skiddaw. He was also learning that the weather changed daily, a challenge for farmers, though perhaps not so severe a challenge as drought or flood. After an excellent breakfast, which the astute proprietor had served on an extra-large plate after learning of Don's background, he wandered outside to explore his village surroundings. Underneath his casual jacket he wore a Merino wool polo-necked sweater he had bought in Bradford to cope with the cool September air.

Soon, he was gazing in awe at the village's variety – modern bungalows, imposing hillside houses, plain terraces, small, colourful cottages, impossibly narrow roads; the cluttered, higgledy-piggledy arrangement of everything, the age of everything, the tiny humped-back bridge, the random stonework. There were hedges and walls everywhere, people apparently seeking privacy from their very close neighbour. Where he came from there were no hedges or walls, privacy being provided by space, the only boundaries being marked by a few stakes or a wire.

He loved the way the village was tucked into the base of the surrounding hills, like a sheep sheltering from the weather. The whole scene was so picturesque he felt as if he were on a Disney film-set and seven dwarfs would soon appear out of their tiny cottages and dance around the streets. The people – pale, heavily clothed and surprisingly cheerful – seemed too modern for the old film-set. Everything was so different from the villages in Queensland, which were arranged on regular grid systems, where the properties were large verandahed bungalows, or houses built on stilts in the flood regions, where the suntanned people wore shorts, went bare-footed, where you needed a car to get around such was the distance between the houses. He found it fascinating that all these people, although thousands of miles apart and living such dissimilar lives, came from the same stock.

One of his wishes was to visit an old English pub to sample the infamous warm beer so he was delighted to come across the Royal Oak in the centre of the village. He checked its opening times and made a mental note to ask for a pint rather than a schooner when he came back to sample the brew. He knew now he was going to enjoy his visit to the old country. Already he felt at home in this beautiful corner of it. He was, after all, still in Queen's land.

Chapter 19

Since their meeting two weeks ago in Keswick police station Ben had continually pestered Peter Murphy about how the police search for Stott and Babalato was progressing, and the review of their files of unexplained deaths in the last two years.

Peter had told him that an extensive survey of all hotels and guest houses in the Lakes had revealed no contact with Stott or Babalato, which more or less confirmed his theory that they had moved out of the area. All police stations throughout the country had now been issued with their descriptions and circumstances, and the search continued on a national basis.

With regard to the review of the files, Peter had been slightly evasive. Ben assumed it was probably due to lack of information. It seemed obvious, however, that little, if anything, had been unearthed. Had anything significant been discovered, there was no doubt in Ben's mind that Peter would have been shouting about it, particularly if it supported his theories about Stott.

It was at times like these that Ben wished he had been a detective. He would have loved to sit with a pile of files and slowly sift through them searching for that vital clue that solved the case. He had, more or less, done that with the

Hector Snodd case, using the files provided by Sophie Lund and her boys. His own database of facts extracted from those files had been the catalyst to identifying and finding Snodd. It had been exhausting but very rewarding work, and Ben had been surprised to find that he had a gift for it.

If nothing emerged in the next few weeks, he intended to ask Peter if he could help. He knew the chances of the CID taking him up on his offer were practically zero, but he would ask anyway.

Nothing untoward had happened to Helen or himself in those two weeks and he was beginning to believe that Stott had indeed left the area. He was, however, still not *certain* of anything. The discovery of the body of Mr Colin Grant on Loughrigg Fell had cast another shadow over the Lakes. It seemed to be an accident, but if it was murder it wasn't *certain* that it was part of a sequence or that Hamish Stott was involved. There were too many unknowns for Ben to come up with theories, never mind conclusions.

He had busied himself with his work for *The Tribune* which had recently, along with every newspaper in the country, been asked to publish photographs of Hamish Stott and Samuela Babalato together with the usual message about the police wishing to speak to them to help them with their enquiries into the death of Daniel Tulip of Windermere. This in itself should have ensured that Stott had left the area.

Ben had also managed to produce a half-decent watercolour painting which had won the approval of tutor, Roger Coulson. Sucking on his unlit pipe and squinting through his glasses as he inspected each detail, Coulson had murmured, "Mmm… good… good… frame it… sell it." A man of very few words, this was one of his longer sentences.

The painting depicted a view down the length of Bassenthwaite Lake on a misty, atmospheric day, with a single tree and a wooden fence terminating in the lake being the foreground interest. The mid and far distant features had blurred edges – ideal for watercolour washes. But, as always, it was the foreground detail that worried him. How to depict thousands of tree leaves with a few delicately placed, variously coloured and textured washes was a skill that had evaded him up till now. This time he just went for it, and more by luck than judgement he pulled it off.

Today he had delivered the painting to the Keswick gallery, picked up some books from the library and it was late afternoon when he headed towards Borrowdale to interview a farmer he had met at the recent agricultural show. He had an appointment with him at six o'clock, the earliest the farmer could see him.

Ben never tired of a trip to Borrowdale, an elemental Lake District journey. Here came a captivating lake, colourful fells, towering cliffs, natural woods, meandering river, quaint villages, fields full of grazing animals. The farmer, Geoff Stokes, had won some prestigious awards for his meat products and was now supplying top hotels in London as well as the Lakes. It was a good-news story which Sue Burrows would give prominence to in *The Tribune*.

Geoff Stokes's story was an interesting one and it was an hour later that Ben came away with his notebook full of text and his camera full of shots of Geoff and the farm. Ben looked forward to putting it all together at home, first thing in the morning.

Arriving back at the cottage at twenty to eight, the late September evening already darkening, Ben had a sudden adrenaline surge when he saw that Helen's car was not in its usual place. She had said she would be back from the Grasmere project by mid-afternoon. Even allowing for some interim shopping in Keswick she should have been back long before now. Ben brought his car to an abrupt, gravel-shifting halt, and rushed from his car. The cottage was in darkness and both doors were closed.

Chapter 20

Don Ivison drew back the curtains with some trepidation. What would the weather be like on his second day in the Lakes? He was pleased to find the sun shining and no heavy clouds over Skiddaw, though he knew by now this might not last throughout the day. Last night, after dining on local sirloin steak, noticing the subtle difference from the taste of his own cattle's meat, he spent a pleasant evening in the hotel's lounge bar where he mixed with the proprietor and a few guests and locals. They were a much quieter group than the mob he was used to back home, but there was no shortage of good humour and he had resented the tiredness that suddenly swept over him and sent him to bed early.

His pain control drugs got him through the night without distress and he was feeling well when he set off to see where his great-great-grandfather had lived.

The journey, travelling north alongside Bassenthwaite Lake, and then west towards the coast, was very scenic, but Don was so intent on avoiding the other traffic that he saw little detail. He continued, however, to be fascinated by the immaculately trimmed hedges that lined the roads and surrounded the tiny fields. It didn't look like farming land to him, more like a large, well-tended garden. Who had the time and money to do all that trimming? Why was the grazing land divided into such small areas?

His heart started to pound when he saw the sign reading *Eaglesfield*. The stress of driving had now been joined by the excitement of seeing his families' roots. His grandfather had told him that a farm just outside the village was the birthplace of Fletcher Christian of *Mutiny on the Bounty* fame, who had gone to school with a certain William Wordsworth in the nearby town of Cockermouth. It was just possible, he said, that Don's great-great-grandfather, Henry, had been working on that very farm when he stole the lamb that sent him to Australia.

Fletcher Christian had been sailing in the Bounty off the Australian southern Pacific Ocean some 60 years before Henry's arrival in Australia, but the thought that two ordinary men from this small Cumbrian village had finished up so far from home, in the same part of the world, seemed, to Don, to be incredible, somehow sad, and yet romantic.

Doing his own research before visiting the village, Don had learned that the village was also the birthplace of the brilliant eighteenth-century chemist and physicist, John Dalton, born just two years after Fletcher Christian. His list of achievements was remarkable, including being the founder of atomic theory.

It was, therefore, with great anticipation, and a little pride – in spite of the convict connection – that Don stopped the car and started to walk around the village.

Two hours later he arrived, breathlessly, back at the car. He had found three working farms, incredibly small by his standards, a small village-green, a pub called the Black Cock

Inn, and the same randomly distributed selection of houses, cottages and narrow roads he had seen in Braithwaite, albeit without the spectacular backdrop.

What had attracted most of his attention was the age of some of the stone cottages. He could imagine that they were the type of cottages that Henry had lived in. At one stage he had stopped outside of one, and imagined young Henry coming out dressed in tattered clothes, wearing a cloth cap and heavy boots, making his way to work on the farm; having to steal to survive, being caught, put in prison, and then shipped out to Australia in conditions not fit for animals. The inhumanity of that age, of the authorities, of the ruling class was hard for Don to comprehend. He had suddenly found tears in his eyes, and as the mood of pity swept through him it tricked him into feeling sorry for himself – his illness, and the ever-present void left by Kathy – and he had started to weep freely. He had to rest his back against the cottage wall and take out his handkerchief and pretend that he had a fly in his eye when a passer-by said hello.

Back at the car, feeling physically tired but somehow mentally refreshed by his outpouring, Don decided to brave the nearby town of Cockermouth to get a much needed cup of coffee, and some more incredibly expensive petrol.

Ten minutes later he was regretting the decision as he sat in a queue of traffic that moved very slowly through the town's streets. He came to a T-junction, turned right, and glimpsed a sign about Wordsworth's house as he straightened up. This street was wider and tree-lined and there were shops, and he realised he was probably in the town's main street. There were vehicles everywhere, and there was nowhere to park, but he spotted a P sign and followed the procession until he entered a car park. Here he had to circulate until he found a space and he was mightily relieved when he was able to climb out of the car and relieve the tension in his body.

He locked the car and started to walk.

"Excuse me," a voice shouted.

Don turned. A thin, refined looking man was beckoning to him. "I hope you don't mind… you seem to have forgotten to pay."

"Pay?" Don frowned.

"Your parking fee," the man explained, pointing out a machine some metres away.

"You have to pay to park?" Don queried. "In a small country town like this?"

"'Fraid so," said the man, now recognising Don's accent. "I take it you don't pay in Australia?"

"Not in country towns you don't… not bloody likely. They're all competing with each other for customers. They practically pay you to visit their town… there's always some sort of incentive to attract you in."

"I wish," the man said.

"Why do they do it here," Don queried. "It'll put people off coming. Are all country towns like this? Do they all charge for parking?"

"It's the council," the man explained.

"Well vote the bastards out," Don growled, firmly. "They don't know what they're doing."

"The next lot would be the same," the man insisted. "They all charge. It's been going on for years."

"What about the people who work in the town, in the shops and offices, they don't have to pay, do they?" Don asked.

"Yep, they all have to pay," the man said, resignedly.

"So, let me get this right," Don said, disbelievingly. "People here are paying a fortune for their heavily-taxed petrol to get to work, then they are effectively fined for parking at work, and also fined for doing their shopping?"

"Taxed," the man corrected.

"Taxed, fined, what's the difference? It's bloody madness," Don snarled. "How do you expect your economy to flourish if you tax people for going to work, leave them with less money to spend, then tax them again when they go to spend what they have left?" He was surprised at how angry he felt at a situation that did not concern him and which would be a distant memory in a few days' time. Then he remembered the endless fights he had had with authorities back home over taxes and regulations, leaving him at one point shouting in court that he was working for the bloody government and not for himself, and he knew where his anger originated.

"The parking attendant's coming," the man said, pointing out a small, stocky man in a dark uniform and peaked cap. "You'd better get a ticket or you'll be fined."

"Jesus," Don shouted. "It's like living in a bloody police state." But he followed the man to the machine and, with his help, obtained a ticket and put it in his car window.

They walked together across the car park, Don glancing with contempt at the uniformed symbol of authority that passed them. "This is no good, mate," Don advised his new companion. "You can't go on living like this, in small houses, all crammed together... no space... being fined for going to work, fined for doing your shopping. It's time you gave this away, mate. Time you all went walkabout and came over to Oz...we've got loads of space over there."

"If only," the man said. "Your government won't let many of us in. You've got some of the strictest immigration rules in the world."

Don slowed down and nodded his head in acknowledgement. "Yeah... you're right mate. I forgot. Bloody governments... bloody politicians... stupid bastards!"

The man started to peel away. "I'm going this way," he said. "Nice meeting you..."

Don caught up with him and crushed his pale, thin hand with his grilled sausages. "Thanks mate," he said, with some feeling. "Don't let the bastards win. Keep fighting."

The man gave him the limp smile of the long-defeated and turned and walked away.

After his coffee, Don found his way out of Cockermouth and headed for Bassenthwaite Lake. He parked his car at Dubwath, and went for a stroll along the shore of the lake. The weather stayed fine for him and he enjoyed the walk, away from the crowds and the traffic, his 70-year-old eyes as entranced as a child's by the beauty of his surroundings.

Inevitably, tiredness moved in and told him to go back to the hotel to rest.

He slept in his room for about an hour, not bothering to undress, but sliding under the quilt to keep warm. With time to kill before dinner he decided to stroll into the village to sample the beer in the Royal Oak.

The traditional beer was not as warm as he had been led to believe, but its taste took some getting used to after drinking ice-cold lager all his life. A few men were gathered in a corner watching a football match on television. He sat down close to them and soon had their attention when he scoffed at the players' play-acting as they rolled around in apparent agony, something which had led most Australians to call it a game for Sheilas, Wogs and Poofters. Don made it clear that soccer, as he called it, was no match for the manly game of rugby which he and most Aussies preferred. The watching men took it all in good heart and gave him some abuse in return and they all settled into an amiable evening of chatting and drinking. When Don bought the next round of drinks for everybody in the bar, something he often did for his staff back home, he was made even more welcome. And when he found that one of the bar staff was from New South Wales he got the feeling that he was in for a good night.

Three hours later he swayed out of the pub, and stood in the car park as though on a heaving deck. He had tried to leave earlier, tried to control his intake, but such was the hospitality thrust upon him he felt he had to stay and partake. He had switched from beer to lager, hoping his body would cope better with something it was used to, but the volume consumed, and the lack of food, had made him as drunk as he used to get as a young man after a long hot week on the cattle station.

It was very dark once away from the glow of the pub, and Don hoped he was going the right way as he started back to the hotel. He squinted through the darkness, his deep eye wrinkles folding like an accordion. An involuntary hiccup shook his chest. He walked very slowly and stiffly, like Frankenstein's monster, as he struggled to keep in a straight line, an occasional wobble and a full side-step becoming impossible to control. Part of him felt ashamed at his condition, but part of him said: "*what the hell, there's not going to be many more nights like this left... and I'm on holiday*".

His recollection was that the route was about a quarter of a mile long and had a couple of bends and not much pavement, the roads being too narrow for them and cars. Halfway along a narrow stretch a car passed him, horn blaring, warning him to keep to the side. He didn't jump with shock, his senses having been anaesthetised.

Shortly afterwards, he rounded a bend and caught sight of an illuminated sign in the distance. He stopped and squinted and slowly read "Middle Ruddings Hotel". He set off walking again, a silly smile on his face, when a fast moving vehicle struck him from behind and sent him hurtling into one of the many stone walls he had noticed on his first day. In the split-second of life left in him the synapses in his brain managed to convey a silent message of thanks to the driver for saving him from a long, miserable exit.

Chapter 21

It was dark inside the cottage. Ben stood still for a moment and listened, hoping he might hear Helen. The silence seemed to intensify the darkness. Ben started to shiver though it wasn't cold. He rushed from room to room turning on the lights, looking everywhere. No Helen.

Without her presence the cottage always seemed empty. This time the emptiness was palpable and brought back terrible memories of the day that Snodd had taken her. It hadn't happened again, had it? Had Peter been right after all? Stott was reliving his father's life, he had said. He already had a Filipino girlfriend, he was suspected of at least one murder, maybe many more. Abducting Helen would just be part of the cycle to his crazy mind.

But it didn't look as though she had been taken from the cottage, her car wasn't there. Stott could have taken the car at the same time as Helen – from the cottage. It was unlikely that he owned a car on his wages. Ben's mind was beginning to whirl.

He rushed to the hall phone and dialled Helen's mobile. No answer. He left a message, trying not to sound too concerned, "It's only me. I'm at home. It's quarter to eight and I'm wondering where you are. Give me a ring a.s.a.p. please…"

She has a panic button. Why did she not press her panic button?

He decided to phone the Grasmere hotel first, find out what time she had left, then phone the police, check if she had used her panic button. Helen had left him the hotel's number on a slip of paper. He rummaged through the pile of papers lying on the telephone table, many with notes and doodles from long ago which should have been thrown away.

He couldn't find it... it was all a jumble... which number was it... he was speeding up... he was panicking. He grabbed the yellow pages from the nearby cupboard. *Hotels... hotels... hotels... got them. What was the hotel's name? The bloody name? Can't remember... look for Grasmere numbers... there's hundreds of numbers... keep calm and just do it... the print is too small... where's my reading glasses... upstairs...Christ!* He ran upstairs, the thump of his feet on the risers matching the drum in his heart. He found his glasses on his desk. *Should have brought the directory up... used the upstairs phone... too late.* He skipped two steps at a time, back downstairs, grabbed the directory and ran his finger down the page. *At last a Grasmere number... but it's not the hotel... I'll know it when I see it... another one... no...another one... don't think so... another one... yes... yes... why the hell didn't I remember it.*

He grabbed the phone and started to hit the buttons. He heard a distant noise. *An engine... a car's engine.* Then a faint hissing sound. Closer now. Tyres on gravel. *She's back. But it might be the police answering her panic alarm.* Ben threw the phone down and rushed outside.

It was Helen's car. For a split second Ben imagined a policeman stepping out of it, a dreadful look on his face. But it was Helen who stepped out of it, carrying her briefcase – smiling as usual. The tension left his body so quickly he thought he might collapse. His body seemed to shrink; his clothes suddenly too big for him. He didn't know whether to laugh or cry. He did neither. He found himself shouting clichés, "Where the hell have you been? I've been worried sick. Why didn't you answer your phone?" He wanted to rush to her, hold her tight, but something held him back. She had to be punished, didn't she, for causing him so much worry?

Helen put down her briefcase, walked quickly towards him, and put her arms around him. She could sense the utter relief in his body. Only now did she fully understand the situation, and though she had done nothing wrong, she said quietly, "I'm sorry."

That was all it took. His arms went around her back and his cheek came down to rest against her head and all was well again in their world. They clung together for a minute or two until hearts and minds were in sync, and they became as one again. They knew when to break apart without having to speak, and together they picked up the briefcase and locked the car and walked hand in hand into the cottage.

Not long after they had first met, Ben, who at that time fancied himself as a poet, had looked deep into Helen's eyes and declared: "I think we will become a poem that is word perfect. Remove one word and we will not exist."

They had in fact, over the years become more like a jigsaw puzzle – people of many parts, of many colours, who daily scattered themselves across the landscape of life, then gathered themselves together again to form a single entity.

There was no great mystery connected to Helen's lateness. It had been caused by the mundane delays often experienced in busy hotels due to managers and staff being pulled in many directions. Meetings had been put back, contractors had not turned up on time, drawings had been mislaid and so on – all very routine. She hadn't phoned Ben to let him know she'd be late because she knew he had a late appointment at the Borrowdale farm, and she still expected to be back before him. As it transpired, only a few minutes had separated their arrival back at the cottage. The drama had been caused by the fear instilled by Stott's presence at their home, reviving terrible memories of his father.

She had not answered his last call to her mobile because she had been in the car, saw that the call was from home, and knew she would be back shortly to reply in person.

Later that night, with some Mahler adagios and a glass of whisky to finally settle him down, Ben helped Helen to tidy up the pile of papers that cluttered the hall telephone table. Ninety percent of it was binned, including the slip of paper carrying the Grasmere hotel's number along with many others. Helen agreed that it was difficult to see clearly, having jotted it down in a hurry, and wrote it out again in very clear, large numbers on a new A4 sheet, along with the numbers of other, less important contracts she was dealing with. She also took Ben's mobile and keyed the numbers into his contact list. They promised each other they would phone more often during the day to check that all was well, then they went to bed and cuddled and listened to the owl until sleep took over.

Ben had just finished breakfast when the phone rang. "'Morning Ben, finished dipping your soldiers yet?" Sue Burrows said, in her deceptively lazy tone. It belied a very quick brain and astute business acumen.

"No soldiers on parade this morning, Sue," Ben quipped. "Just porridge, and I have a matted pullover to prove it."

"Yuk, spare me the details. Are you busy this morning? There's been a 'hit-and-run' over at Braithwaite, happened last night, tourist from Australia dead. Can you get over there and cover it? The police will still be there probably, they can fill you in... anyway you know what to do..."

"Yes, I'll get straight over, Sue. Do you know whereabouts exactly?"

"Close to the Middle Ruddings Hotel, apparently. He was staying there."

"On my way. And don't worry, I'll change my pullover."

The scene of Don Ivison's death had been taped off and a police constable, who Ben knew, stood guard. The constable was able to give Ben some of the basic details, and added the information that a couple who had been standing outside the hotel last night said they saw what they thought was a Land Rover-type vehicle go speeding past shortly before another car pulled up and sought help to deal with the body on the road.

Ben made his way to the hotel where he found two police cars in the car park, and was told by the receptionist that all guests were being interviewed individually in the lounge.

Ben was able to obtain a brief interview with the hotel proprietor, who gave him some background information on Mr Ivison together with some favourable personal comments.

Next, Ben walked to the Royal Oak and met the landlord. After praising Mr Ivison – Don – for his geniality, and expressing sadness at his demise, the landlord hinted, diplomatically, that Don had been drunk when he left the pub. This put a slightly different angle on the event. It may not have been the driver's fault. But with the vehicle not stopping it was still unquestionably a 'hit-and-run'.

Ben finally returned to the taped-off area, took a couple of photographs, and looked around. Although there was no pavement in the area, the road was wider here than at other places along the route. A careful driver should have been able to pass a pedestrian easily, even in the dark. That, of course, assumed that the pedestrian did not stagger across the road in front of you. But, whatever the circumstance, why would you not stop? Perhaps the driver had been drunk as well. No doubt the police would be looking out for Land Rover-type vehicles in the area, particularly those with signs of damage at the front.

Ben left the scene, and headed for home where he would write up the story and take it and the photographs to Sue the next morning; he had two days to go before deadline. If there were no more urgent calls, he planned to spend the afternoon on his latest painting. As he drove along, he thought about the poor man's family in Australia. Life was inordinately cruel at times. Why did we cling to it so fiercely?

Helen was still at home when he returned. She was due to go to work in the afternoon, but she was busy mixing his favourite cake, while doing her consultancy work on the laptop, on the kitchen table. This was her idea of a morning off. He kissed her cheek as he passed through the kitchen, cunningly sneaking his index finger into the cake-mix at the same time, and carried on through the hall and up the stairs, licking his finger. He knew that, so far, he had been one of the lucky ones.

Chapter 22

Having delivered his 'hit-and-run' report and photographs to the Tribune office, where he also enjoyed a coffee and chat with Sue Burrows while picking up some new work, Ben made his way to Keswick police station to see if Sergeant Murphy was available.

"Five minutes, Ben," Peter said, firmly, inviting Ben to take a chair, while glancing at his watch to emphasise the point.

Ben had never been impressed by these overt displays of busyness. They were usually employed by incompetent people trying to impress, and were insulting to the person addressed, intimating to them that they were not as important as the people or event that lay ahead. Perhaps Peter needed to go on yet another course, which seemed to be the only way basic social skills seemed to be learned these days. However, Peter was not incompetent as far as Ben knew, so he put his internal rant to one side as he sat down.

"Just a word about that 'hit-and-run' at Braithwaite," he opened. "Any news? Any bent Land Rovers been found?"

"No, not a thing," Peter said. "No more witnesses came forward, and enquiries about the Land Rover are progressing, as we say."

"Did you visit the scene yourself?"

"Yes?" Peter's frown queried the question.

"Did you notice that the road was wide where the event occurred? The driver should have been able to avoid the victim – Mr Ivison – even though Ivison was drunk and possibly in the middle of the road."

"Agreed, Ben. We noted the width of the road and came to the same conclusion. But it's just conjecture. We have no knowledge of what really happened. Bottom line is it doesn't matter where Mr Ivison was on that road. It's why did the driver not stop? We need to find him or her. They might have just panicked or they could be hiding something else they don't want us to know about."

"If you don't find them will you be adding this case to your files of unexplained deaths?" Ben asked.

"Very unlikely. We know how the man died."

"What if it was deliberate? What if it was murder?"

Peter sighed. "Here we go again. That imagination of yours. If we had to assume that every road accident was a possible murder we would spend all our time investigating nothing but road accidents. Do us all a favour, Ben, and go and find another outlet for your imagination. How about writing children's stories. I've heard they pay well."

Ignoring the put-down, Ben went on, "How are the unexplained deaths investigations coming along? Have you heard anything from CID yet?"

"Nothing yet, and before you ask, there's no news about Stott either." Peter paused and looked thoughtful, as though he was debating with himself whether to tell Ben something else. Finally, he said, "They've added one more case recently. One that you will remember well. You covered it in the paper... about a year ago. It's not an unexplained death as such, because no body has been found. Remember Mrs Elizabeth Lamb from Lorton?"

"Certainly do," Ben affirmed. "The story kept you, me, and the mountain rescue teams busy for the best part of a month. Terrible thing to just disappear. The family must still be traumatised."

"Yes... terrible. In cases like this most people would rather have a dead body than not know what happened to them." Peter started to rise from his seat as he said this. He was calling the audience to an end.

Ben followed suit and let Peter off the hook by saying, "Right, time I was pushing off. Thanks for the info, Peter."

"Cheers, Ben," Peter said, as he busied himself with some papers. "See you next Saturday, weather permitting."

Ben took his leave, and stepped outside into early October sunshine. He hoped it would last until Saturday. It wasn't just the golf he was looking forward to, but the chance to keep pestering Peter about the unexplained death cases, in the vain hope that he might let him help in some way.

Back home, in his office, Ben searched through his box files where he kept copies of reports he had written down the years. He limited these to what could be considered as important local events. He also kept the occasional piece which had been particularly well written, though the event may have been trivial. He could see himself thumbing through these in his old age when his powers were waning and he needed a reminder that he had once done good work: a little ego boost.

It didn't take him long to find the report he had written a year ago, in late September, about the disappearance of Elizabeth Lamb. It was the last of his three reports on the case and summarised the situation at that time. The two photographs included in the story were not very good. One was a head and shoulders photograph of Mrs Lamb which he had obtained from the family. The caption under the photograph read: "STILL MISSING: *Elizabeth Lamb, of Lorton.*" The other photograph taken in late September mist was of a number of vehicles parked on the grass verge on the bend of a road. The caption under this photograph read: "MAJOR OPERATION: *Some of the mountain rescue team vehicles involved in the search for Elizabeth Lamb.*"

The report looked longer than Ben remembered. He started to read, mainly to remind himself of the detail and perhaps spot something worth following up, but he also knew his critical eye would be at work to see if he could have improved the piece.

STILL NO SIGHTINGS OF MISSING MUM

The search for a missing mother-of-two, who has not been seen since September 3, has been one of the most extensive undertaken in Cumbria. More than 70 people, police sniffer dogs and an RAF helicopter searched the countryside looking for Elizabeth Lamb, 42, of Lorton, near Cockermouth.

The search, led by mountain rescue teams, was called off on Tuesday, but police said they would continue a missing person's enquiry and would actively look for Mrs Lamb, whose red Honda Civic was found close to Thornbeck Forest on the day after she disappeared.

Mrs Lamb, who has two children aged 11 and 13, was said by her husband, Nigel, to be in good spirits before her disappearance. She is described as 5ft 7in, tall and slim with straight, short hair. She was last seen wearing a dark green fleece jacket, brown wool hat, casual black trousers and walking boots. She had left her home in Lorton to go for her regular walk which, apparently, was usually taken within a few miles of Lorton; Crummock Water and Thornbeck Forest were, according to her husband, two of her favourites. A keen walker, Mrs Lamb is a member of Keswick Rambling Club.

Speaking for Cockermouth Mountain Rescue Team, team leader, John Smart, said members had spent five days looking for Mrs Lamb, as well as dealing with other call-outs. They had been helped by other mountain rescue teams from Patterdale, Keswick, Penrith, Wasdale and Langdale. Mr Smart said: "This has been one of the biggest searches for a number of years. I have never called on five other teams to assist before, and we certainly appreciate all the help they have provided. Things have been intensive recently. As well as the search for Mrs Lamb, we have had two fatalities on Blencathra and a man missing on Helvellyn, so resources have been very stretched."

As well as the mountain rescue teams, the search has involved police search advisors, a police helicopter, and specialist search dogs capable of picking up ground scent. Searches have been conducted near Mrs Lamb's home at Lorton, around Crummock Water, Buttermere, Thornbeck forest and surrounding areas.

Police have also issued appeals at local guest houses, hotels and transport providers, and carried out extensive house-to-house enquiries.

Mr Smart said: "Each day has become more frustrating as we could not find a trace of her. Until the police receive more intelligence we cannot do much more, but if new information comes to light, we will go out again."

A spokesman for Cumbria police said: "We have officers still looking for Mrs Lamb and we are still talking to relatives and friends who might provide further leads. So far we have been unable to pinpoint her location. We do not know where she is, but it is unlikely she will have survived if she has been out on the fells all this time."

Anyone who has any information that might assist the police in locating Mrs Lamb should call Cumbria police on 0845 3300 247.

Ben noticed he had missed out the colour of Mrs Lamb's hair in his description of her and wondered whether it was his omission or whether he had not been given it. He gave himself a black mark for not asking. The rest of it was a bit jerky in places, but he forgave himself for that, guessing it was probably produced in a hurry.

The only information he spotted that might be worth revisiting was the fact that she was a member of Keswick Rambling Club. No doubt her family and friends had been questioned *ad infinitum* by the police looking for leads. But perhaps they had not been so diligent with the Rambling Club members. In Ben's experience people often shared information and problems with relative strangers or casual acquaintances rather than family or close friends. It was just possible that, without knowing it, a member of the Rambling Club was in possession of some information that could lead to Mrs Lamb's whereabouts, or explain the reason for her disappearance. It was this kind of concentration on small detail which had helped Ben track down Hector Snodd, and he knew he would be unable to resist applying it to Mrs Lamb's case.

The fact that the police had now added this case to their list of unexplained deaths meant that they thought she could have been one of Stott's victims. They obviously had Stott earmarked for most of them. Ben was not so sure.

He booted up his computer and googled "Keswick Rambling Club", feeling that small surge of excitement he always got when he set off to solve a puzzle, be it a crime or a crossword. If he could track down information that led to the solving of Mrs Lamb's case, maybe the police would let him help with the others. Now that would be exciting!

Chapter 23

Christian names can be surprisingly important. Charlotte Ambler thought hers was responsible for the way her life evolved. When a toddler, her parents called her Charlotte but as soon as she started school, entering the world of texts and jargon, where you switch on the ac, have an oj, and lol, she was inevitably reduced to Charlie. This had the effect of making her feel slightly boyish. Her problem was then compounded by finding that she was good at sport, out-running, jumping, swimming and playing most of the other girls.

She soon became known as a tomboy and eventually played football for the school's under eleven team, the other ten players being boys. At home, in Manchester, her son-less father encouraged her sporting prowess and took her camping, walking, climbing, cycling, fishing and to the local football matches.

Later, at university, studying computer software design and marketing, she took a lot of ribbing from the other girls as she donned her tracksuit to go running or rowing while they went downtown to "have a good time". As a result she developed a thick skin, and a steely determination to do better than them academically. She succeeded.

Within 12 months of leaving university she had started her own online company, FIB (Fun In Britain), offering sport and adventure holidays in Britain to overseas customers. By the age of 35 she had 54 franchised operators under her company's umbrella, and a turnover of millions. At this point she was approached by a national holiday/leisure company who offered to buy her company for two million pounds. She talked them up to three and a half million and sold the company.

Still unattached, she decided it was time to see the world, and hopefully "have a good time". She didn't know how long she would travel or what she would do when she returned. For once in her life she was going to relax and let the winds of fate take her where they might.

During the next four years she climbed in the Rockies and the Andes, saw bears and condors; hunted narwhals alongside Inuits in Canada; dived in the Middle East and on the Great Barrier Reef; caught marlin, blue-fin tuna and yellow-tailed kingfish while sailing in the South Pacific; tracked the big cats and rhinos on safari in Kenya; visited temples in India, the Great Wall of China, the Kremlin in Russia and the Vatican in Italy. She lost her virginity in Brazil during the Mardi Gras celebrations, unable to recall who to. She paid for a male escort in Paris to dine with her at Maxim's restaurant on the rue Royale. She belly-danced in Turkey, skied in Austria, bungee-jumped in New Zealand, wild-water rafted in Thailand, walked to Everest base-camp in Nepal, swam in the Amazon in Peru, and camped with a nomadic tribe in the Sahara Desert.

Intermittent, fleeting visits were made to Manchester to "touch base" and check on her parents. One such visit, ostensibly made to share her 40th birthday with her parents, finally put paid to her wanderings. During the visit her mother died suddenly, and she decided to stay in Manchester to support her ageing father.

Before settling down to life in Britain again, and getting back into business, she decided to take her father on a short holiday to the Lake District. She hoped it would cheer both of them up after their loss. The Lakes had been like a second home when she was young. Camping weekends and holidays were spent there. With the outstanding guide-books of A. Wainwright to help them they had climbed every fell, and walked two-week circulars. She remembered her father telling her that Mr Wainwright was a genius who would be as famous as Wordsworth one day. They had also fished and swam in the lakes.

Because her father was no longer capable of fell-walking and because it was October, reputedly the best time of year to start pike fishing, she decided to base themselves near Bassenthwaite Lake and spend some days trying to catch one of the big ones for which the lake was famous. Her father still had in his garage all the rods and tackle they had used all those years ago. They would need some new 15-pound line, wire traces, swivels, treble hooks, lures and dead bait, but the basic kit was still usable.

Having obtained their fishing permits from the Tourist Information Centre in Keswick, they made their way to the eastern shore of Bassenthwaite Lake and started fishing on a typically fine October morning on the southern point of

Scarness Bay, a place they had fished with success before, a place where the beauty of the surroundings was ample compensation when the fish didn't bite. Charlotte was delighted to see her father come to life as he rigged up his rod, and she felt those familiar hunting stirrings herself.

They both cast out their paternoster, floated dead-bait rigs, laid the rods on their supports and settled back in their folding canvas chairs to watch their floats with eagle intensity. Half an hour later Charlotte glanced at her father to see if he wanted to share her flask of coffee, and found him asleep. And that set the tone for the rest of the day. Spells of intensive float watching, through protective sunglasses, were followed by bouts of dozing, Charlotte also becoming susceptible in mid afternoon.

They broke up their somnolence with occasional periods of retrieval to check on and renew the bait. The only other interruption to their languid day was a pleasant chat with a passing walker who stopped to ask if they had caught anything. At the end of a fruitless but very relaxing day they made their way back to their hotel near Overwater Tarn, where they filled the long, dark October evening by dining, reading, and dozing again, the Lake District air apparently containing some form of tranquiliser.

The next day they visited the tackle shop in Keswick and bought two bite indicators. Now they could relax and doze off without missing a bite. They decided to try their luck about 100 metres south of Scarness Bay on a straight stretch of shore, another place they had fished before.

The weather was kind to them again, some sparse, high-level cloud being the only interloper in a heaven of pale blue. Three-quarters of an hour after their first cast her father dozed off again. He was still asleep when his bite indicator went off. Charlotte leapt to her feet and shouted, "Dad! Dad!" She picked up the rod, engaged the reel, pointed the rod at the fish and began to wind in smoothly and quickly. Suddenly she felt the weight of the fish and she pulled the rod firmly back to set the hooks. She maintained the pressure on the rod as she handed it over to her father who, by this time, had struggled to his feet. Together, like two children, they watched excitedly as he wound the line in. Charlotte picked up the large landing net and walked into the shallow water. She didn't care about getting wet, she was intent on landing the fish properly. Now she could see it – a pike – relatively small, but still a big fish. It came in peacefully, with just an occasional flick of its powerful tail, then she had it in the net.

Splashing to the shore, Charlotte deposited the pike gently onto the grass. Using her protective mesh glove, she used the forceps-and-hand technique to remove the hooks from its mouth, then stood back to let her father admire it. He had a big grin on his face as he leaned down to study the fish. "Nice one Dad," Charlotte said.

Her father didn't speak, but went on gazing at the fish. Then he turned slowly and he had tears in his eyes. He stepped towards her and put his arms around her and said, "Thanks love… for everything."

As she stood, with his arms around her, Charlotte believed she knew the cause of his tears. Still in mourning, he was now thinking of his own mortality, of how few times like this there were left to share. This, mixed with the happy memories of their time together when she was a little girl, a time that had just been recreated. Charlotte felt the moment herself. Closing her eyes and resting her head against his chest, she felt thirty years slip away and she was ten years old again and feeling safe and loved.

Their long embrace was developing into a reverie when her father whispered, "We'd better put him back, love."

They drew apart, both blinking the tears from their eyes. Charlotte bent down and, using a wet piece of cloth, gently picked up the fish with both hands. She showed it to her father. "What do you reckon, five or six pounds?"

"Let's say six," her father smiled.

They had been hoping to catch something closer to twenty-six pounds, but nevertheless this was a nice young fish, and hopefully the start of better things to come. Charlotte carried it into the water, bent down and let the fish rest in the water with her hands supporting its belly. It stayed there for a few seconds then suddenly swam off, powerfully.

The rest of the day was fish-less but still enjoyable. There was lunch to eat, which always tasted better in the open air, wildlife to see, strolls to be taken along the shore, tackle and methods to change to try to optimise their chances of catching a big one. Yesterday's walker turned up again and listened with interest when they told him about their catch. He told them he lived locally and conveyed the bad news that the lake had not produced a large pike for a number of years. He tempered this with the opinion that some big ones probably still existed but had become so used to anglers that they were too wary to be caught. Before he left, he wished them luck and, handing over his card, asked them to contact him if they succeeded in catching a big one. He said he would put it in the local paper. His card told them he was a journalist for *The Keswick Tribune.*

That night, back at the hotel her father started coughing and wheezing. They had probably stayed out too long in the chill evening air. The clocks had gone back and it was now dark at five o'clock. They had, as did fishers all over the world, hung on until the last minute in the hope of landing a fish.

The next morning, Charlotte was relieved to find that her father's coughing had not worsened. She insisted, however, that he should spend the day in the warm hotel. He reluctantly agreed, and counter-insisted that she went out on her own and brought him back a record pike, or rather a photograph of one. She also agreed, reluctantly.

Having seen her father settled in his room with a good book, Charlotte enquired at Reception about the hire of boats on the lake. She wanted to try fishing in the deeper water. She was told that, there were no boats available for public hire, but she could have use of the hotel's boat which was permanently moored in the water off a jetty within the premises of the sailing club.

An hour later she was in the boat, moving away from the sailing club jetty, pulling strongly and smoothly on the oars, enjoying the seesawing sound of wood on metal and the gentle plash of the oars as they entered the water. Initially, she had hesitated about going out at all because the lake was shrouded in a dense mist. Or was it cloud? The steep fells on either side of the lake had a way of pulling clouds down to sit on the lake's surface while the sun could be shining in a clear sky a few metres above them.

Charlotte's hesitation hadn't lasted long. She was always up for a new experience, and she was desperate to catch a big pike to please her father. Now, as she moved towards the centre of the lake she was starting to enjoy the fact that she couldn't see either shore. She was lost in her own little world far from the madding crowd. She recalled a misty morning on the Amazon and imagined she could hear again the raucous calls of South American parrots and see again the black caymans sliding into the water from the riverbank looking like man-made military weapons.

She stopped rowing while she fixed her dead bait on the treble hooks then cast out over the rear of the boat, resting the rod on the rear transom. All she could hear as she started to row again was the faraway hiss of traffic on the A66 running along the western shore; not quite as exotic as the sound of parrots, but useful in determining her distance from the shore. Her intention was to troll about a mile down the centre of the lake and return, and if not successful, to stay in the centre and fish from the stationary boat.

The first mile passed uneventfully, Charlotte's disappointment at the paucity of fish being mitigated by the pleasure the rowing was giving her. It had been a few years since she had rowed seriously and she had forgotten how therapeutic it could be, the repetitive rhythm leading you into a soporific peacefulness.

The return journey was well underway when she got a bite. The peace was shattered as she clumsily docked the oars and lunged at the rod, excitement pulsing through her. Again, she waited until she felt the weight of the fish before she pulled up on the rod. She had it. It didn't feel very big. But nothing would ever feel big again compared to a marlin. Smoothly and quickly she reeled it in, netted it, and lifted it into the boat. It was bigger than she had imagined – maybe ten pounds. Not bad. Hurriedly she took her camera from her backpack and, placing her foot next to the pike to give it scale, she took a couple of photographs. At least she had something to show for her efforts, to show Dad. He would be pleased.

Now, as she gazed at the beautiful fish, she went through her glowing phase, an inexplicable feeling she always got when for a brief moment in time she and another creature shared their lives. She knew it was probably nonsensical, the fish would have a brain the size of a sugar grain, but she couldn't help it, she always felt a connection, something almost electrical passing between them, the cause of her glow.

Gently, she removed the hooks and returned the pike to the water, her glow fading as she watched it flick its tail and dive into the depths. She fixed another dead bait onto the hooks, cast out again and started to row again. The mist had started to thin slightly as the day's temperature rose, but she still could not see either shore. The hiss of the A66 traffic seemed louder now so she may have drifted closer to the western shore or there could simply be more traffic on the road. Either way, she decided to stay where she was as she stopped rowing and started to fish from the stationary boat. She knew from past experience that the western side of the lake was the deepest and hopefully the home of a big one waiting for some easy lunch.

She lost track of time as she sat nursing the rod in her hands, staring out across the glassy water, glad that she had remembered to take a foam cushion. Gradually, she drifted into a trance-like state, not thinking, her eyes blankly staring at nothing in particular.

Something moved in the corner of her right eye. Like a sleepy cat, she turned her head slowly towards the movement. A narrow, black oily ripple in the water seemed to be emerging from the mist. No… it was something solid… moving smoothly towards her… an animal? For a moment she was back in South America again, watching an anaconda swim.

As it grew closer she could see that it was actually a swimmer in a black wetsuit, wearing a black swim-hat, and goggles. The swimmer's front crawl technique looked good – head low, reaching arms, smooth entry in line with the shoulders, long pull, good breathing. Judging by the speed the gap was closing, Charlotte guessed that the swimmer was also wearing fins, though she couldn't see them.

The swimmer was clearly heading straight for her. Charlotte was intrigued, mildly excited. She sat up straight, blinked herself alert again, and put down her fishing rod. It would be nice to have a chat with a fellow adventurer in the middle of a mist-shrouded lake. *Might be another local with some good advice about the state of the lake's fishing.*

Nearing the boat, the swimmer stopped, raised a hand and waved. Charlotte couldn't make out whether the swimmer was male or female. Automatically, she waved back, then readied herself for the expected boat movement if the swimmer held onto it for a rest or a chat or both.

The swimmer closed in and, as expected, grasped the boat with both hands. Masculine hands. The boat rocked slightly. Knowing how swimming hats muffle sound, Charlotte shouted a cheery, "Hello."

The swimmer did not lift his head or reply. Beneath his glistening wet-suit, his shoulders were heaving slightly. He was obviously getting his breath back. Suddenly, his body reared upwards, then plunged back into the water, his hands pulling the side of the boat down with him. Charlotte gasped with shock as she lost her balance, her arms and legs becoming tentacles searching for something to hold on to. In the split second that the boat levelled again, she managed to grab both sides of the boat. Her rod clattered across the floor. She heard something splash into the water – her tackle box. The man continued to rock the boat viciously, rearing up and plunging down, apparently unable to turn the boat over completely. She gripped the sides with all her strength as her body was flung about, bruising her thighs and legs.

As the rocking continued, the man staring ahead, seemingly in some kind of robotic rhythm, she realised she would not be able to hang on much longer as her arm muscles tired. She needed to do something else; she needed to take the initiative. She checked his position in relation to herself. He was roughly in the centre of the boat, out of range of her arms, but not out of range of her feet.

The next time the boat levelled out, leaving his head and shoulders exposed, she swung her left leg across to try to kick him on the head. She caught him on the neck, his wetsuit, unfortunately, absorbing some of the blow. He shouted, left loose of the boat, and put his hand to his neck. Then he swam a few metres away and trod water. Charlotte braced herself for the next attack, kicking her legs in the air to show him that she was ready to fight.

He came straight towards her this time. She didn't know whether to use her fists to repel him or grip the boat's sides again and use her feet. She decided on the latter. He swam right up beside her and started to prise the fingers of her right hand from the boat's edge. She brought her left fist over to hit him on top of his head, but he saw it coming and caught her wrist with his right hand. He pulled her towards him and she had to let go of the side. He lurched backwards and pulled her out of the boat, into the water on top of him.

The shock of the cold water numbed Charlotte's reactions and he was able to move from under her, take hold of her, and push her down deeper. Then he put his feet on her shoulders and pushed her even deeper. Charlotte was stunned and disorientated. She had to clear her head. She had to think like a wild animal, like the marlin, the tuna, who fought frantically for survival. Visibility was poor. She didn't know which way she was facing as she regained her equilibrium. But she was not panicking. Before starting her adventure company she had attended numerous life-saving courses run by the Royal Life Saving Society, culminating in receiving an ER-AS qualification for supervisors of aquatic activities on open water. Left unmolested she knew she could survive. She was a strong swimmer, she wouldn't drown. But she would not be able to out-swim him if he came after her; he had fins on his feet, and she was impeded by her clothing. A plan flashed into her mind. It was very risky, but it was her only chance.

She swam two strokes underwater to put a small distance between them when she came up. Then she kicked her way to the surface, remained vertical, and immediately started to thrash at the water with uncoordinated arm movements, while gasping for breath. While doing this, she spotted him a few metres away, holding the boat's rope. He appeared to be stationary, waiting and watching. During the life-saving courses, she had taken her turn at being "the body", so she knew how to pretend. She went under again and kicked up again, repeating the performance; dramatically thrusting her head up to reach for air, thrashing her arms helplessly, going down again. She didn't scream or shout for help in case he swam over to silence her. She came up one more time, more slowly, clearly weakening, barely able to lift her arms, head trying desperately to stay up but losing the battle. Finally, she allowed herself to slip below, leaving one hand grasping at the air for dramatic effect.

Having taken a big gulp of air before slipping under, she now tucked her head into position and started to swim away. She knew she would have to remove most of her clothes to accomplish the long surface swim that lay ahead, but right now she was glad of their weight which helped to keep her under the water. She swam as strongly as she could, hoping that when she had to surface again either he had moved away or the mist was thick enough to hide her from his view.

The water was bitterly cold, thrusting invisible icicles into her body, causing pain right through to her bones. A toothache-like throb pulsed in her temples. Her arms were already tired from two hours of rowing, fishing and holding on to the sides of the boat. But she gritted her teeth and forced herself to keep swimming as long as possible. This was life and death.

With her lungs at bursting point, she finally surfaced. She came up gently, trying not to disturb the water, keeping everything below her mouth under the water. She fought to minimise the sound of the gasp that her lungs had to make, and partially succeeded.

She spotted him immediately, about 25 metres away. He had moved away from the boat. It took her a few heart-stopping seconds to work out that he was facing away from her, that he was in fact swimming away from her. A few splashes as his fins broke the surface told her that he was trying to swim quickly. He must be making his getaway, believing he had seen her drown. Her plan had worked. She couldn't sigh with relief because she was still gasping. She felt the urge to cry, but knew she couldn't afford to until she was safe on land. She still had a long swim ahead and the cold was a deadly enemy.

She kept a wary eye on him until he was barely discernible in the mist, then she turned onto her back and floated for a few seconds, allowing her breathing to recover. While floating, she thought about returning to the boat, but soon dismissed the idea. She didn't think she had enough strength to pull herself up and into the boat, and her instincts told her to get as far away as possible.

Treading water, she began to remove her clothes, starting with her trainers which had Velcro fasteners. Next came her heavy jacket, then her trousers and jumper. She blessed the many days of training she had done to perfect the removal techniques. She left herself with T-shirt, bra, pants and socks.

Now, with a time-check on her watch, a deep breath, and a determined mind, she set off swimming in what she hoped was the direction of the eastern shore. She knew that swimming in a straight line, without anything to guide her or aim at, was very difficult; many swimmers found themselves going round in circles in such circumstances. She also knew she had no alternative but to keep going until a sight or a sound guided her. Her consolation amid this fear was that her front crawl swimming stroke was very evenly balanced. She did not have one arm pull stronger than the other, a common occurrence among swimmers, and the cause of going round in circles.

The first 15 minutes passed relatively comfortably, the initial pain of the cold water subsiding as the effort of swimming pumped warm blood around her body. She paused occasionally to listen for… anything – the sound of a tractor in a field, a child shouting, a distant car – but nothing came to her rescue. The hiss of traffic from the western shore had disappeared which at least told her she was swimming away from the maniac.

Five minutes later, and the cold started to take over her body again. She started to shiver as she swam, the start of hypothermia. As long as she shivered she would be alright; it meant the body was still producing heat. If the shivering stopped she knew she was in serious trouble, the body core would lose temperature, and she would become physically uncoordinated and mentally confused.

A few more minutes went by. She began to lose hope. What if she was swimming in a perfectly straight line, but that line was north to south, down the length of the lake, not the width? What if the shore was only 100 metres away, but she was swimming parallel to it and would never reach it? Should she make a sharp turn to the left to check out that possibility? Her numbed brain was pondering the question when she heard a bell ring. For a moment she thought she might be hallucinating – the effect of hypothermia. But she heard it again. It was quite loud. It was almost straight ahead. It sounded like a church bell. There was only one church on the shore of Bassenthwaite. It had to be St Bega's, on the east shore. Her spirits soared as she heard the bell continue chiming. It was Sunday. She had forgotten.

Another few metres and she could see a giant shape through the mist. It had to be a mountain – Ullock Pike? Yes, and now she could see the church sitting in the meadow in front of the mountain. She was too exhausted to shout or laugh or even smile, and too numb to cry. All she could do was concentrate on keeping going until she felt the ground beneath her feet.

Two minutes later, fortunate to still be shivering, she felt her left hand touch a smooth stone. She stopped swimming, stood up and tried to walk through the thigh-deep water. Her legs had little feeling left in them and she fell occasionally as she slipped on the underwater stones. She was too numb to feel the pain when her knees and legs hit the stones. No doubt she would be covered in bruises when her ordeal was over.

She had just stepped off the tiny pebbled beach onto the meadow grass in front of the church when a well-dressed elderly couple arrived at her side and caught her as she collapsed. They helped her gently to the ground, wrapped her in their jackets, and the man went for help while the woman stayed with her.

Chapter 24

Having come in like Dr Jekyll, October decided to go out like Mr Hyde. Heavy rain and a fierce wind flung themselves at the cottage. Its ancient stones and slates glistened and came to life, as though refreshed by a morning shower. The cast-iron gutters and pipes caught the rain, gargled with it, and spat it down the drains. A feisty robin preened itself in the splashes.

Ben had made quick dashes outside to feed the birds and carry Helen's gear to her car, adding "watch out for the potholes" to his warning list as he saw her off. He was now comfortably ensconced in his office, and having done a couple of hours' work for *The Tribune*, was busy reading an email from the secretary of the Keswick Rambling Club. She had attached a list of all their members, together with phone numbers, as he had requested. He would now be able to spend some serious time revisiting the disappearance of Elizabeth Lamb. Her membership of the rambling club was his starting point.

He glanced down the names, and was surprised at how many he recognised. He had always thought of himself and Helen as incomers, knowing that a few years in the Lakes did not usually qualify you as a local, but this list made him feel like one. It contained a couple of friends and a few acquaintances – a good place to start his investigation. He downloaded the documents to the printer and ran them off.

He was highlighting the names he recognised with a yellow marker pen when he heard a car arrive on the gravel. He left the office and went downstairs, reminding himself to make coffee before he went back up again.

He reached the back door just as the bell rang. He was surprised to find Bill, standing with hunched shoulders, trying to avoid the rain. He ushered him in, quickly.

"Great day for ducks," Bill growled, taking out his handkerchief to wipe the rain from his forehead.

"Take a seat," Ben offered, indicating the chairs at the kitchen table as he moved to fill the kettle. "Fancy a coffee?"

"Yes… please." Bill sat in his chair sideways-on at the table, one elbow resting on it. He had an awkward bulkiness about him, as if he didn't fit anywhere and was ready to move at any moment. He gently moved the small vase of flowers on the table away from him.

"Milk, two sugars," Ben said, as he placed two cups on the table and sat down opposite him.

"Ta." Bill took a quick sip, and then another one. He seemed flustered.

"A rare pleasure, Bill" Ben enthused. "Wife kicked you out? Sick of being a golf widow?"

"I wish," Bill half-smiled. "No, I've just come straight from the station. I sometimes pop in for a chat when I'm in Keswick, see how they are coping without me."

"And how are they coping without you?"

"Listen," Bill said, urgently, ignoring Ben's question, "I've just left Peter. He had just returned from the cottage hospital where he had been interviewing a woman. She says she was attacked by a swimmer while she was boat-fishing on Bassenthwaite. She says he rocked the boat and pulled her out and tried to drown her. Fortunately for her, she was a trained lifesaver and a strong swimmer. She pretended to drown and he swam off. She had a long swim to reach the shore and was suffering from mild hypothermia when she came out near St Bega's. A couple of churchgoers spotted her and drove her to the hospital."

"Bloody hell!" Ben exclaimed. "Right on my doorstep. When did it happen?"

"Sunday. It was misty, remember."

"Yes… I didn't go for my usual walk because of it. I wonder if it was the woman I met a couple of times, fishing on the shore with her father. They said they were from Manchester. They're the only people I've seen at the lake recently."

"Sounds like it. Her father was with her in the hospital. He'd been back at their hotel nursing a cold, so she was out on her own."

"Did she give a description of the man?"

"Not one you could work with. He was wearing a wet suit, hat and goggles and his body was mostly underwater, so she couldn't even guess his height. She said he seemed about average build, but she couldn't be sure."

"What do you reckon – another Giles Innes?" Ben raised his eyebrows, questioningly. Bill had dismissed Giles Innes's death as accidental.

"Possibly." Bill's tone was reluctant.

"They never found that swimmer in Windermere did they?"

"No." Bill shuffled in his chair.

Ben took a drink of his coffee. "What does Peter think?"

"He didn't say. He was handing it over to CID when I left."

"I wonder if he still thinks Stott is out of the area? I've never been convinced that he is."

"But he must be, Ben," Bill pleaded. "How can two people, one an Asian, stay undetected in the Lakes for weeks on end? What are they doing for money? Where are they hiding?"

"I don't know, but desperate people find ways of coping we wouldn't think about," Ben offered.

"Desperate people usually make a run for it." Bill countered.

"Not if they are compulsively connected to a place. If Stott *is* reliving his father's life, this is where he has to be to do it."

"But Snodd didn't go round pulling people out of boats, he attacked them on the fell tops, and it turned out he had a motive. Tulip, Innes and this woman seem to have been chosen at random."

Ben sipped his coffee, studiously. "But these attacks could also have a motive. We just haven't found it yet. Or maybe they *are* random victims. Maybe Stott just wants to kill the same number of people his father killed, regardless of method used. Maybe he has a list and I'm the last one on it, the only genuine motive he has, saved for the big finale. Trouble is, we don't know how many people are on that list, or how many, if any, he has killed, so I don't know if I'm safe for a while or next to go. Bottom line is we don't actually *know* anything. What facts have we actually got to go on? Both Tulip's and Innes's deaths could well have been accidents. Sunday's episode on the lake is the only fact we have, and even that cannot be proved if there are no witnesses. Assuming the woman is telling the truth, it could have been anybody who attacked her – a jilted lover, a wronged business partner, anybody. It doesn't sound like a random attack does it? A fully equipped swimmer in the lake in cold October water? It sounds planned to me. Whoever it was must have known her movements. How would Stott know her movements? For all we know, Stott and his girlfriend could be in the Philippines right now." Ben paused, and frowned in concentration.

"Then there are all those unexplained deaths that the police are re-examining to take into account," he continued. "Truth is, Bill, we just don't know enough. If it isn't Stott, then God help us, we have to start from scratch."

"Jesus, Ben," Bill snorted, "don't go bringing other suspects in. If murders have taken place it has to be Stott, even if it's hard to believe he is still in the area. How many other madmen or sons of madmen can there be out there? Every policeman in the country is looking for him. They just need a lucky break and they'll have him, you'll see."

Ben lifted his cup from the table and stood up. "Well, I'm not going to wait for the police to have a lucky break," he said, decisively. "If it is Stott, I'm definitely on his list. He didn't pay us two visits to check on our health. Maybe Sunday's attack on that woman was another warning that he was close to me, that he could pounce at any time. Now I feel like a lamb who has heard the wolf howl and is waiting for it to come in the dark. If he is trying to frighten me before killing me he is succeeding. I can't sit around here waiting for him. I can't risk Helen getting hurt. We are going to have to move."

"That's a bit drastic, Ben."

"So is death."

"I was going to say maybe I could help; you know, provide a bit of protection. I know the police can't act until something happens, but I could. I'm still pretty handy at the rough stuff."

"Oh really! And what have you been knocking about lately, apart from a golf ball?"

"The warehouse work can be heavy at times. It keeps me strong."

Ben smiled, "It's really great of you to offer, Bill, but how could I possibly accept? What if I did and something happened to you? How would I live with myself? What if he came armed and you were killed? No – thanks, but no thanks, Bill."

Bill drained the last of his coffee and carried his cup to the sink. "Where will you go?"

"Not sure yet. Relatives, friends, hotel. I'll have to discuss it with Helen. But it can't be too far away, we both have work commitments here. What we need is security, not distance."

"And Peter and me don't want to start buying our own beer," Bill added.

"That too," Ben smiled, and then hurried on as another decision came to mind. "And between you and me, Bill, I'm not going to wait for the police reports on those unexplained deaths. I'm going to start my own investigations. I know I've got very little to go on. I don't even know which cases the police are investigating. But I can have a good guess at some of them. Over the past couple of years I've written reports on many of the accidents, particularly in the north Lakes. I can start there. Obviously I won't have all the information the police files contain. I'll only have the bare facts like names and addresses, places of accidents etc, but they give me a start. I just *have* to do something, Bill. You know me, I can't just sit around waiting for other people to do things."

"And thank God for that," Bill said, generously. "If it hadn't been for you we would have missed Snodd. Listen, if I hear anything when I'm having a cuppa in the station, I'll let you know. I won't break the law, but I'll do what I can to help."

"Thanks Bill, that's great. And thanks for coming round... telling me what happened on Sunday. Reminds me, I'll have to try to get an interview with the woman before she leaves her hotel. Any idea which hotel?"

"Overwater, I think."

"Did you get her name?"

Bill hesitated. "....Peter mentioned a name, but I can't remember... I should have written it down."

"Never mind, I'll phone Peter later."

Bill turned towards the door. "Better get going, I'm working in a couple of hours. You okay for golf this week?"

"Should be… unless I find another place quickly and we start moving. I'll phone you if I can't make it."

"Right." Bill opened the back door and dashed out into the rain.

That night Helen agreed that it was time to move, and they spent the night making a list of people and places that might prove helpful or suitable.

The following morning, Ben managed to obtain an interview with Charlotte Ambler at the hotel, having first learned her name from Peter and her whereabouts from the cottage hospital. She and her father were about to leave for home. She looked remarkably well considering her ordeal and she answered his questions with assurance. She even joked about having caught a bigger one than expected. He asked for, and received, her home contact details in case he needed to ask her more questions later, when he was working on his file of accidental deaths.

Ben wrote up the report at home and took it immediately into *The Tribune* office. While discussing its contents with Sue Burrows he mentioned his, and Helen's, decision to move from the cottage. After sympathising with their problem and expressing her hope that they would stay in the area, Sue came up with a suggestion. She reminded Ben that her family had built up a number of businesses over the years. As well as the newspaper they owned a garage, a tea room, an off-licence and a medium-sized hotel overlooking the market place – The Dog and Gun. The top floor of the hotel had originally been used as the owner's accommodation, but it was now used as occasional holiday accommodation for the Burrows' relatives when they visited the Lakes. Sue looked after the bookings and was able to tell Ben that it was free until next July, a period of 7 months. If other relatives wanted to book later on, she said she would accommodate them in the hotel or at home. She insisted that there would be no charge other than a contribution towards normal household costs such as heating etc.

That evening, Ben discussed Sue's suggestion with Helen. She agreed that it was a perfect solution, providing as it did, the security of a busy hotel in a busy town centre, making unobserved access almost impossible, as well as their need to be near their work. And, being fully furnished and equipped, it meant they had only clothes, office equipment, food and personal items to transfer, a task easily achieved with their two cars. The fact that neither of them liked living in a town was irrelevant in the circumstances. That night they started drawing up their lists of things to take. Ben's first item was: *golf clubs*.

Chapter 25

The number of things we believe we cannot live without rises exponentially with age and the speed of technological development. Thus, two people who thought of themselves as simple country folk finished up having to make seven car journeys between their home and the Dog and Gun Hotel just to take their "essentials" with them. Most of the journeys took place at night after work, in the dark, and that coupled with having to carry everything up two flights of stairs meant that at the end of three days Helen and Ben were very tired. Their physical decline became matched by a mental fragility as they wrestled with the seemingly impossible task of being able to make telephone contact with a sentient human being within the bowels of the giant utility corporations. Trying to inform the corporation's call-centre staff of their simple move, and make suitable transfer arrangements had, they learned, become a trial of persistence and sanity that only the very strong survived – a modern version of survival of the fittest.

Having survived these trials without becoming gibbering idiots, they sailed into calmer waters on day four, their last day, and found themselves about to say a temporary farewell to their beloved cottage in a relatively relaxed frame of mind.

That night, sitting beside their blazing log fire, watching Helen reading while he listened to a Brahms concert, Ben realised how much they would miss it. It was their home in every sense of the word, a place that gave them a deep-seated feeling of belonging. Surrounded by natural beauty and wildlife, it had become their haven of peace and tranquillity in a world which, judging from the news and their own observations, was permanently teetering on the brink of chaos.

A cloud of melancholy drifted across Ben's mind at the thought of leaving, aided no doubt by the sad beauty of Brahms' 2nd piano concerto and the glass of whisky in his hand. He glanced at Helen, wondering if she could sense his mood; he didn't want to transfer it to her. She had sensed his gaze, and smiled at him over the top of her book. When he didn't speak, she returned to her reading, changing her sitting position and adjusting her glasses as she did so. She seemed to be able to take all situations in her stride, no matter how stressful. Sometimes Ben wondered if she had a secret stash of serenity pills hidden away.

In an attempt to rid himself of his mood, Ben tried to think of the positive things that would accrue from living in the town centre. Closer to *The Tribune* office, the theatre, Derwentwater, post office, library, pubs, restaurants, supermarket. This was all good – when he needed them – but it also meant he would be closer to their crowds, noise and congestion when he didn't need them, when he wanted space to be alone, to be able to think without interruption, to walk without having to dodge people and traffic. After this sequence of thoughts Ben's mood had not improved and he knew he would not be truly happy again until they could return to the cottage.

The end of the piano concerto coincided with the emptying of Ben's glass, and brought him out of his reverie into present reality. He needed a refill. Some immature instinct told him that he deserved compensation for the turmoil of having to move house.

As he rose to seek his top-up he noticed that the fire was dwindling. He glanced at the log basket on the hearth. He had forgotten to fill it. The hassle of the last few days had, clearly, affected his routines. "I'm going to get some logs," he said, as he picked up the log basket and moved towards the kitchen door.

Helen peered over her book. "Be careful out there. You've got your alarm haven't you?"

Ben eased the cords out from under the neck of his pullover and pulled out the alarm so that it hung, visibly, on his chest.

"Take your eight iron as well," Helen insisted.

"I'll be alright," Ben scoffed. "I'll leave it for you."

"You'll need a coat on, it's freezing out there."

"Yes mother," Ben smiled, as he left the room.

In a hall cupboard Ben found his favourite old sheepskin jacket that he had bought over 20 years ago. Back then, in a rare fit of devil-may-care they had bought a second-hand sports car and two sheepskin jackets to keep them warm when the top was down. The jackets had, of course, outlasted the car, and Helen had kept hers for about 12 years before disposing of it. Ben, however, had hung on to his, knowing that it would always be useful for the type of cold, dirty job he was now about to embark on. Wrapping himself in its thick warmth, he checked that the small torch was in its pocket, then walked through to the kitchen and went out through the back door. A small oblong of diffused light from the kitchen window made a light patch on the lawn, otherwise total darkness reigned. He paused for a moment to take in the vast display of stars, remembering now that this would be something else he would have to forego when in the town centre, the street lights being an artificial barrier to the night sky.

The log store stood a few metres away from the garden shed, both at the far end of the 20-metre long lawn. Both had been built and left by the previous owner of the cottage. The log store was a simple long, low box-like structure made of wooden planks spaced apart to let the air circulate. It had three closed sides and a roof made of timber tiles. Its closed back faced west to keep out the majority of the rain driven by the prevailing wind. The open front gave easy access to the logs, which Ben stacked neatly inside to make full use of the space.

Ben made his way across the lawn via intermittent stepping stones, also provided by the previous owner. Before reaching the end of the stones, he veered to the left, over the lawn; a shortcut to the log store that, over the years, had damaged the grass, Ben promising himself to do something about it – one day.

On reaching the store, Ben put his basket and torch on the ground, the beam providing just enough light to see the logs. He bent down and picked out two logs and placed them in the basket. As he bent to take two more, a sudden dazzling light lit up the whole area. His heart took an adrenaline hit. He turned, quickly, nervously, to find the cause. A roe deer stood motionless in front of the garden shed, apparently frozen with fear. It had obviously triggered the security light that Ben had installed on the shed following a brief spate of burglaries in the area a couple of years ago. Ben gave a sigh of relief and would have carried on admiring the deer had he not suddenly become aware that his was not the only shadow being cast by the light. Alongside his own shadow was that of someone or something else, the shadows being distorted by the shape of the log store. For the moment, neither shadow moved. Then Ben spun around, ducked and pressed his alarm all in one movement. At least, that was his intention. The alarm got pressed, but his spin and duck were just underway when a massive blow struck him between the shoulder blades. He slumped to the ground, a sickening pain convulsing his body. He felt bile rising in his throat, saw stars flash behind his eyes, as he fought to remain conscious. Willing his mind to forget the pain, he rolled onto his back and emerged with his right hand clutching his alarm. He shouted to the figure that lurked over him, indiscernible due to the light behind him and the hood over his head: "I've pressed this alarm. The police will be here in minutes."

The man hesitated for what seemed like an eternity, then apparently made up his mind and lifted his club-like weapon to strike again. At that moment, the back door of the cottage crashed open and a figure came racing across the lawn, roaring like a highland trooper, brandishing some kind of steel weapon. The man froze in the striking position, hesitated, then lowered his club and ran off into the darkness.

Helen reached Ben's side, laid the golf club on the ground, and took hold of his hand. She was breathing heavily and seemed unable to speak, as if she daren't ask him if he was all right in case the answer was no. Her hands were trembling.

"I'm okay," Ben grimaced. "I'm okay. Hit on the back, hurts like hell, but I don't think anything's broken." He tried to ease himself up off the ground, but his right arm didn't like having weight put on it. He moaned with the pain.

"Let's see if you can sit up," Helen said, shakily, and moved behind him.

Using his left arm as a lever, and with Helen's help, Ben managed to reach a sitting position. From there, with Helen's help, it was relatively easy to gain his standing position.

Helen picked up the eight iron, then supported Ben on his left side. "Right, let's get you back inside."

They moved slowly across the lawn, Helen glancing around nervously, afraid of the man's return. "Don't worry," Ben joked, "he's not coming back. You frightened the life out of me, never mind him."

They reached the cottage door just as the garden shed security light went out. Helen helped Ben to sit down at the kitchen table, helped him remove his sheepskin jacket, then, at Ben's insistence, went into the hall to phone the police.

In spite of the throbbing pain between his shoulder blades, Ben knew he was extremely lucky. If that blow had landed on his head he would have died. A sequence of chance happenings and an amazing wife had saved his life. He owed his life to an old sheepskin jacket, a deer, and another dear – Dear Helen. What a woman. What a performance. But how did she know he was in danger?

"It was your mobile," she explained, after she had sat down opposite him and told him that the police were on their way, and that road blocks were being set up around the lake and on major arteries. "You left it on the coffee table in the lounge. When I answered it and realised it was the police answering your alarm, I just dropped it and ran into the kitchen and picked up the golf club and ran out. When I saw you on the ground all I knew was that that man had to die. I was going to kill him and nothing would have stopped me."

"You were magnificent," Ben said. "Terrifying, but magnificent. Where did that roar come from? You sounded like an animal."

"We are animals," Helen pointed out, quietly. "Animals protect their mates."

"He must have sensed your determination," Ben said. "You saved my life, sweetheart."

"All part of the service," Helen smiled, as she rose from her chair. "Fancy a cup of tea while we wait for the cops."

Two days later, having spent one of them in the cottage hospital, where x-rays showed that nothing was broken, with severe bruising of the trapezius muscle being diagnosed as his only problem, Ben and Helen were busy acquainting themselves with their new home. It was a typical open-plan apartment – lounge, dining area and kitchen all in one large space – all furnished with typical second-hand "holiday furniture". It was a far cry from their small, cosy rooms, carefully furnished in a traditional style. "At least we can still see Skiddaw over the rooftops," Helen said, as she stood at a window overlooking the marketplace. As always, she looked for the positive in things.

"And Catbells and Grizedale Pike out the back", Ben added, trying to match her positivity, though not feeling it. The shock of the attack, the long interviews with the police, the pain and the house move had left him feeling like the victim of a stampede. But the thing that depressed him most was the realisation that another enemy had emerged. The attacker was not Hamish Stott. He had not seen the man's face, but he had seen that he was not small or thin, and Helen had confirmed that the man was too tall and well built to be Stott. Both agreed that the speed of his departure and the way he ran indicated somebody under 35.

The police roadblocks had failed to come up with a likely candidate, which was not surprising given the large number of back roads and lanes the man could have used once he had left Scarness Lane and reached the A591.

Peter, and subsequent CID officers, had scratched their heads at the news that it wasn't Stott. They had even questioned Ben about his past, wondering if he had ever been involved with criminal situations other than the Hector Snodd case. Ben's negative answer had led to a detective sergeant proposing that the man could have been employed by Stott, or be a friend of Stott's, who was doing the dirty work for him since Stott himself would have been picked up if he had shown his face in the area. With Stott coming from a gangland area of Edinburgh, and also having old army mates to call on, this proposal had gained wide acceptance among the gathering. But not by Ben, though he didn't voice his doubts. In his opinion, a genuine hard man or a professional hitman would not have run off when faced by a woman. She would have become nothing more than "collateral damage" to him. This led Ben to believe that the man who attacked him was neither professional nor "hard". The attacker did not want to hurt Helen, just him. But who the hell was he? This was a puzzle that needed to be solved quickly. This was personal and deadly. It would have to take priority over Elizabeth Lamb and the accidental deaths. Could they be connected, or were they separate?

Towards the end of the police interviews, Ben and Helen had been offered the chance to go to a police safe-house, which would be many miles away in another county. When they said they preferred to stick with the Dog and Gun Hotel, the police had called Sue Burrows in and asked her how, in view of recent events, she and the hotel staff felt about housing them. Sue explained that the staff, who were mostly locals, had all been told about the situation and they were actually looking forward to "protecting" Ben and Helen who were well known and popular in the town. Unable to dissuade Sue, the police said they would be writing to her, pointing out the fact that they had advised a different course of action, namely that Mr and Mrs Foxley should be housed in a police safe-house. All agreed that, at the very least, the move should buy the police more time to track down the attacker.

After a lengthy discussion on the pros and cons, all parties agreed that news of the attack should appear in *The Tribune*. It might, they hoped, provide another "layer of protection" by the community. Ben had reservations about being the centre of attention in the town, but Helen overruled him, saying, "It's better to be constantly stared at than constantly dead."

Chapter 26

Ben opened his eyes and, momentarily, had no idea where he was. The light of day and the sound of traffic further confused him. Sleeping late would explain the light, but where did the traffic noise come from? A glance around his strange new bedroom soon answered his question. His watch told him it was 9.15. The void beside him told him that Helen was already up and about.

His back protested as he eased himself into a sitting position on the bed. He had taken painkillers, and tried to sleep on his side for most of the night, but he remembered how restless it had been. The pain, and his churning mind working *ad nauseam* on the mystery of who his attacker could be, had given him a night to remember.

As he swivelled his legs onto the floor he noticed the paper and pen on his bedside cabinet, and recalled that at some point in that long night he had written a note. He picked up the sheet of A4 and somewhere near the centre of the otherwise blank page he had written one word – *Lund?*

The night's long brain-scan had confirmed to him that he had not had any dubious dealings with the criminal fraternity other than with the Hector Snodd case. Except for a random maniac, his attacker had to be associated with that case. Stott had been discounted on this occasion, so that only left his connection with Sophie Lund. It had been a tenuous, long-distance connection that had seemed unreal at times, almost imagined. The only time he had met her, in a Keswick hotel, he had wondered if she was on drugs. Her suspicion that a government minister had been assassinated on Skiddaw because of his knowledge of an international nuclear scandal had struck him as bizarre at best, crazy at worst.

When, having employed him to investigate her suspicions, Sophie had supplied him with data which, she said, "her boys" had obtained by hacking into police records, Ben had become seriously concerned about what he was getting into. Eventually, when Ben had proved that the minister had died at the hands of a serial killer and that his death had nothing to do with the nuclear industry, he had been questioned by senior police officers about the source of his information. With a hint of threat in his tone, one of the plain-clothes officers had finally offered him a deal. "Tell us who hacked into our computers and we will (a) not charge you with being in possession of confidential police records, and (b) expect you to remain silent when we tell the media that it was the police who caught Snodd after months of investigation. You must play the part of an innocent bystander whose wife was kidnapped by Snodd."

Believing he was doing the right thing, Ben had agreed to their deal and given them Sophie Lund's name, but he explained that he did not know who did the hacking for her, only that she called them "her boys".

Shortly after revealing Sophie Lund's name to the police, she had been found dead in her London flat. The police blamed burglars. Ben had been shocked and left wondering if her nuclear story might, after all, have had some truth in it. He had not, however, pursued the question as he had already booked a long holiday on a remote Greek island, a place where Helen and he could recover from their ordeal at the hands of Mr Snodd.

It was during their time on the island, without newspapers, television, radio or telephone, that Sophie Lund's son Dominic and his colleagues in "Robin Hood" had been arrested. Ben had been unaware of their existence or their arrest until their trial 11 months later, which made the national news. He had followed it with intense interest, keen to learn at last the identity and character of Sophie's "boys", one of whom was precisely that – her boy – Dominic. It had been fascinating, and shocking, to learn of the extent of their hacking activities – international companies, and government ministries as well as the police records they had obtained for Sophie, to give to Ben. Ben still did not know whether Sophie had told Dominic and friends why she wanted the police records, or if she had mentioned his name as the eventual recipient. If she *had* told them about him, he now saw it was possible that they had put two and two together and realised that it had been Ben who "betrayed" Sophie to the police. A cause for anger and retribution certainly, from their point of view. But murder?

This was where Ben's analysis came to a grinding halt. They may have a motive, but they certainly didn't have an opportunity. They were all still in prison weren't they? Dominic, the ringleader, had been sentenced to 12 years and the others to 10 years each. That had all been about five or six years ago, Ben felt, though he realised his judgement of the passage of time had deteriorated as he got older. He would check it out, get the exact sentence details. He was aware that some prisoners were released before their full sentence was served, but he didn't know how this was decided, or by how much a sentence could be reduced. He had a vague idea that it was only a couple of years that was taken off. Again, he would check it out.

That afternoon he telephoned Peter and passed on his thoughts about the "Robin Hood" boys possibly having a motive to attack him, and asked if he would check on the details of their prison sentences. Peter immediately gave him the alarming news that all sentences classed as "determinate" were automatically served half in prison and half outside "on licence", under the supervision of the probation service.

Peter followed that up two hours later with the news that two of the "boys" had been out of prison for almost two years, which almost certainly ruled them out as Ben's attacker, and Dominic Lund had been released 11 months ago. He was now living on his own in a flat in London, and had immediately set himself up as a self-employed IT security consultant. Ironically, one of his first customers was the Ministry of Defence. According to his probation officer the terms of his probation were relatively lax since he was not considered to be a danger to the public. He was not allowed to have contact with his two former colleagues. He was not allowed to leave the country, and he had to report once a month to his probation officer.

"So," Peter concluded, "if he is your attacker why did it take him 11 months before he decided to do it? Doesn't seem very plausible does it?"

"Not on the face of it," Ben agreed. "But who knows what factors decide these things. Are the London police going to question him about his movements at the time of the attack?"

"I don't know," Peter hesitated. "I've passed it all on to CID. Whether they act on it is up to them. I think they still have a mate of Stott down as favourite, and frankly, so do I."

"Surely, in the circumstances, they must check him out," Ben insisted.

"They might, they might not," Peter said, flatly. "There is nothing certain in your theory, no absolute facts to work on, and local CID are reluctant to ask the Met for favours unless they are sure of their facts. The Met, as you can imagine, are very busy boys."

"Great," Ben fumed. "So my safety depends on the internal politics of police cooperation."

"Off the record, Ben," Peter said, sympathetically, "it's the one aspect of police work that bothers me. Cooperation between forces is not as good as it should be. When I'm a Chief Constable I intend to do something about it. Meanwhile, I'll keep pushing CID to ask the Met to interview Lund, how's that?"

What a shrewd operator Peter is, Ben thought. *He takes criticism in his stride and offers something back that he presents as a favour. No doubt he will be a Chief Constable one day, or even a politician.*

"Thanks," was all Ben could come up with, by now feeling defeated.

That evening, when Helen returned from work, Ben made no mention of his suspicions about Lund or his conversation with Peter. He didn't want to heap any more worry onto her. Genuine though these concerns were, Ben knew that he was still hiding the main reason for his omission. The reality was that, after all these years, he had still not disclosed to Helen his contact with Sophie Lund.

Chapter 27

Dominic Lund sat staring at his computer screen. Unshaven, hung-over, he had not moved for at least five minutes. A cigarette had smoked itself to extinction in an overflowing ashtray on his desk, the bad habit picked up during his time in prison. He was supposed to be working; supposed to be finishing a security system for an important client; had promised it for later that day. But he couldn't concentrate. His mind kept replaying his failed trip to Cumbria.

He had planned it like a military campaign. In and out quickly had been his intention, leaving no trace or clues. A morning train from London to Carlisle. A hire car from Carlisle to Bassenthwaite. Wait near the Foxley's cottage for evening darkness. Attack and kill Ben Foxley at the first opportunity. Return by car to Carlisle. Same night train from Carlisle back to London.

If an opportunity did not arise on the first day, he would return to London and do it all again later. He did not want to be traced via hotel accommodation. He had set up verbal explanations for his absence with friends and acquaintances, which could be used as an alibi if needed. He had studied maps of Cumbria to find alternative routes back to Carlisle from Bassenthwaite should things go wrong and the police got involved and put up roadblocks. He had decided that once he left Scarness Lane and reached the A591 he would take the minor road via Orthwaite to Caldbeck, then the B5299, passing through Dalston to Carlisle. At least that part of his plan had worked.

Foiled by a fucking deer, a fucking alarm and an irate wife. He was glad he had picked up another bad habit in prison – profanity – it helped him to express his deep frustration. *How the hell could I plan for that? Why was he wearing that alarm? Was I expected? Had I been spotted during the summer when I was shadowing him? If so, better not try it again.*

He had already decided not to try again when he learned that the police had indeed been called in, and set a roadblock. Police involvement was the stopper. The risk of being caught and sent back to prison was something he could not countenance. He would rather die than go back to prison. He would have to content himself with the memory of striking his enemy a vicious blow, one that he hoped would cause Foxley injury and pain for at least six years. A thought suddenly struck him – *perhaps I could also cause him some financial pain.*

Hacking into Foxley's bank account would be relatively easy, but he would have to confer with Alberto and Vyan before doing so. Although the terms of their probation forbade them to meet they were constantly in touch via computer and phone, and occasionally met at night when London was asleep. Ostensibly working as individual security consultants in various areas of London, they were in fact still a team who shared information, helped each other in their legitimate business endeavours, and when money was needed, continued to relieve foreign wealthy individual's bank accounts of small amounts. No hacking was done without the three of them agreeing on its merits and risks. *No time like the present*, Dominic thought, as he saved and closed his current project window, opened an email, addressed it to Alberto and Vyan and headed it "Prop 374", their shorthand for Hacking Proposition No. 374.

He had completed his introduction when a knock on the apartment door interrupted him. As a precaution he closed the email before rising to answer the door. Because he was not expecting anybody he took the further precaution of shouting, "Who is it?"

"Police, Mr Lund. Open the door please." The tone was authoritative and demanding.

Alert and fearful as a cornered fox, Dominic opened the door. Three men wearing paint-stained white overalls and decorator baseball caps, rushed in, grabbing hold of him as they did so. They were too strong to resist, their surgical-gloves aiding their vice-like grips. They dragged Dominic to a chair, sat him down, snapped a chloroform ampoule under his nose. With two of them holding him, the third man forced Dominic's mouth open and slowly poured in the contents of what appeared to be a half bottle of whisky. As he passed into unconsciousness, Dominic swallowed the liquid involuntarily. The men carried Dominic to his bedroom, laid him on the unmade bed, put the empty bottle in his right hand and went off to search the apartment. The three laptop computers they found were placed in a soiled heavy-duty plastic sack they had brought with them.

Normally they would have simply copied the information held on the computers using USB Flash drives, but time was of the essence, and it was almost certain that these computers would be heavily protected. Back at HQ some boffin armed with the latest COFEE (Computer Online Forensic Evidence Extractor) app would soon extract the necessary information.

One of the men took a set of iPod earphones out of his pocket and placed them over his ears. As they left the apartment, carrying the sack, the man with the earphones walked ahead, girating his body and head as though listening to lively pop music. The other two followed, pointing at him, laughing and joking at his ungainly movements. Out on the street the three jolly decorators dumped the sack in the back of their battered old, unmarked, pick-up, and in no apparent hurry climbed aboard and drove off slowly.

Later that day a motorcycle messenger left the headquarters of MI6 in Vauxhall Cross and delivered an envelope to the Foreign and Commonwealth office in King Charles Street. Shortly afterwards, Sir Hugh Peters, the new head of MI5 at Thames House activated his direct line to the new Home Secretary.

An hour later, both the Foreign Secretary and the Home Secretary reported to 10 Downing Street where they told the recently elected Conservative Prime Minister that his request to "tidy up the Operation Pluto file" (a job that his predecessor had failed to do) had been successfully carried out. All three "paragraphs" had been removed. Blame would be diverted to a gang of Russian hackers. "Good", said the Prime Minister. "At long last we have some good news for the President. He will be relieved."

Chapter 28

The death on the same day of three members of the once notorious hackers – Robin Hood – made headline news and appeared on Ben's computer homepage the day after the event. Alberto Sousa had been found sitting on a park bench near his London home, a small puncture hole in his temple. Vyan Chetana had been struck by a white van as he crossed the road outside his home. Two witnesses had noted the van's number. It turned out to be meaningless. Dominic Lund had been found dead in his flat. The police said that a crude attempt had been made to make his death look like alcohol poisoning caused by a binge-drinking session. But blood tests revealed traces of a fast-acting poison that deteriorates in the blood stream after two days, then becomes untraceable. This poison first came to the notice of British authorities during the Cold War in the Soviet era when used by the Russian KGB to silence their enemies. Rumours were already circulating that this had been the work of an infamous gang of Russian hackers who were ambitious and ruthless, and saw Robin Hood as rivals.

Ben was shocked, relieved and puzzled. Shocked at the sudden murder of three people on the streets of London; relieved that, though he was not absolutely certain that they were involved in the recent attack on him, he could now discount them as a possible source of future attacks; puzzled at the timing of their deaths – just after the attack on him – and at the rumour that Russian hackers were responsible.

Had the Metropolitan Police followed up on the information Peter passed down the line? Why would hackers kill each other? It all seemed implausible, but what did he know about what went on in the fight to access and dominate the new world of virtual reality; his was the simple world of open space – not cyberspace. Ben switched off his computer and decided to take a short walk to the police station.

Emerging from the hotel apartment into the cobbled-street hustle of Keswick market-place was a strange new morning experience: surrounded by buildings – not trees; the chatter of people – not birds; the sound of cars – not tractors; the smell of food – not foliage. It was market day and the place was buzzing with stallholders setting up and early-morning shoppers getting in before the car-parks filled up. The cobbles were strewn with a thousand boxes containing everything from fruit to clothes to books. Weather-beaten stallholders chatted and joked as they heaved their wares from the boxes to the stalls, seemingly apathetic to the slight drizzle that added to the grey autumnal mood. Ben was struck by the contrast between the simplicity and timelessness of this scene and the complex new computer-dominated world that was occupying his brain, even as he dodged a backing van. The sudden movement caused the quiet pain between his shoulder blades to become louder. Gingerly, he made his way across the wet cobbles, rounded the historic Moot Hall, and weaving slalom-like among the scattered boxes, finally turned into the relative peace of Bank Street. It was all going to take some getting used to.

"I've been expecting you," Peter said, as Ben hung up his waterproof jacket and sat down. "We got the word from CID yesterday afternoon. I've been phoning round ever since." He paused, as though not sure how to continue.

"And?" Ben encouraged.

"I think I'm as mystified as you must be," Peter said, quietly. "I'm not hearing much that makes any sense. Three of them on the same day, at different locations. It's obviously a targeted hit by a big organisation, but which organisation? And before you ask, the Met had not been to see them before they died. The Met's involvement only started when they got an anonymous phone call reporting a disturbance at Dominic Lund's flat. When they got there they found Lund dead on his bed, but no sign of a disturbance. Somebody had wanted him to be found as soon as possible…"

"The poison," Ben interrupted.

"What!?"

"The poison," Ben emphasised. The report I read this morning said that it deteriorated after two days then became untraceable. They wanted the cause of death to be known."

"That doesn't make sense," Peter pointed out.

"It does if you are trying to frame somebody," Ben suggested. He paused to see if Peter was following his line of thought.

Peter frowned, "You mean somebody was trying to frame the Russian hackers?"

"Exactly," Ben concluded. "Russian poison found, rumours about Russian hackers on the news already. Does anybody know where these rumours started? I bet they are as untraceable as that poison."

"You might be right," Peter concluded, "but all that does is add to the confusion. It doesn't tell us who did the killing, and why. And try as I might I cannot see any connection between the recent attack on you and these deaths."

"There has to be a connection," Ben insisted. "And I think its roots go way back to the Snodd case. Remember, at the end of the Snodd case I told the police that Sophie Lund and her boys had been hacking into police records. Two days later she was found shot in her flat. Police blamed burglars. Nobody was ever convicted for that crime. Now this. All her boys found dead, just after I was attacked by, I believe, Dominic Lund. Police are at the scene, then a rumour starts about Russian hackers…"

"You can't believe the police are involved," Peter said, incredulously.

"I don't discount it," Ben said, solemnly. "The world has changed. We used to put our trust in the police, priests, doctors, politicians, judges, bankers, virtually anybody in authority. Not anymore. One of the benefits of this age of instant news is that people in authority can no longer cover their tracks, hide their misdemeanours. They have all been exposed at one time or another. People no longer automatically trust them; the age of innocence is over."

"The police don't go around killing people," Peter stressed, vehemently. "You've lost the plot."

"I haven't lost it, Peter," Ben said, calmly. "I'm trying to find it. It may not be the police directly, but I have a feeling they have some involvement, probably at a very high level."

"This is turning into a pointless discussion," Peter snapped. "Until somebody comes up with some hard facts, some proof, then all this is conjecture."

"You're right," Ben conceded. "And the chances of you or me finding out what really happened in London is about as good as me getting a hole-in-one on Saturday. Are you playing?"

"… I doubt it," Peter said, caught out by the sudden change in subject. "Not if it keeps on raining. The course will be too boggy."

"Mmm… could be," Ben reflected. As he rose from his seat the pain in his back sent him a reminder. "I forgot," he grimaced, "I won't be playing either."

"You won't be going back home, will you?" Peter said, quickly. It sounded more like an order than a question. "You cannot rely on the fact that Lund is dead. You don't know for sure that he was your attacker. We still think it was somebody associated with Stott—"

Ben held up his hand. "Don't worry, we won't be going back yet. I appreciate your concern. If it was only up to me I would go back, but I cannot risk anything happening to Helen. So we are staying put at the Dog and Gun until Stott is found."

"And don't get too relaxed there either," Peter warned. "Keep your eyes and ears open. If he's determined who knows what he'll try next. And tell Helen as well."

"Yes Sergeant," Ben said, as he gave Peter a mock salute and moved to collect his coat.

Back in the hotel apartment, having picked up an irresistible pork pie for his lunch on his way back through the market stalls, reflecting that it might not be so bad living in the town after all, Ben set about preparing the ground for his own investigations into the recent spate of unexplained deaths. He was aware that it was a daunting prospect. How far back to go? Who to include and exclude? So little information. So few facts; so few clues. No police files to work with. Yet he felt he had little choice but to attempt to find the answers. There wasn't only his curiosity and love of a challenge to satisfy. His own life could be at stake.

However, he had been in a similar situation when he started investigating the Snodd killings, and he had managed to solve that terrible puzzle. That had been achieved mostly by perspiration rather than inspiration, a bit of luck, and that indefinable thing he called "the vibrations", which occur when you concentrate intently on a given subject. He had also studied basic police investigation procedures based on the WHY WHEN WHERE HOW system, the critical and most difficult question to answer being WHY. To answer that you had to identify the victim and then link the victim to the killer... somehow. If, as it was beginning to appear, one person was responsible for a number of murders – a serial killer – then it was vital to identify the *type* of victim the killer chooses since the victims tend not to be known personally by the killer but usually have something in common, the commonality often being very vague and difficult to detect, though it can often be simple in retrospect because the killer is usually simple-minded. He had picked up this information and much more from the excellent book *The Serial Killers – a study in the psychology of violence* by Colin Wilson and Donald Seaman. Investigation into the victims' backgrounds to search for commonality had been his first step on the Snodd case and was again where he intended to start.

The big difference between this and the Snodd case was that there was already a suspect on the board – Stott. If Stott had been on a killing spree then it should help the search for the link between victim and killer. But if Stott had just been notching up numbers to match his father then a link would not be there to find. And the presence of Stott as a suspect could also be a hindrance. It could close minds to the possibility of another killer; it could deflect thought processes from seeking out new avenues. Ben knew he must guard against this, that he must keep his mind open to *all* possibilities. He also knew he must remember to "study the minutiae of events in all cases".

Ben sighed as he slumped into the chair facing his computer. Though he enjoyed the prospect of an intellectual challenge, he knew he was about to set off on a long, difficult journey, that he would have to forego some of his usual activities such as painting, and that success was far from certain.

He had set up his computer on a desk in the spare bedroom at the rear of the apartment, the desk being in front of a window that afforded a glorious view across the rooftops of Keswick to take in a sweep of fells from Grizedale Pike to Catbells. By now the drizzle had stopped and the overall blanket of grey cloud had been ripped into shreds of tattered grey rags. Through the cloud gaps shafts of sunlight arrowed down like spotlights from heaven, highlighting crags and trees and heather, turning the russet bracken into glowing orange. Had Ben not been so familiar with this scene he would have found it almost impossible to tear his eyes away. As it was he found comfort in the fact that at any given time on his long journey he could lift his head and refresh his mind, clear his clogged-up brain with a dose of natural beauty beyond compare.

He booted up the computer and started to compile the same database document he had created at the beginning of the Snodd case, a place where he could record some basic facts and statistics about each of the "possible victims", which would enable him to search for commonalities between them. He typed in the headings: NAME. ADDRESS. SEX. AGE. HEIGHT. WEIGHT. NATIONALITY. OCCUPATION. MARRIED. SINGLE. RETIRED. DIVORCED. CHILDREN. RELIGION. POLITICS. MEMBER OF. HOBBIES. TRAVEL. SPORT. MILITARY. RELATIVES. ENEMIES. LOC OF DEATH.

On a separate page, headed simply – CLUES – he typed:

1. Land Rover? (D. Ivison).

2. Man of medium height and build? (C. Ambler).

His journey had started. Deciding on who to include on the list and finding ways of obtaining information on each of them was going to take days of work, mostly involving the searching of newspaper archives. He half-smiled to himself as he realised what he really needed was a good computer hacker to get into the police files. Instead, all he was going to start with was a good cup of coffee. He made his way to the kitchen.

Chapter 29

Two days later, Ben was on his way to the *Tribune* office to start his search of the archives when he literally bumped into Bill in Station Street. Ben had been walking along, deep in thought as usual (he always did his best thinking while walking) and Bill had stepped out of the newsagent with his head buried in a newspaper.

Apologies over, Bill persuaded Ben to join him in a nearby speciality coffee shop by announcing, "I've got a bit of news for you." It needed that sentence to get Ben into the type of place he usually avoided like the plague, not being keen on handing over what used to be his monthly mortgage repayment for a small cup of ridiculously named dark liquid which had simply been called coffee once upon a sensible time. From the menu of 15 meaningless choices Ben selected *Flat White* which sounded the nearest to plain coffee. Bill ordered something called *Bombon* which he had "discovered" while on holiday in Spain. On arrival, in a glass, it looked disgusting, with a thick layer of what appeared to be pus or glue having separated out into the bottom of the glass. When Bill explained that this was sweetened condensed milk lying underneath an espresso, with a large blob of cream on top, Ben knew it would also taste disgusting.

Clearly ignoring the millions of pounds his government spends on health warnings, Bill also ordered a huge chunk of chocolate gateau, which Ben had the dubious pleasure of seeing being masticated while Bill told his story. Ben assumed it would be something to do with the recent dramatic events in London, and was surprised when Bill said, "I was in the station earlier on. They've had some feedback on that attack on the woman on Bassenthwaite Lake."

Ben took a notebook and pen from his inside jacket pocket, his back sending out a twinge of pain as he did so.

Bill continued, "Remember the police asked for people to contact them if they had seen anybody wearing a wetsuit near the lake or in the vicinity of the A66 that day?"

"Yes, I put that in my report in *The Tribune*."

"Well, a lorry driver from Chester has been in touch... read it in one of the nationals. He says he was driving south on the A66 that day. He says it was misty so he had his lights on and his eyes peeled. He says he saw a man in a wetsuit come through a lake-side gate and open the back door of a vehicle parked in one of the lay-bys on the A66. He was carrying those flipper things. Says he was pretty sure it was a Land Rover." Bill paused for effect and took a sip of his drink.

"The Braithwaite hit and run..." Ben started.

"Exactly," Bill enthused. "That's a Land Rover reported seen on both cases."

"Has there been any joy yet on tracing the Braithwaite Land Rover?" Ben asked.

"Not that I know of. Peter reckons it's like looking for a needle in a haystack. Cumbria's the second biggest county in the country and it's nearly all farmland; there are thousands of farmers, most with Land Rovers, and most of them are bashed about a bit so it would be hard to find one that wasn't dented. On top of that you've got millions of visitors passing through—"

"I get the picture," Ben interrupted. "Any description of this bloke on the A66?"

"Just that he was on the smallish side, the driver said. But everything looks small from a lorry driver's seat, doesn't it, so I wouldn't put too much store on that one. Apparently he still had his swim-hat and goggles on, probably in case somebody saw him…" Bill paused for a second, then, "Stott is small, isn't he… but where the hell would he get a Land Rover?"

"With his background I expect he would have no trouble stealing one," Ben offered, though he still wasn't sure that Stott was the only candidate. "I suppose the police are checking on any stolen Land Rover cases?"

Bill took a sizeable bite of his gateau before he answered, "I expect so, Ben, but I don't know for sure." On each of the words beginning with "s" a slight spurt of chocolate crumbs came out of his mouth.

Ben wished he had ordered a bib. "It's so frustrating not knowing what's going on," he sighed. "I've started on my own investigations like I said I would, but I only have a few names. And I have so little information I'm almost certain to fail. If I only knew which files the police were reopening I could work on the full picture." He looked at Bill, earnestly. "I don't suppose you—"

Bill held up the palm of his left hand. "Hold it," he smiled. He had a piece of chocolate cake stuck to his top-left lateral incisor giving the appearance of a missing tooth. "I told you I would help but wouldn't break the law."

"I know I'll never see what's in the files," Ben barged on, "but if I just had a list of the names on the files I would know I wasn't wasting my time on cases the police aren't interested in. We would, in effect, be working in tandem."

Bill dabbed up the crumbs on his plate with a moistened middle right finger. "Actually..." he smiled again, looking like a character in a Dickens novel, "I think I might be able to help with that."

"Really?"

"I think I'll be able to get a list of names out of Peter. I'm pretty sure he'll have a list; he keeps pestering CID for info all the time; sometimes I think he's also doing his own thing on this, trying to beat the CID to the draw. He's very ambitious, you know. If he could crack this case before the CID he would be well on the road to promotion. If I tell him that you will share any leads you get and, if you happen to crack the case, hand the answer over to him so he can claim it, then I'm pretty certain he'll go along with it. You might not always get along, but he respects your capabilities after the Snodd case."

"And if he doesn't?"

Bill seemed to grow in his chair. "Remember, I used to be his boss. I know what makes him tick. He'll do anything to get ahead… he'll do it all right. Are you happy to hand it over to him if you crack it?"

"Absolutely. The last thing I want is to be the centre of a media circus."

"Okay, then leave it to me. I'll get back to you as soon as I can." Bill turned his attention to his half-finished coffee and lifted it to his lips.

"That's great, Bill, thanks." Ben rose from the table, leaving most of his coffee, picking up the bill as he did so. The pain in his back throbbed. "I'll get this," he said, as cheerfully as he could. "You'd better check your gnashers before you go out, you'll frighten the kids."

Chapter 30

A man wearing a light-grey anorak and cloth cap sat on a seat situated halfway up the steep eastern slope of Catbells, overlooking Derwentwater. The seat, a simple two metre long oblong of Lakeland slate placed across supporting pillars, was dedicated, by means of an inscribed plaque set into the face of a crag just behind the seat. The plaque read:

TO THE MEMORY OF
SIR HUGH WALPOLE CBE
OF BRACKENBURN
THIS SEAT IS ERECTED BY HIS FRIEND
HAROLD CHEEVERS
SEPTEMBER 1941

The famous novelist had lived in the house called Brackenburn, which sat just 100 metres below the seat, when he had written his epic story of a Cumberland family – *The Herries Chronicles*.

Sticking out from under his cap, the man's white hair flicked in the breeze that came across the lake from the east; causing him to abandon his attempt to light his pipe. Peering through his glasses he concentrated on the opposite shore, where woodland covered the narrow strip of land between Walla Crag and the lake and continued southwards, clinging to the cliffs around Lodore Falls, and onwards through the Jaws of Borrowdale as far as his eyes could see. In late autumnal sunshine it was a scene of exceptional beauty. Collectively, the trees had apparently decided to follow the advice of another literary giant – Dylan Thomas – whose famous poem demanded:

Do not go gentle into that good night,
Old age should burn and rave at close of day;
Rage, rage against the dying of the light.

The trees were all burning and raving and raging in a final frenzy of colour as they fought against the dying light of summer. Soon they would be mere skeletons clinging to life until the light of spring filled their veins with sap again.

It was this spectacle that brought the man to the slopes of Catbells at this time every year. Each year he brought his sketch-pad and pencils and tried to capture the scene, its shapes and proportions, and make notes of colours to be applied at a later date. Otherwise, it was not the sort of place he would normally frequent. Its popularity with tourists meant that there were always people to be seen whatever the time of year. And with people came cars, and pollution and… An airforce fighter-jet hurtled past his eyes, at about the same level, its sudden, inhuman roar shattering the peace, assaulting his ears. Another one followed closely behind, destroying the tranquil air; the pair gone in seconds, coldly indifferent to their savagery.

Can humanity sink any lower, he wondered. Creating monstrous machines whose sole purpose is to destroy other humans. The practice of using England's most beautiful landscape in which to train to do this was, no doubt, a trifling matter of minor inconvenience to the warmongers.

The man was consumed with rage. The senses he used – that all artists use – to attempt to capture a place, a moment in time, had been deadened by the noisy intrusion. He quivered as he stood and started to pack away his equipment.

With a final look around from his lofty viewpoint, the man set off walking along the track that would eventually lead him to the road into Grange Village, then on to the main valley road where he planned to catch the bus. He had only taken a few steps when, to his dismay, he saw someone walking along the track towards him. The man lowered his head to avoid eye contact.

Chapter 31

"November the fifth has changed beyond all recognition," Ben typed onto his computer screen. "When I was a boy kids did everything for themselves – collected wood, cardboard, old tyres, built a bonfire on every spare bit of ground around town, bought their own fireworks, lit the fire and kept it going, lit the fireworks – frightening the life out of each other with bangers – and stayed out in the freezing night until their parents shouted them in or came looking for them. Bonfire night was a big night, a night never forgotten.

"Now, we have one or two large public bonfires organised by the local authority where the child is brought along in a car by its parents and stands dutifully watching from a great distance as a man from the fire brigade dressed like an astronaut lights the fire and the fireworks. No doubt the Senior Coordinating Officers of the council's Planning, Fire, Health, Risk Assessment, and Insurance departments have spent months organising them. Some councils have even instigated "bonfire patrols" in which council employees are paid to patrol the town and confiscate any "illegal" personal bonfires; probably the same councils who plead they are short of money.

"At this rate the time cannot be far away when children will only be allowed to attend if they are wearing matching, sponsored, fire-retardant uniforms, safety helmets and goggles, and are accompanied by an adult who can produce a certificate showing that he/she has passed the local authority "Fire and Accident Awareness Procedures" examination. Or, worse still, there will be no real bonfires allowed, and children will have to watch virtual bonfires on their latest electronic gadgets."

Ben paused and looked out the window, over the Keswick rooftops, and watched the weak November light start to fade behind Grizedale Pike. Large flocks of jackdaws made surging waves in the sky, like wind on water. It was late afternoon, yet there was nothing visually to tell you that today was November the fifth. No early bonfires or bangs instigated by excited kids just home from school. All would be patiently waiting for the organised one which would start at precisely the advertised time. It was this contrast which had given him his subject for the article.

Sue had phoned him yesterday, pointed out that news was thin, and asked him to come up with a one-thousand-word filler piece on any subject he cared to write about. Invariably, he took the opportunity to ridicule the banality and fatuity of the modern world compared to the relative sanity of his youth.

An hour later he had finished the piece and emailed it to *The Tribune*. Sue would probably look at it the following morning, and edit out some of his more scathing comments.

After closing down the computer, Ben entered the kitchen and found Helen unwrapping bags of fish and chips she had picked up on her return from work. She commented on this particular consolation of living in town. They were both regularly pointing out the positive things to take from their move, a sure sign that they were desperately missing their home.

Dinner passed quietly, the quiet thrum of the traffic outside, the distant thud of doors in the hotel being closed too forcibly, being occasionally interrupted by their muted conversation speculating about events at the cottage. How the birds were coping without their regular feeding? Would the gutter and down-pipe in the corner near the bathroom window be blocked again with leaves? They agreed the only certainty was that the hall would be freshly carpeted with junk-mail. This brought a further agreement to visit the cottage together within the next few days to check on things. Neither should go alone.

After dinner, Ben returned to his computer. He was keen to get on with his investigation. Bill had been as good as his word and had brought him the shortlist of files that the police were working on; cases which, due to the appearance of Hamish Stott in the area about eighteen months ago, they now regarded as "unexplained deaths".

Peter had passed the information to Bill with the proviso that should it be discovered that Ben had been given access, then Bill would have to admit to "obtaining" the information while visiting the office, leaving Peter uninvolved. Peter, of course, still expected Ben to pass over any information he discovered and to claim the credit should Ben solve the case. "He's looking after number one again," Bill had said. "He's sure to go far."

Having booted up his computer, Ben went straight into the "victim" database he had just finished compiling, which now included the names supplied by Peter via Bill. His eyes scanned down looking for any obvious commonalities:

Innes, Giles – Windermere – Male – 67 – English – Married – Retired – etc.

Tulip, Daniel – Bowness – Male – 45 – English – Divorced – Chef

Grant, Colin – Suffolk – Male – 64 – English – Married – P. Office

Nelson, Ian – Derbyshire – Male – 35 – Welsh – Single – R. Climber

Ivison, Donald – Queensland – Male – 70 – Australian – Divorced – Farmer

Ambler, Charlotte – Manchester – Female – 40 – English – Single – Business

Harris, Wayne – Carlisle – Male – 19 – English – Single – Unemployed

Wilkinson, Alan – Gretna – Male – 18 – Scottish – Single – Unemployed

Robinson, Cynthia – Hastings – Female – 27 - English – Single – Volunteer

West, Phillip – Inverness – Male – 39 – Scottish – Divorced – Photographer

Lamb, Elizabeth – Lorton – Female – 42 – English – Married – Housewife

Foxley, Ben – Scarness – Male – 58 – English – Married – F.L. Journalist

NOTES: C. Ambler included though not dead; was a target.

E. Lamb included by police though no body found – on suspicion.

B. Foxley included as possible future target – on suspicion.

Ben also updated his CLUES list with:

3. Small man in wetsuit seen A66 (truck driver) – C. Ambler case

4. Land Rover seen in A66 lay-by (truck driver) – C. Ambler & D. Ivison cases.

5. B.F. & H. Foxley find note at cottage "HS LIVES ON" – suspect H. Stott.

6. Swimmer seen in Windermere – not traced – G. Innes case.

7. H. Foxley sees H Stott in cottage garden – now known to be son of serial killer Hector Snodd.

8. Braithwaite road wide – car contact avoidable – D Ivison case.

9. B. Foxley attacked at cottage. Man not H Stott. B.F. theory – Dominic Lund and/or associates. Police say attacker is associate of H. Stott.

10. D. Lund and 2 associates found dead in London? B.F. theory – police involved as in S. Lund death years ago. Ref nuclear case.

This first scan revealed no obvious connections. It was a mixture of different sexes, ages, locations, occupations, marital status. They had died in a variety of ways from drowning to falls from crags to car strike to car crash.

Something might be made in the future of the fact that no victims were found in the region of the western fells. All were found in an approximate corridor running from Bassenthwaite in the north to Windermere in the south, with offshoots into Borrowdale and Langdale.

Ben had been surprised to see the names of Wayne Harris and Alan Wilkinson on the police list. He had written a report for *The Tribune* when they had been found dead in their stolen car, which had obviously gone off the dirt road and smashed into trees in Thornbeck Forest. It had been a clear case of two joyriding tearaways losing control. He had visited the scene of the crash and been shocked at the damage to the car. He was told that the youths had been badly mutilated by the car's metal and glass.

He had queried their inclusion when Bill handed over the list, and Bill recalled that there had been questions asked by CID about deep marks on the track some 50 metres before the crash scene. The marks occurred opposite a track lay-by where large stacks of cut timber were stored ready for loading onto lorries. Though the obvious conclusion would be that the marks were caused by loading activities, the police could not rule out the possibility that one or more logs had been on the track at the time of the accident. Whether they had been placed there deliberately was the big unknown.

Ben, who prided himself on his observation skills, had not noticed these marks when at the scene, and had given credit to the police. "They're not all plodders like me you know," Bill had joked, and paused, clearly waiting for Ben to contradict him.

"Obviously," Ben had grinned.

"Bastard," Bill had grinned back.

There were, of course, lots of blank spaces in the database, representing Ben's lack of information. A space he was particularly keen to fill was "MEMBER OF". It had been this information that had cracked the Snodd case when Ben had discovered that all the victims had been members of environmental organisations or charities.

Ben continued to visually analyse the information that he did have, but after an hour with no outcome decided to call it a night. He shut down the computer, sighed, took off his glasses and rubbed his eyes. He would have to start gathering information to fill in those spaces. It was going to be a long, painstaking process. He looked out of the window. All he could see were the lights of the town. Beyond them the fells lay asleep in absolute darkness. Ben decided to follow suit.

They were having their 10 o'clock coffee, Helen almost ready to leave, when the phone rang. Helen answered it. "Hello... yes, good morning... yes, send him up... thank you."

She turned to Ben. "That was Reception. Bill is on his way up."

"Early bird," Ben observed, as he stood up and checked in a mirror that he was tidily dressed. He sometimes worked in his dressing gown and remained unshaven until late morning. This was not one of those days.

Ben had the door open, and Helen a cup of coffee ready, before Bill appeared in the doorway, breathing heavily. "You're safe up here alright," he gasped. "Bloody villain would have a heart attack before he reached you."

"It's only two flights, Bill," Ben scoffed, as he ushered him in and indicated that he should sit at the kitchen table.

"Aye, but they're steep 'uns," Bill countered, as he sat down. Helen put a cup of coffee in front of him, and she and Ben joined him at the table.

Bill pulled a folded sheet of A4 from his inside pocket and unfolded it. "I've got another one for your database," he said seriously, as he glanced at the paper.

"Another one?"

"Yesterday... Catbells. Man's body found at the bottom of a crag just below Walpole's seat." He glanced again at the paper. "Peter gave us this, this morning. I was in the station early. Looks like he was an artist... on holiday... staying at The Bridge Hotel in Buttermere...."

"That's where I'm going this afternoon," Helen interjected involuntarily.

Ignoring the interruption, Bill pushed the paper over to Ben who studied it. "John Appleton... from Dorset... 76," he read out in a reverential whisper. "Multiple injuries including broken back... found by passing couple of walkers... body recovered by Keswick MR team." He glanced up at Bill with questions in his eyes.

"No, no witnesses, nothing. And a very unlikely place for an accident," Bill responded. "You know that path... it's absolutely flat and wide enough for a bus. Most likely a jump or a push, but you don't usually take your artist's gear with you if you're intending suicide, so a push is favourite."

"Could have been natural causes," Ben pointed out. "Heart attack or something – has the post-mortem been done yet?"

"I don't think so, but I'll try to find out."

"So Peter reckons this will be going on the list, does he?"

"Absolutely."

"Then on the database it will go until I hear different. God! Didn't that sound awful… so impersonal, unfeeling…"

"It happens, Ben. Don't knock yourself. The more death you see and hear about, the less if affects you. It has to or we'd all go mad."

Helen stood up. "I'll have to go." She moved across to the lounge area where her coat and briefcase lay on an armchair.

"When will you be back?" Ben shouted.

"I'm at Penrith and Appleby this morning," she said, as she picked up her things and moved to the door. And I have a three o'clock appointment at Buttermere, so it might be six when I get back."

"It's dark at six," Ben said.

"Don't worry, I'll get away as soon as I can. You know I don't like driving in the dark, particularly on those narrow roads."

"Watch out for the sheep and the cows and the—" Ben started.

"Bye dear." Helen blew him a kiss. "Nice to see you Bill." And she was gone.

Chapter 32

Helen's mood lifted as she drove out of Keswick on the A66 heading for Penrith and Appleby. Sombre thoughts about the conversation around the kitchen table gradually dissipated as Blencathra came into view and brought back memories of great days climbing its slopes. The majesty of the mountains always put things back in perspective, making problems seem as small as humans are to them.

She was about to start one of what she called her "bread and butter" mornings; mornings in which her part-time role as an External Verifier for the Royal Life Saving Society meant that she would be carrying out routine duties that would not tax her too much. The work of inspecting swimming pools was similar to that of a hotel inspector, checking that normal operating procedures, emergency action plans, staffing levels and qualifications etc, were all up to date. Her afternoon at Buttermere would be completely different. Here she would be answering leading questions put by management in an effort to win the job of consultant on a new swimming pool project which The Bridge Hotel was planning to build.

As expected, her morning's work went fairly routinely, though one of the pools would require a further visit to ensure that lax staff training procedures had improved, and after a late lunch in an Appleby coffee shop she set off to keep her three o'clock appointment at Buttermere.

During the one and a quarter hour journey Helen found her mind wandering across a broad spectrum of subjects, though she was careful to avoid thinking about the predicament she and Ben found themselves in as they tried to make the best of their exile from their beloved cottage.

As she approached Blencathra once more she started to think how lucky she was to have a job in the leisure industry, a job that enabled her to drive on such a beautiful journey, with the best yet to come. At times like this she found herself struggling to disagree with Ben who scoffed at the artificial creation of the leisure industry, a term he derided as an oxymoron. There was no doubt that since the decline of traditional manufacturing, a mixture of human ingenuity and stupidity had created a number of new so-called "industries". Fashion, entertainment, cosmetics, leisure had replaced steel, shipbuilding, transport, engineering. In Ben's opinion these were not industries but frivolities, cleverly designed to part people from their hard-earned money. He found it incomprehensible that people could now make a living as a "nail consultant".

Helen could not deny that swimming, which in her childhood had amounted to the simple pleasure of donning a costume, jumping into water and having fun, had now become a huge bureaucratic business with hundreds of regulations and dozens of companies offering thousands of products for purchase, including such essentials as underwater MP3 players with headphones and anti-fog drops for your goggles. Nor could she deny that this artificially created complexity had provided her with a good living and so she went along with it.

Rounding the "magic corner" once more as she cruised into the Vale of Keswick, Helen's thoughts were, as usual, swept aside by the irresistible attraction of the scenery. Even on a dull day it was transcendent. Bypassing Keswick, she drove towards Braithwaite before turning off into the village of Portinscale. Time was getting short so she had decided to take the more direct route to Buttermere over Newlands Pass, a narrow, winding, mountain road that, hopefully, would be quiet on this cloudy November afternoon.

Like all Lake District passes, the road demanded full concentration as it climbed steeply, clung precariously to fell-sides and played host to meandering sheep and the occasional fellow driver. Reaching the highest point, the 'Hause', Helen found herself literally in the clouds, but it wasn't long before she was able to switch off her lights and start the long descent into Buttermere.

Although she had driven on this road and visited Buttermere many times, Helen could not help being enthralled yet again by the scene that unfolded below her. This, she understood, was the essential magic of the Lake District; its incredible difference from the rest of England's landscape; a place so astonishingly beautiful that no matter how many times you see it, and you live within it, you remain in constant awe of it.

The old village of Buttermere sits in a valley on a narrow strip of farmland, completely surrounded by steep, high, rugged fells. There is something almost Tibetan about the scene. Rough stone walls separate small fields and career up and across the fells with impossible verticality. Stone farms, stone barns, stone houses, stone church, stone hotels huddle together in this lonely outpost. Around the dark eye of the lake trees lend a softening quality to the picture. But raise the eyes and an alpine ruggedness takes over and there is a sense that this is not a place for the faint-hearted or the city softie. It is here in this majestic arena that the inimitable Alfred Wainwright chose to spend eternity, his ashes strewn on a fell called Haystacks situated at the eastern head of the valley.

It was five minutes to three when Helen pulled into the hotel car park. A slight drizzle had started to fall. Helen grabbed her briefcase and hurried towards the hotel, an angular three-storey building that had once been a mill, crushing the corn, barley and oats once farmed in the valley. Its old, rugged exterior gave way to a warm, welcoming interior as Helen made her way to Reception.

Not for the first time her meeting was delayed. Today's reason was that the owners, who lived in Brighton, had been delayed by traffic problems. This was conveyed to her by an attentive manager who provided her with coffee and biscuits while she waited in the lounge.

The owners turned up at five minutes to four, the meeting went well, and Helen came away feeling good about her prospects of winning the contract. The downside was that it was now approaching five thirty, it was dark and the drizzle had turned to steady rain. Helen was a confident driver in towns and on motorways but hesitant on narrow roads, particularly in the dark. She didn't fancy returning to

Keswick over Newlands Pass in the dark, with the possibility that the clouds had lowered even further. She decided to take the longer but easier driving route along the valley to Lorton Village then over Whinlatter Pass to Braithwaite and on to Keswick.

Before setting off, Helen phoned Ben to let him know she would be late. He, of course, ended their brief conversation by reminding her to "mind the cows and the sheep and the druggies and the..." The signal had gone, as it often did in Lakeland valleys.

She switched on her lights and wipers and started to pull out of the car park. As she did, she noticed another car's lights come on and the car move into line behind her. She had not seen anybody enter the car park while she phoned Ben so she assumed that whoever it was must have already been sitting in their car. Normally, she would have taken no notice; the driver could have being doing any number of things before setting off – reading, writing, phoning – but times were not normal, people were being killed, Ben had been attacked, she had seen Hamish Stott in their garden. It was no wonder, therefore, that, as they left the car park in convoy, her heart was beating faster than normal, her hands gripped the wheel more tightly, and her senses were on full alert.

The first mile involved sharp twists and turns through the woods that marked the border between Buttermere and Crummock Water. As she swung round the bends her headlights picked out the tree trunks, looking like the gnarled legs of giants; now to her left came a long cast-iron fence, symbol of an old estate. Then she was in a clear run along the banks of Crummock Water, one of her favourite swimming lakes, but now a cold, dark place of death should she move her wheels one metre to the left. She switched the wipers on to the fast setting and leaned forward, peering through the smeared window, concentrating on the road, not daring to look at the dark void to her left.

The car following stayed well back; about 50 metres away. Either he didn't want to risk having his number plate seen or he was a local and knew that it was sensible to stay back on a narrow road that contained passing places, the passing places often only being capable of accommodating one car.

After a section of dead-slow hair-pin bends around a rock outcrop, Helen put her foot down as the road width improved on the last section along the length of Crummock Water. She could sense Grassmoor Fell towering above her right shoulder. Then it was back to a narrow, winding section through trees until she came to a junction which took her onto the main Lorton Valley road. She turned right and headed for Lorton Village. In her rear mirror she saw the other car also turn right, rather than left to Loweswater.

The following car was still about 50 metres back when she reached Lorton and turned right to join the road which ran over Whinlatter Pass. At this point there were a number of choices of destination, the main one being straight on to Cockermouth and surrounding villages. Again, the car behind followed her.

Helen was becoming increasingly worried. The four-mile road ahead was full of climbs and bends, but it was a wider road, a road where the following car could safely draw alongside or pass and force her to stop, or worse still, force her off the road. And at 6 o'clock on a wet November night there was a good chance that no other vehicles would be using it – no witnesses, no help.

Her worries increased as she started the climb out of Lorton Valley. The car behind made no attempt to pull up closer or to pass her, even though the road was wide. She deliberately slowed down to allow it to pass, but it remained 50 metres back. She was in no doubt now that she was being pursued rather than followed.

As she approached the highest point of the pass so the western extremities of Thornbeck Forest wrapped its cloak of trees around the road, adding to the darkness, and her sense of foreboding. On a rare straight stretch it was like driving down the aisle of a large unlit cathedral.

When her headlights picked out a sign announcing "Thornbeck Visitor Centre", Helen had a spur-of-the-moment idea. She decided to test him again; to make sure once and for all that he was following her. She speeded up to put more distance between them, then on reaching the visitor centre she turned into the centre's large car park, which was separated from the road by a thin strip of trees. It was completely empty and unlit. If he followed her into there, she would be certain.

Only as she swung her car around to face the entrance did she realise what a stupid thing she had done. Fear must have scrambled her brain. She had given him the perfect opportunity to attack her in a place that was hidden from the road. She gripped the steering wheel tightly, her body tensing, as she waited to see if the lights of his car came flooding into the car park. Then she realised she had left her own lights on, announcing her whereabouts. *What an idiot!* Her left hand crashed into the steering wheel in her haste to switch them off. At that precise moment she saw his car lights pass by on the other side of the strip of trees; he had not turned into the car park.

Her relief was momentary. What if he had spotted her lights as he had passed the car park entrance, but hadn't had time to turn in? Maybe he was turning his car around now and would reappear at any moment. She put her sidelights on and drove into the farthest, darkest corner of the car park, underneath overhanging trees. She stopped and put out her lights. If he did come back he would not find her in the same place. She might have a chance to dash out past him. In total darkness and utter silence, she held her breath... and kept on holding it... and kept on holding it... and the lights did not come. She let out a loud, head back, mouth open, eyes closed expulsion of relief and waited for her heart to stop racing.

Her hands were trembling slightly when, a few minutes later, she turned the ignition key, switched on her lights and wipers, and drove out onto the main road again. She had imagined the whole thing. *Stupid woman. Weak woman. Don't tell Ben, he thinks you're an Amazon warrior after that display in the garden. He'd want you to stop working late, and he's got enough on his plate. So come on, pull yourself together and get a grip.*

Motivation session over, Helen started to relax as the road wound its way down the eastern side of the pass towards the village of Braithwaite. She pressed the button to turn on the radio, which was almost always tuned to a classical music station. Some light Mozart would go down well. She got Elgar which was even better.

As she let his exquisite cello concerto sweep away her tension, she started to wonder what kind of person drove a car in such an unusual manner, staying so far behind, not overtaking when invited. Suddenly she had it. It was herself thirty years ago. It was not a man but a young woman, probably a staff member at the hotel, her first job. The car was an old one bought by her parents to get her to work and back. She had just passed her driving test. She was nervous, maybe even sat in the hotel car park until somebody else drove out, then used them as a guide and a source of comfort on what were undoubtedly dangerous roads. Now Helen started to feel slightly guilty. The girl had lost her guide. She was on her own. At least there wasn't far to go and there were street lights in Braithwaite and between Braithwaite and Keswick.

She rounded yet another bend, came to a straight tree-less section and knew she was passing a long lay-by on her left where an ice-cream van parked all through the summer to serve the multitude of tourists who pulled in to take advantage of the great views over Bassenthwaite Lake. Without trees in the vicinity the darkness was not so intense here and as she drove alongside the lay-by she noticed a car parked in it. It appeared to be empty. Perhaps it had been abandoned, or maybe a fell walker was late getting down off the fells. Looking in her rear-view mirror as she swept on down the slope, she saw the parked car's lights come on, and it pulled out onto the road behind her. *MY GOD!*

From this point the road plunged steeply down a mile long section of bends, ending in the village of Braithwaite. Helen put her foot down and, braking at the last moment, screeched around the bends. For a minute she thought she had lost him, but then she watched in horror as his lights drew closer and settled down about 50 metres behind. She felt like the proverbial rabbit.

Who is he? What is he trying to achieve? Did he have a pre-planned place where he would make his move? Or was he following her so that she would lead him to Ben? That was more likely; Ben was clearly a target.

On reaching Braithwaite, Helen took a crumb of comfort from the fact that there were street lights and people; surely he would not try anything in these circumstances. She was tempted to take refuge in the village pub, phone Ben and wait for him to come and get her. But she daren't risk bringing Ben out into the open. That could be playing into the pursuer's hands; that might be his plan. Ben would be safer where he was, in the hotel apartment. Even if she led the pursuer to him, Ben would have a better chance of defending himself in the apartment than out in the dark night.

The car followed her through the narrow streets of the village until she emerged onto the A66 and turned right towards Keswick – just over a mile to go. He had kept further back in the well-lit areas so she had not managed to read his number-plate.

Turning off the A66 into Keswick, Helen watched him follow in her mirror. She had thought about driving on, trying to lose him somewhere out on the dark roads so that she did not lead him to Ben, but gradually realised the futility of that. She could run out of petrol, strand herself, put herself in danger. And, most importantly, the man in the car had managed to follow her today; he would be able to follow her on other days and she would forever be looking in her mirror. Best to bring things to a head; to get things over with. Get the police involved and turn the tables – perhaps set a trap for the man.

Helen abandoned these constructive thoughts as she approached the busy town centre and negotiated a right turn on a traffic roundabout that took her behind the market square. Here she turned into the large public car park that served the town centre and was immediately behind the Dog and Gun Hotel. Separate from the public spaces were a few private spaces allocated to the hotel and it was here that she parked.

By this time she had given up keeping an eye on her pursuer, his car becoming engulfed in the melee of town centre traffic, and she did not know whether he had followed her into the car park. She concentrated on grabbing her briefcase and getting out of her car as fast as she could. She ran towards the narrow alley that cut through the buildings and led to the market place and the entrance to the hotel. Approaching the alley, she looked behind her. There was no pursuer. Breathing heavily, she slowed down and started to walk. She entered the semi-dark alley, which relied on light filtering through from the market place on one side and the car park on the other side. Suddenly, a door in the right-hand wall of the alley opened and a man stepped in front of her. All she could see was a figure outlined by the lights in the market place. Helen half-screamed, half snarled as she swung her briefcase at the man's head. The man turned as he stepped back and the blow caught him between his shoulder blades. "Bloody hell", he roared with pain, as he retreated further into the alley. Helen recognised the voice.

Chapter 33

Ben lay face down on the bed, stripped to the waist. Helen laid a tea-towel across his bruised back, and placed two bags of frozen peas on the towel. "How's that?" she enquired.

"Did you ever think of joining the SS?" Ben moaned.

"You mean the SAS?"

"No, the SS. They had a lot of violent, cruel women in their ranks. You would have gone far, probably made Obergruppenführer."

"It's your own fault," Helen insisted. "You shouldn't leap out at people in dark alleys."

"Leap? When have you seen me leap, lately? I struggle to get out of bed some mornings."

"What's an obergroopen…thingy anyway?"

"A general."

"Mmm, yes, I like the sound of that. I quite fancy wearing a monocle and going around whipping lower ranks and prisoners with my riding crop."

"And your briefcase."

"That, too." Helen stepped away from the bed. "Do you want a cup of tea, or something stronger?"

"Tea, please and easy on the strychnine."

Helen made her way to the lounge. Here she double-checked that the main apartment door was locked before heading to the kitchen. She was still feeling a bit shaky and vulnerable after her ordeal in the car even though it had ended well; although Ben might think otherwise. He explained that he had kept a lookout for her car through the back bedroom window which overlooked the public car park. On seeing her arrive, he had come down to meet her in case she had shopping to carry up – she often did. He had taken the short cut through the back of the hotel into the backyard which gave access to the alley through that door. Helen knew about the door, having used it when transferring their essentials from the cottage, but she didn't like going through the dark backyard full of bins and hotel detritus, and it was usually locked from the inside.

Her swipe with the briefcase had reignited the pain in Ben's existing bruises which had been getting better by the day. After listening to her numerous apologies and to her detailed retelling of her nightmare journey, Ben had said he was proud of the way she had coped and defended herself but pleaded with her to phone him if ever she got into a similar situation again.

After quizzing her about the details of the pursuing car and learning that it was "definitely not the shape of a Land Rover, just an ordinary, fairly big car", and telling Helen that they should report it to Peter in the morning, Ben had succumbed to her treatment of his bruises and tried to make light of it as always.

When Helen returned with the tea, Ben eased himself into a sitting position, his back resting against the headboard. "Well, mein Obergruppenführer," he said, "now that you have me naked in your bed, do you have any other fiendish tortures you wish to inflict?"

Helen walked to the window, and with the exaggerated, quick movements of the military whipped the curtains together. She swivelled quickly on her heels, clicked them together, and looked at him with a sneer on her face. "Vee hef vays of making you scream," she hissed, as she approached the bed.

Chapter 34

Sergeant Peter Murphy was his usual non-committal self when Helen and Ben called at the station next morning to relay Helen's experience on the road. He appeared to be sympathetic as he listened and made lots of notes, but when the story was over he told them that, though they were right to report it, nothing could be done because no offence had taken place. A report would be written up and all station staff would be informed, but no specific action could be taken.

It was more or less what Ben had expected, but Helen was not happy. Somehow, Peter had managed to turn her frightening experience into a routine matter that could be filed and forgotten about; it felt as though the matter had been dismissed too easily, that she herself had been dismissed as a neurotic woman.

As they walked back to the apartment through Keswick's busy marketplace, all the while discussing Peter's attitude, Ben noticed that Helen was constantly turning her head to see who was in their vicinity, to see if they were being followed. Ben put his arm around her shoulders, a protective urge sweeping through him. He vowed to himself to work harder. He needed to get this thing solved as soon as possible.

Back at his computer, Ben turned his attention to his database once more. It now contained the name recently given by Bill - artist John Appleton from Dorset. The addition of this new name had done nothing to change the whole picture – commonality still did not appear to be present in any shape or form.

Ben had been working hard recently and had succeeded in filling some, but not all, of the blanks on his database. He had used newspaper and library archives, tried Google a few times but mostly used the good old telephone to track down family and friends of the deceased. Some had been more forthcoming than others, the others being mainly the relatives of the more recently deceased who were still too upset to answer all his questions. Nevertheless, he now had far fewer blanks on his database and he hoped that there was now enough information for him to delve into and find that elusive interconnection which almost always existed between victims of a repeat killer.

Unlike the Snodd case, he had been disappointed to find no overall commonality under the MEMBER OF heading. The nearest he had come to finding any obvious commonality was under the HOBBIES heading where, surprise surprise, seven of the ten deceased listed "Fell Walking".

With the search for obvious commonality now abandoned, Ben had recently embarked on a detailed analysis of all aspects of the names on the list – just the names, not their histories. He was treating them simply as letters or objects in a word game, looking for anything unusual, any pairings, matchings, coincidences, anagrams, reversals, etc.

One of his methods was to pick out a victim's name at random and start from there – e.g. C. Robinson. Robinson was the unlikely name of a Lake District mountain. Were there any other victims with names of mountains? He knew there was a Mount Grant in America. Nelson had a column named after him – did he also have a mountain somewhere? Yes, there was a Mount Nelson in Canada. Google also showed him Mount Ambler in the USA, Mount Wilkinson in USA, Mount Innes in Antarctica, and Mount Appleton in USA By this time Ben had been getting excited, but no other matches were found and he moved on.

He considered the possibility of the name's combined initials being an anagram for some other meaningful words. He listed both Christian and surname initials and analysed them separately and collectively. With so few vowels in each list, the best he could come up with was "badged or cadged" in the Christian name list and "Thawing or Waiting" in the surname list – forget it and move on.

And so he spent hour after hour, randomly stirring, mixing and matching, adding and subtracting, delving and seeking. His desk-side waste bin started to fill up with crumpled scraps of paper and coffee breaks became more frequent. Most people would have given up by now, but Ben had the advantage of knowing that persistent effort usually brought its rewards. He had learned this lesson the hard way when he had been over-burdened with work in his previous life in industrial management. Somehow, with supreme effort and application he had managed to keep all the balls in the air and come out with successful conclusions. His brain had been hard-wired by that experience and now it still functioned like a mini-computer, able to absorb and analyse a lot of data without faltering.

Until he had exhausted all possible permutations which might result in the discovery of a link between the victims, Ben would plough on with his search. He would squeeze the database until every last drop of information had dripped out and been analysed, and it could be discarded like a dry rag.

There remained, of course, the possibility that there were no links between the victims, that they had been selected randomly, that the killer was just going for numbers, building a portfolio of death to make himself famous, or if it was Hamish Stott – to match his father. Ben recalled that Hector Snodd was known to have killed 15 people. If that was the number Stott was aiming to match, he wasn't finished yet.

Chapter 35

It was to be a day of relaxation. Ben needed a break after two intense days of concentration, without anything to show for it. He had gone to the library and then he was going to the golf club where he planned to have lunch. In the afternoon he was going to walk a round with Bill and Peter. His bruised back wouldn't allow him to swing a club yet, but the exercise would do him good and he could update on any information Peter might have about the police investigations.

Helen usually recharged her batteries by going for a long walk or spending a couple of hours in a local hotel swimming pool, where during a hundred-length swimming session her mind would empty and she would turn into an automaton. A sauna usually completed her relaxation. But not today. She had to do her Christmas baking today; she had already left it late. She usually had it finished by late October, giving the cake and puddings time to mature before Christmas.

She had already amassed the ingredients in previous weeks and now they waited for her magic touch in various containers around the kitchen, including some of the fruit for the cake which she had soaked in brandy overnight. It was not a chore to Helen. She had always enjoyed cooking and baking, using her hands as well as her head, creating pleasure for others as well as herself.

She started the session by making a batch of mincemeat – mixing currants, raisins, sugar, suet, chopped apples, candied peel and spices in a large bowl. She spooned this into old jam jars she had sterilised, then capped the jars with wax papers and sealed the tops with elastic bands. This mincemeat would be put aside until needed on Christmas Eve, when it would be turned into fresh mince pies.

Next she mixed up all the ingredients for the Christmas pudding using a recipe on a handwritten piece of paper handed down by her grandmother. Helen had to refer to this worn, stained piece of paper frequently to get the quantities right and to remember to use breadcrumbs rather than flour, and to finish off with a good splash of rum. One day she would have to transfer the recipe to her computer, but until it actually fell to pieces she wanted to keep using it; it brought back happy memories of her childhood.

The mix complete, she transferred it to the large pudding bowl and covered that with greaseproof paper and a damp cloth. She would leave this mix to mature overnight then steam it for eight hours tomorrow. She had appointments tomorrow so Ben would have to "babysit" it - topping up the water as it evaporated.

Lunch followed, after which she found herself dozing off for half an hour, a luxury she didn't usually allow herself. *Must be getting old.*

Time to make the cake mix. She assembled all the ingredients, but when she looked for the recipe book she always used, one whose spine cover had disintegrated due to regular use, she couldn't find it. She must have forgotten to bring it with her from the cottage. *I am getting old.* She had also forgotten the silicone mould shaped like a Christmas tree which produced a cake for decoration of the table, only to be consumed after the main cake was gone.

Helen slumped into a chair and sighed. They had agreed not to go to the cottage alone. But Ben wouldn't be back for hours. She was on a roll and she wanted to get the baking finished; she had a busy week ahead. The thought of putting all the stuff away and starting again in a few days' time was unbearable. It was only fifteen minutes' drive to the cottage. She would be back long before Ben returned from the golf club. The decision was made, but she would play it safe. She went into the lounge, grabbed a piece of paper off the telephone table and wrote *"Gone to cottage for recipe book. At 2 o'clock. Back before you can read this. Love S.S. Obermydeadbody"* She put the note on the kitchen table, hurriedly discarded her apron, and retrieved the cottage back door key from a kitchen drawer. Then she donned a coat and scarf in the bedroom, and made her way out of the apartment.

An assortment of emotions ran through Helen as she drove the familiar road to the cottage. Guilt, at going without Ben. Happy, to be going home, however short the stay. Sad that she had to go back to the apartment. The damp, grey November weather didn't enhance her mood as she turned off the A591 onto the narrow lane which led to Scarness.

Pulling up outside the cottage she was struck by how cold and unwelcoming it looked, as if it had been abandoned and was sulking. Getting out of the car, she felt as though she was a stranger to the place, that the cottage and all of its surroundings were as foreign and remote as a highland bothy. It was the silence, she finally decided. After the hustle and noise of Keswick this place was as quiet as a church.

All surfaces, including the lawn, were covered with wet, rust-coloured leaves. Groups of them had collected in heaps, like sweepings up of scrap metal. The bare, twiggy branches of the huge surrounding trees drooped down like the arms of dejected people. There were no birds to be seen or heard, no squirrels, no distant sound of a tractor or the moan of a cow. Somewhere, a timid drip of water had the temerity to ripple the saturating silence.

Helen shivered as she took the key from her pocket and opened the back door. She took the key out, stepped inside, closed the door, placed the key in the lock and turned it. There was a slightly musty smell in the air, like the distemper smell found in old, damp houses. The cottage was old, so even though they had programmed the central heating to come on occasionally, it had clearly not been enough to stop the old wall coating from reannouncing its presence after many years.

Helen stepped into the kitchen, and switched on a light, the grey November afternoon not providing enough through the small kitchen window. A bearded man was sitting at the kitchen table. Helen stared at him for two disbelieving seconds. *Ben will kill me.* Then she screamed.

Chapter 36

Ben arrived back at the apartment just before five o'clock. He was in good spirits having enjoyed the walk around the golf course in spite of the gloomy weather. Most importantly, he had some news that he was keen to pass on to Helen. He couldn't wait to see her reaction. He anticipated that it would be a mixture of anger and relief.

There was, therefore, a feeling of anti-climax as well as anger when he found her note on the kitchen table. She had done it again – taken a risk – broken an agreement. She was too headstrong for her own good. When would she learn? He thought her recent fright in the car would have taught her a lesson but apparently not. Part of him admired her spirit and bravery; she wasn't the little eye-fluttering woman who relied on her man when things got tough. But part of him was seething with anger. It wasn't just her life she was risking. It was also his. Without her he might as well be dead.

Still wearing his outdoor clothes, he went into the lounge and checked the answer machine – no messages. He punched the cottage phone number, realising as soon as the engaged tone sounded that they had transferred the calls and he was, therefore, phoning himself. He punched her mobile number. A trilling sound came from the kitchen area. He walked to the kitchen and found her mobile on a worktop. She rarely went anywhere without it. Either she had simply forgotten it, or she didn't think it was worth taking for what should have been an absence of only half an hour.

She had now been absent for three hours. He tried to stay calm, not jump to conclusions. She had a habit of turning up with that smile on her face, and all would be forgotten and forgiven. He was dying to take a bath, having sweated his way around the golf course in layers of weather protection, and he could murder a pot of tea. Should he do both these things, wait for her, and be nice and relaxed as he listened to her explanation on her return. Or should he dash out to the cottage now. If he did and he found her baking or cleaning or doing some other innocent activity he would throttle her with his bare hands. But. There was always that but. If she was in danger...

He raced down the hotel stairs and left by the back entrance. Soon he was driving too fast on the A591 and being flashed because he only had sidelights on. He thought by now that his mind would also be racing, but it wasn't. For some inexplicable reason it had become fixated on the way Helen had signed the note – *SS Obermydeadbody*. It was meant as a joke, of course, and she hadn't intended that he should see it. But now that he had seen it, a picture had become fixed in his mind. It was of him kneeling down over her dead body.

Darkness was spreading its inky tentacles as he completed the drive down the lane and pulled up some 50 metres short of the cottage. He was taking no chances; he didn't want to announce his arrival by driving onto the gravel. He got out of the car, lifted the boot, and armed himself with his sand wedge; his golf clubs being permanently resident in the boot since the move to the apartment. There was just enough light to see his way ahead.

As he reached the cottage, he saw Helen's parked car and lights shining out of the kitchen and lounge windows. All seemed to be well. He approached the back door, tried to open it, and found it locked. *Sensible.* He knocked on the door.

It was taking a long time to be answered, and he was about to move to look through the kitchen window, when the door opened.

Helen smiled, looked at the golf club in his hand, and the smile vanished. "I knew you'd come," she said, hesitantly, as she stepped aside to let Ben in.

Once inside, Ben turned on her and demanded, "What's going on? Why have you stayed here? Why didn't you phone? We agreed we wouldn't come here on our own didn't we?" His voice rose with each question.

Helen moved towards him and took hold of his left hand. She was wearing her serious face. "I want you to promise to stay calm and not get angry."

"You haven't scraped the car again have you?"

Helen let out a weak laugh, "No…" She hesitated, then, "We have a visitor in the lounge… you might not be pleased to see him. I want you to promise not to use that thing in your hand."

Ben didn't wait for her to finish. *She was too trusting, sometimes naïve; qualities that people took advantage of.* He pulled his left hand from hers and tightening his grip on his golf club, marched into the lounge. Helen hurried after him.

A small, thin man in a crumpled grey suit stood by the fireplace. His long brown hair was tied in a ponytail and his pale face was obscured by a dense beard and moustache, making it difficult to guess his age. He exuded an air of reticence. He could be a tramp recently kitted out at a charity shop, a professor of quantum physics or a poet, Ben thought. He was probably some kind of itinerant who Helen had felt sorry for and taken in to feed. The main thing was that he looked non-threatening. But Ben remained alert. Before he had a chance to speak, Helen said, "Allow me to introduce Mr Hamish Stott."

Chapter 37

Ben found himself taking a step backwards and lowering himself into his favourite fireside chair, giving himself time to recover, time to think. Hamish Stott was in their cottage, standing right in front of him. Ben stared at him, unable to find any words. Caution told him to hang on to his golf club.

Hamish Stott remained standing, head down looking at the floor, like a boy waiting outside the head-master's office awaiting his punishment.

Helen broke the silence. "Why don't you sit down Hamish, and I'll bring us all a cup of tea."

Ben's head swivelled. "Hamish?"

"He doesn't like being called Mr Stott. Do you want some tea? Only powdered milk, I'm afraid?" Helen had already turned towards the kitchen door, anticipating his reply.

Ben still looked shell-shocked. "Why didn't you phone me?"

Helen turned in the doorway. "And tell you Hamish Stott was here, in our cottage? You would have brought the police with you, and I didn't want you to. You'll see why after you have spoken to Hamish."

Ben shook his head in disbelief. "God! I hope you're right."

Helen smiled. "I'll get the tea."

His tongue now loosened, Ben turned his attention to the man sitting only a few feet away. How could this small, timid-looking man have been the centre of his universe for the past few months? How could he be one of the most wanted men in the country, his photograph in every police station, on every computer screen? He didn't look as though he could swat a fly; could he really be a killer? Of course he could, his father had been small and insignificant, yet he had left a trail of death. Ben would keep up his guard; he would not be lulled into a false sense of security; would not be charmed, though that looked unlikely.

"So…" Ben found himself saying, feeling as though he was back in his industrial management job, about to interview an unlikely candidate, "…what are you doing here, what do you want?" Hurriedly, he added, "And tell me why I shouldn't phone the police right now?"

Hamish Stott sat stiffly in his chair, almost to attention, apparently not knowing what to do with his hands. Eventually they came to rest on his knees which were close together, like a woman's. "I'm sorry to bother you," he started, then paused as if pondering which of Ben's three questions he needed to answer first.

Ben was surprised at the throaty depth of his voice and guessed he might have started smoking in his cot.

"I'm expectin' you to call the polis… but if you could hang on til tomorro'… give me time to get hame."

"Where's home?"

"Isle o' Barra… Outer Hebrides." 'Outer' sounded like 'ooter'.

"How long have you lived there?" Ben leaned forward. The answer to this simple question was vitally important.

Stott was slow to answer. "…Aw, months and months. Ever since we left here, left Windermere. Seems ages ago."

To make absolutely sure, Ben rephrased the question. "So you haven't been in the Lake District for the past six months?"

Stott shook his head. "Naw."

Ben did his best to hide his excitement at this news. Assuming Stott could prove what he said, many assumptions had been wrong, although there was still the slight possibility that Stott had hired somebody to do his dirty work. The fact that Stott was now sitting in front of him made even this possibility seem unlikely.

"You said "we"?" Ben enquired.

"Aye, me and Sami… she's my wife now… they can't send her back now."

"So how have you and Sami been coping on Barra?" Ben probed, needing to hear details that sounded authentic before giving Stott the benefit of the doubt. "I understand you are AWOL from the army. It's hard to find work without National Insurance numbers and the like?"

"We had nae bother. I'd been to Barra the first six months I went AWOL. I got work at a hotel there before I came down here to the Lakes. I went back there with Sami and they gave us both work… they've been great to us."

"Do the owners of the hotel know you are AWOL?"

"Oh, aye and we told them about Sami's work permit running out. It was them that suggested we get married so Sami needn't worry... they've been brilliant."

"Did they know they could get into trouble by knowingly harbouring somebody who is AWOL?"

"Aye, they knew, but they didn't care. They're religious folk, they don't believe in war and that. They think I did right leaving the army. But it was them that told me the only way I was going to get on in the future without looking over my shoulder was to give myself up, take my punishment, start afresh like."

"Do they know and do you know that the police suspect you of committing murders in the Lakes?"

"Aye I saw it on the telly, and they heard it on the radio. That's when they told me I should give myself up and get it all sorted. They said they would back me up... tell the police I couldnae have done them 'cos I was with them on the island. But I was scared at first. I don't have a good record with the police...in Edinburgh, ye ken, where I lived, and I hate the army and didnae want to go to prison."

"But you have decided to give yourself up now?"

"Aye I need to for Sami, she's feart for me... and what if we have bairns. An' I have to do it for Mr and Mrs Curry, the owners. They've sort of adopted Sami and me. They gave us a wee cottage to rent...and they've promised there'll be a job for me whenever I get back, even if I have to go to prison... an' they'll look after Sami while I'm away..." At this point Stott faltered, and Ben thought he was going to cry.

"They seem like good people," Ben said.

"Aye the best…" Stott faltered again, his voice wavering. "They've been like a mother and faither to Sami and me… we didnae have…" He stopped and blinked as a film formed over his eyes.

Ben hesitated for a moment, then ploughed on, "So why have you come here and not gone straight to the police or the army?"

"I wanted to say sorry… I thought I'd no' get the chance if I went straight to the polis."

"Sorry? For what?

"For puttin' that note in your letter box… an' for scarin' your wife in the garden. I only came that day to say sorry about the note, but your wife screamed so I thought I'd better scram."

"If only you knew how much trouble that note caused," Ben said, grimly. "Why did you do it?"

Stott fidgeted and scratched his head above his right ear. "Aw, it's hard to explain. I'm no' very strong, ye ken, inside like… an' I was tryin' to show myself that I could be tough."

"Bravado?"

"Aye, that's it. Sami and me was havin' trouble with a guy at the Greenstone in Windermere, an' I was tryin' to make myself tougher so I could handle him. I didn't want to let Sami down…"

"This guy was Tulip I take it?"

Stott seemed surprised that Ben knew about the chef. "Tulip… aye, that's him. He was giving us—"

"So you killed him?"

Stott almost jumped out of his seat in his anxiety to express himself. "Naw, naw," he shouted, waving his hands about. "I never killed him, I wanted tae, but I didnae…"

At this point Helen came into the lounge carrying three mugs of tea on a tray. She put the tray on the coffee table beside the sofa, handed two cups out, and kept one for herself as she sat down on the sofa.

Ben took the opportunity to lay his golf club on the floor and take off his outdoor jacket, which he also placed on the floor beside his chair. The room was warm; Helen had obviously put on the central heating some time ago. Settling down again, Ben took a long drink of tea, registering the horrible taste of the powdered milk but keeping it to himself. He looked across at Helen. "I take it you have heard most of this already?"

"Probably, but did I hear Tulip mentioned? We didn't talk about Tulip. Maybe I should leave you to it?"

"No, no, don't go," Ben insisted. "You can double-check Mr Stott's answers, see if he is consistent."

"Hamish's answers," Helen corrected.

Ben looked to the heavens, counted to five, then continued. "So why did you leave Windermere on the very day that Tulip was found in the lake?"

Stott's eyes dropped and he seemed to be gathering himself for a big effort. "I'd been following Tulip. I wanted to dae somethin' to him that would keep him off work for a few weeks… give me an' Sami a break. I hadnae a clue what to dae but I was hopin' for somethin' to come. Anyway, I seen him trip ower his dog's lead an' fall in the lake. I went and had a look in the water but couldnae see anything. It was dark. I should have done somethin' but I didnae... I hated him. When I got back to the hotel I got to thinkin' what if he's dead. The polis will come to the hotel. Somebody on the staff might tell them about Tulip always havin' a go at Sami and me. The polis would question me and find out about me being AWOL an' Sami might also get picked up for havin' an out-of-date work permit. And there was always a chance somebody might have seen me followin' Tulip, or down at the lake where he fell in. We couldnae risk staying so we took off."

"But you didn't go to Barra straight away, did you, because it was two weeks after Tulip died that you appeared in our garden?"

"That's right. We didnae know where to go. We'd a bit of money saved so we got a bus to Workin'ton an' stayed in a cheap B&B for a week. Then I phoned a pal frae the hotel an' he let us sleep on his flat's flair for another week. Then we decided to give Barra a go. Like I said, I called here on that last day to say sorry for leavin' that note."

Ben glanced at Helen to get her reaction. She gave him a raised eyes, shrugged shoulders, sounds reasonable to me, look. Ben took another swig of his tea. He was also convinced by Stott's story, but decided to probe further. "What about Mr Giles Innes? He disappeared off his rowing boat out on Windermere. A swimmer was seen near the scene. The police in Edinburgh discovered that you are a good swimmer. Did you drown Mr Innes as a favour for your boss, Mr Robinson; he hated Innes didn't he?"

Stott suddenly looked very tired. "Aw, Christ, what next? I know nowt about that. I heard about it like everybody else, on the local telly." He shook his head and half-smiled. "If you knew me… *really* knew me… you wouldnae be asking these questions. You'd *know* that I couldnae murder anybody…" There was a hint of regret in his tone. "Puttin' that note through your door was the most dangerous thing I've ever done. I nearly shi—" He stopped abruptly and looked at Helen. "Sorry."

Helen nodded her acknowledgement.

"But you did know that Robinson hated Innes?" Ben persisted.

"Everybody knew," Stott retorted, almost angrily. "He used to go on about it in the bar when he was stocious."

"Fair enough," Ben conceded, momentarily enjoying the use of a word he had frequently heard on their trips to the Highlands. He was running out of questions and starting to feel like an inquisitor who had an innocent man in front of him. But, being Ben, he couldn't let go until all the little details had been tidied up. "How long have you been down here in the Lakes? Where have you been staying?

"This is the third day. I've been stayin' with that pal from the Greenstone."

"Have you been here, at this cottage, waiting for us for three days?"

"Aye."

"Didn't you know we had moved into town?" Ben was about to add "to get away from you", but realised how ridiculous that would sound to Stott.

"Naw, I thought you might be on holiday. I was givin' it a week then I was off."

Ben looked at the clothes Stott was wearing. "You must have been frozen standing out there?"

Stott indicated with a turn of his head. "I've got an anorak hangin' up in the hall out there… an' I stayed out the rain in your garden shed." He glanced guiltily at Helen.

Helen remained silent.

"That shed is locked," Ben accused.

Stott sighed the sigh of a man being asked to explain the obvious. "I've been pickin' locks since I was ten, ye ken. Nae damage like. It still works okay." Again, he looked at Helen to see if she was going to reveal that she had found him in the cottage.

Helen continued drinking her tea, as if she was not aware of Stott's worried eyes.

"Do you own a Land Rover?" Ben suddenly blurted out, having just thought of it.

Stott replied just as quickly, finally revealing the quick-fire banter of the Scottish city. "Oh aye! An' I've got my yacht parked down on the lake next to all the other kitchen assistant's yachts." This was followed by a quietly regretful, "I don't have any kind of car, I cannae even drive."

Ben shuffled in his chair, picked up his cup, took a sip, peered over at Helen, and sighed. "What do you think? What are we going to do with him?"

Helen put her cup down and said, "I think we should accept Hamish's apology. He's caused us a lot of trouble, but he's made a big effort to come here to put things right. Apart from his AWOL problem, as far as I can see he hasn't done anything wrong."

Ben grimaced slightly. "I tend to agree, but it doesn't really matter what we think. The police want him for questioning. He is not officially innocent until the police say so. If they know he has been here talking to us and we just let him walk out, we could be in trouble."

"I just want to get back to Barra before you call the polis," Stott pleaded. "I want them to see me and Sami and the Currys all together, like a family, ye ken. The Currys will tell them the truth an' that."

"How do we—" Ben started.

"We can't stop him from walking out," Helen said. "We can't restrain him."

Ben gave Helen a disapproving look. "I was going to say, how do we *not* tell the police for twenty-four hours?"

"Where's the problem?" Helen snorted. "We do nothing for twenty-four hours; if anybody should understand that it is the police. They haven't exactly shown great urgency towards us these last few months. What are they going to do anyway – slap us in prison? I don't think so. A tiny slap on the wrist maybe, but I can take that and so can you."

Ben said nothing for a long time. Finally, he looked across at Stott and said, "Look, I'm not sure yet how we are going to deal with the police, but that's our problem, we'll think of something. I take it you will be leaving here first thing in the morning?"

"Aye, train to Glasgow. Pal will give us a lift to the station."

"So we'll phone the police tomorrow night about this time. You should be well on your way by then."

"Aye… fair enough. Thanks."

Ben stood up and offered his hand to Stott. "And thank you, Hamish."

Stott stood up and shook hands with Ben. "I never expected to say that," Ben said, "but if you hadn't come down to apologise, this thing could have dragged on for months, even years. And don't worry, I'm sure the police will cross you off their list once they speak to the Currys. As for your AWOL, I don't know anything about the consequences, but I agree with the Currys about facing up to it."

Now Helen stood up, and shook Stott's hand and said, "Thanks. I promise not to scream at you again – twice is enough."

Stott stared at the floor as if embarrassed or overwhelmed or both. He said nothing.

Fifteen minutes later two cars pulled away from the cottage. Helen, complete with recipe book, drove straight to the apartment. Ben gave Stott a lift to a bus stop on the southern outskirts of Keswick. During the journey, Stott told Ben what he had learned about his father during his visit to Thurso. He recalled that a man called MacDonald had told him that his father had been a good husband and a good worker and a good father to his daughter. He had not known he had a son. Stott was clearly desperate to find the best in his father, and when he asked Ben if he had spoken to his father before he died, Ben said that he hadn't, but he had seen no wickedness in his face, just torment. "And," Ben added, "his last word was 'sorry'. Just like his son eh?"

Chapter 38

The last few hours of their "day of relaxation" had been spent in the apartment, discussing the implications of their encounter with Stott. They were free to go home now, weren't they? They had lived under such a cloud of tension for so long that they needed to confirm with each other that this was the case. Yes, they decided eventually, they could go home. Stott had never been a threat, and the man who attacked Ben had been found dead. Of course, Ben had no actual proof that Dominic Lund had been his attacker, but instinctively, he was sure it had been him. Who else could it be? Who else had a motive? It was now inconceivable that any further threat could exist.

Helen had not brought up the subject of her car pursuer, presumably because she didn't think it was relevant to the subject of moving back to the cottage and Ben was keen to let that one lie for the moment; there had been enough excitement for one day.

As their new situation began to dawn on them so their excitement increased at the prospect of moving back to their beloved cottage. Just before turning in for the night, they agreed that they would return in a few days' time after things had settled down and Helen's workload had eased.

The next morning, though the weather outside had not improved, the climate in the apartment had. There was a palpable change of atmosphere as Helen and Ben went about their morning chores. There was a sense of lightness everywhere – in their heads, in their bodies. Neither would have been surprised if the other had started to dance and sing around the breakfast table like they did in old Hollywood musicals.

Ben's happiness was somewhat tempered by the news he had yet to pass to Helen. It was undoubtedly further good news, but there was an element of it that would almost certainly cause her some aggravation. He waited until they were sitting at the kitchen table, drinking their final coffee, having just finished a warming breakfast of porridge and fruit, before he said, "I know who was following you back from Buttermere the other night."

Fortunately, Helen did not have a mouthful of coffee at the time, such was the gasp she emitted. "What? Who? How?"

"It was Bill."

"Bill Unwin?"

"Yes, good old Bill. Peter and I were talking about it on the golf course yesterday, when up pops Bill with his admission. He thought he was being helpful. He said he was looking after you, not following you. He didn't know you had spotted him." Ben laughed. "You can see why he didn't make CID, can't you."

"It wasn't funny. I'll kill him when I see him."

"Poor old Bill. He always means well," Ben mused. "If you remember, he was here, in the apartment, telling me about the artist being found dead on Catbells, when you said you were going to Buttermere that afternoon. Apparently you said you might not be back until six o'clock, and I had expressed my concern that it would be dark by then. Well, Bill had taken all this in and decided, since he had a free afternoon, to go over to Buttermere, do a bit of walking and wait for you to come out of the hotel and shepherd you home. *Shepherd* was exactly the word he used. He said if he had offered his services up front you would have turned him down because you are a self-reliant woman, so he decided to do it without telling you. It was a hell of a thoughtful gesture, don't you think?"

Helen nodded. "Thoughtful, but not thought through. It was a crazy thing to do, and him an ex-policeman? Did you tell him how frightened I had been? Did you tell him it had caused me to attack you with my briefcase?"

"Yes, and he couldn't stop apologising. He was really upset when I told him. It was the last thing he wanted to happen. You know how much Bill likes you – bit of an admirer if you ask me – that's why he was trying to protect you in the first place. He really thought you hadn't seen him. He's a worried man now. He doesn't know how he's going to face you in the future."

Helen sighed. "Oh, I suppose I'll forgive him eventually. Next time you see him, tell him thanks for the thought, but to expect some future punishment for the way it turned out. Tell him the Obergruppenführer is working on a suitable punishment. Let him sweat on that for a while."

"With pleasure," Ben grinned. "He owes me as well for my sore back."

"At least we now have an explanation," Helen conceded. "It's another monkey off our back, thank goodness. I'm sure I would have been looking in my mirror all the time until we got to the bottom of it. And Sergeant Murphy now knows I wasn't being neurotic."

Ben leaned across the table and put a comforting hand on Helen's arm. "Never mind what Peter might have thought. We are in the clear now. All our troubles have suddenly vanished. We can get back to normal. How about celebrating by having a normal walk to Portinscale this lunchtime, a normal visit to that café by the lake, and a normal bowl of hot broth followed by two enormous scones with jam and cream?"

Helen smiled. "Sounds deliciously normal to me."

Later that afternoon, having continued his celebratory mood by having a post-lunch nap, Ben returned to his computer and brought up his database of possible victims. The discovery that Hamish Stott was not a killer did not mean, in Ben's opinion, that the database could be discarded, that all the deaths had indeed been accidents and not murder. The known fact that Charlotte Ambler had been attacked and survived to tell the tale was enough to give credence to the possibility that others had also been attacked, and not been so lucky. Ben, therefore, intended to continue with his investigations until something was proved one way or another. The problem had, of course, become more difficult with Stott out of the picture. Everybody could see that Stott could have had a motive. Now, if there was a killer out there, his motive had yet to be discovered, or worse still, he was killing without a motive.

Ben, meanwhile, decided it was right to remove his name from the database. It had only been included because of an assumed threat from Stott. Next he removed the name of Daniel Tulip whose death, according to Stott (and he believed him) had been accidental. He also removed the name of Charlotte Ambler, deciding that, if she had been the target of a repeat killer, he would know by now that she had not died, and would possibly be seeking a replacement target. Finally, he decided to remove the name of Elizabeth Lamb, simply on the grounds that he wanted to concentrate on certainty. She was missing, but she was not *known* to be dead like the others on the list.

The database, which had numbered 13 "victims", including the recently added John Appleton, was now down to nine. In purely statistical terms Ben was relieved that the task might have become just a little easier and, for the moment at least, he did not have to think in terms of it reaching 15, as surmised when Stott was a suspect. But he would never forget that he was dealing with the destruction of individuals, each life precious, each death bringing chaos and hell to relatives. He *must* never forget.

Later that evening, remembering that due to recent cuts phone calls to Keswick police station were diverted to Penrith after five thirty, Ben phoned Peter at home to tell him about Stott's visit and subsequent departure. As expected, he was not amused. Ben held the phone a few inches away from his ear while Peter let rip. At the end of almost every expression of disbelief, he added "I don't believe it". Ben was tempted to address him as Victor Meldrew, but thought better of it.

In what sounded like it might be his last, and deepest felt, expression of incredulity, Peter pleaded, "Tell me you phoned the hotel on Barra to verify that Stott and Babalato worked there?"

"I didn't feel the need," Ben replied, calmly. "I believed him."

"Didn't feel the need," Peter mocked, his voice rising to a shrill pitch. "You're a bloody—"

"Why don't you do it, Peter?" Ben interrupted. "Then when you pass it on to CID you can demonstrate that you had initiative, that you were on the ball. You might get some brownie points."

"I'll do just that," Peter countered. "And if they don't work there I wouldn't like to be in your shoes."

"Will you let me know what CID intend to do after they have established that Stott is innocent? You know, how it will affect their investigations into the unexplained deaths?"

There was no reply.

Ben envisaged Peter, speechless with anger. "I'll take that as a yes," he said, and put the phone down.

Chapter 39

Mid-November and Keswick marketplace was already adorned with Christmas lights. Tonight the lights were to be switched on by a "celebrity". Much to Ben's relief the celebrity this year was not to be the runner-up of a reality TV contest notorious for its banality, who found it difficult to string two cohesive sentences together during the post-event interview which Ben was expected to carry out.

This year the powers-that-be had managed to obtain the services of Ms Josephine Turner, the popular new presenter of television's *Walking with Wainwright*. Articulate, attractive and professional were the words most often used to describe Ms Turner who had now started to appear on screen in other outdoor programmes. Ben, a fan among many, was quite looking forward to meeting her.

He was not, however, a fan of the modern Christmas, and had not enjoyed spending some of the morning compiling the usual 200-word introduction to *The Tribune's* double-page Christmas Greetings section. He did this by recycling last year's piece, which he had on computer file under "Christmas Crap", changing a few adjectives here and there and finding new ways of expressing the same content. It was a suitably bland piece containing the usual Christmas clichés and platitudes, which Ben was sure nobody read.

In the afternoon, though working in the bedroom at the rear of the apartment, he could hear the constant rumble of traffic and general clatter as traders brought their stalls into the marketplace and erected them.

Later, the inviting smell of burgers and hotdogs and onions somehow found its way into the bedroom, and when Helen returned from work just as it was getting dark, he suggested they should forget about their planned dinner and go down to the marketplace and stuff themselves with whatever took their fancy. Helen agreed with alacrity.

With half an hour to go before the switch-on, they looked out of the lounge window overlooking the marketplace. There were so many canvas stalls it looked like an aerial shot of an Arab village. A big crowd had gathered, seemingly covering every square foot of cobbles. A brass band could be heard playing carols.

A minute later, suitably clad against the cold night air and glad that it wasn't raining, they stepped out into the throng. A smell of curry and fish and chips now mingled with the other food smells. Near the Moot Hall a Jennings brewery dray wagon was being used as a platform on which a choir started to assemble. Getting to the stalls and the food was going to be difficult they could see. It was a question of dodging left and right around stationary people.

Finally, they had sustenance in their hands – Ben's a burger with onions, Helen's a hotdog with coleslaw. They set off trying to make their way around the stalls, occasionally pausing to take in the lights display. Hundreds of silver lights hung from the gutters, replicating icicles. Shop windows were framed in red material with coloured lights surrounding them. Through the windows, Christmas trees could be seen, their variously coloured lights flashing metronomically. Suspended high above the crowds, stretched right across the marketplace at regular intervals, lights had been cleverly arranged to depict the shapes of reindeer and Christmas trees. Silver tassels on every horizontal surface depicted snow.

The choir started to sing and the crowd moved closer to listen. Helen and Ben made their way to the far end of the stalls and found a roped-off area containing a group of real reindeer surrounded by excited, rosy-faced children. Imported from the Highlands for the day, the reindeer looked decidedly unexcited as they sprawled on their beds of hay.

Further on, they came across a small open-fronted marquee in which a presenter from *Radio Cumbria* was interviewing passers-by. Next, they accepted some free samples of cheese from a persistent salesperson and then they stopped at a charity stall to buy cups of tea to wash down their food.

Having done a full tour of the stalls, they edged their way closer to the Moot Hall where the switching-on was to take place at the top of some steps, a stand and microphone indicating the location. A webcam was also active, which would transmit the scene to interested parties around the world.

Ben looked around at the old, colourful, three-storey buildings that surrounded the marketplace and thought, as he often did, that it looked more European than English. This was particularly true in the summer when more people sat outside the cafes than inside. He knew from previous research that the market had been granted its charter in 1276, and that Keswick had had a long and chequered past. A highlight, for him, had been in the eighteenth century when, to a marketplace oozing with mud and grime, men used to bring their wives to sell. Maybe they were the good old days, he joked with himself.

What would those people have made of today's world – of cars, planes, computers, television, radio, telephones – all designed to speed things up, to fill our heads with information? Had humans been able to keep pace with it all without going mad? It was beginning to look doubtful. What would be happening in the marketplace two hundred years from now? He could not imagine.

A man dressed in a bright red ceremonial gown caught his eye and brought him back to the present. The town crier stood at the microphone and said a few words which Ben didn't catch. A ripple of applause followed. Then a group of people assembled themselves at the top of the steps – the mayor and his wife, somebody dressed as Pudsey Bear, two unknowns, and Josephine Turner, standing quietly at the back.

The mayor welcomed everybody to Keswick, thanked them for coming, pointed out that they had been blessed with good weather, thanked the Christmas lights committee for their hard word, presented a girl called Erin with a prize for something, then invited Josephine Turner to step forward to switch on the lights. Applause rang out as she came into full view; there was no doubt about her popularity. She beamed a big smile and waved and shouted

"Hello Keswick" into the microphone. The crowd waved and shouted "hello" in return.

"It's lovely to be here in the Lake District," she started. "Especially in Keswick, which has many happy memories for me. Thank you so much for inviting me." She sounded sincere. "Do you know how lucky you are to live here?" she shouted, holding out her arms to indicate everything around her.

"Ye…es," the crowd shouted back.

"One day I hope to be standing down there with you, when I've finished with this television lark. Would you let me come and live with you?"

A very loud "ye…es" followed. She was pressing all the right buttons, and still sounded genuine.

"Great," she smiled. "Now will you give me a hand to get these lights on? Help me with the countdown?"

"Ye…es."

"Okay, here goes. Ten, nine…"

The crowd join in, "Eight, seven, six, five, four, three, two, one."

She leaned down and flicked a switch, and the lights flashed on and the crowd cheered and applauded.

Ms Turner, the mayor and his wife and a couple of others made their way down the steps and walked to the other end of the Moot Hall, where they entered the part of the building that had been converted into a Tourist Information Office. Here they had arranged a small buffet of tea and snacks while giving journalists the opportunity to meet and question Ms Turner and the mayor.

Ben escorted Helen back to their hotel entrance then made his way to the Tourist Information Office. He already had his notebook and camera with him. When he arrived in the Tourist Office he was surprised to see journalists and photographers from four other Cumbrian newspapers already milling round Josephine Turner. Their editors obviously saw her as good for their sales figures. And it was easy to see why, Ben thought. She was more beautiful in real life than on the screen. This was probably due to her complete lack of make-up. She had the natural beauty of a healthy young woman. There was no dyed hair, no painted fingernails; just healthy skin, shining hair and sparkling blue eyes.

Ben was pleased to see the other journalists; it made his life so much easier. All he had to do was listen as she answered their questions, and take a couple of photographs. He hung to the back of the group and let them get on with it. The questions were the usual mix of the trivial, the personal and the serious, and she took them all in good spirit and did her best to answer them in her velvety voice. Head down, Ben scribbled in his notebook, preferring the written word to recording devices.

"Any questions from the back there?" he heard her say.

He looked up and she was smiling at him. "You haven't asked any questions?"

She was a pro alright, making sure all the journalists went away satisfied, Ben thought. But he also thought that her courtesy came naturally. He leaned forward slightly and asked, "What is your opinion of Alfred Wainwright?"

"Absolutely remarkable," came her immediate reply. "He had such amazing energy, such commitment, such dedication. A great walker and a great writer. And all those drawings. They are so detailed, so perfect. Maybe he was a genius. I don't know, I'm not qualified to say." She looked at Ben and opened her eyes wide as if to ask if that was enough.

"Thank you," Ben said, and leaned back again.

A few more questions were asked and answered, and then she held up her hands and said, "Do you mind if I call it a day, guys. I'm whacked. I've had a busy week. Thanks very much for coming."

Totally smitten, the assembled journalists stepped back immediately and put away their gear quietly and thanked her, and left the Tourist Office with smiles on their faces.

Shortly afterwards, Josephine Turner left the Tourist Office and made her way to the central car park where she had left her car. She was watched intently by a man standing alone in the shadowed doorway of an outdoor shop. His eyes were slits of concentration behind his glasses. He was wearing a light-grey anorak. A cloth cap was perched on top of his unruly white hair.

Chapter 40

Josephine Turner opened her car door, got in and sat perfectly still with her eyes closed for about a minute. She was getting used to these personal appearances, but they were never easy. Being in the public eye meant being alert at all times and it drained her energy.

She opened her eyes, took a deep breath, switched on the engine, and started to smile as she pulled out of the car park. There was lots to look forward to over the next couple of days. Rather than book into a hotel, which would have meant more contact with the public, she had booked a self-catering apartment situated two miles out of Keswick. It was part of a complex of apartments which had been converted from a mansion house. It sat on the lower slopes of Skiddaw near the village of Applethwaite. Five-star luxury its website boasted.

This was why she had brought her car rather than use the train; she needed to carry food and other essentials for a two-night stay. She had already been to the complex, arriving in late afternoon, obtained the key from Reception, offloaded the food into the fridge and freezer, and taken a ten-minute nap before driving into Keswick for the switch-on.

Now, all she wanted to do was relax in her luxurious surroundings, open a bottle of wine, and take a long shower in that heavenly bathroom.

Away from the lights of the town, the countryside wrapped itself in a blanket of total darkness. There was no moon, so all she could see was that which appeared in her headlight's glare as she drove up the steep, narrow lane that led to the complex.

Pulling into the car park, she recalled how impressed she had been with the place earlier in the day. The imposing mansion house had been built into the slope of the steep fell, cutting out the land to create the horizontal space. The same had been done with the large formal gardens which sat in front of the mansion, about twenty feet below the level of the mansion. Large stone-retaining walls had been built all around the garden to obviate any future land slips. It was now promoted online as "The Walled Garden". Wide stone steps allowed people to walk between the two levels.

The car park was on the top level and it was surrounded by waist-high walls to prevent visitors from driving over the edge, but allowing them to look into the gardens below and see the distant fells beyond.

Josephine parked in front of the wall and made her way, aided by the lights on the outside of the main building, to her apartment. She heard another vehicle pull into the car park as she opened the apartment door.

Once inside she kicked off her shoes, enjoyed the under-floor heating on her cold feet, threw her outdoor coat and scarf over one of the sumptuous sofas, and headed for the kitchen area. She opened the fridge and took out one of the three bottles of Vionta Albarino she had brought with her. It made an excellent aperitif as well as going well with the chicken salad she had planned for dinner.

Soon she was curled up in the corner of a sofa, her half-full glass of wine sitting on a side table while she replied to three texts and two calls – four business, one personal. Once that was over she felt free and relaxed. She gulped down the remainder of the wine, topped it up in the kitchen, then headed for the bathroom that was en suite to the bedroom she had chosen.

She took her time in the bedroom, enjoying the caress of the deep pile carpet on her bare feet as she walked about discarding her clothes while taking intermittent sips of wine.

The glass was emptied before she went into the bathroom. Here, she picked one of the large white towels from the pile and draped it over the ladder radiator. Selecting soap and shampoo from a range of luxury brands displayed on glass shelves, she stepped into the shower enclosure.

Five minutes later, her body felt warm, clean and cosseted. She took the shampoo and started on her long hair. Soon her head was covered in lather which ran down her face causing her to close her eyes.

When, after rinsing, she opened her eyes, she saw a man's face staring at her through the glass. His nose was squashed flat against the glass, his eyes wide and wild, his mouth twisted in a vicious snarl. She gasped as adrenaline stabbed into her heart, shocking the whole of her body. Automatically, she backed into a corner of the shower, covering herself with her hands. She felt panic welling up inside her.

The man's face withdrew slowly. Then appeared again, suddenly, at the shower door. The door opened slowly. She saw a powerful, hairy, hand. And then a distorted, vicious, face appeared. "How ya doin' bonny lass?" it said.

"Christ, Dave, I am going to kill you," Josephine shouted, as she picked up the empty shampoo bottle and threw it at him. It hit him on the cheek, but he didn't flinch.

"You left the door open, pet," he explained in his Geordie accent. "Just as well it was me and not some pervert, like. His eyes roamed up and down her body. "Mind, you're looking well. Though I'm not too keen on that beard you're wearing."

Automatically, Josephine's hand went to her chin. It came away with a blob of lather that had not rinsed away. "I am seriously thinking of cancelling your invitation," she said. "That was not funny. I was terrified."

"Aye, I noticed a couple of big goose-pimples."

Angry though she was, she couldn't help but laugh. If that had been a man from London he would probably have apologised and begged forgiveness and she would have been slightly irritated by his weakness. Dave made jokes and stood his ground and by doing so implied that she was strong enough to take care of herself. In a way, he was paying her a compliment. Anyway, angry or not, she had no intention of letting this spoil a weekend she had been looking forward to for two months.

She had phoned Dave as soon as she received the invitation from the Keswick lights committee, and asked him if he would care to join her for a discreet weekend of passion. His reply had, of course, contained quips about switching him on anytime and lighting his bulb, but they finally got round to making their arrangements. Dave was to arrive in the dark and leave in the dark two days later. They were not to be seen in public together. It more or less meant that they would be imprisoned in the apartment for two days, but neither of them baulked at that prospect.

Having apparently calmed down, Josephine suddenly swivelled, turned the cold tap on full pressure, grabbed the shower-head and turning back, aimed it at Dave. In an instant his head and shoulders were soaked and yelling profanities, he backed out of the shower doorway.

Smiling at her sweet revenge, Josephine turned both taps off and exited the shower. Dave was drying his face and hair on a towel. He smiled at her. "Nice one, Jo. That makes us even. Shake on it." He held out his right hand.

Jo stepped towards him and shook his hand, but he didn't let go and pulled her closer. His expression changed. "It's so good to see you again" he said, seriously, before placing his damp lips gently against hers.

When they parted, Jo said, "Let me get dried and dressed, and I'll see you in the lounge in a few minutes." She was still slightly annoyed at the manner of his intrusion, otherwise she would have been tempted to stay entangled in the bathroom and let nature take its course. But she knew her annoyance would soon dissipate, given time and a couple of glasses of wine. "There's some wine in the fridge," she pointed out. "Why don't you—"

"Best place for it," Dave interrupted, as he turned to go. "I've brought some whisky."

Now she didn't know if his curtness indicated his feeling of rejection, or if it was just his normal way of getting on with things. She guessed the latter. This was the problem with people whose knowledge of each other was little more than carnal. She hoped to ease the problem over the next two days. You can't stay in bed for forty-eight hours. Can you?

Fifteen minutes later, with her hair dried, and wearing casual trousers and a pale blue cashmere sweater, Jo entered the lounge to find Dave lying on one of the sofas, his head on a cushion, his eyes closed. He was now wearing a dry, dark brown, polo-neck sweater. An empty whisky glass sat on a side table. She tip-toed up to him, bent down close to his right ear, and shouted, "Action!"

The whole of the trunk of his body jumped in the air and fell back again, as if it had suffered an electric shock. His eyes flew open – alert, searching. He must have been asleep judging by his reaction. "Gotcha!" Jo grinned. "*Now* we are even."

Hand on his heart, Dave slowly swivelled his feet off the sofa and sat back. "Bloody hell, Jo, you nearly had a corpse on your hands there. I was away with the fairies."

"Still think it's funny?" Jo queried, smugly.

There was a split second of hesitation before Dave replied, "Oh aye."

Quickly recovering his composure, Dave tapped the cushion beside him and said, "Howay sit down Jo and tell us what you've been up to lately." He had clearly picked up her *let's take things slowly* signal; let's talk and break bread, let's behave in a civilised manner – before we tear each other's clothes off.

And they did just that. They talked and drank and ate dinner and drank, and, like all new lovers, went to bed early.

It was ten minutes to midnight when Jo found herself squinting at her watch-face in the darkened bedroom. A throbbing pain behind her eyes and temples explained the reason for her wakening. It was no stranger to her these days. The stress of her marriage and high-pressure demands of her job had started to take its toll. Sleepless nights and caffeine-filled mornings had become the norm.

To compound the problem, her husband had introduced her to depressants to help her sleep, and then to stimulants to get her through the day. "Uppers and downers", he rationalised. "Everybody uses them".

She had started to rely on them, use them habitually. The downside was occasional dehydration and severe headaches. Now, she also took painkillers for the headaches.

She touched the bedside table-lamp once. It glowed gently, just enough to allow her to look across the bed and see Dave looking like he had been hit by a train. He had been tired when he arrived, and now he was obviously dead to the world.

The pain throbbed on, beating a louder drum every time she moved. She knew from experience it would not go away of its own accord; it had to be killed by the painkillers. Fighting her tiredness, she eased herself out of bed and trudged, unsteadily, into the bathroom. The sudden, bright light hurt her eyes. She filled a glass with cold water and gulped it down; its coldness and the cold night air making her naked body shiver. It was at this point that she realised she had left her pills in the car. She carried all of them – uppers, downers and painkillers – in their separate bottles in an old makeup bag which went everywhere with her, in the glove compartment of the car.

The thought of having to get dressed and go outside into a cold November night, appalled her. But she knew she would have to; the pain would not stop otherwise. She wended her way into the lounge, put on the light, and found her trousers on the floor where their love-making had begun. She struggled into her trousers and then her shoes which she had kicked off earlier, and made her way to the hall. Here, she put on her coat, checked that the car keys were in the right-hand pocket, and wrapped her scarf around her neck.

Before going out, she paused. All was quiet. Dave had not been disturbed. She switched on the outside light that would help her to see her way to the car park. She opened the door, stepped outside and closed the door.

Chapter 41

Ben sat in his favourite armchair in front of the blazing log fire he had just topped up. The room was disgracefully warm. He had a book in his lap, a glass of whisky within reach and Sergei Rachmaninov in the background. Across the room, Helen sat in her chair under the reading lamp, the light creating a luminous halo behind her. She was reading intently, her glasses edging down her nose. Occasionally, during the evening, she had looked over at him and smiled, and his heart had swollen as it did when he was young.

They were back in their beloved cottage, back to their usual routines, and all was well again. Ben felt like purring. He envied the cat's ability. It was five days since Helen had announced that her workload had slackened sufficiently to give them time to pack up and leave the apartment. They had celebrated their last night in Keswick with a visit to their favourite fish and chip shop, knowing that this pleasure would be curtailed in the future.

It was nine days since the body of Josephine Turner had been found in the walled garden of the luxury apartment complex. Nine days in which Ben felt that history was repeating itself as he watched the media hordes swarm into Keswick. A television personality was now as newsworthy as a government minister apparently, perhaps more so, though minister Jack Fraser and his wife Elaine had also attracted international attention.

Ben had been caught up in the melee. He had been in the media crowd that visited the garden, took photographs, interviewed complex staff, searched for a story, an angle. The truth would be left to the police, the pathologist and the coroner. The resultant articles he produced for *The Tribune* appeared dull in comparison with the nationals who, with their armies of researchers, had managed to find in three days almost everything that Josephine and her famous husband had said and done in the last ten years.

Until the facts came out, speculation had been the name of the game. The rift between them had been well known in media circles. Had her husband followed her to Cumbria to kill her far away from home? Or had he followed her to reconcile with her, found her with another man, and then killed her? Had Jo used this trip for a final fling with her lover before ending it all? What about the other man, Dave? Had they had a lovers' row? Had he followed Jo out to the car park, thrown her over the wall to the garden path below, and returned to bed to appear innocently asleep when her body was found early the following morning by a member of staff?

The newspaper headlines matched the inanity of some of the conjecture. **"Jo sleepwalks to her death"**; **"Did Jo fall for Dave?"**; **"She fell on a fell"**; **"Jo's final fling?"**; **A fall or a lover's leap?"** Perhaps the most tasteless was: **"Not tonight, Josephine"**.

When the post mortem findings were published at the coroner's inquest they did nothing to stop the conjecture. If anything, they added to it. Cause of death was inconclusive, the coroner announced. There was no doubting that she had suffered multiple injuries, including a broken neck and contusions to the brain, caused by her fall of 20 feet from the car park onto the stone pathway that ran around the walled garden, but the pathologist had also commented on the wound to her skull that was separate from other wounds on her skull, which he deemed to have been caused by her head-first contact with the path. And he pointed out that her eyes had been bloodshot and bulging slightly, which were symptoms of suffocation. However, the fact that she had been drinking heavily cast doubts over the certainty of this prognosis. Slight traces of drugs had been found in her blood, which matched those found in the glove compartment of her car.

As a result of these findings, the coroner had adjourned the inquest to enable further investigations by the police. Ben had had a couple of meetings about the case with Peter at the station and with Peter and Bill at the golf club. Their debates on the matter had reached no firm conclusions but all felt that "unlawful killing" would eventually be the coroner's verdict, given the pathologist's report. All they could do now was await the findings of the CID investigation.

Ben had been genuinely saddened by the death of Josephine Turner. It reminded him of the death of Tessa Coleman, the artist found dead on Bilberry Shelf, beneath Dalehead Crags; one of Snodd's last victims. He had known both women only slightly yet their beauty and personality had won a place in his heart. They had both brought light into the world; light that should have lasted a lifetime, not be extinguished so soon, so cruelly.

He had also been angry at the media, particularly that part of it to which he belonged – the newspapers. The term *news*-paper should be withdrawn from some of the nationals he felt. The reporting of the news – true facts – had virtually been discarded. They were now little more than sensation-seeking purveyors of gossip and speculation. By insinuation and innuendo they ruined the reputations of people who did not deserve it. Such was Ben's disgust, he felt as though his beautiful little town had been infested with rats. He was delighted, therefore, when, after a few days, he saw them pack their bags and scurry off, noses twitching, to their next assignments.

One of the last things Ben had done before leaving the apartment was to enter Josephine Turner's name and known details on his database. Though nothing was yet proved, it seemed to him very unlikely that an accident or suicide could have caused her death. Having seen her smile and looked into her sparkling eyes that very night he would have sworn that she was happy and forward-looking, not suicidal. And yet, experience told him that the face was just a mask, a mask that can hide reality: a smile – sorrow; a scowl – happiness. Did we not all play the part of Pagliacci some of the time? Were we not all painted clowns?

After entering her details, Ben had spent a few hours trying to work out whether her inclusion on the database had made any impact on his search for patterns, commonality, motives. Nothing caught his attention. If there was a serial killer at large, he was not leaving any noticeable signature.

At the end of this session it suddenly occurred to Ben that it might not be possible to see any connections until the deaths stopped, until all the murders had been committed. How in God's name would he know when that had occurred? Would it ever occur? The killer might not have an end in sight. He still didn't even know if everybody on his database *had* been murdered. And the almost certain exclusion of Hamish Stott as a suspect made everything even less clear.

As he closed down his computer for the last time in the apartment, Ben had glanced out of the bedroom window. The usual scene of beauty and serenity had been obliterated by late November fog. This was how his search was going to be from now on. It was going to be like driving in the fog. Without lights.

Chapter 42

Ben had decided years ago that December was a time for the closing of eyes and ears and the gritting of teeth, as the sights and sounds of the industry called Christmas were thrust into the consciousness of everybody by all means possible. Outbreaks of war, earthquake disasters, assassination of innocents, even England winning a football match, were all relegated to also-rans in the media. How could they possibly compare in importance with news about the discounts on offer at supermarkets, the name of a new perfume, what is going to be No.1 in the charts, and the latest electronic gadget that allowed you to copy stuff off your television onto your desktop, onto your laptop, onto your tablet, onto your smart-phone, and then send it via Facebook to Twitter to U-tube which could then send it to outer-space and back to your television – all for just £359.99.

There was no escape from it, so he shut down his senses whenever it was possible and safe to do so, and gritted his teeth whenever it was impossible to do so. The situation was made worse by the fact that Sue expected him to cover every event, large or small, spawned by or associated with this "season of celebration", a euphemism surely, to all except the shopkeepers.

The net effect was that he travelled through December in a kind of mental torment, his brain wanting to shutdown to avoid the nonsense, yet required to function to record it for other people to read.

To preserve his sanity he took every opportunity between weekday events to "disappear" into the fells for as long as his schedule allowed. Why couldn't Christmas be in June when we could spend our evenings outdoors until bedtime, instead of being held prisoners of the dark, and thus become sitting targets for the sharks in suits?

At weekends he spent virtually all his time on the mountain tops, as far away from the town and shops and crowds as possible. Here, among the bog and the rock, the snow and the ice, the whipping wind and urgent rain, the crag and the heather, the climb and the slide, the cold and the tears, the sweat and the wet, the hot drink and food, the map and the compass, the boots and the thumb-stick, he found what he was looking for – freedom, the dangerous thrill of raw nature, and most of all – reality.

Helen, on the other hand, although equally disparaging of the commercial juggernaut that Christmas had become, still liked to preserve the simple, old traditions and therefore spent some time shopping and cooking, resulting in the day itself being an agreeable one of good food, small presents and relaxation.

Once over, however, Ben felt a palpable sense of relief and release. The madness was over for another year, the great white company executives would order their new yachts, the loan sharks would polish their knuckledusters, the credit card bosses would calculate their bonuses, the turkey farmers would book their cruises, normality would return, frenetic consumers would metamorphose back into calm people again, their sanity would return and they would function normally once more. And he would have the time and patience to get back to his detective work; the work on his database that had barely been touched for a month.

It was actually the third of January before Ben got back to the database. The Christmas and New Year holiday period had brought its usual batch of unprepared walkers venturing onto the snow-capped fells without crampons or ice-axes. The resultant slips and falls had caused the call-out of the mountain rescue teams on four occasions. One of them, sadly, had been a fatality – a fall of six hundred feet. Reporting on these accidents, and routine New Year stuff, had extended Ben's time away from his investigations.

Now, at last, he could get back to it. He was keen to see if the information Peter had given him a few days ago affected the database or his list of clues. Peter had informed him that Hamish Stott had been extensively questioned by the Highland police, now called the Northern Constabulary, both at his home on the Isle of Barra and at the Western Isles Area Command headquarters at Stornoway on the Isle of Lewis. They had then brought him down to Penrith police headquarters where he had undergone further questioning. Both forces agreed that his employers at the hotel on Barra were reliable "witnesses" whose statements had provided Stott with an incontestable alibi for the time he was suspected of still being in the Lake District. Stott had also provided them with sound alibis for some of the days (but not all – not remembering what he had been doing on those days) on which other "unexplained deaths" had occurred in the past 18 months. They had reached the obvious conclusion, therefore, that he could not be held responsible for any of the deaths that occurred on the days for which he had alibis, which were the majority on their list.

Because of this and because of any evidence to the contrary, and because he had volunteered the information, they were also prepared to believe him when he told them that he had seen chef Daniel Tulip trip and fall into the lake. It was, therefore, sensible to assume that he had not committed any murders at all and commenting on his timid and cooperative manner, they agreed that even if charges were made regarding Tulip's death, no jury in the land would find him guilty. He was, therefore, free to go.

As soon as he had stepped outside the police headquarters he had been rearrested and charged with being AWOL. He was eventually handed over to the military police who came to Penrith to take him away. His current status was not known.

Peter had gone on to say that the innocence of Stott had thrown a whole new light on the entire "unexplained deaths" investigations. So far, the investigations had turned up nothing to suggest that a serial killer was operating, and now senior officers were wondering if the mere presence of the son of Snodd, a serial killer, had panicked them into thinking it was history repeating itself. They had decided, therefore, to put most of those investigations "on the back burner", and transfer the people who had been working on them to the cases where they had "something to go on". These included the drowning of Giles Innes in Windermere, whose case had been revitalised since the swimmer attack on Charlotte Ambler; the attack on Charlotte Ambler on Bassenthwaite Lake which was self-evident; the hit-and-run death of Don Ivison because the witnessing of a Land Rover-type vehicle near the scene coincided with the witnessing of a Land Rover in the Charlotte Ambler case; and the recent death of Josephine Turner where the coroner has asked for police investigation following the pathologist's inconclusive findings.

The attack on Ben at his cottage, which they had put down to Stott or an accomplice, had also been put on the back burner, since they were now ready to accept Ben's proposition that it had been carried out by Dominic Lund or one of his associates, all of whom were now dead.

Ben had been glad that Hamish Stott had been cleared by the police and he hoped the military would take it easy on him. In spite of all the trouble he had caused, inadvertently sometimes, Ben felt that Stott was a young man who "needed a break", as the USA put it.

He thought the police were unwise, however, to put the majority of "unexplained deaths" cases on the back burner. Just because they had not found any evidence yet did not mean that it did not exist; it could be lying on their files right now, without them being aware of its significance. He would love to get his hands on those files. And didn't the sheer number of cases of "accidental" deaths in such a quiet, rural area speak volumes about the probability that some were not accidents. The one *certainty* was that Charlotte

Ambler had been attacked by somebody trying to make it look like an accidental drowning. Just like Giles Innes. Ben couldn't believe it was a coincidence. How many more "accidents" had that person arranged?

He therefore fully intended to carry on with his investigations into all the cases on his database. First of all he decided to check out the CLUES list to see how they had been affected by recent events. Of the 10 clues, he found he could safely remove four – clues 5, 7, 9 and 10. These related to events involving Stott, which Stott had cleared up, and to the attack on himself, which he did not intend to spend any more time on, being confident in his Lund thesis. He did, however, have to add a new clue: 11. Separate blow to head & possible suffocation (pathologist) J. Turner case.

He now turned his attention once again to analysis – to commonality. Having not found complete commonality under any heading he decided to select the commonality that was most frequent and see where that took him. He would work on the initial assumptions that his database might not be complete, or the killer had not been able to achieve total commonality up to this point, or the killer had more than one commonality criterion when selecting victims.

The most common factor he had found amongst the ten victims was that seven of them were *outsiders*. They did not reside in the Lake District. Two of the three *insiders* – Askew and Wilkinson – were Cumbrians, but lived outside the national park where all the deaths had taken place, so they could be recategorised as *outsiders*. And it could be argued that the one victim who did live in the Lake District was originally an *outsider* – Giles Innes of Windermere. All of which could lead to the conclusion that the killer was somebody born and bred in the Lake District who was intent on discouraging tourists and newcomers. It was a phenomenon found in desirable areas all around the world, though the methods used were not usually so draconian. Up until now, however, Ben had been unaware of any such activity in the Lake District. But maybe the problems of housing affordability and availability, due to the influx of wealthy outsiders, had finally tipped a local man over the edge?

As he contemplated the mammoth undertaking necessary to screen the 40,000 people who lived in the Lake District, in order to find a disgruntled person who had been born in the area, swam well and owned a Land Rover, it suddenly occurred to Ben that the person need not be a born-and-bred local. The wish to keep out tourists and incomers could equally apply to an existing incomer; one who had found his little piece of paradise and now wanted to keep others out; wanted to keep it as exclusive as possible. Are not immigrants often equally or on occasion, even more anti-immigration than nationals?

If it came down to it, Ben concluded, if all other avenues of investigation had been tried and failed, screening might eventually have to take place. But it would have to be a police operation, for time and legal reasons. It was beyond his capabilities and scope and at this point he didn't even know if this theory was correct. There were dozens of other theories to consider before selecting some to put on a short list for detailed examination. So he decided to continue seeking out theories and listing them, before going on to take them to their detailed conclusions. Ah! Happy New Year indeed; challenging days were here again.

Chapter 43

The people of Cumberland and Westmorland – collectively known as Cumbrians since amalgamation in 1974 – are, as Ben and Helen have found, very tolerant people. Having been isolated for centuries by their geography we might have expected a modicum of insularity in their nature. But not so. For many decades now they have witnessed their land being invaded and occupied by outsiders and with few exceptions have made them welcome. They are now so used to the rest of the world wanting to own a part of England's most beautiful landscape – the Lake District – that they scarcely raise their eyebrows when more outsiders come to join them.

So why was there such excitement when a couple arrived in the Bassenthwaite Lake area? Was it their exotic appearance? Was it his flashing eyes and powerful chest? Was it her brooding looks and graceful movement? Or was it the strange house they built in the forest on the side of a steep fell overlooking the lake; a house made entirely of random, intertwined pieces of wood.

It was all these things and the facts that the house was high in a tree and they ate only fish and they flew rather than walked.

The arrival of the first ospreys to nest in England for 150 years had indeed caused a stir when it happened in 2001 and their continued presence ever since, fledging chicks every year, had unleashed an amazing amount of interest in their daily lives. More than 100,000 visitors now came each year to see them. 90 volunteers and a small group of permanent staff looked after them, driving them to the viewing points, giving talks and film shows in a visitor centre, protecting the nests when the birds flew off to Africa for the winter. It was estimated that the birds were responsible for bringing over half a million pounds every year into the local economy.

But not everybody was as thrilled as the bird-watchers and the money-makers. Not everybody liked the commercialisation of this natural event. The forest ranger didn't like it one bit. His life had changed dramatically since the arrival of the birds. His job had changed from being a slow-paced, behind the scenes provider of equipment and services to enable walkers and educational parties of schoolchildren to enjoy the natural attractions of the forest, to being an upfront, smiling, greeting performer for the benefit of the camera-carrying hordes who arrived by the busload.

Why *did* humans have to interfere with nature, he questioned? Why did they have to possess and change everything they see and in the process usually destroy it? It was as if the ospreys were being wrapped in plastic and put on display like a convenience food in a supermarket. Add in the recent policy of making the forest open to all-comers for recreational activities he judged more suited to Blackpool

Pleasure Beach and his haven of peace and quiet had been transformed into what he saw as bedlam.

This was not what he had bargained for when he went into the forestry service 23 years ago. He had been attracted to the work by the prospect of being on his own, away from people, close to nature; isolated from the overcrowding, clamour and falsities of urban life – of modern life. His house in the middle of the forest had come with the job. Its perfect position on the steep side of the fell meant that he could see the mountains on the other side of the lake as well as his immediate surroundings. It had been his idyllic retreat at the end of a quiet, fulfilling day. It was incapable of receiving a television signal without a special aerial, so he and his wife Ruth had gladly spent the evenings gardening, talking and reading. Badgers, owls, foxes, deer, ravens, buzzards and countless small birds were their welcome neighbours.

Now he saw it as a refuge from a noisy, commercialised, distasteful day and now he had nobody to share it with. Ruth had left two years ago. She had been content until the ospreys came. She had loved the forests and the mountains. She had been glad to share his quiet life. But when, over the years, he had become more and more miserable and angry because of the change in his job; when he had increasingly sought solace in the bottle and drunkenly snarled at her, ignored her, bullied her, she had packed her bags.

The terrible irony was that he loved the ospreys. He was thrilled that they had returned after 150 years. He loved to watch them fly and dive for fish and feed the chicks. He was happy to take his turn at guarding the nest. He would have been happy to see all the animals that had disappeared down the centuries return to the forest – wolves, bears, lynx, pine martins, boar, eagles, bats and birds.

It was what the ospreys had attracted that he hated – people. Too many people. Like a plague of ever-increasing ants they were spreading across the earth, eating, breeding, taking, using, discarding, destroying, killing. Now, as well as swarming all over Wainwright's sacred fells, they were marching into his precious forest like a football crowd in a cathedral. It was a sacrilege.

It seemed to him that nothing had gone right since the coming of the birds. Like winged harbingers of doom, they had brought him misery and depression. Fortified with alcohol he had retreated into his own world, a world full of anger and darkness in which only one god-like man was worthy.

Chapter 44

Global warming, climate change, El Nino, greenhouse gases, solar variation: whether singularly or in combination, these phenomena were apparently causing the coldest winter the Lake District had seen for years. Rain in the Lakes was commonplace, as were floods, and snow on the mountain tops. But thick snow in the valleys, particularly snow that hung around for weeks, was a comparative rarity.

The new year had started with a whisper; the snow quieting all the sounds of the valleys – the tractors taking hay out to the herds, the traffic slewing along the winding lanes, the footfall in the streets.

Helen, not confident on slippery roads, stayed at home as much as possible, dealing with her clients by phone and email. She was surprised to find she accomplished much more than she expected and decided to spend more time working from home in the future, after the snow had gone.

Ben, however, had to get out to where the stories were. And the weather was throwing up plenty. Road crashes, burst pipes, animal rescues, human falls, ice-skating on Derwentwater, skiing on Skiddaw, helicopter food drops to isolated farms, power failures and their effects, etc, etc. Unlike Helen, he was confident on the roads and had always felt a quiet thrill when driving his 4 x 4 in snow conditions;

it was such a break from the routine, a stimulating challenge.

The challenge he had set himself on his database had had to take a back seat while he concentrated on his paid job and he had only managed a few hours on his theory list, when first January and then February, literally slipped by.

March, with the snow on the retreat, gave him more time and he spent many hours poring over his database, thinking and analysing. He led himself down many "promising roads" only to find they were eventually "blind alleys".

Ben's tenacity was being tested to the limit and he was beginning to lose heart when Peter came up with some information which reinvigorated him. Peter had learned, belatedly, from CID that when questioning guests at the holiday complex where Josephine Turner had died, one of them reported having spotted an old Land Rover in the car park that night. He was an accountant for a large, private company, on holiday with his wife and he had received a phone call from his boss that night asking him to produce some financial forecasts for one of their divisions by the next morning. Such calls were normal in his company, at his level, which was why he always carried his laptop, even on holiday. He had gone out to his car to get the laptop from the boot, and while walking across the dimly lit car park had noticed the Land Rover. He said he noticed it because he was an unashamed "petrol-head", driving a top of the range BMW, and taking a passing interest in most vehicles he came across. The old Land Rover stood out, even in the half-light, because the car park was usually full of cars like his – upmarket saloons and 4 x 4's. He had assumed it was a staff vehicle, probably the gardener's, who for an unknown reason had not used the staff car park on the other side of the complex.

The accountant had not noticed anybody in the Land Rover, nor had he taken note of the number plate, but he did identify it as a Defender 90, the type of workhorse that farmers use. It did not belong to any of the other guests or staff, and none of them had noticed it, either because they hadn't ventured out into the car park that night or, not being petrol-heads, it had simply not caught their attention.

The news reinvigorated Ben in that it confirmed his search was meaningful and was becoming increasingly urgent. It also confirmed the probability that Josephine Turner had been murdered, and this had the opposite effect – a depressing sadness that there was a human being out there capable of brutally killing the beautiful and the innocent.

On further reflection about the news, Ben realised that it did not affect his database. The news concerned the killer not the victims. But he did have a new clue to enter on his list: 12. Land Rover 90 seen in car park on night of death (Accountant) – J. Turner case.

Peter went on to swear Ben to secrecy about the discovery. The police did not want news about the Land Rover made public. The Police National Computer had already supplied them with a list of owner names and addresses of all Defender 90's registered in Cumbria, and they had a team working their way through it, starting with addresses in the Lake District.

Chapter 45

"Luck affects everything. Let your hook always be cast; in the stream where you least expect it there will be a fish". So wrote the Roman poet, Ovid. This was the ancient version of Ben's own theory about luck, that when you work at something hard enough you set up some sort of energy – he called it a vibration – that somehow led you to success, from a direction you were not expecting.

Ben's hook had been cast for a further month, tortuously searching, thinking, analysing. He was getting to hate the sight of his office, and the unblinking square-eyed monster that sat on his desk, staring at him, challenging him to do better. Spring was making an appearance, its extravagant bursts of new life seemingly mocking the tired old man he had become. He wanted to go outside and enjoy the buds bursting, the grass stirring, the lambs frolicking, the birds singing, but felt duty-bound to stick to the task he had set himself. How would he feel if he gave up and another body was found? The trouble was, he was getting nowhere. And, according to Peter, the police were also getting nowhere.

His latest session over, he switched off the monster, and swivelled his chair away from the desk. Frustrated and dejected, he remained in his seat and stared at the floor. Then, unthinkingly, his eyes came up and stared at his surrounds. In the corner, a single bed for guests; close by, a wardrobe, a chest of drawers. On the walls, three of his own paintings – two oils and a watercolour – all of the Lake District landscape. The majority of the walls were home to bookshelves, bulging with books of all shapes and sizes.

As often happened when his brain had ceased thinking, his eyes wandered across shapes and objects, counting them, noticing their order. Downstairs, when switched off, he frequently found his eyes counting the random shapes and numbers of the stones in the fire surround. Repeat patterns on wallpaper, curtains and tiles were also likely to be stared at and counted. He assumed it was a fairly common phenomenon. At least he hoped it was. Perhaps it was a sign that active brains never truly switch off.

Now his eyes wandered across his nearest bookcase. It was quite orderly in general with non-fiction and fiction separated, and books grouped where appropriate, but of course it was not orderly when it came to shape or colour, and it was these variations that were attracting his eyes. Fat, thin, tall, short, black, brown…along the rows of books his eyes went. He just let them wander from shelf to shelf. There was something therapeutic about it, and at times it felt almost like a need; like a runner needs a cool-down jog before stopping completely.

His eyes came to a stop for a moment when he came across a group of books all the same size and colour. He found that he was looking at the famous seven volumes of Wainwright's *Pictorial Guides To The Lakeland Fells*. Here he paused, and for a few moments relived the pleasure these books had given him over the years. From the simple act of walking in the hills, Alfred Wainwright had created a literary world of beauty. They were not just brilliant guide books with wonderful drawings, they were poetical and philosophical works of art.

As he looked at them, Ben noticed, for the first time, that one of them did not carry Wainwright's name down the spine. Six of them carried the book title, such as THE WESTERN FELLS, and also carried Wainwright's name, but this one only said THE NORTHERN FELLS. Always keen to find the explanation for everything, Ben rose from his chair and, using both hands, lifted the block of books from the shelf and carried them to his desk.

He laid them in a horizontal pile on the desk and, sitting down, picked up THE NORTHERN FELLS and one other. Turning to the publisher's information at the beginning of each book, he found the explanation. THE NORTHERN FELLS had been published by Westmorland Gazette, and the others by Michael Joseph Ltd. Clearly Ben had bought them at different times, and the earlier Westmorland Gazette books had not carried Wainwright's name on the spine.

Mystery over, Ben was about to return the books to the shelf when he felt a tug on his line. Sitting right in front of him, on the book's spines, in horizontal repetition the word WAINWRIGHT nibbled at his brain. Not the name, just the word – the collection of letters. Had he not been looking at these same letters for the past few months? His pulse quickened. Better not get too excited; he was tired, his synapses might not be firing on all cylinders.

Scanning his desk he soon found a paper copy of the list of names on his database. With a pen he jotted down the first letter of each surname: I from Innes, G from Grant, N from Nelson, I from Ivison, H from Harris, W from Wilkinson, R from Robinson, W from West, A from Appleton, T from Turner. He looked at the row of letters - I G N I H W R W A T – and very slowly and carefully crossed each letter out as he transcribed them into W A I N W R I G H T. He held his breath in disbelief. It had been an anagram all along. He had tried anagrams to no avail when he had thirteen names on the list, and then again when the list came down to ten names. But his recent attempt had been half-hearted when he saw that there were two W's, two I's and only three vowels. He had been unable to find anything better than "waiting", and had made the mistake of looking only for words, instead of words *and* names. Now here it was. The fish had swum downstream and taken his ever-ready hook. The vibration had worked again.

He sat staring at the letters in front of him, not sure how to react. He had been right. There was a commonality to find among the victims. There must be a serial killer out there. The confirmation of this horrific fact was tempered by the elation he felt at having solved the problem. He was elated but too tired to shout in triumph and there was also that feeling of anti-climax when a journey is over, a conclusion reached.

He knew, of course, that it was the conclusion of his analysis, not of the solving of the murders. Why were the victims being killed in the name of Wainwright? What was going on in the mind of the killer? Was he offering them as some sort of sacrifice to the great man? Was he building Wainwright's name out of the bodies of outsiders as punishment for intruding on his beloved Lake District? Whatever the reason, it was clear that Wainwright held a central place in the killer's psyche.

Would there be more murders to come? Would the killer now be looking for an initial A for Alfred or, worse still, the whole Christian name, ALFRED. The sooner Ben got this information to the police the better.

He would be giving the police a target to aim at. They would be looking for somebody who was writing Alfred Wainwright's name in blood, somebody obsessed with him, somebody clearly insane. There would be many new avenues to explore. Too many for one man to cope with when time was of the essence. It was time to give Peter his moment of glory.

Peter tried to look calm and professional as he sat behind his desk while Ben divulged all that he had found, but Ben could sense the nervous energy coming across the desk. He envisaged Peter passing this pot of gold to his superiors and taking the credit. This would almost certainly clinch his transfer to CID. So be it; that was the deal. The good thing was that Peter would now be involved with, or at least kept closely informed of, the progress of future investigations. And surely he would pass this on.

Ben suggested that the police should contact all organisations which a Wainwright enthusiast might attend or support. He suggested contacting *The Wainwright Society*, an organisation described on its website as "dedicated to keeping alive the fell-walking traditions promoted by A.W." Formed in 2002, it now had approximately 1000 members. Could "our man" be one of them? All members would, of course, be Wainwright enthusiasts, but could one of them have become obsessed by him, and believed he was carrying out his wishes to preserve the peace and tranquillity of this special place?

There were dozens of rambling, fell-walking and environmental groups to consider such as *The Friends of the Lake District*, and *The Lake District Fellowship*. As he mentioned the last name, Ben was suddenly reminded that Giles Innes had been the chairman of that organisation. Could there be a connection there? Was the killer a local member who had taken a severe dislike to their arrogant "outsider" chairman who had breezed in and taken over in a very short time? Had he then continued getting rid of other outsiders?

Ben also suggested contacting Cumbria's speciality bookshops which catered for collectors and lovers of old books. Would not somebody who was obsessed with Wainwright have collected all of his books over the years? Where did he buy them? Would a shop owner remember that one of his regular customers was a particularly intense admirer of Wainwright?

With so many organisations to contact Ben realised it could take the police a long time before results, if any, came through. He, in the meantime, was going to read-up on obsession and try to learn where excessive hero-worship came from and where it could lead. Hopefully, it would give him a greater understanding of the *type* of person they were looking for.

Chapter 46

Helen was thrilled when Ben finally got round to telling her about his breakthrough, and that he had handed it over to the police. Without wishing to diminish the importance of his discovery, she was mostly thrilled at the prospect of getting her husband back. He had started looking like a gaunt prisoner who had been refused parole as he emerged from his office every day. Now, hopefully, they could get back to something approaching normality.

Her hopes were short lived. Just after breaking the news, Ben asked, "How many oddballs do you know in the *Friends*?" He was referring to the organisation *The Friends of the Lake District* of which Helen was still a member, even though her membership had been the cause of her terrifying ordeal with Hector Snodd. Ben was not a member of *Friends* or any other environmental organisation, mostly out of personal choice, but also because his job as a journalist required him to write unbiased reports.

"Oddballs?" Helen frowned.

"You know what I mean. People with weird hobbies or habits. Train-spotters, stamp collectors, collectors of anything, watchers of *Strictly Come Dancing*, drinkers of herbal tea, early morning swimmers, *Daily Mail* readers."

"They're all like that."

"What?"

"Just kidding. Why?"

"The police are going to be questioning all organisations where somebody obsessed by Wainwright might hang out. They will be asking if you have any obsessive-type personalities in your midst, discreetly of course."

"What if the person they ask is the killer and misleads them?"

Ben smiled. "They will be misled. Now come on, let's try and help the police by analysing your lot for them."

"Oh, that's impossible!" Helen insisted. "How can you draw conclusions from *any* kind of behaviour? We are all unreadable... unpredictable. Anyway, I don't know anybody intimately enough to even hazard a guess. Everybody I know loves Wainwright, but I couldn't point to anybody who idolises him."

"Fair enough... but that's only your immediate reaction. Have a think about it and then let me know if anybody comes to mind."

"I thought you'd handed all this over to the police?"

"I have. Well, all the donkey-work and the footwork. But I'm still staying in touch with Peter about it. I can't just wash my hands of it now."

"I should have known," Helen sighed. "Ah, well, a leopard can't change its spots. I'll have a think, but don't hold your breath."

"Ta."

"By the way, I bumped into Bill in the supermarket yesterday. Poor bloke was so embarrassed. He couldn't stop apologising for following me from Buttermere. I told him it was all my fault, that it was my nervousness and imagination that had caused the problem. Which is true. He had only been trying to help. I thanked him for being so considerate, and insisted he pop in for a cuppa next time he's passing. He seemed relieved and went off smiling."

"And so he would," Ben smiled. "You know he's your biggest fan. Anyway, well done you. I'm off to learn all about obsession now."

Obsession, Ben found, was like most medical conditions – multi-faceted. When present in acts of hero-worship it varied tremendously from teenage idolisation of a pop singer to a recognised psychological condition called "hero-worship syndrome", a condition wherein, at its most severe, the object of worship becomes the central figure in your life. The hero is usually the embodiment of what the individual strives to be but manages to approximate only on those occasions when the "better self" is in the ascendancy. The individual feels inferior to his or her hero and tries to mimic or copy the hero. The hero provides a model, sometimes simplifying decision-making by the authority of a lifestyle and code offered for imitation, or aggravating the conflict inherent in an unattainable ideal.

It was possible, Ben read, to worship a hero and endow him/her with qualities more fantasised than real without making a pathological break with reality. But hero-worship did become a pathological condition when the border between the self and the object of veneration broke down, at which point the individual effectively became his own hero.

Noticeable in this pathological condition was the obsessive's accelerating retreat from reality.

At this point, Ben picked up the phone and rang Peter. He told him about his study of obsession and highlighted the fact that a pathological hero worshipper can often mimic or copy their hero. With this in mind, he suggested that the police should re-examine all witness statements on all ten cases to see if any witness had reported seeing anybody who somehow – by dress, walk, voice, mannerisms – reminded them of Wainwright.

Peter pointed out that there would be hundreds of statements to plough through because as well as "direct" witnesses, the police always sought out "indirect" witnesses – people who had been in the area that day, but were not directly aware of the incident. The more the merrier, had been Ben's response.

Ben finished his reading in no doubt that obsessive hero-worship could lead to a total breakdown of a person's character and reality. Could that lead to the committing of murders? Apparently, yes, if the person's character was already flawed with other problem conditions, such as narcissism. Obsessive narcissists appeared often in the list of modern serial killers.

Ben didn't know, of course, if this was such a case, but he could see that somebody in that pathological condition, not in touch with reality, could do things he *thought* his hero would like to have done, or would like his "twin" to do on his behalf. Had the killer mistaken Wainwright's well-known love of animals and aversion to crowds as a deep-seated hatred of people, and was now doing what he thought Wainwright wanted to do – get rid of them? It would be a travesty if this was the case, because even though Wainwright had given most of his money to animal charities, he was not a misanthrope; he just preferred walking on his own. And even if he had been a misanthrope it could be safely assumed that he did not want people killed.

It was at about this time that all Cumbrian newspapers were invited to a press conference at Police Headquarters in Penrith. Ben guessed it would be to do with his Wainwright information, passed through by Peter. Ben went on behalf of *The Tribune* and heard the head of Crime Command, Chief Superintendent John Baker, issue a statement. In it, he stated that information recently received led them to believe that a number of deaths in the Lake District over the past two years, which had been assumed to be accidental, now needed to be recategorised as unlawful killing. Speaking in a deliberate monotone, he went on to say that they believed the number was in the region of ten, and they were working on the assumption that one person was responsible for the killings. What sounded like a single, loud gasp swept the room. After the gasp, came a barrage of questions. The Chief Superintendent held up his hands, asked them to leave questions until the end of his statement, and carried on in his monotone. As a result of these developments a special team of senior investigating officers, including some from other areas, had been set up under his overall command. He said that they already had a number of important leads in the case, and expressed confidence that they would soon bring it to a satisfactory conclusion. In the meantime he asked the public not to panic. But he also recommended that they did not walk, boat or swim alone and whatever the activity, to try to avoid doing it unaccompanied.

As John Baker concluded, Ben noted that he had not mentioned the Wainwright connection. Clearly, he did not want the killer to know that they knew.

Ben also noted that he had not warned people with the initials A L F R E D to take extra precautions, presumably because this would also give the game away. This could be seen as gambling with people's lives, and Ben sincerely hoped that the killer would be found before another dead body with one of those initials. If another body was found before the killer, Ben would be as guilty as the police for not forewarning them. He was not sure how he would deal with that.

Statement over, the Chief Superintendent allowed questions:

"Is this connected to the attack on Charlotte Ambler on Bassenthwaite Lake?"

"Yes."

"Is Josephine Turner one of the victims?"

"We believe so."

"When can we have a full list of victims?"

"After further consultation with relatives."

"Have we got a genuine serial killer in our midst?"

"If that is the term your newspaper wishes to use, yes."

"How is he killing them?"

"We would prefer not to publicise that at this stage, nor do we know if it is a he."

"Why did the police not spot this earlier?"

"Because the deaths looked like accidents and there was nothing to indicate otherwise."

"Why are you confident you will close the case quickly – what are your leads?"

"You should know better than to ask that question."

And so it went on for another fifteen minutes, until one of the Chief Superintendent's sidekicks, clearly acting on preconceived instructions, leaned over and whispered something in the Superintendent's ear. At which point, he held up his hand to stop the next question, stood up, announced that he had to go, and thanked everybody for coming. Question time was over.

Chapter 47

Six thirty on a mid-April evening and the forest ranger was already drunk. He had finished work early and hit the bottle as soon as he got home. Now, on a mild, cloud-free evening he stood outside his house and peered, glassy-eyed, at the empty, pale blue sky. He was pleased to see the emptiness. He didn't want to see anything move. He didn't want to see that unmistakable wingspan effortlessly glide across his world. He wished them no harm, but he hoped their journey from Africa this year had been difficult; difficult enough to throw them off course, to take them to another lake, another county, another country. They were overdue and his fingers were crossed. He hated the prospect of another summer of bedlam.

He did a lot of hating these days. Without it he knew he would be a pathetic creature, an empty shell. In his numbed alcoholic state he was aware that it was hate that kept him alive, gave him strength and purpose.

During the relatively quiet winter months he had watched with revulsion as more of the forest had been set aside for the amusement of people. They had even created a new position – Recreation Manager. More children's play zones, another orienteering course, new mountain-bike trails. In they would come with their machines and their gaudy clothes, destroying the plants, killing the insects, frightening the birds, leaving their rubbish.

But he had not wasted those months. During those dark, cold days he had managed to do some more culling of the herd. Three more letters had been added. Altogether, since the arrival of the Ospreys last spring, he had obtained the letters I A I G T and thus managed to complete his surname. All he needed now was another A for his Christian name (he never used his full Christian name), and the project would be complete. His altar to the great man would stand as a work of art equal to that produced by the man himself.

He wondered, though, if his search for the final A would have to be delayed. The police were now sniffing around like a pack of trail hounds. From his seat on a bus, he had seen them pulling over Land Rovers at a lay-by. He was curious to know what had put them on the trail. He had only used his Land Rover three times, when absolutely necessary – twice in the dark and once in the mist – and he had taken the extra precaution of smearing mud over the bodywork to cover the Forestry Commission logos and the number plates. All the other times he had used the bus and his legs, just like the great man did. Even if it had been spotted once or twice it was certain that the Land Rover's number-plate had not been read, otherwise the police would already be knocking at his door. Without the number-plate details he was confident the police could not trace him. This was because all Forestry Commission fleet vehicles were purchased centrally by their Mechanical Engineering Services department, and fitted out with additions and modifications for forestry work, before being sent to site.

His Land Rover had been registered by their workshops in Stirling, Scotland. So, he was safe for the moment, but he couldn't take any risks; he would not be taking his Land Rover out of the forest for a long time.

Lowering his eyes from the sky, satisfied that another Osprey-free day had passed, he decided to lie low for a while. There was no hurry. The great man never hurried. He took things slowly. He studied things while smoking his pipe, then made good decisions. He would understand it was time for caution when the hounds were out. He would wait until they had gone away, then he would march out and complete his project.

He stepped back inside his house, into the small hallway. The two dogs that had followed him out, padded silently behind him. In the hall they were met by three cats. Through a door immediately to his left he entered the large garage. The Forestry Commission had built the house in the 1950s shortly after carrying out their first ever powered ropeway extraction test in the forest, which speeded up hillside extraction. Being a public body, they had not skimped on expenditure and the house was a substantial three-bedroom, two-storey building, with an integral garage, over which one of the front bedrooms sat. It had been set into a cutaway in the steep hillside, with views to the front across the access track to the valley beyond, and surrounded on all other sides by forest.

The forest had grown to such an extent over the years that the house now seemed to be part of it, buried within its dark, damp overhangs, the roof covered with a thick, multi-coloured layer of mosses, ferns growing from the gutters, the roughcast walls covered in green mildew and streaks of rust. Pools of stagnant water lay all over the surrounding ground, rarely drying out in the sunless air. The house had the appearance of a wrecked ship lying on a coral reef, gradually being absorbed into its surroundings.

Inside the garage, which was windowless, he switched on the light and immediately grinned when he saw his surroundings. After his wife had left he had spent every spare moment changing the garage from a dirty, utilitarian, space into a spotlessly clean, white-painted chapel of worship. Above the altar, which he had built at the far end of the chapel, hung a large, blown-up photograph of the object of his worship – Alfred Wainwright. He had selected a photograph of the great man when he was quite old, when he had finally decided to show his face to the public. It was the image that most people now had of him – wearing a cloth cap, metal rimmed spectacles, light grey anorak – collar upturned, a steel-stemmed pipe clamped between his teeth, his white hair bulging out from under his cap, and also travelling, neatly-trimmed, down his cheeks. His age gave him *gravitas* and a look of quiet wisdom that perfectly matched the writing in his books. As always, when entering the chapel, the forest ranger bowed his head to his hero.

The white walls all around the chapel were covered with Wainwright memorabilia, from photographs to press cuttings to favourite extracts from his books, which the ranger had enlarged so that he could read them every day and remember them off by heart. On one wall he had built shelves which held all 59 of Wainwright's books. He had covered the floor with green linoleum and placed a large brown rug over it – the colours of nature. On the rug, in the centre of the floor, facing the altar, sat an old brown armchair. Beside it, a side table, a standing lamp, an electric fire, and three metal water-bowls for the animals. Here he sat, when the mood took him, and drank his beer, and read the great man's words, and confirmed that only they knew where humanity was going wrong. They understood that the human race was the most destructive force in the world, its insatiable appetite for instant gratification eventually resulting in the destruction of the things it most desired. Humans were incapable of learning from history, from experience, and carried on their indifferent savagery even after the carnage of wars. They were little more than dressed-up apes, continually finding new ways to grunt at each other, to kill each other. Not content with annihilating each other, their multitudes were now destroying nature – the forests, the rivers, the lakes, the animals, the fish, the birds, the air we breathe, the very things needed for life itself. And now they had brought their predatory behaviour to his forest, to his doorstep. The whole land of Wainwright was now under siege. If this precious land was to survive, if nature was to survive, they had to be controlled. They had to be culled.

At one stage the ranger had thought of installing a fridge to store his alcohol, but then decided it was not in keeping with a chapel, and so he made a trip to the kitchen every time he topped up. He did this now, his entourage of animals following. In the kitchen two more cats, stretched sleepily on a table, watched disinterestedly as he filled his glass with beer from a can taken from the fridge. The rattle of the can as it joined the pile in the bin caused one of the cats to reopen half an eye. At his feet, on the stained, red tiled floor, the two dogs licked their empty food bowls and looked up for more. He ignored their pleading eyes and lolling tongues and carried his glass back to the chapel. One dog and two cats followed him.

He sat down in the armchair, drank some beer, and let his eyes wander over his handiwork. He was proud of the altar he had built; a simple, natural structure in keeping with the man it honoured. He had taken 11 one-inch-thick by one-foot-wide timber boards and cut them in five pairs to different lengths, with the remaining single board being the longest. Arranging them against the wall with the smallest pair in opposite corners, then adding the next longest pair on the inside of those, and so on until the gap in the centre was filled with the longest piece, he had constructed what appeared from the front to be a series of steps leading from both corners of the floor rising up to a single top step, a pyramid of steps. The whole eleven-foot-wide by seven-foot-tall structure was screwed to a wooden frame he had bolted to the wall and above it hung the large photograph of his hero.

Close to the top of each board he had carved the letters of the great man's name as and when he had obtained them. Each letter was deeply carved and took up a space of nine inches square. He had applied black bitumen paint into each carved letter, making them stand out against the timber and the white wall. All letters had now been carved and painted save for one board in the bottom left hand corner which awaited the final A for Alfred. He never tired of looking at the altar and confirming to himself that it was indeed a work of art.

As he continued drinking, becoming less focussed, less interested in his surroundings, he found himself thinking back to the event that had started him on his new, important life.

For a number of Sundays, while out on his afternoon walk through the forest, or while sketching, he had been disturbed and angered by a pair of joy-riders who appeared every Sunday at the same time, tearing along the forest roads at great speed, creating noise and flying debris. Twice they had roared past him, blasting the horn, sticking two fingers up and yelling some inanity through the open car window. Incensed by their behaviour, he had set about laying a trap for them.

One Sunday, just after lunch, he had selected a section of the forest road which they always drove along, and where he had seen a pile of cut logs awaiting pick up in a purpose-made lay-by. He had heaved three logs, each about eight feet long, off the pile and laid them across the road at six-metre intervals, the idea being that the car would just be recovering from the first impact when it would strike the next log and so on, hopefully frightening the life out of the occupants and maybe damaging their car.

After setting it up he had gone for a stroll up a fire-break and then back again, and was starting to sketch when they turned up. He had been shocked to see the fatal result of his trap but not displeased. In fact he had been delighted. He had replaced the logs on the pile in the lay-by and smiled all the way home. And when, a few days later, he read that their names were Askew and Wilkinson – their initials A.W. – the same as the great man's, he saw it as a sign that their deaths were meaningful, had purpose. They would be the basis for a memorial to the great man, a memorial built out of those who would destroy his legacy. And he had been chosen to build it.

Later, when the police, trying to find witnesses to the crash, had questioned him along with everybody else who was in the forest that day, he had simply pleaded ignorance. He had seen and heard nothing; he had been enjoying his Sunday afternoon nap. It was all so easy. Arranging deaths to look like accidents would continue to be easy.

Chapter 48

Ben hoped it was the lull before the storm. After more or less handing everything over to the police, he felt like a becalmed yacht on a windless sea. Released from its perpetual machinations his brain had gladly slipped down the gears and was now as relaxed as a purring kitten. He finally got to see, hear, smell the remainder of spring as he accompanied Helen on long walks by the lakes and over the fells.

It was a dry spring as usual. The lakes had dropped their water-levels, indecently exposing their grey bottoms. The ghylls no longer punctuated the fells like white exclamation marks, their absence revealing the crooked cavities behind their gushing smiles. As if emasculated, the dwindling rivers had lost their drive and meandered aimlessly, stopping to waltz with every stone along the way. Ben was happy to see the lambs, hear the birds, smell the fresh green bracken as it pushed its way through last year's rusted carpet.

He enrolled again in his art lessons, being welcomed back by tutor Roger Coulson, whose ever-lengthening white hair made him look more than ever like Albert Einstein.

But all the while his ear was waiting for a phone call from Peter, or even Bill after talking with Peter. The police had expressed confidence that the leads they had would soon lead them to an arrest. They had a very large team at work. Ben was waiting to hear their results. He was waiting for the storm to break, for the killer to be revealed.

And nothing happened. The phone didn't ring. Peter had nothing worthwhile to report when they met for golf. Using a proforma for consistency, the police had interviewed over three hundred Land Rover 90 owners in Cumbria, using the TIE process (Trace, Interview and Eliminate), and nothing suspicious had emerged. They had checked all of the camera-operated ANPR (Automatic Number Plate Readers) located around the county, which register passing vehicles then upload their details into an intelligence database. They had also checked all local CCTV systems. Nothing had emerged from these checks. And, so far, nothing had come from contact with the *Wainwright Society* or specialist booksellers.

Helen was pestering him to take a holiday. She wanted to go again to Sutherland, to see the wide-open spaces, the beautiful white beaches, the strange, thimble-shaped mountains; to breathe the clean, clear air coming down from the Arctic. She thought it would do him good to get away from it all for a while, to let that great emptiness of the north release the tight coil of expectation she could sense within him. But he wouldn't go. He felt he couldn't go. Not until this job was done. How could you go on holiday when somebody capable of cold bloodedly destroying Josephine Turner was roaming free?

Having lost that battle, Helen, with typical feminine guile, used her "defeat" as a means to get him to do some spring cleaning. "Since you won't go on holiday and you now have time on your hands…"

Outmanoeuvred, Ben set about doing those things that a British spring demands, particularly after a severe winter. Lawns to de-moss, gutters to de-leaf, paintwork to wash down, joints to refill, cracks to repair, mildew to remove, garden furniture to varnish, hedges and shrubs to tidy up, rubbish to burn, windows to clean.

After the imprisonment of winter, Ben enjoyed working outdoors, using his hands instead of his brain, finding company and entertainment in the antics of the pheasants and mallards, discovering nests with chicks in the hedges, hearing the buzzards, watching the geese formations overhead, feeling the spring of spring.

Two weeks of concentrated effort later, he looked on the results with satisfaction. Helen, after pointing out that he had "not quite" cleaned the windows to her standards, went on to give the rest of his work her tick of approval. Then she asked him to go inside and clean out his office.

The next day he was sitting in his office chair, contemplating where to start, when the phone rang.

"Finally got something," Peter said. "Don't get excited, it just confirms your theory, but it doesn't solve anything."

"What is it?" Ben *was* excited; getting a theory confirmed was as exciting as it got these days.

"They ploughed through all the witness statements on the ten cases and came across two sightings of an old man who looked like Wainwright. A walker on Loughrigg Fell, where Colin Grant's body was found, said he passed an old man wearing an old fashioned cap and anorak. He also noticed white sideburns. He didn't witness anything suspicious, he was just describing who he had seen on the fell that day."

"The second witness, on the John Appleton case, actually mentioned Wainwright's name. He said he had been walking on Catbells that day and had passed an old man who looked like Wainwright. That's all the statement said, so they went to interview him at his home in Appleby. He wasn't able to recall all the detail, but he confirmed that an old man who reminded him of Wainwright had passed him. He says he stood out because he looked so old-fashioned. He said he was dressed for a stroll in a park rather than on the fells. He remembered the white sideburns, and glasses, and his trousers tucked into his socks."

"I take it this witness hadn't seen anything suspicious either?" Ben queried.

"No."

"Did they say whether this old man was short or tall, thin or fat?"

There was a short pause. Peter was obviously reading. "One says medium height, medium build, the other says about six foot, medium build. Which is pretty close."

Ben was trying to think of another question when Peter said, "Doesn't sound very promising, does it? How many old codgers do you know who can swim out into a lake and turn a boat over?"

"I wouldn't dismiss it completely," Ben suggested. "Helen tells me there are some real tough pensioners out there; people who have swum all their lives and still train every day. We also have the possibility – far-fetched I grant you – that he isn't an old man, but a younger man wearing a disguise. Remember, if this person is obsessed with Wainwright and wants to look like him, he would have to make some alteration to his appearance no matter how old he is."

"Mmm, possible; far-fetched as you say, but possible."

"There *has* to be something in this, don't you think," Ben stressed. "The same person sighted at two of the ten cases?"

"Could just be coincidence," Peter said. "It happens all the time. And with neither of the witnesses having seen anything suspicious, the sightings couldn't be used as evidence of a crime anyway."

"So why are you telling me this?" Ben snapped in frustration, immediately regretting his tone.

"Just to let you know that I am passing on everything I get. There has been so little to report. I wanted you to know that I wasn't holding anything back."

"Right… yes… thanks Peter, I appreciate it. As you say, it's not going well is it, nothing to report for weeks."

"Catch you later, Ben." The line went dead.

"Blast!" Ben cursed, as he put the phone down. He didn't want to get on the wrong side of Peter.

Returning to his chores, Ben set about tidying up the shelves alongside his desk which carried the usual office accoutrements – copy paper, laminator machine and paper, files, maps, address book, boxes of printer inks, reading lamp and sundry document files.

Then he turned to the plethora of documents spread all over the spare bed, it being a too useful place to park things until needed rather than file them away. As always, he was surprised at how much stuff, which seemed important at the time, could now be thrown away, having outlived their necessity or relevance. The wastepaper basket started to bulge.

After tidying up a small side table covered in newspapers and magazines, held down with paperweights and an old pewter beer mug full of pens, pencils and highlighters, Ben turned his attention to a pile of cardboard boxes of varying sizes which had accumulated in a corner. One or two he would keep; most he would remove to the recycling bin outside.

Finally, he got down to tidying up his desk, on which sat his computer monitor, keyboard and associated printer. Under and around these items were scattered eight separate piles of paper, the significance of their separateness gradually fading as time passed. Ben sat down and painstakingly went through each pile, reading each document to assess its keep-worthiness. Inevitably, the wastepaper basket couldn't cope and had to be emptied before he could continue.

He was approaching the bottom of a pile that sat in front of the printer when he came across the list containing the names of members of Keswick Rambling Club, which he had requested from the membership secretary seven months ago. He had intended returning to the case of Elizabeth Lamb of Lorton who had disappeared and never been found, but other events had taken over. The case as well as the list had faded to the bottom of the pile. On the list he had highlighted, in yellow, the names of a few members he had intended to contact to question them about Mrs Lamb. He had been hoping one of them might have a snippet of information which Mrs Lamb may have privately shared with them, which they had not given to the police and which would give him a lead as to her whereabouts, be she alive or dead.

Ben sat staring at the list, wondering whether to bin it or to consider taking up the cause again. Mrs Lamb had been missing now for over two years; the trail was inevitably getting colder. He was still marginally involved with the Wainwright case, and Helen would kill him if he took it on after just giving himself and her, some spare time again.

Yet it was against his nature to give up on a challenge, particularly one that could be so rewarding if he succeeded. Eventually, he decided to compromise. He would take up the challenge again, but not now. He would wait a month or two, spend some summer months with Helen, hope the Wainwright case would end and then he would go back to the search for Mrs Lamb.

He was about to put the list in his IN tray (i.e. the pile just to the right of the monitor) when he remembered that at one time Mrs Lamb's case had been included among the "accidental deaths" files of the police, based on the assumption that she could have been one of Stott's victims. Ben had also included her on his database at one time for the same reason. Being a stickler for thoroughness (almost to the point of obsession, he thought ruefully), Ben now had no choice but to run her case through his mind again, now that Stott had been replaced by a killer obsessed with Wainwright.

At first glance she did not appear to be connected to the Wainwright case. She was not an outsider, having been born and bred in the Lake District. And her surname's initial – L – did not fit the surname criteria. The name WAINWRIGHT, anyway, had been completed. And since he was always known as A Wainwright the letter A was probably the only one the killer had plans on collecting, if he had plans at all.

But what if he was going for the full Christian name – ALFRED? Then she did meet the criteria. What if the killer had already disposed of other people with initials matching the Christian name, but their bodies had also not been found? Ben was becoming excited and horrified at the same time. She *could* be connected to the Wainwright case; there *could* be more bodies to be found. If that was the case then the Missing Persons Bureau data would have to be consulted.

It was equally possible that the fact she was a local was enough to *protect* her from any inclusion in the killer's plan.

It was also possible that she was the killer's *only* victim so far in his search for matches to ALFRED, and therefore there could be five victims yet to come.

Warming to the task, Ben's brain now threw up another frightening, though unlikely, possibility. What if it wasn't Elizabeth Lamb's surname that attracted the killer, but her Christian name? The name *Elizabeth* was often abbreviated to *Betty* – the name of Wainwright's wife. What if the killer had abducted Elizabeth Lamb so that he could live with his own version of *Betty*? Ben couldn't decide if this was good news or bad news. Elizabeth Lamb could still be alive, but what state would she be in if she had been held captive for two years by an insane killer?

Without looking for further variables, Ben decided that Elizabeth Lamb's case could *not* now be put on the back burner. It needed immediate investigation along with the other cases. Keen as he was to get stuck into it himself, he knew he had to hand it over to the police. He also had a promise to Helen to keep.

It took about fifteen minutes to pass on all of his thoughts and theories about Elizabeth Lamb's case to Peter, listen to Peter's usual questioning of his theories and then agree that it should be passed on to CID. Ben knew this would mean more brownie points for Peter in his quest to join them and wondered what personal embellishments Peter would make to his submission in order to make it look like the thinking had come from him. Deep in his heart, though, Ben didn't really care about these peripheral matters. What *really* mattered to him was stopping the killing.

It took Ben a further ten minutes to pass on his latest discovery to Helen, whose face took on a look of resignation as he took her through his theoretical possibilities. He spent another five minutes trying to persuade her that since he had passed it to the police he would not be getting involved himself. When he had finished, the look on Helen's face had not changed.

Chapter 49

Breakfast over, Helen was getting ready to go to work; she had a full day ahead of her, a mixture of the routine and the new. She was not sure when she would get home.

"There's some shepherd's pie in the fridge," she said. "Can you do some fresh veg to go with it?"

Ben was sitting comfortably, still in his dressing gown, listening to a radio voice tell him some stories. They were the usual horror stories from around the world, but the polished indifference with which the voice relayed them helped to make them sound as routine as milk with cornflakes. "Will do," he said.

"Are you going for a walk today?" Helen asked. She knew he didn't have much work on.

Ben switched off the radio. "I was thinking of giving Thornbeck Forest a try; long time since I've walked over there."

Helen glared at him. "You are so predictable."

"What do you mean?"

"Don't play the innocent. Elizabeth Lamb's car was parked near Thornbeck Forest when she went missing, wasn't it?"

Ben held up his hands. "Okay, guilty as charged. But where's the harm. I'm going walking anyway. Might as well walk there as anywhere."

"But what do you expect to find after all this time? The forest was searched for weeks by the Mountain Rescue teams and the police?"

"I'll probably find nothing," Ben said. "But remember, they were looking for a walker, Mrs Lamb, who had gone missing in the winter. A not uncommon event. They were searching a forest which is on the slope of a 1800-feet-high fell. It is full of crags and ravines and undulations. They would be expecting Mrs Lamb to have slipped or fallen. They would be expecting to find her body somewhere in the forest, having died of her injuries or hypothermia." Ben paused, assuming his meaning was clear.

"And...?" Helen frowned.

Ben couldn't stifle his sigh. It was not an impatient sigh, but an habitual one; one that he frequently made before having to explain things that were crystal clear in *his* head but not, apparently, in other heads. "They were not looking for somebody they suspected of having been abducted. Consequently their search was probably limited to the forest itself and would not include a thorough search of the few houses that are in and around the edge of the forest. I would guess they paid each house a visit to ask if the occupiers had seen Mrs Lamb, and they might have made a cursory search, but I doubt if they would have made a comprehensive one."

"Why don't you find out... ask Peter?"

Ben hesitated. "No, I've already handed it over. What I'm doing today is not worth involving him. It's just an informal walkabout to see where Mrs Lamb might have come close to properties. If I find any I'll make a list and hand that over to Peter."

"And what if the abductor, if one exists, doesn't live in or near the forest? What if she was abducted by a man in a car who grabbed her and drove off to Land's End?"

"Even better, we get to walk along the Cornish coastal path again."

Seeing the threat of violence in Helen's eyes, Ben quickly added, "I will have had a pleasant afternoon's walk in the fresh air: the time will not have been wasted."

Helen shook her head, the look of resignation returning. "I don't know why I waste *my* time. I can't win, can I?"

Ben sensed more than resignation. "You're not worried, are you?"

"Of course I'm worried. I worry every time you just go out for a walk, never mind trying to find serial killers at the same time. You're always getting into scrapes: remember that time on Dalehead when you came back all scratched and bruised. And it's not long ago, is it, since you were attacked in our garden."

"Don't forget the briefcase attack…"

Helen exploded. "Be serious, Ben! You are not getting any younger. You have to grow up sometime and stop playing Harrison Ford."

"I'd have preferred Sherlock Holmes."

"There you go again."

"Sorry."

Helen turned away and started to gather her work things together. "I'm always very careful," Ben pleaded to her back.

"I always take my compass and my whistle and my trusty thumb-stick."

Helen, with brief case in hand, turned in the doorway and said, "You know what you can do with your bloody thumb-stick." And she slammed the door behind her.

Ben felt guilty. He had misjudged the situation. He usually got away with playing down problems, joking away serious matters. They had become so close over the years, so involved with each other, their nuances could be transmitted, received and understood without conversation. Yet this time, even with conversation, he had got it wrong. Swearing meant she had been hurt – the last thing he would have wished for.

Now he realised he was also forgetting their morning routine. He leapt from the sofa, dashed out of the back door, and was just in time to see the car pull away. He shouted, "Drive carefully...mind the sheep and the cows and the..." He waved as the car picked up speed, and through the back window he thought he saw Helen's hand wave back.

Before going back in, Ben surveyed the surrounding scene. It promised to be a nice day – the blue sky played hide-and-seek behind light cloud, pushed along by a gentle breeze. The trees were now showing off their full complement of leaves, their faint scents losing out to the smell of the May blossoms, which along with the swifts and house martins were now appearing in April, thanks, they said, to climate change. On the fells, the pale winter pinks and rusts were almost gone; over-painted with shades of summer green. There were no mallards or pheasants on the lawn. They were following their seasonal urges down by the lake, and in the shaded woods.

Ben walked back into the kitchen and approached the small mirror that hung on the wall above the radiator. He peered into it, stroking his unshaven chin, pushing his uncombed hair roughly into place. *Harrison Ford eh?* He squinted his eyes and gritted his teeth to make his jaw look more solid. "A man's gotta do what a man's gotta do," he drawled to his reflection. It rewarded him, as he moved closer, with a close-up of the receding hairline at his temples, going grey. He didn't need reminding about the spreading waistline. He relaxed the squint and the gritted teeth, took on a superior air, and in a clipped Oxford accent said, "Elementary, my dear Watson." Without doubt, and with a touch of regret, he concluded he was more like Holmes than Ford. Anyway, whoever he was like, he had decided to go through with his visit to Thornbeck Forest in the afternoon. Those Hollywood writers had been right: in spite of the pleadings of the "little lady", a man did have to do what a man had to do.

Having spent most of the morning writing up items of news for *The Tribune*, including the recent return of the Bassenthwaite Ospreys, and the completion of the new sewage scheme whose diversions had tested the patience of Keswick's drivers for many weeks, Ben ended it by re-hanging a sagging kitchen cupboard door, and changing a dead light bulb in the hall. He needed to score some brownie points with Helen.

After lunch and a little nap, he booted up his computer and clicked on Google Earth. He wanted to take a birds-eye view of Thornbeck Forest to see where all the forest roads were. As he zoomed in, as though flying a helicopter over the area, he was surprised to see how many roads there were. They came into the forest from all directions and snaked around the forest in convoluted twists and turns looking like contour lines on an ordnance survey map. This was probably because they had no choice but to follow the same line as the contours, the land in this forest among mountains being so diverse and complicated. Some of the roads performed circular tours, others went off into the hills and stopped suddenly; others were joining roads between them; others were small add-ons, like a tail on a dog. There were straight horizontal stretches and long climbing/descending sections full of hair-pin bends.

Ben had also been hoping to see the houses in the forest, but all he saw were approximate shapes and outlines. He knew he needed the actual address names to pinpoint them, although it was possible that their remoteness had precluded them from a visit from Google's roadside camera cars.

Looking at the extent and complexity of the roads, Ben decided it would take too long to walk around all of them. He would have to use the car. Over the years he had become familiar with some of the ways into the forest, their entrances usually having a single wooden pole barrier across the road to deter tourists from entering in the wrong place. However, only some of them had warning signs such as *No unauthorised vehicles allowed beyond this point,* and it was well known that locals took their cars in for their Sunday afternoon stroll. Unfortunately, so did the occasional joy-rider.

It had been years since Ben and Helen had walked in the forest even though it was close to home. They, like most fell-walkers, preferred the open fells where magnificent views were available all the time, on the ascent and descent. Only occasionally in the forest did you come across an open space where views were possible.

It was about two thirty when Ben finally set out in his car. He wrote a note to that effect and left it on the kitchen table for Helen. He was wearing his walking boots just in case he needed to do some, and carried his usual outdoor stuff in a small backpack. He placed it and some waterproofs in the boot.

Mrs Lamb's car had been found in a small public parking space about 100 metres into the forest, at its northernmost edge. Ben arrived there at about three o'clock. He was familiar with this small corner of the forest, often walking through it as an alternative way off one of his favourite fells. He knew, therefore, that shortly after passing the public car park he would come across a sign announcing: *No unauthorised vehicles allowed beyond this point.* Another sign warned walkers that there was an electricity substation ahead. There was, however, no barrier at this point and Ben carried on until he reached a familiar large clearing, roughly the size of a football pitch. This had been a Forestry Commission depot for many years. It contained numerous large timber and metal/brick storage buildings, piles of cut timber, loading and turning bays, a horizontal oil tank, a derelict petrol pump and a pair of semi-detached houses with small front gardens. One of the houses had an old Ford Fiesta standing to one side. There appeared to be no activity going on; the place was devoid of people. At the far end of the depot Ben could see a pole barrier and further signs warning vehicles not to proceed further along the forest road.

Ben stopped his car just past the two semis and tried to look nonchalant as he left the car and strolled back towards them. The weather had stayed kind all day and both houses had washing hanging out on lines, both bearing children's clothes as well as adults'. Some abandoned plastic toys were visible in one of the gardens, and a trampoline in the other. Through the front window of the semi on his left Ben could see a woman sitting with her back to the window, her stooped, concentrated posture telling him that she was working on a laptop, though he couldn't see it.

As he turned to walk back to his car, a woman aged about thirty appeared from the back of the house on the right and got into the blue car. She appeared to be lost in thought and took no notice of Ben as she swept quickly past him. *Late for the school run,* was Ben's immediate thought.

These normal domestic scenes, with women and children present, meant almost certainly that the killer did not live here, and that Elizabeth Lamb was not being held captive in either of these houses. And yet, nothing could be discounted since the activities of Fred and Rose West showed the world there were no limits to human depravity. Mrs Lamb had probably walked past these houses; they had to be searched. Back in the car, Ben made a note in his notebook and marked the location on a map of the forest he had downloaded and printed before leaving home.

He drove on to the far end of the depot, got out of the car, lifted and swung the pole barrier out of the way, drove forward, replaced the barrier, and set off to drive through the winding, dark canyons of the forest.

*

The cats skidded on the kitchen floor in their haste to get out; the dogs yelped and whined. Their post-lunch siesta had been noisily disturbed by the sound of one metal can being violently introduced to many.

The forest ranger watched the can bounce off the top of the pile and roll onto the tiled floor. He picked up his beer, lurched from the kitchen to the hall, from the hall into the chapel. He banged his glass down on the side table and slumped into the armchair. He had been doing this since lunchtime - two hours ago. The bastards had fired him. Two pen-pushing bastards in suits.

The new Area Manager, an accountant, whose bulbous face, double chin and burgeoning stomach told of years of physical inactivity, had been brought in five months ago to "maximise the introduction and effectiveness of our new mission statement, and optimise fiscal opportunities and profit outcomes." To the ranger, this imported American jargon epitomised all that was wrong with today's so-called "march of progress". He recalled Wainwright's sceptical words (*The Northern Fells, Bakestall 3*) "…but nobody ever tells us where it is marching". Not only was the peace of the forest being destroyed by it, so was the English language.

The *'Human Resources'* Manager, a baby-faced twenty-something in an immaculate dark blue suit, white shirt, and college tie sat alongside the Area Manager as he was told, "we will have to let you go" – more American crap – meaning "you are fucking fired". Twenty-four years ago he had been hired by a sixty-year-old *Personnel* Manager who had worked his way up from the forest floor; whose handshake proved it.

He had already had two warnings about his bad time-keeping, surly manner with clients (there had been complaints in the suggestions box), general lack of enthusiasm, untidy appearance etc etc. "You are clearly not keen to join us on our exciting new journey," the Area Manager said. "The rest of the team are all systems go, but you have been dragging your feet in the background. Your general behaviour leads us to believe you are drinking heavily, which is a danger to yourself and to others. We can't allow this to continue. We can't carry passengers." The Human Resources Manager chipped in with, "Because of your long-service history, we have decided to make your position redundant rather than terminate your employment. This means you will receive a substantial redundancy payment as well as your one month's notice salary."

"During your notice period we expect you to hand over your duties to the new Recreation Manager and assist him in any way you can," the Area Manager concluded.

As he sat listening to the two suit-clad know-nothings, the forest ranger felt his lava rising. His world was about to fall apart. His life in the forest was coming to an end. Worst of all, it was being taken away by these stupid bastards and people like them. In a flash of foresight, he saw himself pushing aside the desk that separated them, placing his hands around their throats, and slowly strangling them. These little men didn't know who they were dealing with. *His* mission statement was almost complete; now he was thinking of adding to it.

But he had controlled his anger then; decided to save it for later. Their turn would come. Revenge was sweeter when deliberately delayed; gave you time to savour it. He was sitting doing that right now.

He had returned to his house immediately after the meeting. There was no way he was going to do any more work; no way he was going to assist a Recreation Manager. He had changed from his work clothes into his Wainwright gear, fed the occupants, grabbed his first beer and moved into the chapel. Here he sat, peering at the altar through his glasses, sucking on his pipe, seeking inspiration from the great man, gradually merging with him. He had not eaten.

*

Ben swung his car round yet another hair-pin bend, then put his foot down as he climbed another hill. He was starting to enjoy himself; began to see himself as one of those rally drivers who tore along forest roads, skidding sideways as they took the corners, splattering the spectators with debris. He could afford to let his imagination wander because he was pretty certain he wouldn't find any more houses within this central area of the forest; he was just going through the motions, being his usually thorough self.

He was cruising along a straight stretch when his mobile rang. He braked to a halt at the same time as taking the phone from his pocket.

"Where are you?" Helen asked. Her voice was distant, faint; typical Lake District reception.

"In Thornbeck Forest."

"Where exactly?"

"Are you checking on me? Do you think I'm out with me fancy woman?"

"Just tell me."

"I don't know, somewhere in the middle I guess. Shouldn't be too long before I reach the Visitor Centre. I might stop there for a cuppa. Where are you?"

"Grasmere, having my tea break right now. Sorry for slamming out like that, I was just worried about you, and you weren't taking me seriously. Nothing new there I suppose."

"What's with all this worrying all of a sudden?"

"I don't know, I just have a feeling something bad is going to happen."

"It is. I'm going to knock all this worrying nonsense out of your head. There's going to be some domestic violence when you get home tonight."

Helen started to laugh, but suddenly stopped. A long silence followed.

"Are you still there?" Ben enquired.

"Yes, I... I'd better get going. Enjoy your cuppa... see you later. Take care."

She was gone before Ben had time to say goodbye. He put his phone back in his pocket and for a moment sat and stared out of the car window. Something? She hadn't explained why she wanted to know *exactly* where he was.

A movement in the roadside ditch caught his eye. A flurry of fur and then stillness. A stoat ran off with a mouse in its mouth.

Ben started the car and continued his journey through the forest. Another ten minutes passed without incident. As he expected, there were no more houses to be seen. Five more minutes brought him to the large car park of the Visitor Centre.

It was more than half full. People were milling around, coming and going between the car park and the large main building. Cycles were being loaded on and off roof-racks. Cyclists in their skin-tight clothes and protective headwear looked like aliens off a film set.

Ben parked up, headed for the café, enjoyed a pot of tea and treated himself to a scone with jam. Surrounded by families on holiday, dressed in their outdoor gear, cheerfully ignoring their little darlings while they ran all over the place, Ben began to feel uncomfortable. He felt like an unwelcome stranger, a black stain on a white sheet. They were here to relax, have fun, forget their work, their worries. They had apparently forgotten, or chosen to ignore, the media publicity about the killer in the Lake District; somebody who could be watching them right now, planning his next attack. Ben felt he should stand up and shout some kind of warning. But they wouldn't thank him for spoiling their holiday. The best thing he could do was remove himself from their presence, take his darkness away from them, get back into the forest where darkness was not a stranger.

Leaving the café, which was an integral part of the large retail building, Ben looked around at the other buildings – cycle shop, toilet block, lecture room etc. All should be searched he reckoned; Mrs Lamb could have passed this way. He made a brief note in his notebook, adding in brackets – *check all V.C. staff were questioned*. Marking the map wasn't necessary.

Back on the main forest road, he drove a quarter of a mile before pulling into another clearing he was familiar with. This was another Forestry Commission depot, smaller than the first and probably used as offices judging by the holiday lodge type of timber buildings. On the edge of the clearing stood another pair of semi-detached houses, identical to those in the first depot. Ben parked his car and started to walk towards the semis. He saw a face watching him from one of the office buildings. The face moved and shortly afterwards the office door opened. "Can I help you?" said a balding man, with rolled-up shirt sleeves, in a tone that implied more "bugger off" than any genuine offer of assistance. He was probably tired of telling tourists they had taken the wrong turn for the Visitor Centre.

Not wanting to explain his purpose, Ben said, innocently, "I take it this isn't the Visitor Centre?"

"Four hundred yards up the road," the man stated, flatly, like an actor doing his 43rd take. He pointed his finger in the direction, then stood waiting while Ben returned to his car. Only when Ben was driving out of the clearing did he turn and go back into his office.

It didn't matter. Back on the road, Ben stopped and made a note that the semis and the offices should be searched. Again, no mark on the map was necessary. Moving on, it wasn't long before he came to a fork in the road. The left branch seemed to swing back into the area of forest from which he had just come, while the right probably led to a separate flank of forest which filled a valley and also covered the lower reaches of a neighbouring mountain. Ben took the left fork, thinking it best to complete one section of forest before moving onto another. The road climbed gently across the slope of the fell before suddenly coming to a junction near the fell top. It was clearly one of the short roads that cut across between main routes. Ben turned right and enjoyed a view of the lake as the road dropped in a straight line down the fell. Halfway down the fell, Ben saw a right-hand bend ahead. As he slowed to take it, he noticed a minor road on his left, with a pole barrier across it. He slowed to a halt at the barrier, and read PRIVATE – NO PUBLIC ACCESS. He assumed this must be one of those little add-on roads he had seen on Google Earth – a tail on a dog.

Whatever it was, it needed investigating. Ben got out of the car and approached the barrier. He was about to lift it and swing it out of the way when he saw that it was secured to the support with a chain and lock. He gave it a try, but it wouldn't budge. He returned to the car and parked it close to the side of the road, leaving enough space for other vehicles to pass. He locked the car, ducked under the pole barrier, and set off on foot along the minor road. It started off as a long straight road, the land dropping away to his right, affording occasional views of the lake through gaps in the trees, with the land on his left climbing steeply up the fell.

Now he was enjoying himself, stretching his legs after the confinement of the car, inhaling the subtle redolence of the trees, hearing coal tits twittering, a buzzard keening overhead. He had walked about 300 metres when he saw what appeared to be a small clearing ahead.

Ben got a shock when he entered the clearing. It was like walking into an abandoned builders' merchant yard. There were small stacks of bricks, half-open bags of cement, coils of wire, trailing ropes, slates, tiles, wooden pallets, copper pipe, plastic drainage pipe etc, all scattered about, all covered with mildew. Stacks of logs of various lengths stood close to a wooden lean-to, which provided cover to an electric saw. The ground here was thick with sawdust.

Most of the clutter lay to the left of a detached house that looked as abandoned as its surroundings. It was tucked into the side of the fell, sheltered by the umbrella of the surrounding trees. Moss covered the roof; the walls were green with mould. About ten metres to the right of the house, there was a large wooden structure. All that was visible was its nearside wall. It looked like it might be a carport, standing sideways-on to the house.

As he got closer to the house, Ben noticed that the signs of neglect included filthy windows covered in cobwebs, grass growing in the gutters and sacks and boxes of refuse overflowing with bottles and cans and kitchen waste. He could see, however, that behind the surface neglect, the house was a good building with a great view of the fells on the other side of the lake. You could probably see the lake itself from the bedroom windows. He guessed it must have been a forest manager's house at one time. It even had an integral garage. Ben assumed that the house was unoccupied, but just in case it was occupied he took a wide berth as he circled around to its right-hand side. He didn't want to disturb anybody.

*

The barking of the dogs woke the forest ranger. They were also scratching at the door. He lifted his head from his chest. He was still slumped in the armchair. His glasses sat, precariously, on the tip of his nose. He pushed them up with his middle finger and looked at his watch. His watch said four thirty-five. His pipe had fallen onto the floor. Bleary-eyed, he eased himself up into a sitting position and reached for it. He put it, shakily, on the side table.

The last thing he could remember was planning to kill the Area Manager, and that other twat if he got the chance, and burn down the Visitor Centre on the day he had to leave the forest. He would show them; he would leave his mark. He would go out in a blaze of glory.

The accidental metaphor went unnoticed as he stared ahead, trying to get his alcohol-ravaged mind to switch on again. Now he realised his body was hot, his skin sweating. His mouth was so dry he had trouble operating its moving parts. His tongue had glued itself to the roof of his mouth and it took a concentrated effort to pry it off. Somebody had installed drums in his temples and was playing a steady, throbbing, beat. He needed water. The animals... the animals... they needed water... and food. He tried to rise quickly but the drum in his head banged louder. He tried again, slowly, and managed to make his way to the door.

The excited animals leapt up as he opened the door, their nails and claws penetrating his trousers, scratching his thighs. "DOWN," he managed to shout, his throat catching with the effort. They followed him, rubbing against his ankles, as he shuffled along the hall and into the kitchen.

His feet kicked and crushed discarded cans as he levered a stained cup from the pile on the draining board, filled it with water and gulped it down. He filled the kettle with water and slowly went around the animals' drink bowls and topped them up. Next, he opened four cans of dog and cat food, and went around and spooned the contents into their bowls. All of the animals settled down to the urgent task of eating and drinking. Except one. The young mongrel was a fairly new member of the family. It had stayed in the hall, and stood beside the front door barking at it. It must have heard something outside.

The forest ranger leaned over the kitchen sink and looked through the smeared window, turning his head to the right, towards the front of the house. A man came into view, walking slowly, glancing around like a sightseeing tourist. The initial shock of seeing somebody soon dissipated. Stupid, lost, tourists occasionally came by. He would soon be gone. While at the sink, the forest ranger filled his cup again, and drank the water slowly while watching the man outside. *The cheeky bugger's still coming. He's heading for the back of the house. What the hell does he want? If he thinks the house is empty and he's on the rob he has a surprise coming. I'll have the bastard's guts if he picks something up.*

The man approached the carport, glanced in, and suddenly stopped, his back to the house. He seemed to be taking something out of his inside jacket pocket. It looked as though he was writing something. *SHIT, he's taking down the number of the Land Rover. NO, can't have that... can't have that. I'm stuffed if that gets out...*

Without stopping to think, the forest ranger moved to the back door, and picked up the long-handled log splitter that always stood leaning against the wall, behind the door. It was a new Swedish one he had bought recently, with a long, smooth hickory shaft and a special steel head that weighed 2.4kg. It was a beauty, making splitting the logs as easy as cracking eggs. It was going to be messy.

*

The barking of the dogs stopped Ben in his tracks. He stood still for a couple of minutes. When nobody came out or appeared at a window, he assumed the dogs were alone in the house, waiting for their master's return. He continued his circumnavigation of the house, deciding to check out what was round the back. He drew alongside what he could now see was indeed a carport. He glanced inside. Standing in the shadowed space was a Land Rover Defender 90. Ben stopped breathing. It had an unfamiliar number plate. It had not been registered in Cumbria. Quickly, he pulled his notebook and pen from his inside pocket. His hands were almost trembling as he wrote down the number. He put the notebook back in his pocket and was reaching for his mobile when he heard a crashing noise behind him. He turned and saw a white-haired man coming out of the house towards him, the door having been flung open. Three barking dogs spilled out behind him. Next, he spotted the axe in the man's hand, and even from a distance he could see a wild, jaundiced, madness in the man's eyes. There was no doubting the man's intention.

The man started to circle to Ben's left, the snarling dogs following him. Ben wondered why, as he backed away to his right. He found out immediately when he turned to run. There seemed to be nowhere to run to. All the cut-away fell side behind the carport and to the rear of the house had been shored up with a concrete retaining wall almost as high as the house eaves. But there should be a gap round the back, between the house and the retaining wall. Ben ran 15 metres to find out. It was blocked with rubbish – fencing, mattresses, bed, old furniture, rusting fridge, rolls of rotting carpet etc. He didn't think he could scramble over it, it was too unstable and imposing. Anyway, he didn't have time.

Now, completely terrified, his body buzzing with adrenaline, Ben turned to face the man. The man came towards him, slowly, menacingly, his axe hanging loose in his right hand, almost touching the ground, the dogs barking ferociously at his side. There was a slight uncertainty in his gait, as though he was drunk. Suddenly, when about five metres away, the man stopped like a frozen statue, and stared at Ben. Then he blinked and shook his head and kept coming. In that moment Ben noticed how odd he looked. Something about him looked unreal, artificial. For a second there was even something vaguely familiar about him.

As the man came ever closer, Ben felt time slow down. He continued to back away, waiting for the man to lunge. As he did so, his mind decided to trip out. One second it was filled with pure fear, another, it went blank – absolutely empty and unstressed – as if he was strolling around his garden. Then a thousand thoughts and pictures fought to take over, flashing across his mind like lightning bolts. Most of them contained Helen. *God…what will happen to Helen? I'm sorry Helen, I should have listened to you.* He suddenly realised he had spoken the words out loud, not only thought them.

The man didn't seem to be in a hurry. He was following Ben's dodging movements slowly, plodding along like an experienced boxer gradually edging his opponent into a corner. The dogs continued beside him, creating a snarling, bared-teeth barrier. Ben felt like a sheep being rounded up. At times there was a sneer on the man's face. Ben didn't know if it was a sneer of hatred or of enjoyment.

He kept looking around for something to use to protect himself, but there was just small general detritus in the area, nothing substantial enough to ward off a blow from a steel axe. As he retreated into the corner formed where the side and back retaining walls met, he noticed an old steel dustbin that contained a small, withering tree. Quickly, he dashed back to it, knocked it over, pulled the tree out, spilling the soil out in the process. He picked it up, holding both ends, ignoring the jagged, rusting steel that was now cutting into his right hand, and held it, horizontally, in front of his chest. He stood and waited. There was nowhere left to run.

The man came close and swung his axe. The blow almost destroyed the bin. It pushed the impact area inwards until it struck the opposite side, sending Ben reeling backwards, dropping the remains of the bin as he did so. He felt as if he had been hit by a charging rhino. He gasped as his lungs contracted. Pain rippled across his chest. He felt his notebook push into his ribs. He managed to stay on his feet, but staggered backwards until he felt the wall at his back. The man started to wind the axe up again…

"OI!" A very loud voice stopped the action. The man turned. The dogs stopped barking. Ben, clutching his chest, looked past the man and saw another man, about 20 metres away, coming towards them. A burly man, marching quickly, almost like a soldier on parade. Ben knew that walk. It was Bill. "Watch out, Bill," Ben shouted, "he's got an axe."

"I'll take that," Bill shouted, holding his hand out as he continued to close.

The man spread his legs apart and hefted the axe up, like a baseball player ready to strike.

"Get back, Bill, he'll kill you," Ben shouted.

Bill kept coming with his hand still out. "I'll take that," he shouted again, in a voice of uncompromising authority. By now the dogs had run to Bill and surrounded him, snarling and barking. Bill ignored them and kept his eyes on the man.

The man tensed, ready to swing the axe.

Bill never stopped marching. He continued right up to the man, swung his right foot and kicked the man between his legs. The man roared with pain, doubled up, dropped the axe, and held both hands to his genitals. Bill swung his right fist in a powerful pendulum-like action and struck the man on the side of the head. He went down as though shot.

Bill checked the man's head position to make sure his airways were clear, and then walked over to Ben, examining his right hand as he did so. "You okay, mate?" he said, making it sound like a routine enquiry after a coughing spell.

"Jesus, Bill," Ben wheezed. "You've just saved my life. I've never seen anything so brave. Christ, you could have been killed." For a moment the thought of what he had just seen, just experienced, overwhelmed Ben, and he couldn't speak. A minute ago he could have been lying dead on the ground. Then along comes Bill, good old Bill, not too bright Bill, and does the most amazing thing Ben has ever seen, and saves his life. Ben felt humble and guilty. He was lost for words. He reached out and put his arms around Bill and, wincing with pain, hugged him. Bill stood, embarrassed, not sure what to do with his arms. "Thanks, mate," Ben whispered, "I'll never forget this."

Bill pulled out of the embrace, obviously keen to restore manliness to the situation. "Let's get that joker tied up before he wakes up." He started to walk towards the man, who was now surrounded by quiet, puzzled dogs.

Ben followed, saying, as he held his chest, "Can you manage on your own? I think I might have a cracked rib or two."

"No bother. You find somewhere to sit and stay still."

Bill searched the area and eventually found some suitable rope, underneath a tarpaulin that played host to pools of stagnant water, no doubt home to the eggs of summer's biting insects. He took the rope to the man. Ben was looking down at him. The man's hair looked strangely out of place. Ben started to reach down towards it. "Don't touch him," Bill warned, as he dropped the rope and pulled out his mobile. He proceeded to take some photographs of the man as he lay unconscious, the axe close by. "Need to get some shots to prove why I had to hit him," Bill explained. "With these and you as a witness I have a good chance of avoiding prosecution."

"Are you serious?"

"Semi. Should be okay if this guy's got form."

"I think you'll find he's our killer," Ben said, quietly.

Bill looked at him. "Are *you* serious?"

Ben nodded. "Take a look in that carport. There's a Defender 90. I was taking down its number when he attacked me."

Bill looked from Ben to the man while the news sank in. "Better get the crazy gang up here," he said, with authority. "Can you phone them while I tie him up? Tell them we need the works – forensics, detectives, at least four uniformed men, a medic, possibly an ambulance, the RSPCA with a van, and some steel cutters or a chainsaw for that pole barrier.

Ben took out his phone and tried to ring Peter. The signal was poor. He walked away from the house towards the lake and tried again. Better. He got through to Peter and quickly relayed the location, the story, and Bill's list of requirements. Behind Peter's business-like response, in which he promised men would be there within twenty minutes, Ben could sense his excitement. He could almost see him racing down the corridor shouting "We've got him! We've got him".

Ben walked back to rejoin Bill and found he had the man tied up. It looked like the job of an expert. The ankles were tied together, as were the hands, and a connecting piece of rope was tied between the two, ostensibly making it impossible for the man to move his limbs independently. While tying him, Bill had laid him out on his back, the formality of the new position looking slightly incongruous.

Ben again noticed that the man's hair seemed to have moved slightly, and this time Bill did not stop him as he knelt on one knee to examine the man. There was a small gap underneath the unkempt white hair on his forehead. Ben leaned over and put the little finger of his left hand into the entrance of the small gap. He wiggled his finger slightly and saw the hair start to move en masse. Easing his finger further into the gap and wiggling harder, Ben felt slightly queasy as he saw the whole thatch start to lift. It was obviously a wig. He continued easing the wig off, revealing what appeared to be a bald head, but which he then saw was some sort of fine material cap.

By now, Bill was bending down, watching with his mouth open. Ben lifted the wig until he reached the right ear, at which point the wig became stuck. Ben applied a bit of force and was surprised to see the white sideburns on the man's face start to lift off. As they came off completely, he could see they had been placed over a flap of the wig positioned just in front of the ear. Now the wig was free to move it came off easily along with the right sideburn. Ben repeated the activity on the left ear and soon had the entire wig and sideburns removed. Bill's mouth was still open.

As Ben started to peel back the remaining fine cap material, the man's eyes began to stir. His body twitched slightly and he moaned quietly. Ben completed the removal quickly. Just as the cap came off completely, revealing a full head of short, dark hair, the man's eyes opened fully.

"Good heavens," Ben said, realising as he said it that he had taken classic British understatement to new heights. He was looking into the eyes – the blurred, jaundiced eyes – of his art classmate, Alan Williams.

"You know him?" Bill queried.

Ben rose off his knee, and backed away, staring in disbelief. "Yes, we go… we went… to the same art lessons. He never said boo to a goose, he was a real loner. I remember ages ago he mentioned he worked for the Forestry Commission, but he didn't go into detail. That was about all we ever got out of him. The rest of us put it down to shyness and left him alone. Christ, it's just struck me, his name - Alan Williams – another A.W. That's probably what got him started. And he was always trying to improve his drawing rather than his painting. No doubt he wanted to be as good as Wainwright. Now I know why he suddenly stopped when he got close to me – he recognised me."

Alan Williams was starting to struggle against his bonds, but without much energy. He continued to moan: the left side of his face was now badly swollen. Bill looked down and said, "You're wasting your time. The police will be here in ten minutes. Might as well make yourself comfortable while you're waiting. I'll bring you a head cushion." With that, Bill walked over to one of the piles of junk and returned with a soiled armchair cushion. He pushed it under Williams's head. "Want some water?" Bill asked.

Williams nodded.

Bill ambled over to the back door, followed by the three dogs, who followed him in, no doubt thinking they were going to be fed. Bill returned without the dogs, but with a cup of water. He held Williams's head while he drank the water. He left the cup on the floor.

Ben meanwhile, had found a pile of logs on which it was possible to sit. As Bill joined him, Ben finally got to ask his questions. "How the hell did you know I was here? How did you find me? What made you come here?"

"Your wonderful wife," Bill said, simply. "She probably told you we bumped into each other at the supermarket the other day. What she didn't tell you was that she asked me, when I had the time, to keep an eye on you. She phoned me this morning and told me you were coming over here this afternoon. I told her I had nothing special on today, so I would get myself over and park in the Visitor Centre and hope to pick you up from there. She phoned me later in the afternoon and told me roughly where you were. I saw you come into the Visitor Centre and I followed you out. Must have done a better job this time, because you obviously didn't see me. Then I saw your car parked on the side of the road and the rest is history, as they say."

There was a long silence then Bill added, "That's some woman you've got there."

Ben sat, head down, reflecting on his luck. "I know," he said, eventually.

Another silence followed. The place became almost eerily quiet. Even Williams had stopped moaning. Ben and Bill sat side by side, staring into space, both needing to collect themselves after their exertions.

Eventually coming out of his trance, Ben remembered his next question. "Where did you learn to tackle an armed man like that? You were incredible"

Bill made a dismissive snort. "Manchester... before I came up here. That's where I learned why it's called a police *force* and not a police service. You can have all your clever, analytical people – no offence, Ben – and your university graduates, but as often as not it's plain brute force that saves the day... that protects the public."

"But what you did was *exceptionally* brave. Surely you weren't..."

"It's not that difficult once you've been trained," Bill protested. "You see, anybody with a weapon *knows* they are in charge of the situation. When you approach them like I did, with authority, as if *I* was in charge, and show them you are not scared and order them to do things, a bit of doubt creeps into their mind... it distracts them, makes them think. And then when you get close they always expect you to stop and take up some sort of fighting stance. So in the split second they are waiting for this to happen you get in first."

"That's all very well in theory, Bill," Ben said, "but in my book it still takes enormous courage to carry it out. I'll never forget it. And no offence taken by the way"

"We'd make a good team wouldn't we," Bill joked. "You do the analytical stuff and find the villains and I'll do the heavy stuff. We could set up as private investigators."

"Oh no! No thanks, Bill," Ben stressed. "I'd rather imitate a Constable with a paintbrush than a truncheon."

"Very droll."

"Actually," Ben went on, "I think we might still have some investigating work to do here. Before we go we should search that house thoroughly. There's an outside chance that Elizabeth Lamb is in there."

Bill looked sideways at him. "What makes you think that?"

"Just a theoretical possibility. I told Peter about it recently."

"I'll go ask the man himself, see if we can save some time." Bill was off his seat and on his way before Ben could reply. Shortly afterwards he saw Bill lean down and ask the question. And he heard Williams reply, "Fuck off."

Bill returned and sat down again. "He wasn't very cooperative," he said. "Anyway, we can't go in there searching, it's a possible crime scene. We'll have to wait for the gang to arrive."

Right on cue, the first police car arrived and three uniformed officers emerged. Bill seemed to know them and went to greet them. Ben sat back and watched Bill take them over to Williams. They were carrying handcuffs. Another car arrived and three plain-clothed men got out; one obviously the older and senior, probably a Detective Chief Inspector. They made their way over to the others and a conversation ensued. At one stage he saw Bill pointing to the house and assumed he was telling them about Elizabeth Lamb.

It suddenly struck Ben that, from a journalist's point of view, he was in the rare and privileged position of being present at the arrest of a major criminal. This was a big story. As well as writing it up for *The Tribune*, he could make money with the nationals. He couldn't write himself into the investigating story, because he had promised Peter that side of things, but he could write it as if he had happened on the scene. He would do that. And he would make Bill the hero of the story. They had been walking together, old pals, when they happened on the scene. They had stopped to look at the Land Rover, knowing the police were checking all owners, when they were attacked by Williams with an axe. Bill had dealt with him exactly as seen. He would be a local and national hero and rightly so. Ben took out his mobile and started to wander about the area taking shots of everything. He would get the interviews later. He returned to his seat, took out his notebook and started to write what he saw happening in front of him.

Over the next hour he saw two more cars arrive, disgorging people who dressed themselves in white jumpsuits, complete with hoods and boots, before entering the house. Forensics, he presumed. Two RSPCA men arrived and took away the dogs and cats in their van. Williams was next to go in a police van, after being examined by a doctor. The stand-by ambulance was dismissed. The same doctor examined Ben, gave him a couple of painkillers and arranged for him to be x-rayed at Keswick Hospital the next morning. Ben recorded these comings and goings with his mobile camera.

Bill was on his feet most of the time, acting as a sort of go-between, telling Ben what he thought was happening. He brought him back reports of a stinking house, and a garage full of Wainwright stuff including some kind of carved altar. Ben would be allowed in to take photographs after forensics had finished, perhaps tomorrow.

Dusk was setting in when Bill told him they were starting to search the house thoroughly. A short while later he reported that a police constable had spotted that the outside of the garage was about two metres longer than the inside. They were about to dismantle the altar to see if there was access behind it to the extra space. They were also investigating the bedroom floor above the garage.

Ben was starting to feel cold in the evening air, but he couldn't tear himself away. He walked up and down, trying to keep warm. He rang home to tell Helen he was running late. She wasn't in so he left a message on the machine. He didn't mention the drama of the day.

Suddenly there were shouts and raised voices and a general sense of excitement. Slowly this dissipated, and for about five minutes there was absolute silence. And during the silence Ben saw a female police constable emerge from the front door. She was arm-linked to a pale, thin, shabbily dressed, middle-aged woman, who was arm-linked on the other side to another officer. They supported the woman as they slowly led her to one of the police cars, where she was gently eased into the back seat. The car soon drove off.

Bill came running back. "It was her! It was Elizabeth Lamb," he said. His eyes were wet with tears. "She was in a terrible state, but she's alive, Ben, she's alive." And then he forgot himself and pulled Ben up off his seat and wrapped his arms around him.

Chapter 50

The following four days passed in a whirl of frantic activity:

Helen took Ben to Keswick Cottage Hospital for an early morning x-ray. Diagnosis – two hairline cracks, plus bruising. Cure – time plus painkillers.

Ben declined a five-figure offer for his story from a disreputable tabloid newspaper but accepted a four-figure offer from a reputable one. He made Bill the star. He had briefed Bill on how he was going to present the story, and Bill had agreed that it was the best way, otherwise it would have been difficult to explain what they were both doing there.

Ben wrote his piece for *The Tribune*, again making Bill the star and mentioning the outstanding contribution of local police sergeant Peter Murphy.

Keswick was again invaded by the national media. Ben, Bill and Peter were all interviewed on numerous occasions. During his interviews, Chief Superintendent John Baker commended Peter on his exceptional work during the investigation, pointing out that, due to Peter's work, the police had been planning to search the houses in Thornbeck Forest and would have arrested Alan Williams and found Mrs Lamb had it not been for their "accidental" discovery by Mr Foxley and Mr Unwin.

During those four days Bill became one of the best-known people in the entire country because, unlike Ben, he accepted a five-figure sum from a tabloid to tell his story. The headline read - *RETIRED COP DOWNS AXE-WIELDING SERIAL KILLER – Read His Story.*

Elizabeth Lamb had been taken to hospital suffering from malnutrition and associated problems. Her condition was described as serious but not critical. Her family, who had also been subjected to the media frenzy, was at her bedside.

On the morning of the fourth day, the media started to drift away. Soon the story would be forgotten and life would get back to normal, though for Bill it was clearly never going to be the same again. He would be a local celebrity for the rest of his life.

Helen came out of the shadows and informed Ben that, two days ago, she had received a letter from Hamish Stott. He was writing to thank them for their kindness. He said he had been dishonourably discharged from the army, but it didn't bother him. He was back working in the Isle of Barra hotel and all was well. His wife, Sami, was expecting. If it was a boy he was going to name it Jamie, after his pal, though he hoped he wouldn't swear as much. If it was a girl, the name would be Grace, after the half-sister he never knew.

Ben had suggested that, when he had received payment from the national newspaper, they use the money to fly up to the Isle of Barra to pay them a surprise visit. "I've always fancied flying over the Hebridean Sea, and touching down on that beach landing strip."

Helen had agreed, then added, "Since there will be lots of money left, how about we also, later on, fly to the Great Barrier Reef; I've always wanted to swim there."

Ben had agreed.

On the afternoon of the fourth day, when it was clear that the heat had gone out of the story, as well as the sunny May day, Ben came back into the cottage, having strolled around the garden. "I think it's all over," he sighed with relief. "I think we can get back to normal. Let's celebrate, let's do a Wainwright."

Helen, about to prepare the evening meal, frowned. "What, climb a fell at this time of day?"

"No… let's do what Wainwright used to do at this time of day, after he had climbed a fell. Let's get the bus into Keswick and have some fish and chips."

Helen agreed enthusiastically.

They got dressed, walked to the end of the lane, took the bus into Keswick, enjoyed the delicious fish and chips, and caught the bus back. It dropped them off at the end of the lane, leaving them about a mile to go.

They set off, hand in hand, on a walk they had done hundreds of times. The sun was low in the western sky, about to kiss the top of Sale Fell. Insects were still dancing in the warm, evening air. Luxuriant trees, without a breeze, lined their way like silent sentinels. The sounds of the country – mooing cows, bleating sheep, singing birds, a distant tractor – drifted in from near and far, wrapping them in a blanket of familiarity. Words were not necessary.

They knew what they had around them and between them was wonderful.

When they reached the end of the lane, they stepped off the tarmac onto the gravel that marked the start of their drive. They walked along it, turned a corner and saw their beloved cottage, nestling, like Wordsworth's daffodils, beside the lake, beneath the trees.

------End------

Epilogue

At a subsequent police press conference details were revealed about the small room at the back of the garage where Mrs Elizabeth Lamb had been found. Originally a storeroom, with access via a door within the garage, it had been adapted by Alan Williams into basic living quarters. He had installed a toilet, shower, sink unit, single bed, wardrobe and chair. He had cut a trapdoor entry through the roof into the bedroom above the garage, and installed a fixed aluminium ladder to allow access into the room from above. He had then boarded off the door within the garage and eventually hidden it from view by covering it with the altar. There were no windows in the room, with air being circulated via two wall air vents. Food had been lowered or taken down via the ceiling trapdoor.

*

It was three months before Mrs Lamb was given clearance by medical staff to talk to the police about her experience. They said she was a remarkably resilient woman (from a Cumbrian farming family) who they expected to make a good long-term recovery. The police released details of the information she possessed regarding Williams's method of operation. She said he used to boast to her after a killing, telling her how he had managed to fool the stupid police again.

His method was to use a bus that travelled up and down the A591 corridor, between Keswick and Windermere, with branches off, in order to spread his victims geographically. He sat in pubs, hotels, tourist information offices, visitor centres and the like, to overhear the names of people, particularly the surname. Once he found an initial fitting the name *A Wainwright,* he set about creating his plan of attack. He chose different methods of killing to avoid creating a pattern, but he always made them look accidental. His targets were tourists and incomers as well as high-profile people like Giles Innes who he just did not like, and Josephine Turner, who he had seen "morally abusing the land" and was responsible for increasing tourism to the area.

The only personal details the police released was that Williams always called her Betty in spite of her insistence on Elizabeth and that, initially, he had generally looked after her well, but his attitude had declined as he sank deeper into his alcohol dependence and she was being badly neglected by the time of her rescue.

*

The police also released a medical report (psychologists and psychiatrists) on Alan Williams. The general consensus was that this was a classic case of an obsessive's journey into pathological hero worship, which eventually led to paranoia.

He probably felt an intense and personal bond with his hero, and probably even felt controlled by the voice of the hero, the only person he could trust. His feeling of inferiority to his hero made him try to mimic and copy him. He had probably closely associated himself with his hero long before his pathological behaviour started. This is demonstrated by the fact he had married a woman called Ruth, the name of his hero's first wife. After their separation, it was almost inevitable he would seek a woman called Betty, the name of his hero's second wife, to replace her.

The trigger to his behaviour was a deeply held feeling of the need to protect his cause – the environment – a common cause, these days, of extreme misanthropic behaviour. They pointed out that most serial killers and sociopaths demonstrate misanthropic attitudes. Mistakenly, Williams had associated this attitude with his hero.

*

The police file on the attack on Ben Foxley (in his garden) remains open, though no current investigations are taking place.

*

The murders of three members of the computer hacking team, *Robin Hood,* remain unsolved.

About the Author

After combining a career in industry with that of a freelance writer, Michael Wood now writes full-time. His first Lake District novel *The Fell Walker* achieved wide acclaim and is currently being adapted for the stage. His second novel *Climate Change*, a murder mystery set in Australia and Scotland, was published in 2011.

He lives in Cumbria with his partner Dorothy.